PRAISE FOR

"Jude Berman's debut novel delivers a chillingly realistic near-future portrayal of technology wunderkinds manipulating our political consciousness in a fractured America. Blink your eyes and we could all be living in this cautionary tale."

—MIKE TRIGG, author of *Bit Flip* and *Burner*

"Like Henning Mankell, Elizabeth George, and William Kent Krueger, Jude Berman is keenly aware of the dangers of our contemporary political world. But unlike many writers, she brings ideas about how to combat them—interweaving this futuristic detective thriller with the ancient myths of the *Mahābhārata*, providing both flash and gravitas to compel our attention."

—MARA MILLER, author of *The Garden as an Art*

"Multilayered and inventive, this near-future cautionary tale poses deep questions about the nature of family, integrity, and activism in the digital age that make you want to keep rereading the news. I couldn't put it down."

—SHERI T. JOSEPH, author of *Edge of the Known World*

"Jude Berman's imagination is both epic and personal in this thriller about technology, the fate of the world, and what we as individuals can do about it."

—JEN BRAAKSMA, author of *Evangeline's Heaven* and *Amaranth*

"*The Die* is a fast-paced, fascinating exploration of the dangers of apathy and how to tap into the hero in all of us."

—MEREDITH WALTERS, author of *This Animal Body*

"It pulled me in immediately—and kept defying my expectations and pulling me in further."

—SARAH TOWLE, author of *Crossing the Line: Finding America in the Borderlands*

"*The Die* takes us into uncharted waters, creating a dystopian vision of our world rife with the dangers of authoritarianism and groupthink in what feels like the not-so-distant future."

—EVETTE DAVIS, author of *48 States* and the Dark Horse Trilogy

"Jude Berman expertly juxtaposes a dystopian world of dictatorship and deceit with a millennia-old story. In this cautionary tale about what can happen when democracy is taken for granted, she contrasts themes of fear, oppression, and passivity with those of hope, community, and action. I strongly recommend this fascinating read."

—SUSAN WEISSBACH FRIEDMAN, author of *Klara's Truth*

THE DIE

THE DIE

A NOVEL

JUDE BERMAN

SPARKPRESS

Published by SparkPress, a BookSparks imprint,
A division of SparkPoint Studio, LLC
Phoenix, Arizona, USA, 85007
www.gosparkpress.com

Published 2024
Printed in the United States of America
Print ISBN: 978-1-68463-230-5
E-ISBN: 978-1-68463-231-2
Library of Congress Control Number: 2023913606

Interior design and typeset by Katherine Lloyd, The DESK

Permission granted by Bharatiya Vidya Bhavan to include epigraphs adapted from the *Mahābhārata*, by Kamala Subramaniam (Mumbai, 1988).

to M

CONTENTS

Krishna said, "O Arjuna, when performing an action, never think of the results or the rewards. But neither should you delude yourself that inaction is of benefit to you. Do your work with evenness of mind, remaining indifferent to success or failure. This is yoga."

The princess Draupadi
was born of fire.

THE FLUTE: Darah

The HastinSys café makes a mean mango smoothie. Smooth, sweet, nutritious, with a wicked head of orange froth. A drink to die for. Demolish one and I'll be burning through the beta-test results for the new HSys virtual reality science game. The kids loved it, and their teachers loved how much the kids learned. Writing up the data should be a snap.

As I head down the walkway to the café to fuel up, I spot Keith. He's hurrying toward the parking lot, but not too fast to shoot me a smile. I smile back. The next thing I know, I'm on his self-balancing motorcycle, arms around his waist. We're streaming down the freeway toward Mountain View, rocking out to the electro-techno mix shared through the neurograins embedded in our helmets. My beta-test data? Back-burnered. But no worries, I'll have time to pull it together. And that smoothie . . . well, it'll have to wait too.

This isn't my first visit to Keith's condo. I was there on a Friday after work a few weeks ago. It was a carefree, spontaneous, adrenaline-rousing yet inconsequential one-time-only hookup. The kind of indulgence nobody could object to. Except maybe your grandma. If you have one. I've never met either of mine. But I know they'd oppose any sort of hookup, which to this day remains forbidden in their country. Punishable by death. Even so, I didn't let that—or anything else—bother me afterwards as I drove home alone that Friday, tired but not sleepy, wending up the mountain road to the farm.

Now is the second time.

As before, we pass the galley kitchen and proceed down the long hallway, straight to the back bedroom. Again the holographic parrot in its light cage on the nightstand screeches what sounds like "Ha-pee! Ha-pee! Ha-pee!" I don't know if it's programmed for me or wants the whole world to be happy. Doesn't matter. I'm happy either way.

When they sense a human presence, the strip curtains along the glass wall slide shut, cutting the view of Keith's bed for some seniors at the pool. Turning day into night for us. With one deft motion, he sweeps the rumpled laundry strewn across his bed onto the floor and pulls me down on him.

There is little to say afterwards.

Back at HSys, he parks in a tight spot between two vans. I dismount and assume he will follow. He doesn't. Hoping to prolong the fire between us, I lean against the cycle, my face inches from his, and suggest a pit stop for smoothies. "I heard your stomach growling," I tease. "Don't pretend you're not starving."

A tenseness flickers behind his eyes. At close range, it's impossible to miss. "Darah, I told you."

"Told me what?" I pull back abruptly.

He detaches his smart visor from his helmet, folds it, and stuffs it into his pocket—next to his mini tablet, in its holographic snakeskin case. Then he looks at me straight on, eyes blue and hard like lapis lazuli.

Suddenly I feel like an idiot. Of course I know what he means. Before I left his condo that first evening, we chatted briefly. Mostly small talk, but he made a point of letting me know about Karin. They aren't a couple anymore but still work closely together at HSys. There are a few things it is better Karin doesn't know. We are one of those things. He didn't go into more detail, but he didn't have to. Really it's none of my business. I assured him we're on the same page: two consenting adults, no strings attached. I didn't mention anyone's grandma, but he got the idea. And I meant what I said.

Now as I pivot from him, then dodge between parked vehicles to get away, I wonder how I lost sight of that so quickly.

Back in the office, mango smoothie in hand, I find only Jedd. Unusual for midafternoon. "Where's everyone?" I ask.

"Welcome back, yourself," he says, eyes glued to his screen.

"You're alone?" It's a rhetorical question but it does the trick. He unglues his eyes. As he does, I'm instantly aware of a few windblown hairs loose around my face. Not what you'd expect on someone who wants you to think she merely lost track of time at the café.

If Jedd notices, he doesn't let on. "Beers is at a cybersecurity briefing in the bunker. June's running errands. Don't know where the others went, but they'll be back shortly."

There are five of us. Well, six including me. I came along last, after taking refuge in California just before it declared itself a nation, so the others sometimes still speak of themselves as the five. That doesn't make me any less included, less loved. It's like 5 + 1 = 5. We work together, play together, share a home together. Like siblings. Of course, like siblings, we don't share *everything*. Case in point: where I've been these past couple hours. In general though, you could say that what began as friendship ended up as family.

Our workspace, where we spend most of our waking hours, is a spacious suite on the top floor, equipped with every amenity you could desire: a gaming station, auto-morphing chairs, indi-vidualized climate control, a kitchenette with robotic espresso machine and mini robo-bar, self-cleaning windows with micro-mirror glazing. Never a smudge on those windows. Beneath my feet, the carbon-negative white carpet is always spotless. An array of awards adorns a shelf by the windows. Arranged on it are cod-er-of-the-month plaques as well as trophies for gamer of the year, team player, most original. And my favorite, the high-five prize, which was awarded before I got here but feels like mine anyway. Outside, a real-life pyrotechnic display ignites the sky most eve-nings as the sun sets behind the Santa Cruz Mountains.

Sometimes I have to pinch myself to make sure all this isn't a dream and I won't wake up stressed and scared, back in the dic-tatorship. At first I worried it was just a matter of time before the Dictator found a way to destroy life here too. But he hasn't. Thank god. Most days we focus on work and hardly give him a second thought. Because of all that and so much more, we refer to our workspace as the penthouse.

Jedd persists: "Where were you? Don't you have a report due?"

I take a gulp of smoothie and skip to his second question. "Yep. Whipping it out now."

With that, Jedd goes back to work. As I cross the room to my table by the window, I tuck the loose strands of hair behind my ears. He might not have noticed, but June's another matter. She'd spot a single hair out of place. And expect the full backstory.

The embedded screen on my table wakes up the instant it detects my biometrics. My report on the KnoMor science game is waiting. When Selma, the project lead, left on short notice for an assignment in Japan, she tasked me with submitting the report so a product release manager could be brought on ASAP. If she doesn't return on time, I'm supposed to step in as lead. That's something I've never done before.

By late afternoon, all that remains is to slip in the final graphs.

Because I've been so focused, I hardly noticed Beers and the others as they came and went. I didn't even obsess over whether Keith might text me. Which of course he didn't. But so what? I didn't text him either. Despite my awkward exit from the parking lot—still embarrassing as I recall it now—I kind of like the guy. There's no good reason for this, I just like him. And no one needs to know. Not even Keith.

As I often do at this hour, I point a camera at the sun low over the mountains and project a 3D mirror image onto the display wall, hiding all the graphs and lists that have accumulated over the day. If you still have your nose to the digital grindstone, this signals time to think about quitting. Of course, I could project sunrises and sunsets onto all the walls and ceiling at any hour. But I don't. I'm old-fashioned in that way.

Right on cue, Jedd's chair reclines to give him a better view. Orange and magenta tinge his voluminous cloud of wiry black hair.

Normally I'd also relax, maybe grab a margarita from the robo-bar. But I'm too focused on making up for lost time, putting a wrap on this report. Though I wouldn't admit it to anyone, I'm paying for my earlier escapade. I begin skimming through the graphs on my screen, one final check before fitting them into the text and calling it a day.

Then something catches my eye. "Damn!"

"You're still working?" Jedd sounds surprised.

"No . . . I mean *yes*! Dude, look at this!"

He lifts himself out of his chair and ambles across the room. You'd think he could move a little faster. Except that's not Jedd's style. He may be a quick thinker, but he goes through life with ease. The orange and magenta highlights in his hair fade to rust and maroon, then to black as he stoops to peer over my shoulder. "I see one set of students who played KnoMor. And another who didn't."

"Right. And the gamers should have outperformed the non-gamers."

"Not according to this graph."

"According to the data I saw before, they did."

He frowns. "I thought you just had to whip it out."

"I did."

He clears his throat in a way that says, *I've been around this block.* If I didn't know him so well, I might find it patronizing. "Darah, glitches happen all the time. You know that. Regenerating your graphs should fix everything." His index finger hovers over my document, as if he intends to close it. "This isn't a crisis. Finish it tomorrow."

I'm about to swat away his hand and object that I wanted to finish before leaving and now that's impossible, when a message flashes on the screen. For an instant I think it's from Keith.

Jedd leans closer. "'egg pp prepped,'" he reads aloud. "'when u home?'" Without hesitation, his finger skims across three letters in reply: "'omw'"

Of course, Beers will assume it's *me* saying I'm on my way. Still, Jedd has a point. He rarely sees anything as a crisis, and in this case I have to concede he's right. There's no reason to freak. I'll have time to redo the graphs after we've polished off the eggplant parmesan, or egg pp in Beers's shorthand. "Okay, you win," I say, shutting all my files with one swipe.

As Jedd heads for the door, I dim the display and overhead lights, careful not to cut the Li-Fi, and pop a live image of the constellations onto the ceiling. Under the twinkling of Ursa Major, I pluck a wilted flower off the peace lily on the kitchenette counter, then sling my backpack over one shoulder. Out of habit, I pause at the door to hear the smart lock engage, before crossing the open-space area, its rows of workstations deserted at this hour, to the maglev elevator.

Jedd is already there, slouched against the wall, nose in a video game.

As the cab door slides open, a short man in a pink and tur-quoise shirt hanging untucked over his protruding belly steps out. A six-pack is nestled in the crook of one arm, and he's grunting at whoever is in his ear. From looks alone, you might assume his age to be double mine. In fact, he isn't anywhere near that old.

"Kurt, my man," Jedd says as we squeeze past him. "Working late?"

Kurt stops short but without turning back. "Some of us take our jobs seriously!" He laughs like that's hilarious. Like whoever's in his ear will get the joke. Then as the door is closing, he swivels around, reaches in with his free hand, and grabs my butt. Hard. You wouldn't think someone so unathletic could execute a move like that without getting his hand crushed or dropping a beer.

"Hey!" I yelp.

But the door has shut and we're shooting toward the lobby. Only Jedd can hear me.

He's incredulous. "Tell me the SOB didn't just do that!"

"You saw it," I say, rubbing my rear, as if that will remove the insult.

"That was uncalled-for! You need to report him." Jedd isn't one to tolerate any form of harassment. Or bullying or bigotry or injustice or inequity. He will step up and take action every time. I appreciate that about him.

I've never worked directly with Kurt, but like most people at HSys, he's always seemed friendly enough. He and his group—which includes Keith and Karin—live at the far end of our corridor. Beers likes to refer to them as our distant cousins, as if we share HSys DNA. Make that one kissing cousin now. *Oh*, I think, *that's it*. Keith must have mentioned our hookup, and this is Kurt's disgusting way of letting me know he knows. Except Keith was adamant Karin not find out. Which means Kurt wouldn't know either. So this is all on Kurt.

Jedd's right: he deserves to be reported. HR expects reports to be filed right away. The problem is I've got a data mess on my hands and I'm not about to drop the ball on Selma. The fact that I have a soft spot for Kurt's sidekick has nothing to do with this. I'm not giving him a pass; I'm simply reserving the right to decide when I'll take action.

As we land in the lobby, I assure Jedd that if Kurt so much as touches me again, he's got another thing coming.

We pass through the exit scanner, then hurry along the walkway that transects the lawn in between the three main buildings. Arranged in a horseshoe, each houses a different division. The one in the middle—Building 1—is home to the company's bread-and-butter gaming technologies. Our penthouse is on the sixth floor, facing west. On the right is the R&D center, dedicated to projects involving smart dust and brain-computer interface. The cybersecurity division lives in the low-lying building on the left known as the bunker. Cyberthreats are a constant reality, and nowhere more so than in Silicon Valley. Breaking into and commandeering a major tech company could signal the Dictator's intent to launch a surprise takeover of California. So far there's been no sign of that. HSys remains secure due to the diligence of those in the bunker. They call it the bunker ostensibly because it's lower than the other buildings but also because they go to war every day against a veritable army of hackers and cyber criminals. I've never been inside.

Near the end of the walkway, a fountain shoots arcs from the edge of its circular pool to meet in the center. People like to take food from the café in the R&D building and sit on the surrounding ledge. At twilight, the lights come on and each watery arc sparkles with a different color. It's magical.

A young man is sitting there alone, eyes closed, playing a bamboo flute. He's barefoot, black hair pulled into a man bun at the crown of his head. His oversized T-shirt accentuates rather than hides his bone structure. As he plays, his pursed lips draw down the corners of his mouth. Yet he has the smile of a baby.

I stop dead.

Jedd stops too, but only for a second. He fishes for a few bills in his pocket, places them beside the kid, then sets off toward the parking lot. That eggplant is calling.

I, however, am transfixed. The sound of the flute is as fluid and mesmerizing as the arcs of water. Each wavering, drawn-out note is tender but piercing, joyful but haunting, weeping with happiness. I let them splash over me. Wash through me. Cleanse me. Empty me. I close my eyes and float in the overlapping, ever-expanding pools of sound, each breath pulling me further into my being, into realms I didn't know existed. Everything else in the world around me dies an exquisite death.

For a few moments nothing else matters. No data, no graphs, no report. No hookup. No butt grab. Nothing.

I find Jedd parked in our usual spot in the lot. He's slouched in the front bucket seat, long legs propped against the dashboard where a steering wheel otherwise would be, beneath the faded-pink fuzzy dice June found in the barn and hung here—not because she gambles or she needs good luck but because she could. It's legal in a level-5 fully autonomous car. A car that, for laughs, Jedd once dubbed her chariot. The moniker stuck.

As expected, he's in zombie mode, engrossed in a video game. Most people in his line of work want to unwind at the end of the day. Not Jedd. A game is his means of unwinding. He plays whenever he can. Though he may have to pause his game many times, he never quits till he's won. I once asked what he thought about gaming addictions. It wasn't a personal question, but he got defensive. Called it old-school psychology and insisted playing is his conscious choice. I've noticed that if anyone at work suggests he might be gaming at an inopportune moment, he shrugs and says he's dogfooding. And he gets away with it.

I slide into the other front seat, which is swiveled sideways. "Why do you have June's car?"

"She borrowed mine for her errands."

"Because the chariot's too slow," I say, confirming what we both know: its novelty has long since worn off. June misses zipping past drivers in traffic, racing around curves on the mountain. She resents having to come to a full stop when there isn't any vehicle or pedestrian or cop in sight. If aero cars were more affordable, she'd get one so she wouldn't have to borrow our old-fashioned all-electric vehicles.

Jedd voice-activates the ignition and instructs the chariot to take us home. Then he turns his full attention back on his game. From the clucking under his breath, it's clear he is winning. As per usual.

Nature is what I turn to when I want to unwind. Driving up the mountain, I like to feast my eyes on the vibrancy of the flora. Even the dry, flaxen hillsides here, punctuated by islands of live oak, are more striking than the landscape in Palisades Park, New Jersey, where I grew up. Or Rutgers, where I went to college. So much of the natural world there sleeps for half the year.

It was never a given I would go to college, let alone graduate. But after Rutgers granted a full scholarship, off I went. I wanted to study environmental science. With the climate disaster upending the world—so many people dying, and more suffering—I wanted to be part of the solution. My dream job was at Nanotech Institute, cleaning up the world's diminishing supply of fresh water. I interviewed there in my senior year and was thrilled when they offered a position.

Then everything fell apart. One day a neighbor in Palisades Park called to say Mom was missing. She'd seen immigration officials take Mom away. Before I could contact a lawyer or find out where she was detained, she'd been deported. The Dictator had been getting rid of anyone not born in the country, so we knew the risk existed. Yet when it happened, it was worse than I imagined. No reason was given and no recourse. I could only assume she'd been sent to Afghanistan, from where she'd fled, unmarried and pregnant with me, two decades earlier. There was nothing I could do to get her back. Frigging nothing.

I went home that night and crawled into her bed and lay there, shaking, crying, vomiting. I felt like I was going to die. Neighbors knocked on the door. I didn't answer. Each time they returned, I ignored them. I hated every human being who hadn't put their body between Mom and her abductors.

Finally, days later, I forced myself to get up. Forced food into my mouth. Forced myself to get into my car and drive to Rutgers. I buried my fear and anger and despair. Buried the part of myself that had died. I focused on passing my exams, preparing for my job. That was what Mom would want.

But disaster struck again. This time the government shut down Nanotech for engaging in what it deemed subversive activities. Suddenly I had no plans, no future, no finances. I took the first job I could find: teaching middle school science. I would inspire kids to love the planet. To choose science over conspiracy theories. To understand that "doing their own research" was a euphemism for deluding themselves. A few months into the year, however, the textbook I'd chosen was banned. The school reassigned me to teach a remedial math class. Things went downhill from there. Hate messages attacked me on social media. People I'd never met screamed at me online, "DIE, SCUM!" I was furious. And scared.

I forgot about saving the environment, about saving the kids. Saving myself became my priority. I quit my job, packed my bags, and used what little money I had to buy a ticket to California.

Going to Afghanistan to find Mom wasn't an option. As a woman, I wouldn't be able to work there. Or even leave home by myself. Because women must hide their names, I would no longer be Darah Ahmadi. Besides, I didn't know if Mom was alive. Almost a year had passed without any word from her. But I was doing what I knew she'd want: escaping the dictatorship, fleeing that living hell in which basic rights and freedoms were ripped away from more people every day.

The week after I arrived in the Bay Area, the borders closed. People had started flocking here after the Dictator found the means to extend his term indefinitely. Many years earlier, another president tried the same and failed, but this time it was happening. Democracy was finally and officially over. Too many political and judicial systems had chipped away at it. Too many citizens couldn't be bothered. If they weren't personally in danger, they didn't give a damn. A small but vocal and violent minority even welcomed autocracy.

. The notion of California as a free, independent, democratic country was no longer a hypothetical. No longer a joke. In fact, it became a forgone conclusion after the Dictator himself promoted it. He wasn't serious; he was counting on our quick failure. But he miscalculated.

A few years later, California is thriving. And all the more so since Washington, Oregon, and Hawaii joined forces with us. Of course there were naysayers who chose to migrate east, but we're doing fine without them. Together we have food. We have technology. We have improved schools and free health care and safe streets. Equity and justice are more than buzzwords for our diverse population. We have strong, supportive relationships with many nations. While we aren't immune to the global climate disaster, we do all we can to protect the environment. We have clean air and water. Gorgeous beaches. And movies. Still, there's an underlying fear the Dictator will pull a fast one and take over our democracy. No one can deny that's a threat. Still, with nothing specific to worry about day to day, life here feels pretty darn good.

I landed a job right away because of the demand for teachers to work with the many newly arrived children. No one dictated how I could present scientific facts in the classroom. No one threatened me. I began to relax. And to heal myself—my grief, my anxiety, and the nightmares that tore up my sleep.

June was the first of the five I met. It was a chance encounter in the market, a friendship struck up alongside the beans and carrots in the veggie aisle. The artichokes, actually. I gasped aloud when I saw them. June was putting five into her basket and heard my gasp. I explained that the trade embargo the Dictator had imposed to gain leverage over California meant no one in the States had seen them for ages. She held out the plumpest among hers and insisted I take it. Not long after, she introduced me to Jedd. Perhaps she thought a petite first-gen Afghan American gal and an uber-tall biracial dude would vibe. And maybe we could have. But he was thirty and I was only in my early twenties. Gen alpha meets gen beta. More than that, I was struggling to mend from the trauma I'd been through. After our first date, I found myself becoming friends with the rest of the five. You can't date someone when you feel more like family. And family was what I needed most.

Jedd suggested I upskill for a job at HSys. Initially I was reluctant to leave the school. But the pull of family was stronger. And when I learned HSys had ditched its classic FPS games in favor of the more peaceful genres of puzzles, mazes, simulations, and strategy games, that sealed the deal. I could be happy working there. After a crash course in tech writing, I landed an entry-level position and moved into the penthouse.

Now as the chariot crawls up the switchbacks leading to our farm, I'm not relaxing with nature as usual, not looking for the first star as the city lights fade. No, I'm obsessing over KnoMor. When I first checked, the gamers' scores were thirty points higher than the control scores. I wrote my text based on those results. But when I went back to the data, those gamers had failing scores. Something didn't compute. Tonight I'll regenerate the graphs. Except what if that doesn't fix it? In fact, I've already texted Selma. I reach for my tablet to see if she's replied.

There are only a dozen new texts. Nothing from her. One from Beers says, "egg pp done."

I scroll through my HSys contacts and stop at a pair of lapis eyes. June prefers brown, so these eyes would look hard as rock to her. To me, they're more like liquid gemstones.

Considering we work on the same floor, it's odd Keith and I never had a real conversation—only the two of us—until a few weeks ago. Even then it was brief. I still don't know much about him. We smile and say hi in passing. Slightly flirtatious. And there's the occasional smize at meetings. No one notices because it's only our eyes. On that Friday, when we found ourselves alone in the elevator after work, he looked up from his tablet, in its holo-graphic snakeskin case, and complimented my lapis earrings. I asked if he realized his eyes were the same color. He teased about needing to see the two up close to compare. More banter followed as we exited the cab. One thing led to the next.

We have no history of texts between us. I could change that right now. For starters I type, "ims." But then I think, *I'm sorry . . . for what?* There's nothing to apologize for. So I delete it and instead let my thumb scan the emojis. Grinning? No. Winking? Too flirty. Blowing a kiss? Way too flirty. Angry? Not anymore, not really. I consider asking Jedd's advice. Not that he's a pro at relationships. He keeps his own so much on the down-low I hardly know who they are.

Thumb still on the emojis, unsure if I'm ready for any in-your-face action, I turn to the window. This final stretch of road before the farm's driveway is like a tunnel, with live oaks lining each side, their lower branches grazing the chariot's sunroof as we pass beneath. A warm, dry wind whistles through the leaves. Beers told me that sound has a name: psithurism. For a dude who didn't go to college, he knows the most amazing stuff. Listening to it now, the whistling is eerie yet soothing. Like a flute. A bamboo flute. In this case, nature's flute.

"Hey, Jedd," I say, "did you ever play an instrument?"

He looks up, reorienting himself. "Violin. Fifth grade. If that counts."

I tell him it counts, but I see him as more of a synth or laser harp kind of guy.

"The violin was all Mom," he says with a laugh. "I weaseled out of it as soon as I could." He lowers his legs off the dashboard, folds his tablet. The last quarter mile of dirt driveway has too many potholes for gaming. "What about you?"

Extracurricular lessons were never in Mom's budget. Getting food on the table was hard enough. But I don't want to get into that now, so I say, "I always wanted to play the flute."

"Then get one."

"Maybe I will."

"Do it," he urges. "You won't have to look far for a teacher."

"You mean the kid."

We like to call him the kid. He's a teen and a high school dropout, so he's technically a kid. His real name is Ansirk. The first time I heard him play at the fountain, he pronounced it for me. With an initial drawn-out "A-h-h-n." When I said I'd never heard that name, he said his mother liked to do things backwards. I'm not sure what he meant.

"I'll bet he could use some pocket money," Jedd says.

It's never been clear how the kid earns money, if he even does. Or how he feeds and clothes himself or where he sleeps every night. Or why he's always smiling.

"I'll say this," Jedd adds, as we step out of the chariot and he greets the black dog that's already running circles around him. "You could probably learn a lot more from that kid than just how to play a flute. We all could."

Yudhishtira, eldest of the Pandava princes
and rightful heir to the throne of Hastinapura,
was known for never telling a lie.

THE FAMILY: Jedd

At dinnertime whoever's at home makes the effort to wait until everyone else arrives so we can eat together. Tonight Darah and I find the others gathered around the communal kitchen table, salivating over a pan of steaming hot eggplant in marinara, glazed with mozzarella and parmesan and sprinkled with basil. If it weren't for Beers, the rest of us would subsist on boxed food from the café. But Beers lives for his cuisine; more than that, he lives to nourish us with it. As soon as he sees us now, he dishes out six plates, then lets us serve ourselves from a bowl of mixed greens and a tray with focaccia and condiments.

It's a warm evening, so we head to the porch, which wraps around three sides of our old Victorian farmhouse in the hills above Cupertino. My spot is the hammock, strung between two posts at the corner nearest the towering redwood. I like to sit sideways, legs dangling over the edge as I eat, then flip up my feet so I can relax while I digest. The others sit in Adirondack chairs. Except for Nick and Zack. Their spot is the wicker loveseat hung from chains in front of the window. Dharma makes his rounds, sniffing everyone's dish, then crawls under the hammock. He's ready for any crumbs I let fall through the mesh.

With everyone settled, Beers turns to me: "Hear the news, Jedd?"

Because the free press is banned in the States, we follow California sources, which do their best to sort truth from lies. One of us checks the latest on the way home and fills the others in. Usually it's Beers. I'd rather dig into a good game, but his security mindset keeps him alert to threats both near and far.

"No," I say. "What's up?"

"The Dick has doubled down on the border."

"Really?" I wasn't expecting that. The border's been closed for years. There's no reason to escalate now.

"His drones in Nevada and Arizona are programmed to shoot on sight," Beers says.

"And Idaho," Nick adds.

"How do we know?"

Beers says California tracking systems picked up the intel. There haven't been any deaths, but it's just a matter of time.

"Used to be the borders were closed to prevent people from entering the States," June says. "Now he wants to prevent them from leaving."

I chew in silence as I consider this. We've told ourselves for years the Dictator can't say or do anything to shock us more, and then he finds a way to do exactly that. Life just got harder for anyone hoping to flee to California. To offset what I know everyone's feeling, I offer the first silver lining that comes to mind: "Let's take this as a sign the Dictator isn't about to invade." The fact that I don't repeat Beers's choice epithet doesn't mean I consider him any less of a dick.

"How do you figure that?" Beers asks.

"Why close down access to California if you plan to take it over anyway?" I counter. I'm about to speculate further but stop myself. We each have our own ways of dealing with world events. Though I prefer to avoid the tumult of the news cycle, I see the value of staying informed, analyzing events, anticipating where things are headed. June is politically minded, so she likes to weigh in. Beers is into it more for the drama; he'll get worked up and fret over bad news for days. At which point someone will remind him we can't change whatever's bugging him. There are things we can change and things we can't. Now, for instance, it isn't as if we can do anything to deter the Dictator if he's determined to move on California. Besides, we try to minimize talk about him in front of Darah. She's come a long way but will likely never be as desensitized as the rest of us. Understandably, considering what happened to her mother. So I let June refocus us. I suspect she has some office chitchat on her mind.

She does. "I'm wondering," she says, "how you responded to Kurt."

"Responded to what?" Beers asks.

The rest of us give blank looks.

She stares at me in disbelief. "Jedd, you're always the first in our pod to get invites."

A few years ago HSys adopted a structure of affinity pods, based on the belief that having supportive pod-mates is more valuable than having them all work on related tasks. It puts us about one step up from an ad-hocracy, but people like it. We five naturally formed a pod and Darah joined us. Pods are supposed to be egalitarian, but that doesn't mean they're leaderless. Everyone considers me our leader. I'm the reflective one, the one who can solve problems and chart a clear course. The one who's level-headed, no matter what shit's thrown at us. Who will never tell a lie. Beers goes so far as to call me the family sage.

That might be how others see me. It isn't how I see myself. Of course I like when people say I'm a good leader. And I am one at times, can't deny that. It's my nature. But I don't want it to define me. I try not to place myself above or even apart from others or be an old-school leader who insists everything must funnel through me. I do my best to be fair and honest and respectful and hear others out when we disagree. June might take issue with that. She takes issue with nearly everything. Being contrarian is like eating and breathing to her. If you asked me to describe myself, I'd say I'm a playful kind of guy. I like to point out my birth name is Yehudi, in honor of another type of player—the violinist Yehudi Menuhin, whose recordings my mother listened to when she was young. She had high hopes I'd be that kind of player.

Yet music's never been my thing. When she signed me up for violin lessons in fifth grade, I refused to practice. Instead I found a bargaining chip. "If you let me ditch violin and join the chess club," I said, "I won't fight you about a bar mitzvah."

She said she had no idea I didn't want a bar mitzvah. Pleading ignorance was her fallback as a single parent. She often kept me in check by saying, "Yehudi, if your dad were here . . ." This was not one of those times. There was no reason to believe he'd care about a bar mitzvah. In fact, he was the one who taught me chess. Told me the world needed more grandmasters of African descent. We played every time I saw him.

I took my bargain a step further: "If I beat the top high school chess player, then can I join?"

My mother agreed, confident the odds of a fifth grader losing to a senior were in her favor. But they weren't, and I became the youngest member of the chess club. I played chess before school, after school, during meals, while doing homework, while studying Hebrew. I played in my dreams at night. I was obsessed with the history of chess computers, like Deep Blue and Deep Thought, and envisioned a career path set in silicon. Even so, I never imagined playing AI-supported games on a mini tablet that fit in my pocket. Or in a holographic world I set up in my bedroom.

By the time I got to UC Berkeley, I was chessed-out, ready

for new games. I feasted on computer science courses, especially game design. At the start of senior year, a friend offered me a programming gig at HSys I couldn't resist. It was time for Yehudi to morph into Jedi. The supposed musician turned space warrior. Ironically, while my HSys coworkers were thinking *Star Wars* when they called me Jedi, the name actually stemmed from Yehudi, the Hebrew word for Jew. Those years of Hebrew school had paid off after all.

Soon my salary dwarfed what I'd expected to earn after college. I outgrew being Jedi, the whiz kid. People simply called me Jedd. It sounded more mature.

I'm not one to brag, but the truth is I can program anything you might conjure up. Give me an idea, and I'll turn it into code. Code that works. If I'm not writing code, I'm probably deep in a video game. When someone is trying to find me, they're usually told to look for the lanky dude with the big Afro, the geekier, darker-skinned Bob Dylan doppelgänger with his nose in a video game. I won't dispute any of that. Except perhaps to say that comparing me to a musician will never ring true.

Any full disclosure isn't complete without a confession. I like playing games a little too much. To be honest, more than a little. I'm incapable of refusing a challenge, even if it comes with poor odds. That's because I've beaten the odds so many times. It's what I do. Once I get started, I can't stop myself. And you can't stop me. Fortunately most people have too much respect for my gaming to try.

"No, June," I say now, "nothing from Kurt."

"Double-check?"

All eyes fall on me as I pull out my tablet to confirm. The only new text is from Naomi. We've been trying to connect, but our schedules haven't lined up. I'll reply to her after dinner. "Nope, nothing."

Beers turns back to June. "So, what does Kurt want?"

"He's calling a superpod."

Meetings of two or more pods, called superpods, allow for in-person contact outside one's own pod. That can be sharing results and getting reactions to a project or gaining more diverse perspectives on a new idea. Kurt is in marketing and often runs superpod demos to get feedback. Sometimes superpods are no more than an officially sanctioned way to let off steam.

"Go ahead," I say, "give us the deets."

June holds up her tablet and reads aloud: "Your pod is invited to a superpod on Thursday at 9 a.m. Funnest game ever!"

Beers frowns. "That doesn't tell us much."

"Sounds like a demo," I say. Not that that tells us much.

"Funnest?" Nick snorts. "Who talks like that?"

"Kurt does," June says. "He wants us to think the game is fun."

Beers reaches over the arm of his chair and snatches June's tablet. "I'll bet he means funest—you know, *fyü*-nest. As in portending evil. Or causing death. As in death by superpod!"

June grabs her tablet back. "You know obscure words the rest of us don't. You're a crossword fiend. Kurt isn't. Trust me, this is just him being obnoxious."

"Yeah, probably," Beers says, falling back on his chair.

"The guy can be obnoxious, no doubt about it," I say. The last demo we attended showcased an olfactory smart cream. Not exactly cutting edge. While I thought it might enhance an intergalactic experience, Beers pronounced it a no-go for facial hair. He needed a full carton of wipes to get rid of the goo, but not before Kurt had made a crude remark about his whiskers.

"Obnoxious, pushy, even boorish," June says. "But not portending evil."

"He grabbed my butt earlier," Darah says quietly, almost as if she doesn't want us to hear.

"It's true," I say. "I was there."

Of course everyone wants the details, so she explains. It

happened really fast as we were entering the elevator. Kurt grabbed her. He acted like it was a prank, but it was uncalled for.

"Frankly, I'm not surprised." June says she's noticed Kurt gets away with dubious behavior. People—present company included—like his quirky marketing style, his knack for getting results. He gets the benefit of the doubt because he stops short of crossing any lines.

"Grabbing Darah crosses a line," Nick says.

Zack seconds that and asks the question on everyone's mind: "How do we respond?"

"First things first," Beers says. "Darah files a complaint with HR."

"Tonight," I say.

She whirls around. "And lose focus on my report? I don't think so."

Beers frowns. "You'd rather let it go? Just do nothing?" For someone who considers himself a man of action, restraint is an anathema.

"I'm saying what I do and when is *my* call," she counters. "Not yours. Not anyone else's."

June backs her up. "Beers, it's her call. Next time someone grabs your butt—"

"Fair enough," Beers says before June can complete the scenario; it's easy to imagine what that might look like. "But the rest of us could still take action."

June asks what he has in mind.

"Boycott the superpod."

"That would send a message," I say.

The others are nodding.

Darah nixes the idea.

I'm not sure why, except that, as June said, people tend to go easy on Kurt. He certainly doesn't deserve it now. "If that's what you want, Darah," I say. "We'll take your lead on this."

"Since I got the invite," June says when it's clear we aren't boy-cotting, "I should go."

"Then I'll go too," I say. You won't find me passing up a chance to run through the virgin territory of a new video game. Besides, it will allow me to keep tabs on whatever nonsense Kurt might be up to.

The others confirm they'll be there.

Except Darah. She won't commit to anything till her report is done. "If you can clean up without me," she says, "I'll get on it now."

I'm about to tell her to chill, as I did at the penthouse, but I know she'll sleep better after seeing that regenerating her graphs did the trick. "No problem," I say. "We've got it covered."

I'm on for wet mopping tonight. You'd think our robo-mop could handle that, but the thing spooks the dog so much we never use it anymore. So while the others do the initial cleanup, I stay in the hammock and text Naomi: "lunch tmw?"

She gets right back: "noon?"

"@café," I text. And we're on.

Because he cooked, Beers isn't on cleanup. When he plops down on the loveseat, I ask about his day.

None of us would have ended up living together if Beers hadn't come along. I met him the day he started as an assistant chef at the HSys café. He was hard to miss behind the counter at six feet and three hundred pounds, with his prematurely bald-ing head and broad smile. You might call him overweight, but his pounds come with the punch of a Sumo wrestler. He rarely does any formal exercise; he's innately strong. At the end of lunch that day, he wandered over to the table where June and I were sit-ting and introduced himself. I thought he was making small talk when he asked about a video game that had him stumped, but when he thanked me for my advice the next day, it was clear his interest was genuine.

What was less clear was why he'd taken a job at HSys in the first place. Independently wealthy, he had no need to work, especially during a time when jobs were vanishing at the rate of *Panthera leo* in Africa. Once when I pressed him, he claimed a job was his best chance to find a wife. By then I knew him well enough to know that was a joke. I think it's fair to say we all view marriage as too twentieth century.

Beers wasn't in the café long before he moved to the security team. His first assignment was in the bunker, so we didn't see much of him—until he decided to learn programming. Autodidact that he is, he could have done it on his own. But instead he proposed a trade with June: he'd teach her cooking if she'd teach him coding. She agreed. Judging by the amount of time she spends in the kitchen, he got the better end of the deal. He was a quick study and soon knew all sorts of tricks and shortcuts. June says he could write code in his sleep if he had to. The only issue is he isn't methodical. If you ask him how he solved a problem, he can't tell you. He says it just went off like a bomb in his brain.

Our move to Beers's place was a result of my craving for a canine companion. Having a dog was impractical while living with roomies in the city, spending long hours at work, often not making it home to sleep.

Beers decided to fix that. "Bro," he said one day, "if you're serious about a pooch, come live with me. There's plenty of room at my place."

I knew by then that even if it sounded at times like Beers had a bit of a savior complex, he didn't. He was being his legit generous self. But a move to the farm was big for me, having grown up on the asphalt turf of a city, so I had to verify: "You mean that?"

"Totes!" he said. "And June and Nick and Zack should come too."

So we did. Beers lived alone in a sprawling five-bedroom house on thirty acres, inherited from his family, who made their fortune in Cupertino's wine country some generations back. Perhaps because it had an old barn, Beers called it his farm. It wasn't actually a farm though. By the time the house fell into his hands, it was run down. He fixed up the kitchen and one bedroom, which was all he needed. After the rest of us moved in, we did more to spruce things up. Even now there's always a project underway—refurbishing the cedar-barrel hot tub or installing a bigger battery for solar storage or painting a mural in the bathroom. The farm is fully on the grid, so we enjoy all the amenities that come with the internet of things. Yet when we land here each night, it feels kind of like retiring into an earlier century. We like it that way.

I found Dharma at the Silicon Valley Humane Society. When he gazed up at me, his forlorn puppy eyes begging me to do the right thing and take him home, I instantly knew his name. Dharma means right action. You could say that committing the right action in every circumstance is my motto in life. I have a companion to remind me of that.

Now, after Beers has told me everything about his humdrum day, the conversation turns to Darah. "She seems stressed," he says.

I can't deny that.

"Anything I should know?"

"You mean besides what she told us?"

"Bro," he says, pulling his face into a frown, "I need to know if I should be concerned."

I hesitate. Beers has excellent radar. And a habit of being protective of anyone who's smaller than he is, which is all of us. He's probably noticed Darah hasn't been quite herself these past few weeks. News about the Dictator isn't worse than usual, and as far as I know, she isn't having nightmares. Still, she seems easily distracted. She eats too many lunches al desko, takes longer to get stuff done, spaces out. Like today when she went MIA for a couple hours when she had a major report due. But it isn't my place to bring that up. Whatever she wants us to know, she'll tell us. On her own time. "You know how she is," I say. "If she sees a problem, she'll hammer at it till it's handled."

Beers doesn't write reports, but he understands what can go awry with data. He asks if she's checked her source files.

"As we speak."

"Hopefully that takes care of it."

I'm about to quantify that hope as north of fifty percent when Darah bursts onto the porch, screen door slamming behind her. "That was quick," I say cheerily—until I see the distress on her face. "What's wrong?"

She collapses beside Beers. "I couldn't fix the graphs. There are no other data to regenerate them. I dug through everything!"

My first thought is she doesn't know her way around the HSys cloud as well as I assumed. "Are you sure?"

She sits up, tense and alert. "You don't believe me?"

If I have doubts, this isn't the moment to express them. She needs our support. I tell her I believe her. We all believe her.

I get that Darah has a lot riding on this report. She could be named lead on her next project if all goes well. Her job could be on the line if it doesn't. I don't see the latter happening, but I'm ready to sort out her data myself if need be. Folks at HSys ask me to do stuff like that all the time. Still, there has to be a simpler solution. I ask if she's reached out to Selma.

She says yes, but Selma hasn't replied.

At this point, the others emerge from the kitchen. June expects me to start mopping, but I tell her we're dealing with something more urgent. Mopping can wait. Then I turn back to Darah and say I didn't mean to mislead her. I honestly thought regenerating the graphs would fix this.

"Why assume that?" June is quick to jump in even though she doesn't know anything about the report or graphs in question.

"Because usually that's all it takes," I'm as quick to reply.

June bristles. "*Usually*? Sounds like you're leaving key variables out of your probability calculation. I mean, think of all the reasons data can be wrong."

"That's what we're discussing," I say.

June isn't satisfied. So we're off and running, bickering about Darah's data while the others wait for one of us to call a cease-fire. This isn't uncommon. We've squabbled and nitpicked since our days at Cal, when we took the same algorithm theory course. There's more than one way to optimize any algorithm, and we inevitably chose different routes, then got embroiled in a debate over their respective merits. She argued for the quickest route. I favored the most elegant one. To this day she's known for being fast. Whereas I might write the most intelligible code, she can out-code me based on sheer speed combined with dogged endurance. I've seen her produce a thousand lines of stellar code before lunch.

When I met June, she still went by her childhood name, Rose Bush. But all the years of teasing had worn her down, and she was ready for my suggestion: Why not take your mom's last name? Or use your middle name? She chose both. Legally she became R. June Liu. Or just June to friends.

During our early days at HSys, we found ourselves on projects together. Dating wasn't an option; we'd tried and failed at that while sparring over algorithmic theory. I often crashed on her couch after work so I didn't have to drive to my apartment in the city. Other than grumbling about the dirty clothes I left lying around, she was happy to have me. I watched as she blew through a string of boyfriends. Not that I was a factor in those breakups. The men were older, with high-paying jobs and homes of their own, so none ever stopped by and noticed me on the couch. My theory—which I knew better than to share with June—was that her problem stemmed from her arresting beauty. Her black hair, reaching to her waist, and flawless skin turned heads wherever she went. Even now in her thirties and only a few inches shorter than me, she maintains the willowy grace of a teen model. I've noticed some people hesitate to get close to anyone they see as a paragon of beauty. Others dare to get close but become antagonistic. I avoid being in either camp.

"Let's quit the bickering," I say now. "It's not helping Darah."

"Fine," says June. "We'll have to agree to disagree. You suspect a random harmless cyber hiccup. I'm thinking more like . . . foul play."

"Foul play?" Darah says, voice rising. "You think someone purposely messed with my data?"

June shrugs. "Either that or it was bad from the start."

"So you think *I* messed up?"

"I didn't say that."

"You implied it." Darah may be gen beta, but she doesn't have June's tech expertise, so it's harder to defend herself. But she holds her ground. She says she saw the positive results. On her screen. With her own eyes. The kids who played KnoMor excelled in science. The game worked! Besides, all the data were autogenerated. It isn't like anyone would ever manually enter test scores.

"True," says June. "But there's no such thing as fail-safe data."

Beers is nodding. "I agree. We can't rule out a cybersecurity breach."

"Hold on!" Nick says.

Heads turn toward the porch steps, where he and Zack are sitting.

"You're talking about a cyberattack?" Zack says.

"On a science game?"

"For real?"

It's not unusual for Nick and Zack to listen more than they speak, at least initially. They're the quiet ones in our family. When one doesn't say anything, the other doesn't either. They're alike in so many ways. They even look alike: the same height, both slim, with aquiline noses and dark blond hair, both equally nerdy. Both wear vintage Harry Potter glasses. I didn't meet them until they came to HSys, but they've been inseparable since middle school: always got the same grades, liked the same video games, had the same friends. At HSys they both work as graphic artists. Nick has a flair for concept design and Zack is an expert at 3D modeling, but their skill sets are interchangeable, and they always end up working on the same projects. Wherever they go, everyone loves them, and loves them both equally.

In a six-person family, it wouldn't feel right for some to pair off in exclusive dyads. These two are the exception. They merged into the entity NicknZack—with a self-designed graphic meme to prove it—before any of us met them, so there's no awkwardness about it now.

They're always up for a prank. When Beers started at HSys, they pretended to be twins. He believed them. Started calling them "the twins." They got a good laugh out of it. As did the rest of us. By the time they admitted the truth to him, everyone was calling them the twins. We still do.

They're also quite psychic. Each knows what the other is thinking. That's one reason they're so quiet: they don't need to speak much to share their thoughts. They've developed a knack for foreseeing the future and making predictions. It tends to be about something trivial, like who'll get a phone call or win at basketball. Occasionally they go bigger. Like predicting the Dictator will be invincible till some "little guy" comes out of nowhere and dethrones him. Of course that's all in jest. Or wishful thinking. No one really believes some little guy from nowheresville is going to overthrow the Dictator.

"Thanks," I say now. Their reaction has given me a reason to intervene, to dial things back. "You're right, we can't just scream cyberattack. Not without more info. *But,*" I add before June or Beers can shoot me down, "I hear your concerns. I do."

Beers makes a low grunt, as he does when he wants to do something, take some sort of action, but that's not our best option in the moment. He knows he'll be outvoted if he pushes.

"You're scaring me," Darah says.

I can see from the tightening in her eyes that's not an exaggeration. So I back off a little. "I know you'd like a solution right away. We all would. It's hard to live with uncertainty. But we need to see how this plays out. Starting with what you hear from Selma."

"Okay," Darah says. "But you can't let this go."

"Trust me, we won't," June says.

"No, we won't," I echo. "Promise."

Our family discussions are always lively. We get in the mud together, roll with the punches, and come out more unified as a result, clear about whatever action is needed and ready to do it together. If that right action is still unclear, we sit with the ambiguity. We continue dialoguing. To survive in this crazy world, you need family like that.

The twins stand up and start to head inside, then pause in front of Darah. I sense a prediction on its way.

So does she. "Please, if this is about my job, I'm not ready to hear it."

The twins look at each other for a second, then Zack says, "It isn't."

She perks up. "Okay, then what?"

"It's a warning," Nick says. "About someone."

"We don't know who it is," Zack interjects.

"Right," says Nick. "The warning is that this person isn't who you think they are."

The Kaurava prince said to Arjuna,
"Take aim and tell me what you see."
The young Pandava archer replied,
"I see only the eye of the bird."

FIRST SHOT FIRED: June

I'm not in the habit of waiting when the others get up late or even dawdle a few extra secs over breakfast. I like fast. That's my life: *fast.* If I have a busy day ahead, I double-check that my smart shoes and accessories are color coordinated and not set to sparkle, then hop in the chariot and off I go. As soon as 6G became standard and all the ethical issues of level-5 cars were solved, I bought one. Unfortunately, I failed to consider its speed. Or lack of. One thing it's not is fast.

This morning Darah left before any of us woke up. Which means we'll be taking three vehicles between the six of us. Not very ecological. I know that. She knows that. But sometimes it's too hard to sync everyone's schedules.

Alone in the chariot, I get busy with the messages piling up on my tablet. Of course, my virtual assistant has been programmed to respond with clever (and sometimes witty) replies to most of what lands in my inbox. Even so, while answering the few that require a personal touch—the VA is trained to identify those—I like to peek at the rest to see what's been etched in electrons. Now what catches my eye is a text from Kurt asking for confirmation I'll be at the superpod. My VA has handled it with a simple thumbs up. For a second, I consider amending that with "sorry, something came up." I don't though. Am I excited about Kurt's superpod? No. Especially not after Darah's revelation. The creep grabbed her butt, for god's sake. But she made it clear she prefers to play it cool with him. That in a nutshell is the difference between Darah and me. I'd have put him on blast. But it's her call and I'll honor that. The way I see it, I'm attending Kurt's superpod as a professional duty. Plus there's always a chance the new game will live up to its hype and be fun. Or challenging. In fact, challenging is my idea of fun.

I didn't plan on a career in gaming. At Yale, I intended to major in political science, to learn how to save our democracy. The country had been teetering on the edge, as one state after another did away with free and fair elections. You had to be comatose not to read the writing on the wall. But most people—even many my age, whose futures were at stake—looked the other way. They didn't care enough to follow the news or vote, let alone take any kind of social or political or ecological action. As far as they were concerned, politicians were dirt. Even aspiring to become one made you dirt.

Once I asked a classmate to help us get voters to the polls. He literally laughed in my face. "Work on an election that's already decided? Surely you don't believe the Kool-Aid we're supposed to drink in poli-sci is a lived reality."

"Actually," I said, "I want to make sure democracy is our lived reality. That's why I'm doing what I'm doing."

Another time I invited a friend to a protest where a famous climate activist was speaking. I saw it as a chance to raise our voices, to tell the government they must do more. The friend blew me off. She already had plans for a pedicure before her yoga class.

Still, I didn't stop talking about the state of the world. About the despair I was feeling. About actions we could take to make a difference. Invariably, friends listened for two secs before changing the subject. The worse things got, the less they wanted to know. I was determined to be different.

To me, politics isn't dirty. It's simply the civilized alternative to violence as the means for selecting a government. Of course, it doesn't guarantee democracy. But you can't have democracy unless enough people engage in political action. Voting is the barest minimum. I think it should be mandatory.

While volunteering for one election, I was assigned to data management. Not that I was a data whiz, but we pitched in however we could. When our system was hacked, I found myself without the skills to fix or even understand what went wrong. The candidate lost despite a groundswell of popular support. Everyone agreed: the results didn't add up. But we couldn't prove it. Recognizing how much more I needed to learn, I transferred to UC Berkeley's accelerated-degree program in computer science.

After I graduated, I still intended to go into politics. Even more so as we witnessed the free press under attack, opposition leaders jailed on false charges, protesters shot in the streets. Shot in schools. Snatched from their homes. California felt like a safe oasis, though we never knew for how long. College wasn't free yet, and I'd run up a large debt while studying data systems and artificial intelligence. I ended up taking a job at HSys, thinking I'd pay it off and then go back East and work for the resistance. Maybe run for office someday.

All that got derailed by the Dictator. Sometimes people in California ask, "Why don't those Mericans in the States resist, as many did initially? Why don't they fight back?" The answer is obvious: look at what happened to my activist friends. Disappeared. A few lucky ones resurfaced in Canada or Mexico, but most vanished without a trace. Of course, the resistance hasn't stopped entirely. But it's gone so deep underground you wouldn't know it exists. My own activism as a student means I'd face arrest if caught trying to enter the States. Because of that, I haven't visited my family in years.

Fortunately I've come to appreciate life at HSys. Yes, there are far more important things than gaming, and one day I'll find a way to do them. But for now I avoid dwelling on all the ugly, unjust, deplorable, despicable, horrific, unconscionable things that continue to go down. Things I'm powerless to change. At Yale, a few of my friends used to say, "Rose, I'm glad you're political. Glad you're an activist. Someone has to be." I told them I wished *they'd* step up too, do their part. Stop passing it off as someone else's business. These days, though, none of us knows what to do to fix this insane world. Even if the Dictator were ousted, we couldn't repair all the damage. We wouldn't know where to start. So I do the only thing that makes sense: I stay busy in my personal sphere, grateful to be safe in a free country, earning good money at a job that keeps me on my toes.

More texts are coming in as the chariot enters the HSys lot. But I'm not reading them. Almost before the chariot's auto shutoff has emitted its final blink, I'm sprinting between parked cars and through a side entrance, then cutting across the lawn and up the central walkway. Like I said, fast.

A patch of Monet's waterlilies drifts across the display wall as I burst into the penthouse. Darah likes to throw up calming images before the wall gets cluttered with diagrams and lists. I walk over to the table by the window, where she's deep in her report, earbuds turned on, probably listening to a nature sounds app. She is the only person I've ever heard hum along with nature sounds.

"Hey there," I say.

She gives a little jump. "June! I didn't hear you come in."

The two empty coffee cups by her screen tell me she didn't get much sleep. Hopefully I didn't add to that by giving her a hard time last night. I tend to give people a hard time. I can be nasty. Downright nasty if I have to be. I don't necessarily think I'm bugging them, but they think so. And tell me later. Except for Jedd, who never hesitates to tell me then and there. When I was a kid, my mother told me women who spoke up freely used to be seen as repugnant. They were shunned, humiliated for voicing opinions. She insisted all that had changed. "Rose, speak your mind!" was a mantra of hers. I listened. And spoke up. Refused to let others get the last word. I dreamed of being a politician whose speech empowered the lives of many. Even before I got to college, though, I realized she was wrong: how women were treated hadn't changed that much.

I continued to speak up when I got to HSys but also began doing damage control if someone was offended. Don't get me wrong, I don't give a pass to every idiot who finds me intimidating. I'm talking about friends. Like now, with Darah. I pour myself a coffee, then take a seat across the table and ask how it's going.

She turns off her earbuds. "I reached Selma."

"Good. So how will you handle the data?" I rein in my instinct to provide an answer—my own answer—to that question.

"She said to spin it."

"How?"

"Play up the teachers' feedback."

"And downplay the stats?"

"Yeah." She pauses. "She didn't mention a cyberattack. She's confident in our results."

That's Darah's way of letting me know she didn't appreciate the possible scenario I was pushing last night. I should probably back off a bit, reassure her it was pure conjecture. But it's nine o'clock and the others are here and ready to troop down to the superpod, so I just ask if she's coming.

She shakes her head.

I promise we'll fill her in later. "If you want, I can tell Kurt you're sorry—"

"I don't want," she says quickly. "And I'm not sorry."

"Got it." I smile. "I'll give him a kick in the balls for you."

"That's more like it," she says without a smile.

Superpods are popular, well-attended, often boisterous events. I assumed Kurt's pod—roughly twenty of them—would be here, drinking coffee, checking tablets, milling around when we walked in. But there are only a handful, quietly seated. Apparently no other pods were invited. I slip into an empty chair in front of Karin and Keith. I've heard her refer to him as the father of her kid, but I don't think they live together. Not that that's unusual.

This office is set up much like the penthouse, except smaller and with fewer amenities, though their pod is larger. Many of the pod-mates either work remotely or inhabit a workstation in the open-space area. Safe to say, the latter is a source of friction.

When we're all settled, Kurt scans the room. His eyes stop at the empty seat beside me. "Who's missing?"

"Darah," Keith says. Almost like he expected her not to come. At least he remembers who's in our pod.

Kurt crosses his arms so they rest on his belly and locks eyes with me. "All the people who count are here." He dims the windows, and a banner with "VRcher" in neon red pops onto the display wall. "This is your first look at our next blockbuster. Promised it would be fun, didn't I?"

I glance at Beers to see if he caught that: just fun, nothing evil. But he's fixed on Kurt.

"Here's how it will go. You'll put on this helmet." He holds up what looks like a limp purple nylon ski cap. "Orient yourself. Then look for the bird and take aim. Don't shoot till I tell you to." He pauses. "Got it?"

I'm tempted to ask if it's a first-person shooter game. We all know HSys no longer supports FPSs. But I figure that'll be clear in a minute.

Jedd points to the helmet. "Does it fit all kinds of hair?"

"Designed with your hair in mind." Kurt stretches the helmet to demo its elasticity, then adds, "And your skin color."

"Purple?" Beers says.

I can't tell if Kurt thinks he's being funny or this is how he gets away with microaggressions.

Jedd doesn't dignify him with a response.

No one else has a reaction or a question, so Kurt hands Karin the helmet. She has no problem tucking in her thin blonde hair. The skull cap is opaque purple, and its smart-glass eye shield is a lighter reflective purple. Pretty chic—nothing remotely like those old facebricks.

We watch as a 3D landscape appears on the display wall, the same reality Karin is experiencing in her helmet, only silent. It's a woodland scene, with large trees on either side. Their branches are in constant motion, suggesting a looming storm. A brightly colored parrot swoops low, then rises toward the sky and circles back again. Several squirrels scamper across a branch. Reminds me of classic Walt Disney.

Karin looks like a blindfolded toddler, arms flailing, trying to pin the tail on the donkey.

"Come on!" Kurt encourages her.

She feels around until her arms become steady, and it's obvious she is holding a bow with an arrow cocked. "Dang, this is harder than it looks," she mutters. "Now what?"

"See the parrot?" Kurt prompts.

"Uh-huh."

"Set your mark. Remember, don't shoot. Just say when you're ready."

She fumbles a bit more, then announces she's ready.

"What do you see?"

I'm getting antsy. No one will ever call this slug an FPS, let alone a blockbuster. Shoot, for heaven's sake. It occurs to me Kurt may be waiting for the bird to lift off in flight. But it doesn't.

"What's he waiting for?" I whisper to Jedd.

"No idea," he whispers back.

Karin is still holding her arms raised. "A couple of trees. Some squirrels. A green parrot." She pauses. "That's what I see."

Kurt cuts the display.

She drops her arms and wheels around. "But I didn't shoot."

Kurt dismisses her with a wave of his hand.

She removes the helmet—her hair now plastered to her head—and returns to her seat, grumbling. Can't say I blame her.

"Loser," Kurt says under his breath but loud enough for us to hear.

Jedd and I exchange glances. It doesn't make sense for Kurt to put Karin through all those paces for nothing. And then insult her. I don't recall him acting like this. Obnoxious, yes. Boorish, yes. But abusive? Maybe he has a mean streak we didn't know about— one his pod-mates are used to, judging by their lack of reaction.

Next up is Beers. He gets into the helmet and stands with feet shoulder-width apart, facing the display at ninety degrees. We can see the same woodland. He aligns his bow faster than Karin. "Easy," he says. "I'm ready."

"Not so fast," says Kurt. "What do you see?"

"I see the bird on a wide branch, fluffing its wings. It's about to take off. Let me shoot."

Again it seems Kurt is waiting for the bird to fly. Again it doesn't. Everything else is in motion, but the bird sits there like a block of wood.

"Nope," says Kurt, cutting the display.

I jostle Jedd's arm. "Huh?" I mouth silently.

He raises his eyebrows as if to say, *No clue.*

As Beers sits down, Keith steps forward. "I've got this." He dons the helmet and quickly raises and strings his bow. I suspect he's been through this demo before. He should cinch it.

"What do you see?" Kurt asks, right on cue.

"The tips of my shoes. You need to make this shield snugger at the bottom." He laughs. "Of course I see the parrot. May I shoot?"

"No!" Kurt snarls. He's really hamming it up—so much so it's hard to tell if his act is part of the game. Judging by the titters behind me, his pod-mates think so. I'm not sure how I'll respond when it's my turn. One thing is certain: he isn't going to talk to me like that.

Jedd goes next. "Let's see if I can crack this," he whispers to me.

He has no trouble stuffing his hair into the helmet. As he positions himself, he doesn't fumble like Karin or move swiftly like Keith and Beers. He's deliberate, lining things up as precisely as possible. After a minute he says, "Ready."

"What do you see?" By now it's hard not to snicker at that question.

"The tip of the arrow. It's in perfect alignment with the parrot."

"Nope," Kurt sneers.

There is a low murmur as Jedd sits down. Even if it's a difficult game, he usually figures things out. And doesn't quit until he does.

It is a similar story for the other pod-mates. Kurt doesn't let anyone shoot.

I'm last up.

To my surprise, Kurt turns on the charm. "June," he says with a wink as he hands me the helmet, "show us how this is done."

The helmet is lightweight and fits tightly without being constricting. My hair is too long to tuck in, so I don't even try. I can feel a slight pressure at certain points on my scalp. Probably sensors of some sort. As soon as Kurt activates the display, I'm standing in a majestic forest. I can hear all the ambient sound—the chatter of squirrels, birds calling, the swoosh of the parrot's wings as it flies low. It's a first-class reality job, and I take a minute to enjoy it.

"Ready, June?" Kurt prompts.

A medieval longbow and arrow sit on the ground, and I reach for them. Immediately I see why the others were struggling. It's hard to hold the bow steady enough to nock the arrow. The pieces fall apart if you don't keep them aligned. Even so, it doesn't take me long to nock the arrow, draw the bow, and aim at the bird. "Ready."

"What do you see?"

Given how it's gone for everyone else, I don't expect to be able to shoot. But Kurt's being congenial, so I play along. "The eye of the parrot."

"What else?"

"Nothing."

"Finally, a true shooter. Go, June!"

As I let the arrow fly, the parrot explodes in a blaze of light.

Kurt cheers as I take off my helmet.

Everyone looks duly impressed. Except Karin and Keith, who jump up and start grousing loudly, saying Kurt should have let everyone shoot. The three of them are facing off in front of the display wall as the five of us slip out.

"What a load of crap!" I exclaim as we charge into the penthouse.

Darah looks up from her screen. "That bad, really?"

"Worse," Beers says.

I tell her she's lucky she wasn't there. She didn't miss a thing. Which pretty much sums it up, so I turn to check what my VA has prioritized for the day. Usually I enjoy prolonging the glory of a win. That's the point of winning. In this case, while my VRcher victory may have impressed Kurt, it yielded zero satisfaction for me.

But Darah wants to know what was so awful.

Jedd suggests we take a moment to debrief. He always wants everyone to feel included, and this is no exception.

"We can do it at home," I say.

Jedd responds by calling for a show of hands. I'm outvoted five to one—no surprise there—so we gather on barstools in the kitchenette. Beers activates the espresso machine and breaks open a bag of protein chips. Leave it to him to futz with food at a moment like this.

"Are you thinking what I'm thinking?" Jedd throws out after he has described the basic setup for Darah.

"I'm thinking titanic waste of time." I point out that further talk about the time wasted won't bring it back. It's a valid point but the others ignore me.

"I'm thinking that's one heck of a piece of shelfware," Beers says as he reaches for another handful of chips.

"The bow was a joke," Nick says.

"All you had to do was look at it and it fell apart," Zack adds.

"Why only let June shoot?" Nick says. "And call her a true shooter. What's with that?"

"Your basic charientism," Beers says. Before we can let out a collective huh, he explains: "You know, a taunt disguised as a joke."

"I'm a sharpshooter of parrots," I say, going with the joke.

"A holographic parrot?" Darah sounds surprised. I don't know where she got that idea. None of us mentioned a hologram.

Beers reiterates what Jedd said, that it was a typical immersive VR shooting range, minus the violence. "I could have shot that bird as well as you, Madam Sharpshooter," he says, turning to me. "I'd have shot twice as many in half the time. Facts."

Of course Beers will never beat me at anything based on speed. I take a sip of my latte and point out that beta testers expect to feel engaged. Generating a wealth of feedback can improve a game. Yet Kurt never allowed us to express an opinion or offer suggestions. Not only that, he showed an ugly side of himself I've never seen.

"I couldn't believe his crack about Jedd's skin color," Beers says.

"Some microaggression BS about purple skin," I say, anticipating Darah's question. "He wasn't just obnoxious—he was downright offensive."

"To you?" she asks.

"Not me." I describe how he dialed up the charm when it was my turn. I have no idea why. Maybe he was fishing for a reaction or trying to stick it to someone in his pod.

"Why would he do that?" Darah asks.

"I have no idea," I say again. "Nor apparently did his pod. Most of them weren't there, but the few who were acted like it was no big deal."

"Except Keith and Karin. Did you see how salty they got?" Nick says. "They were at each other's throats before we were out the door."

"We didn't even say goodbye," Zack adds.

Since throwing out the initial question, Jedd has been sitting back and watching us hash it out, waiting for the right moment to jump in. He's always the one to cut through confusion and reveal order where there appears to be only chaos. Sometimes I wish I had his patience, his presence of mind. "Here's what I think," he says, leaning forward, both elbows on the countertop. "I don't know what's up with his pod-mates, but I suspect Kurt doesn't care what we think about VRcher. If he did, he'd have asked for feedback."

"Then why hold a superpod?" I ask.

Jedd looks around the group, as if gauging how we'll react. "Perhaps he was using the superpod to find out something about *us*."

"About us?" Beers echoes. "That's a wild idea. Say more."

"I'm just theorizing, okay?" Jedd says. "Kurt seemed interested in who has the ability to focus and who doesn't. That's why he singled out June. She saw only the eye of the bird. The rest of us were distracted by other details."

"It's smart to take in the whole scene," Beers objects. "I call that being aware."

"Of course. But to hit a target, you need total focus." Jedd pauses. "Either way, I see a bigger problem: none of what we witnessed justifies the expense of creating that game. You don't create a game to *not* shoot; you create a game *to* shoot. And you don't hold a demo to stir up shit between people. There has to be more to this."

"No doubt," I say. "But we're not going to get to the bottom of it now."

I can see Jedd wants to keep talking, but Darah says she needs to get back to her report. So she and the twins head to their workstations. Beers leaves for a shift at the lobby scanner.

As I ball up the empty protein chip bag and toss it in the recycle shaft, my mind is already churning on the code I need to write to eliminate the twenty-millisecond delay in the brain-computer interface for the new Freaks game. BCI is one of my specialties, and I'm eager to get on it.

As I turn to go, Jedd touches my arm.

"What?"

"Something's off, June. No one's about to market that snoozefest. I have to wonder who developed it. And that demo felt like some sort of setup. Or a way to distract us. The question is, a setup for what? Distract us why?"

Usually I like when Jedd pulls me aside and we put our heads together over a tough question. We rarely squabble in such moments. But right now I don't have any answers. It just seems like an ill-conceived game that will never see the light of day. My VA has pinged repeatedly since we got back. It's programmed to escalate to a ping-alarm if it decides I'm ignoring it. I'd like to avoid that.

"Did you notice anything weird when it was your turn?" he says. "Think about it."

I hear the urgency in Jedd's voice. He wouldn't press me unless he had serious concerns. I lower myself back onto a stool and silence my VA so I can mentally review the experience. The helmet was a snug fit. Lightweight. Easy to turn my head. Then I remember the slight points of pressure. "I felt what seemed like sensors on my scalp. Nothing unusual."

He says he noticed that too. "What about when you shot the bird? Anything stand out?"

"It all happened so fast. When I let the arrow fly, there was a bright flash. Almost blinding. You must have seen that on the display wall."

Jedd confirms he saw a flash but wants to know what it was like from my perspective.

I hesitate. It's hard to describe and I want to avoid fabricating a memory. I know VR can have that effect on one's capacity for recall. "It was almost like something happened to my eyes."

"You mean your sight?"

"Perhaps."

"Or your brain?"

"My *brain*?" It's true that sensors in the helmet suggest a BCI technology, but nothing in my experience substantiated that as a component of the game. Aside from the epic Disney visuals, it seemed like your basic aim-and-shoot.

"Maybe your brain," he says. "I'm just speculating. Tell me more about the flash."

Jedd's curiosity is rubbing off. In spite of myself, I'm getting into this. I close my eyes so I can relive the moment more vividly. "It's like . . . I'm looking at the parrot . . . and then I shoot . . . but when the shot hits the bird, something hits my eye. Sort of like a ricochet." I open my eyes and shrug. "It sounds weird, for sure. And it was subtle. That's the best I can describe it."

"Interesting" is all Jedd says. Then his tablet lights up. Someone's waiting for him at the café and he has to jet off, so our chat comes to an abrupt end.

Bheema was the strongest of the Pandavas,
his might equal to that of ten thousand elephants.

UPROOTED: Beers

Since the VRcher superpod I've been asking myself: How fucking bizarre was that? We've all been asking the same thing. Effing creepy, really. Like a video clip you want to unsee but can't. It's been a couple weeks and none of us can get it out of our minds. Not even Darah, who wasn't there. It comes up as we're chatting over coffee. It comes up in the chariot. At dinner. In dumb jokes. Fortunately it hasn't kept us from laughing. It's not like we've become a bunch of agelasts. We do like to laugh. Laughter keeps us sane. Still, we haven't been able to forget that superpod.

To me, this has the classic makings of a security issue. I mean, that's how security issues often develop: you sense something is wrong, but you don't quite know what or why. On the surface, it could appear totally inconsequential. Yet something doesn't click. A person you thought was cool suddenly isn't. Someone says one thing but does something different. Or says one thing to you and something different to someone else, and then you hear about it. So you become vigilant. At least more vigilant than you were already. I have to say though, vigilance for a security guard at HSys is mostly about not dozing off while monitoring a security feed. Or remembering to smile at people as they hurry through a scanner, then apologizing when said scanner buzzes for no good reason. Any serious issues at the company are of the cybernetic kind. Not visible to the naked eye, you could say. That's Jedd's territory. Everyone at HSys knows he's the best. Yet he doesn't have a big head about it. He'd happily spend as much time helping one of us with a project as he'd spend solving an international hack.

In any case, after the VRcher event, I promised the others I'd keep an eye on Kurt.

"Watching for what exactly?" June asked.

"When I suss that out, I'll tell you."

"Sure, Beers, be alert," Jedd said, "but let's not overreact." You can count on that dude to push restraint. It doesn't matter that he's actively voicing his own suspicions about VRcher.

Nor was that demo an isolated event. Kurt attacked Darah the night before, grabbed her like she was a pound of beef.

"I'm taking down the son of a bitch," I said, when Jedd and I were alone. "I swear."

He put the kibosh on that. Maybe he thought I'd go ballistic, pummel Kurt until he begged for mercy. Or worse. And he wouldn't have been wrong.

"Okay, okay, bro," I said. "But I'm keeping an eye out. Like I said."

This is personal for me. Kurt has rubbed me the wrong way since day one, when I was an assistant chef in the HSys café. So has his buddy Keith. Both are so full of themselves. Like a pair of pit bulls. Only difference is Keith stands a good head taller, and his eyes are as hard as rocks. Kurt's eyes are more like cold oatmeal. Karin is the best of the three, which isn't saying much. When any of them look at you, even if they don't open their mouths, you know what they're thinking: "I'm smarter than you. I'm more successful than you. I'm better than you." Their arrogance is smeared across their faces like tomato sauce on pizza.

I've never shared my true feelings about those three with the others at home. There hasn't been a reason to. Instead I call them our cousins. It's my little splash of sarcasm. My way of spitting on their tomato sauce. Even now, after Kurt's butt grab, there is still at least one reason not to say anything: Darah has a thing for Keith. That wasn't hard to figure out. She tries to hide it, but it's obvious. At least to me. I can also tell she doesn't know I know. But I don't want to upset her or look like I'm jealous or anything like that. Because I'm not. So I don't tease her about it.

The twins made an interesting prediction: someone isn't who Darah thinks they are. I assumed it must be Keith. Now I think it could be Kurt. Heck, could be both. Or it could be whoever messed with her KnoMor data. We never ruled out a cyberattack, but she was able to salvage her data and turn in her report. Everything panned out. At least as far as I know. I'm still thinking about NicknZack's prediction though. It was for Darah, but I feel a need to look out for everyone. What affects one affects us all.

Looking after people is what I do. Day to day, it's all about the little stuff. Like right now. On our way to the penthouse, before starting today's crossword puzzle, I activated the espresso machine. So as we walk in, the brew of choice is waiting for each of us. I grab six cups—red for Jedd, turquoise for June, purple for Darah, two yellows for NicknZack, green for me—and pour our coffees, complete with the HSys logo inscribed in the foam.

The others are settling in, chatting, checking calendars, replying to texts. Darah flips between lilies and roses before settling on daisies for the display wall. I'm about to hand out the coffee when five pings go off in quick succession around the room. Along with the sound of chirping crickets, Darah's ringtone.

I reach for my tablet. As do the others.

The text is from upper management and begins with an apology: "We regret this late notice." When it's clear all of us have received the same message, Jedd reads it aloud: "Due to an unexpected critical need for facilities on the sixth floor of Building 1, you are requested to pack your personal and project-specific items and relocate to room 538, effective immediately."

Darah gasps.

He glances at her, then continues: "Packing materials will be delivered to your door. Maintenance will move all boxes before EOD. Again, apologies for any inconvenience. Thank you for your spirit of collaboration and for helping to make HSys the successful company it is today."

"What the fuck!?" You won't hear many curses on Jedd's tongue, but I don't mind swearing if the situation calls for it. Like now. And often when it doesn't.

"There must be some mistake," June says.

"How can they kick us out?" Darah heaves a sigh that ends more like a wail.

The twins are silent. They look anything but pleased. Really, none of us needs this antediluvian corporate crap disrupting our lives. I look at Jedd. "What do you make of this?"

He shakes his head. "Maybe they're emptying the room for maintenance or an upgrade?"

There is a knock at the door. I open to see a robot moving away and a stack of folded packing boxes at my feet. I bring them in and drop them with a thud in the middle of the room. We stare at them, unwilling to admit we may have to suck it up and deal with this.

"Should we scope out room 538?" June asks after a moment. "Maybe it isn't that bad."

"Oh, it's bad all right." As security, I know all the room numbers by heart. Compared with the penthouse, room 538 is a hole in the wall. And that's putting it nicely. I explain that it's a one-person office. On occasion they cram in a couple of interns.

"There are *six* of us." Darah points out the obvious.

"Let's not wig out," Jedd says. "There must be an explanation.

We should speak to someone in the C-suite before we check out the room or pack anything up."

After pods were introduced, those in the C-suite insisted on keeping their status. Since having a corporate hierarchy doesn't mesh with the spirit of affinity groups, that caused a backlash. But they stuck to their guns. Now people mostly ignore them. Which is effective because everyone does it. They're basically empty suits who get their kicks pushing digital paperwork, while everyone else keeps business humming. Of course you can't ignore them when it comes to maintenance issues or hiring and firing. Diddly shit like that. "Whoever made this decision owes us some straight talk," I say. "Jedd, you're the cool head. You should go."

Jedd agrees and June offers to accompany him.

After they leave, the rest of us stand around and stew about our predicament. Without any new information, we really have nothing to say. I figure the coffee is half dead by now, so I toss it and start a fresh pot. The twins stare at their tablets like they're waiting for water to boil. I turn on my crossword puzzle, but I might as well be cross-eyed. So much for being a cruciverbalist. I can't come up with a single word.

Darah fusses with the peace lily, picking off wilted leaves. "You know, Beers," she says, "plants hate to be moved. They hate being uprooted. Even in a temperature-controlled environment, they don't like it."

It doesn't take a genius to realize she isn't just talking about a plant.

"That was a bust," June says as she and Jedd walk into the penthouse more than an hour later. She tosses her tablet on the table and confirms we have to move. For real.

Even Jedd, who prides himself on his knack for smoothing out conflict, looks rattled. "All the furniture stays. And everything that isn't our property or needed for a project, like the text said. We've got to get right on it."

"But *why?*" I want answers but Jedd is already shoveling items off his workspace and into a box, not bothering to sort them out.

"I wish we could've gotten a clear explanation," he says. "All we established is that our space is needed for an urgent project."

"What's that supposed to mean?" Nick asks.

Jedd doesn't look up. "Someone needs more space."

"For *what?*" I press.

"Sorry, we don't know more."

June gives up a few additional deets. Donna O'Donald was the only one around. She made them wait. That's what took so long. And she wasn't very informative. She said someone—she couldn't say who—made the decision last night, and she was out of the loop. We can appeal. That's our only option.

"So let's appeal." I'm not about to surrender the penthouse without a fight.

Jedd points out that could take months. One advantage of pods is they make it easy for those close to an issue to resolve it among themselves. No one bothers with formal appeals anymore. "Too cumbersome. It's not worth it, Beers," he says. "We'd be up against a bureaucratic dinosaur."

"Dinosaur?" I echo. "More like up against the Dick." As soon as the words are out, I regret them. Of course some talk about the Dick can't be helped. Like when we get reports of martial law or people dying as they try to flee to California. Then we can't keep our outrage bottled up. Even if it upsets Darah. But being booted from the penthouse has nothing to do with the Dick. Not even in the same universe of problems. This is one we can actually fix. So I backtrack and suggest we figure out who's pulling the strings. I start assembling boxes and handing them out. "Who needs space so badly?"

"Kurt," says June. "That's my guess."

I toss a box in her direction. "I've had my eye on him since he showed himself to be such a prick at that superpod. Should I kick it up a notch?"

She catches the box but ignores my question. A minute later she adds, "I'm not saying conclusively it's Kurt. Why would he need more space?"

Nick reminds us Kurt's pod is one of the largest. Big pods often split when members have to use workstations in the open-space areas, which can result in hot-desking and create hard feelings for those low on the totem pole.

"Splitting a pod isn't an emergency," I say.

"Unless Kurt's pod-mates got fed up with him," Darah says.

"Or maybe this isn't about a pod," June counters. "Some special project could have an urgent need for space."

"Must be ultra-urgent to warrant giving us the boot," I say. HSys has plenty of stealth projects at any given moment. It's the nature of the business. The name of the game, you could say. If a product doesn't live up to its hype, secrecy saves your butt. But secrecy is no excuse to grab real estate. "If it's in stealth mode, they won't tell us squat," I say.

"That's probably it," Jedd says. "Let's concentrate on packing. We can strategize later."

The six of us scramble for the rest of the day. Having worked in the same space for years, we've put down deep roots. Like home-owners, we've accumulated things we don't realize we still have and aren't ready to toss at a moment's notice. Of course we have virtually no paper. But there are all our awards and trophies, as well as a huge collection of old cables and connectors and headsets and goggles and remote controls and power supplies and random gadgets, not to mention all kinds of sports gear. And Darah's colorful ceramic pots and bottles of plant food. Plus her array of healthy human snacks. She needs twice as many boxes as Nickn-Zack combined. In the final hour, everyone pitches in to help her.

Two robots are waiting in the hallway when I put out the last boxes. After our stuff has been carted off, I sit in my auto-morphing chair for the last time.

Darah goes to the window and gazes out. The sun is still above the mountains, making its way through a layer of pink clouds. I know what she's thinking: there will be so many beautiful sunsets we won't see. Then I notice her shoulders quivering.

I go over and put my arm around her. June stands by her other side. The mood is so somber, you'd think someone died and we're at a wake. An effing funeral.

Finally Jedd suggests we pay a visit to the room that's to be our new home. No point putting it off any longer. Psyched or not, we don't have a choice. So the six of us pick up our tablets and backpacks and a few fragile items. Darah cradles the peace lily in both arms. Then we pile into the elevator, which takes us down one floor, then horizontally to the north wing of the building. It opens in front of room 538.

The access code is already programmed into my tablet. "Holy crackamoli" is all I can say as I hold the door ajar for the others to enter. No one will ever refer to this place as a penthouse.

We survey the scene. The dimensions are a fifth the size of what we're used to. Our boxes—stacked on one side—practically fill the room. There's no display wall, just an old monitor at one end. No kitchenette, not even space for an espresso machine. Only two tables, with five chairs that look like they were rescued from a dentist's waiting room. No carbon-negative white carpet, just heavily scuffed vinyl sheet flooring that looks like it's been here since before I was born. There's a stapler on the floor in one corner. The window looks out on the gray thermoplastic polyolefin roof of the bunker. It's a view ugly enough to broil your eyeballs.

Nick breaks the silence with a series of sneezes. "Musty," he says when he's recovered.

"Looks like no one's been in here," Zack adds.

I go over and pick up the stapler. "When's the last time you saw one of these?"

"I bet my dad still has one." June takes it and turns it over. Some rusty staples fall out.

Darah places the peace lily on the smaller table and drops into one of the chairs, her elbows on the table, chin resting in the palms of her hands.

If we're going to be stuck here and that's her spot, I want to share it with her. I pull up another chair and try it out for size. A real butt squeeze. "I miss the penthouse already," I say.

You might think we originally scored the penthouse due to all our awards. Or because we're such a close-knit pod, such an awesome, awe-inspiring team. But really it was dumb luck. When pods began, there was a lottery for spaces, and that was our draw. Kind of like being born into royalty: you don't have control over your good fortune. Now we don't have control over losing it. It sucks big-time. But we're not going to quit our jobs over it.

Jedd launches into a pep talk, cautioning us not to let this move get us down. There could be reasons we don't know about yet, reasons that make sense. So best to sit tight, not freak out, not assume the worst, stay alert. "Let's not be defined by our penthouse lifestyle. We're better than that," he says. "We can lay low and wait for this to blow over. I'm sure it will."

The twins offer to work remotely. That will free up space. Besides, it's not a biggie: some entire pods have been working remotely for years. Obviously working from the farm isn't an option for me. Since there's nothing more we can do now, I suggest we go home. Get some dinner. Commiserate. We can unpack and get organized tomorrow.

As the six of us move toward the elevator, Jedd stops in his tracks. "I know I said to lay low, but I'm not ready to leave."

I ask what he has in mind.

"I want to see Kurt. Find out what he knows."

"He won't tell you anything," June says. "If he does, it'll be bullshit."

"It's worth a try," Jedd says.

My first reaction is to agree with June. Fuck Kurt's BS. But then I reconsider. Even if we can't trust what he says, we could learn something. I'm a big believer in incidental information. "If you're going, bro," I say, "I'm going with you."

There's a chorus of me toos.

"I appreciate the support," Jedd says, "but we can't march up there en masse. We don't know what's really up or what Kurt's role might be. No more than two of us, please."

It's decided I will go with Jedd while the others leave in the chariot.

"We may be right behind you if he's not there," I say as the others catch a down cab and Jedd and I stand by for one going up.

Bheema said, "Our enemies poisoned me and flung me in the river. But look at me. Did I die? No! Beneath the water, the king of nagas bestowed upon me the force of an entire army. That strength will save us now."

UNDERCUT: Beers

Jedd and I pass the penthouse without turning our heads. Like we never belonged there, never called it home. As we approach Kurt's pod, light is filtering through the door's one-way glass panels.

"You do the talking," I say, as if Jedd weren't already planning on that.

He knocks and the door opens immediately.

Kurt welcomes us with a wide grin. You'd think he was waiting for us. That the dude actually likes us. Super sketch, really. The pile of packing boxes by the door would be hard to miss. Someone is obviously going somewhere. Keith and Karin are in the kitchenette, talking and laughing. They shut up as soon as they realize they have guests. This is the first time all of us have been together since the VRcher superpod. *Crap*, I think, *this is awkward*.

"What's up?" Jedd strikes a casual note, like the two of us are on a stroll through the neighborhood, like we drop by for a chat every evening.

"All good," Kurt declares.

"Couldn't be better." Karin speaks over him.

Keith says nothing.

There's a long pause. Like I said, awkward. I can tell Jedd is giving them dead air, hoping to make them uncomfortable enough to say something remotely relevant. They don't. Finally he breaks the ice himself. "I guess by now you've all heard?"

"That you got displaced?" Kurt twists what's left of his grin into a pout. "Yeah. Sorry about that."

Keith and Karin nod.

There's another pause. More awkward, if that's possible. They're not going to make this easy. Kurt joins Keith and Karin, while Jedd and I stand in the middle of the room. It's your basic face-off. Us against them. I nail my eyes on Kurt, dare him to give us a straight answer. The way he's fidgeting with the six-pack on the counter tells me he feels the pressure. But he won't look me in the eye. Shady as hell. If Jedd can't do it, I'll have to ask the hard questions. Like, *Why'd you fuckers steal our space?*

"Just wondering what you all know," Jedd says.

"Not much. A few rumors." Kurt plucks a beer from the pack and pops it but doesn't offer one to anyone else. Like I'd take his frigging beer.

If Jedd is feeling half as punked as I am, he covers well. He stares at the packing boxes, then turns to Karin. "Sorry if I'm overstepping. But I assumed it's your pod moving into our old space."

"Like I said, it's all good," Kurt says, as if Jedd were addressing him. I can't tell whether he's referring to their pod, their office, a special project, the boxes, his beer, the fact that he considers us losers. Or none of the above.

"Our pod—" Karin exchanges a quick look with Kurt, apparently trying to get their stories straight. It wouldn't make sense to mislead us when we'll find out soon enough if they do move into the penthouse.

"No reason to go anywhere," Kurt says. "I can tell you—"

"Our pod has a dire need for space. You know how it is around here," Karin says, speaking over him. They're contradicting themselves left and right.

Jedd gives a short laugh. "Now I'm really confused."

That does it. I can't hang back any longer. "So," I blurt out, "you stole our space for what? VRcher?" It's not something Jedd would say. But my instinct is to provoke, to agitate, to drop a lit match and step back to see what ignites. It works.

Kurt and Karin object in unison.

"More rumors," he says.

"It's not about VRcher." Karin lowers her voice, as if to inspire trust. Kurt doesn't try to stop her. "Full transparency, here's the deal. VRcher isn't in the pipeline anymore. Our pod is too big, managing too many projects, so some of us are splitting off. We three formed a new pod."

Keith has been watching without a word but now he speaks up. "Management told us to take the room down the hall. You should know, we had nothing to do with it."

"It was a total shock," Kurt says. "I thought we were moving to the basement."

Karin nods agreement, still trying to smooth things over. "We hope you understand."

"Yeah. And definitely stop by for drinks," Kurt says. "After we're settled."

"Bring your whole pod," Keith says.

Kurt revivifies his fake grin and aims it as Jedd. "Drinks," he says, "plus a little gaming."

"No hurt feelings?" Karin adds.

"Of course not," Jedd says. "You all are fam, right?" He makes it sound genuine. No hint of sarcasm. That's not what I want to say. At least a dozen choice phrases are swirling in my head. But there's nothing to be gained by tossing another lit match, so I snuff it. Jedd does a quick calculation, then adds, "We'll be about the same distance away in our new workspace. Except it's not a lateral move."

Everyone laughs at that.

Then Karin shifts into chitchat mode, which we take as our cue to excuse ourselves.

When we get back to the farm, the others are on the front porch finishing off leftover veggie stew. Jedd and I head straight to the kitchen, find clean bowls, and load up. All the effort it took not to stuff Kurt's mouth with a knuckle sandwich must have burned up a lot of calories. I'm famished.

Instead of his usual spot in the hammock, Jedd sits on the floor, Dharma's head on his knee, so everyone can gather close to hear our report. I pull up an Adirondack chair, and between bites we run down our meeting with Kurt. There really isn't much to say. We already suspected his pod was moving into the penthouse. We even discussed the pod splitting. Now all that has been confirmed.

"I get why they'd split," Nick says. "What I don't get is how they snagged our space."

That's the million-dollar question. "The three of them passed it off as a management decision, insisted it was out of their hands," Jedd says.

June shakes her head. "That matches Donna's story. I'm not buying it."

"Me either," I say. "Not for a sec."

Jedd and I discussed this in the car. We agreed Kurt was bluffing when he denied prior knowledge about the penthouse. The guy talks out of both sides of his mouth. If you listen past the stereo BS, it's clear he has an agenda. Pod-mates working on the same project isn't the norm at HSys, yet Kurt and his gang all but admitted to leveraging their project to seize the penthouse. It's an aggressive move.

"You think they have a secret and they're covering?" Nick asks.

"I think the bastards are fricking lying to us." I describe in detail what I observed, how Kurt flashed his pearly whites but wouldn't look me in the eye. Set off red flags big-time. "You noticed it too, Jedd, didn't you?"

He says he did.

"We need to start thinking more strategically. More psychologically," I say. "I'm talking about noticing the tells on someone's face that indicate if it's an honest professional secret or a con."

June is nodding but offers a caveat. Kurt got the Star Sales award for the umpteenth year. He's been around longer than any of us. A pillar of the company. People love him.

I'm not ready to call Kurt invincible. Not on my watch. "So we do what? Kiss up to him?"

"Of course not," Jedd is quick to insert. "If there's a clear case of malfeasance, we won't let it go. But like I said, we don't have all the facts. Yes, we've seen an ugly side to Kurt. Yes, he's feeding us double-talk. Still, we need to keep an open mind. He might not be the reason we lost the penthouse. Really, the only thing he's done inexcusably wrong is grab Darah."

"Okay," I say, though an open mind isn't what I'd recommend. More like a tightly closed fist. "I just wish she'd report him to HR."

Darah has moved to the top of the porch steps, outside our circle, where she's listening quietly. Dharma is by her side, and now I see he's leaning in close, licking her cheeks. She's crying.

When I ask what's wrong, she buries her face in the scruff of his neck and mumbles something about it all being too much.

"Don't worry about Kurt," I say. "I can handle the fucker."

She lifts her head and says more vigorously, "No, Beers. It isn't about Kurt. Or the penthouse. It's *all* the horrible news at once."

"All what news?"

"Somebody please fill us in," Jedd says.

We expand the circle to bring Darah back in, and June steps up to explain. While they were driving home, Darah got a notice about the KnoMor project. Her report was rejected, the project cancelled.

"My god!" I say. "You've been letting us go on and on about Kurt. When were you planning to say something?"

"Wait, there's more," June says. "When we walked in the door, Darah's phone rang. It was Selma calling to say she'd been fired. Her voice was so loud I could hear her from across the room, blaming Darah for everything."

Coming on top of the situation with the penthouse, this feels like whiplash. Sure, projects blow up all the time, but people don't lose their jobs over it. And then to blame Darah, the most diligent, dependable individual you'll ever meet? I hardly know what to say.

Jedd is also struggling to understand. "Selma's a Stanford MBA, super capable. Why not give her another project?"

Darah sits up, wipes her eyes, does her best to collect herself. "She already had another project. That's why she went to Japan. She was let go from that too."

"So she got the axe because some kids failed in science?" Really, the idea is ludicrous.

June offers up more details: KnoMor was killed because some kids didn't perform well, but that's not why Selma was fired. Management accused her of cooking the data to save a botched project.

I turn to Darah. "Do you think she did?"

"What, cook the data?"

"Yeah. Is it a plausible accusation?"

Darah shrugs. "Only if replacing good scores with bad ones can save a project."

"That's absurd," I say. "No one purposely makes scores bad."

"Except someone did." Darah says she doesn't know who, but a theory is forming in her mind.

June reminds us we never ruled out a cyber incident. She's itching to revive that debate, but Jedd isn't interested. He's focused on Darah. "If you have any idea who might have messed with your data, we need to know."

She wipes her eyes again, then exhales sharply, shifting into business mode. "There could still be two sets of scores out there—one showing the gamers did well, the other showing they did poorly."

"I thought you checked all that," I say.

"I did. Multiple times. When I searched for the good scores I'd seen initially, I only found bad scores. But what if someone else was able to see both sets? My theory is that person concluded the good scores were Selma's attempt to fix the bad results. Even if it actually happened the other way around."

"Who had access to your data?" June asks. "Someone in management?"

Darah stops for a second. I guess her thinking didn't get that far. "Maybe. Some execs dislike educational games because they're not as profitable as commercial VR. Doesn't matter if students and teachers rave about them. Or could be someone who views science as a threat to their favorite conspiracy theory. I wouldn't expect that at HSys. Still, you never know."

"But you can't point a finger at anyone?" I say.

"It's just a theory."

Clearly Darah's theory doesn't account for everything, such as how there came to be two sets of scores. Or whether the time stamps were changed. Or why anyone in management would have it in for Selma. My guess is someone else is the real target, and Selma and Darah are merely collateral damage. Since I can't substantiate that, I don't push the point.

Jedd has his head down, his tongue methodically cleaning his teeth as he thinks this through. In situations like this, we look to him for insight. And he knows it. "Again, why does Selma blame you?" he asks.

"She thinks I was in on the data switch. That I torpedoed her project. I told her I had no reason to do that. In fact, it was the opposite: I alerted her the minute I discovered an issue. She didn't get my text because she was asleep in Tokyo. And now she doesn't believe me."

"You know," I say, "you can request an investigation. If Selma hasn't already."

"I'm happy to look into it," Jedd says. "I do that for projects all the time."

Darah likes the idea. Selma, she says, is unlikely to pursue it, because she's already lined up a new job. Given her qualifications, that took a nanosecond.

Jedd promises to dig into the data as soon as we're settled in our new workspace. It's a task he should be able to finish in an hour or so.

That about wraps it up. I'm glad we've taken the pressure off Darah. Not everything has to turn into a worst-case scenario. It's bad enough that we're dealing with two entirely unrelated problems at the same time: the loss of our penthouse and this possible foul play involving Darah's data. Hopefully Jedd can clear up the latter. Call me a stodgy old fart if you like, but life at the farm can't get back to humdrum soon enough for me. I collect everyone's bowls and stack them on top of mine. Since I didn't cook, I'm on for cleanup.

As we're about to disband, Darah turns to the twins. "You warned me someone isn't who I think they are. Could it be a woman?"

"Selma?" Zack asks.

"Possibly," Nick says, "but my bet's on a man."

Krishna took Draupadi's face in his hands.
With one finger, he wiped away her tears.
Nor were his own eyes dry.

HEART SONG: Darah

It's a relief to still have a job. I guess. Better than being fired. Still I don't feel much relief as I plod line by line through my latest assignment: proofreading the HSys annual report. Feels like a huge demotion after KnoMor. And a huge time pig. Not to mention b-o-r-i-n-g.

Nor is that the worst of it. As much as I loved working in the penthouse, I now hate being on the fifth floor. I hate that we were unfairly punished for something we didn't do, a crime we didn't even know we committed. We've been stripped. Jedd and Beers spend a lot of time speculating about why we lost the penthouse and concocting schemes to get it back. But it's all talk. There isn't anything we can do to return to life as it was.

I could cry when I look out over the flat gray expanse of the bunker roof. It doesn't take much to imagine barbed wire coils lining the edges. Armed guards at each corner. No orange and magenta sunsets here. And no display wall to make up for it.

Jedd and June set themselves up at the larger of the two tables; Beers and I share the small one. Most of the day I have it to myself because he is OOO—unlike in the penthouse, where he never looked for excuses to be out of office. Now he takes every excuse to be out of room 538. Not that I blame him. As promised, the twins are working remotely. They do an extra hour of yoga before going to the workspace they created on the south-facing porch. Most days they're still in their yoga sweats when we get home. Arguably they have the best end of the deal.

Room 538 has few of the features we're accustomed to. Not even working Li-Fi. The first morning, Jedd got busy doing upgrades and devising workarounds for the various broken or missing technologies. He said his investigation into my KnoMor data will have to wait until our immediate needs are taken care of.

I understand his call for patience. When life is humming along, patience isn't a big deal. But that isn't the case now. Nothing's humming. Nothing's easy. Even falling asleep at night is hard. A parade of horrors begins its march through my mind the second my head touches the pillow. Dark circles under my eyes stare back at me in the mirror as I dress for work.

I tell myself that the terror I experienced under the dictatorship made me overly sensitive. That being kicked out of the penthouse triggered those memories, but I'll snap back. I'm tough. Even if it feels like I'm not. Besides, losing our workspace is hardly a major crisis. It's nothing compared with having my career snatched away, with being bullied and harassed online. Certainly nothing compared with being deported, like Mom. Or vanishing into thin air, like the immigrant activists I knew. And the dedicated scientists at Nanotech Institute. And those voices we used to rely on for news before they were replaced by official State media. All gone.

I'm not the only one having a reaction. The others are on edge too. Even Jedd, who's so even-tempered, who has the patience of a rock. Last night after everyone had gone to bed, I found him on the sectional sofa, gaming on his mini tablet. I asked when he planned to call it quits.

"When I can't keep my eyes open," he said. Then he told me this wasn't one of his usual video games. It was online gambling, and he couldn't walk away without taking a loss.

"*Real* money?"

"Don't worry," he said. "I've only lost a few bucks. Mostly I win." He said low-stakes online gambling is the one activity that can take his mind off things when life gets chaotic. It's not technically sophisticated like an HSys game but that doesn't matter. It sucks him right in. He's convinced he has the mental prowess to beat the odds, no matter how poor they may be.

I had to promise not to tell the others.

He especially doesn't want June to know. He's afraid she'll call it a gambling addiction, and then they'll get into a debate about whether that's outdated psychology. He chooses to play, he said, and can stop whenever he wants. He's in control. To prove it, he abruptly shut down his game, though it meant swallowing a five-dollar loss, and headed to bed.

I'll never be tempted to gamble. Heck, I don't even play video games for the fun of it. Still, I find myself doing other things, silly things, that make me less efficient at work. I fret over the peace lily more than usual, picking off leaves when they're still healthy. I pull up the constellations on my tablet at odd moments to remind myself how vast the universe is. At least once a day, I take a break from proofreading and log into the KnoMor database. Surprisingly, no one has revoked my access. If my theory is right and someone did see the original set of good data, I should be able to locate it too. So I continue to poke around.

Hopefully Jedd's investigation will shed some light. I want to know who's to blame, even if I never know why they did it. Like knowing who slept with your boyfriend. Or who sold your country's secrets to the enemy. Having such info doesn't wipe away the damage, but it's better than remaining completely in the dark.

It hurt to hear Selma fault me, especially since I tried so hard to support her. If you trust someone, you don't blame them unfairly. You just don't.

Trust has never come easily for me. It certainly didn't help to experience the shattering of trust that was a fact of life under the dictatorship. In school we'd been taught that other countries might be vulnerable but ours was different. We were free. Our rights were protected. If anything went wrong, democracy would self-correct. It was designed to self-correct. It was resilient enough to withstand a bit of backsliding and come out stronger. But then we woke up on that cold, rainy morning in November and learned the government had nullified the election, quashed the opposition. Resistance had been outlawed. Trust had been obliterated. Like a huge boot stomping on ants. To survive, people dug their own anthills and hid in them. With no one left to speak truth to power, any lie could pass unchallenged as fact. Truth ceased to be the bedrock of meaning.

I don't think anyone who has only lived in a democracy—no matter how flawed—can understand the trauma of life under a dictator. Even when you try to explain, they don't get it.

But my issues with trust go further back. They started with Mom. Trust was ripped out of her womb before I was born. Some days she couldn't leave our little apartment, her fear was too strong. As a child, I tried to be a mother to my mother so she could feel more secure in her new country. I tried to convince her we were safe, as if trust grew on the trees in Palisades Park. She wanted to believe me. More than that, I wanted to believe myself. I wanted to be free of the shadow memories lodged like shrapnel in my body since birth, never letting me forget what had happened to Mom.

When I got older, I offered to take her to the Afghan

community center so she wouldn't feel isolated. So we could heal together. We went once. Afterwards she said the people were nice but too old. That was her excuse. I think perhaps she meant too religious. But she herself laid out her carpet and performed salat every day. It's only my generation that has let go of formal religion. If you wanted to put labels on us, you'd say Jedd is Jewish and I'm Muslim. June likes Buddhism. Beers is agnostic. The twins are Christian. But really, none of that matters in our eyes. Each of us relates to spirit in our own way. We don't let our beliefs create barriers between us.

Moving to California has done so much to help me heal. In the past, I watched people turn to their families in times of crisis. After Mom was taken, I had no brothers or sisters, no aunts or uncles or cousins. No grandmas. No one to turn to. Now I have five people I can trust: the five with whom I live. Most of the time I feel that a family, a community, like these five is all I want and all I need.

And now there's Keith. Part of me wants to see him again. If finding a fitting emoji for him was hard before, it would be harder today. Don't think I'm about to text him. I'm not. And the odds of our meeting are low because I come to work late and go home early. I only leave my desk to run down to the café. Some days I don't even do that; I bring food from home or skip lunch altogether. All of which supports the part of me that never wants to see Keith again. Honestly, it's the bigger part. His pod is why I'm stuck in this room.

Today boredom has set in early. It's barely ten o'clock, and I'm staring walleyed at the teensy-tiny numbers in this report's appendix. This isn't the kind of boredom that checking the constellations could fix. It's the kind that settles in like brain fog. Like the fog of PTSD triggered by memories of life under the dictatorship. So I decide to go for the only remedy I know: fresh air. It's too late for midmorning caffeine and too early for lunch, so no one will be hanging around outside.

"Hey," I call over to Jedd and June, "I'm taking a break."

They look surprised.

"If you wait, I'll go with you," June says.

But I don't want to wait.

"All right," she says. "See you in a bit."

Outside, as expected, the common area is deserted. I speedwalk the large loop defined by the lawn's perimeter, taking long strides, arms swinging, picking up speed as I go. Breath quickening. After one loop, my motion and the warmth of the sun have begun to diffuse the brain fog. Yes, I'm safe in California. I have friends, family. A job. I inhale the fresh air, exhale trust. A couple more loops and I'm reinvigorated, ready to tackle those teensy numbers.

As I round the corner by the bunker on my way back to Building 1, still moving fast, a side door pops open and a man steps out, straight into my path. Keith. So much for low odds.

"Hey there!" He sounds casual, like we hooked up yesterday.

I say I'm heading to the office. Not that he needs to know, but I'm flushed from the exercise and don't want him to misread any cues. There's zero chance I'm going anywhere with him.

"So am I," he says.

I continue jogging toward Building 1. If he wants to walk with me, he'll have to keep up.

"I didn't realize how angry you were," he says, falling into step, "till I saw that emoji."

I stop and stare at him. "What emoji?"

"Doesn't matter now," he says. "We're beyond that, right?"

As I pick up my pace again, I recall riding in the chariot with Jedd, thumb hovering some emojis as I considered whether to text Keith. Could I have done it accidentally? All I can do now is insist I didn't send anything. And I'm not angry.

"I'm glad I ran into you," he says. Evidently Karin seeing us together isn't an issue now. "I've been wanting to tell you that I think your pod got the raw end of the deal."

So this is about the penthouse. He wants to apologize. To draw a line between himself and the others.

"I had nothing to do with how it all came down," he continues. "I'm just a guy who crunches numbers."

I'm moving too fast to meet his gaze, but I can see he's squinting at me in a way that suggests he's serious, that he wants me to trust him. I see the benefit of letting him think I do. "Got it."

I sense he has more to say, but we've reached the building. We cross the entryway and step into a waiting elevator cab. For the few seconds we're alone, he smiles at me. The same slightly flirtatious smile that won me over before.

I don't return the smile.

"Darah, it's been crazy busy," he pleads as the door opens on the fifth floor. "You know what it's like."

I step out without looking back as he calls after me, "Catch you later?"

When June asks if I'm feeling better, I nod.

I do feel better. And I'm glad I saw Keith. Seeing him again will be okay too. Because I've proven I can be tough when I need to be. Besides, this is no longer about my feelings for him. It's about the possibility he might disclose something to me, something Kurt didn't tell Jedd and Beers, something that could help return us to the penthouse. The beauty of it is that I've got the upper hand and Keith doesn't realize it.

As I stare down at the bunker roof, I weigh my options. I could alert Jedd and the others that I have a new source of info. They'd be thrilled. And I'd have the satisfaction of knowing they value my help. It doesn't always have to be the others taking risks, doing all the work. Of course I'd have to disclose my source. I'd have to say something about Keith and me. While Jedd probably wouldn't put two and two together, June might. Beers for sure would. And the twins would likely psych it out.

All of which sways me against that option. There *is* no Keith and me. There never really was, and now I know there never will be. I can see that he's not who I thought he was. Like the twins predicted. With everything else going on, no one has mentioned that prediction. But I haven't forgotten.

I quit work as early as I can without June and Jedd asking questions. As I head toward the parking lot, my mind is on Keith. I need to entice him to give up more info. But when? And how? The more I think about it, full-on Mata Hari might be the way to go. No one would expect that in this day and age. Or of me. Some people might not even respect it. But who cares? That may actually work in my favor.

All this has me so preoccupied I almost don't notice the kid as I pass the fountain. He's barefoot, in the same baggy T-shirt, sitting quietly with his flute on his lap. The last time I saw him was the night my data blew up, when I confided to Jedd that I wanted to play the flute. I followed his suggestion and bought one online—a bansuri like the kid's, with bands of red thread at each end. It's been sitting untouched on a shelf in my bedroom.

I run up and tell him. "Please," I say, "can I hire you to teach me?"

"I'm not for sale," he says, laughing.

I guess he doesn't need money, as Jedd assumed. I ask again if he'll teach me, without mentioning payment.

His whole face is smiling as he weighs my request. "Why not?"

I suggest we start right away. If he's free.

He laughs again. Tells me he's free in more ways than one. Which sets him off laughing even more.

It's contagious and I can't help giggling. I say I'm going home and invite him to come.

"Why not?" he says again.

He stashes his flute in his shoulder bag, which I assume holds the sum total of his possessions, and off we go.

The twins, at their workstation on the porch—still in long johns—give a big thumbs up when they see us and hear that I'm getting a flute lesson.

But first I have to give the kid a quick tour.

We start in the kitchen, with its old cast-iron stove coexisting alongside the refrigerated wall oven and solar composter. He runs a finger over the induction charging countertop, then follows me through the living room and into the sunroom, where June likes to work out on the VR flying machine and the twins do yoga on their smart mats. We stand under the giant white bird of paradise, its leaves pushing against the glass ceiling. He observes it all in silence.

Upstairs we peek into each bedroom. Jedd's high-tech canopy bed, with its huge, curved display screen, catches the kid's eye.

I suggest he try it out.

The instant his head touches the pillow, a swarm of space-crafts zoom at him. "Whoa!" he cries, instinctively dodging them. "Didn't expect that!"

"Jedd's games pick up wherever he left off as soon as they detect a live body," I say, suppressing a giggle.

He raises his head a few inches. "Where's the control?"

"It's all eye tracking."

He blinks rapidly, as if that will maneuver the aliens. "One could get used to a life like this," he says as he climbs off the bed, immediately halting the game.

Then, flute in hand, I lead him down the stairs and out the French doors, past the cedar-barrel hot tub, and across the field of dried grass. Soon the rains will turn everything green. After checking out the loft in the barn, we follow the narrow trail that winds along the creek and up to what we call Boulder Point. The highest spot on the land, it's marked by three flat-topped, lichen-covered boulders. The kid perches on one and I on another, and we look out over the golden hillside. A flock of aero cars whizzes below, parallel to the freeway.

"Perfect place for music," he says.

I expect him to show me the positioning for my lips, placement for my fingers, and scales to practice. From what I've read, that's basic. And takes months to learn. But he bypasses all that. His method is simple, improvised, intuitive.

"Play from the heart," he says.

I'm not sure how to do that. And I tell him so.

"Try not to listen with your ears," he says, as if that makes more sense.

I consider it for a moment. "You mean don't worry too much about what I'm doing?"

"That's right. There's no such thing as a wrong sound." He giggles at the thought of a wrong sound, then picks up his flute, cradles it in both hands, and smiles at me. As if he believes the two of us possess wings, and he's just waiting for me to jump off the cliff with my flute and fly.

It's half invitation, half dare. Either way, I accept. Even if it's an unusual way to learn, I want to do this. Raising my flute, I take a tentative breath, then blow out a single long, slow, soft note. It doesn't sound too bad.

He's still smiling.

So I take another breath, play again.

"Let one note lead you to the next," he coaches.

After a bit of screeching and cracking and choking up, the notes start to produce themselves. Like awkward fledglings on a virgin flight over the meadow, they soar and dip and plunge, then rise again.

When he sees I'm getting the hang of it, the kid puts his flute to his lips and casts its sound over the hillside. Adding harmony to the breeze, making the grasses dance.

Back at the house, everyone is gathered in the kitchen as Beers prepares a salad and cornmeal dumplings to go with his black bean soup. As always, it's an abundance of food.

I ask the kid if he will join us. When he hesitates, I promise to take him wherever he wants afterwards. I'm not sure where that might be, and he doesn't say. But he agrees to stay.

During dinner he tells us about himself.

His biological mother was in prison when he was born. He grew up in foster homes and was especially fond of his last mother. She understood his desire to forge his own destiny and trusted him to make sound decisions despite his youth.

I ask why he decided to drop out.

One evening, he says, friends who came over to study ended up binge-watching videos. "Our homework was to calculate the color of sound. I still remember the axiom: doubling the frequency of sound forty times yields a frequency within the parameters of light."

June is impressed. She studied chromesthesia in a neuropsych class at Yale, she says, and they got extra credit for creating an app to convert sound into color.

"I didn't create any apps," he says. "But I did blitz the homework. Middle C was green, G was dark red, E was indigo, F was a faint violet. Before I went to bed, I logged onto my friends' computers and gave them my answers."

"So you cheated," Jedd says.

"Come on," Beers says, "give the kid a break."

I don't want him to feel we're passing judgment, so I ask how that led him to drop out.

"One friend's parents discovered I'd done her homework. They called the principal. I was suspended for a week."

"That's harsh," says Nick.

"Especially if your friend got off with impunity," Zack adds.

"It was a good lesson in accepting the consequences of one's actions," he says with a shrug. His suspension had perks though. He took long walks by the bay, through the marshlands and salt fields, and hiked in the hills, where he tracked a mountain lion, foraged for mushrooms. One day he downloaded a college math text. "Thought it would be fun," he says. "Except I couldn't find anything I didn't already know. After that, I didn't see a reason to go back to school."

"But the world needs people like you," I say.

His response is instant: "Darah, the world still has me. I haven't gone anywhere."

Whenever my students threatened to drop out, I talked to them about the value of education. A philosopher, I said, once called education the midwife of democracy. That was sexy enough to pique most teens' curiosity. But though he's a teen, the kid is my teacher. So I just point out I've never seen him with a tablet.

He admits he gave his up after he dropped out. Hasn't missed it.

"You can borrow one from us anytime," Jedd says. "No doubt you'd put it to good use."

That gives June an idea. "If you're a math savant, are you also a hacker?"

His answer is equivocal: "Could be."

"Meaning you are but won't admit it?" Beers says.

"Or could be but choose not to?" Jedd says.

He nods at the latter. "It's too easy for hackers to cause harm. Even white hats. So I stay clear. Thanks for the offer, but I don't think I'll be needing a tablet."

It's getting late, so I repeat my promise to take him wherever he wants to go.

"Not so fast," says Beers. "Is wherever you're going better than staying here with us?"

The kid laughs. I guess he doesn't have an answer for that.

"I think I can speak for all of us," Beers says. "We want you to stay."

"Not just tonight," Nick says.

"As long as you wish," Zack adds.

"So you'll stay?" I say when he doesn't refuse.

Beers points to the chaise longue under the giant white bird of paradise in the sunroom.

The kid stops him. "Darah showed me your barn. The loft is awesome."

Beers wrinkles his nose. The loft is unheated. No solar electricity. No running water. The roof leaks. It smells. The sunroom, on the other hand, is first-class. The chaise longue is fully reclining, with self-adjusting cushions. Plus it's always warm in there.

The kid stands his ground. "Put me in nature and I've got everything I need."

Normally Beers would demand nothing less than his standard of hospitality. But the kid has a quiet persuasiveness. So it's decided: he will sleep in the loft. We scrounge up some rugs and blankets and pillows and an old kerosene lantern and head out to the barn to arrange his sleeping area. It's modest but I'm sure it's luxurious compared with wherever he's been crashing.

"Zack and I often give little predictions," Nick says as we bid the kid goodnight. "Our message now is a no-brainer."

"We predict none of us will regret having you stay," Zack says.

My bedroom is in the attic, the only open bed when I moved to the farm. To offset the northern exposure, Beers installed a large skylight. I can lie in bed, wrapped in the rust-brown pattu shawl Mom gave me before I left for Rutgers, and study the constellations as I fall asleep.

Tonight I look at the stars and smile. For the past few hours, I haven't given a thought to our lost penthouse or to KnoMor and

Jedd's investigation. I haven't been annoyed at Kurt or worried about how to pry intel from Keith. I haven't been anxious about the Dictator or about anything else in the wide world out there.

Something about the kid has this effect on me. Maybe it's his smile, the way it lingers at the corners of his mouth, ready to blaze across his face at the slightest excuse. Irresistible. When I look at him, I see the purity of an infant. Yet he's wise beyond his years. That may be a cliché but I'm beginning to see how true it is.

The attic window is open, and I can hear the faint sound of a flute. Its notes float through the redwood branches, hang in the cool night air, rise higher and higher into the night sky. I imagine the stars twinkling to this song. As I drift off, my heart is singing.

Yudhishtira said, "The Kauravas invited us to stay in this house made of lacquer. They plan to set fire to it, with us inside, on the fourteenth day of the dark fortnight. The time has come to arrange our escape. Let them believe we have died."

BURN DOWN THE PALACE:
Jedd

I intended to investigate Darah's KnoMor data right after she asked, but the penthouse fiasco took more resources than any of us anticipated. All my projects got backed up. It wouldn't have been fair to prioritize her request because she's my pod-mate. Not to mention fam. So I've been waiting to carve out time.

It's almost four o'clock today when I announce I'm finally ready to get on it. "This won't be difficult," I say, "but I'll need some concentrated head-down time."

They promise to leave me alone. Nothing short of the direst emergency.

"How long?" Darah asks.

"Couple hours max. Definitely before we go home." The task is clear-cut: go in and dig for old versions. It should be obvious which has the original data.

When I first got to HSys, I thought I knew a lot. I was the whiz kid. I was Jedi! But two years in, I moved to the bunker and discovered I wasn't quite the digerati I imagined. Every day our games came under a new attack. Not only were bad actors infecting our products, but they were stealing directly from end users. Fortunately I'm a quick study. I learned to spot the first signs of an attack so I could rush in and prevent further damage. I became really good at it, earning back-to-back MVH awards for most valuable hacker. The most noteworthy was after I nailed a Russian attack on the HSys infrastructure no one else caught.

When pods were introduced, I transferred out of the bunker to form a pod with the five of us. I took my expertise with me and wrote my own job description. I'd been at HSys long enough to earn that. Now I work exclusively on projects of my choosing, doing things I enjoy. I'm not on the cyberwar frontlines anymore, but that's fine. Let the bunker sweat over the latest crisis. I just like solving mysteries. I like finding errors and fixing them, detecting latent threats and destroying them. It's one aspect of my playful nature.

Tracing the history of Darah's data files should be easy-peasy. Neither access nor encryption is an issue. The only unknown is how much digging will be needed if it turns out to be a hacking job. Probably not the work of a pro. Script kiddies and armchair hackers are notoriously poor at hiding their tracks, so it will likely require minimal digging. I'm thinking hand shovel not backhoe.

Two hours later I'm still plugging away. Forget the hand shovel. It'll take an excavator to get to the bottom of the mess I'm seeing. To make matters worse, my tablet is flashing. I'm sure there's at least one text from Naomi, wondering if I'm on my way to jog by the bay with her after work, like I promised. I don't read it. Nor do I stop to explain to the others what's taking so long. To their credit, no one asks. Having agreed to no interruptions, they're honoring that. Still, they're itching for answers. I can feel their inquiring glances ricocheting like stray bullets over my head.

After another hour, Darah breaks the silence. "Looks like you need more time, Jedd."

I lean back and cross my arms. Run my tongue over my front teeth.

"Is there a problem?" June asks.

I hesitate, not wanting to alarm anyone. "I don't have anything to tell you yet," I say. In fact, I could tell them precisely what happened to the KnoMor data and how the students performed on their science evals. But that would raise the kind of alarm I want to avoid.

"I always assumed we'd talk at home," June says.

She's more correct than she realizes: none of what I've unearthed can be discussed here. "I'm about to wrap up," I say. "Go on ahead. I won't be long."

"I'll throw together some sous vide chili," Beers says.

"Sounds good." Now that I've shifted from tracing what happened to the KnoMor data to answering the vastly more complex question of why what I discovered happened, I need to cut myself some slack. Pulling an all-nighter hasn't been in my toolbox for years. I promise again to see them at home. Soon.

"No pressure," Beers says. "We'll keep the chili warm for you."

Driving home after midnight, I know exactly what the others—having sat around all evening without so much as a text from me to say I've been delayed—are thinking: "Where the heck is Jedd? Why didn't the dude quit when he promised?" At least that's what they are thinking if they're not fast asleep. Naomi probably has similar thoughts.

I turn into our driveway, glad my electric engine won't wake anyone. I can't blame them if they've gone to bed. In fact, that would give me quiet time to keep working so I have more to tell them in the morning. If I can stay awake. As I park alongside the chariot, Dharma doesn't come running. Usually he's perched like a sentinel on the porch; now he's probably curled up on the hearth rug, dead to the world.

But then I see light on in the living room. At least one person has waited up. My guess is Darah. It's her data after all.

I tiptoe through the darkened kitchen, past my bowl of chili, sitting stone cold on the counter. Whatever hunger I felt hours ago is long gone. Sleep is what I'm hungry for now. At the doorway to the living room, I stop and survey the scene. It looks like an airport lounge during a late-night flight delay. Beers is slumped in the overstuffed armchair, feet still in their steel-toe boots propped on the coffee table. Darah and June are draped over opposite ends of the sectional, while the twins snuggle on the small sofa. The kid is sitting cross-legged on the hearth rug in front of the inglenook fireplace, eyes closed, flute idle in his lap. Dharma is at his side, asleep.

They all spring to attention when I clear my throat.

Darah says exactly what I expected: "My god, Jedd, where've you been?"

"You said you were close behind us," June says. She and Darah push the throw pillows aside and slide over to make room for me.

I shed my shoes and squeeze between them, bracing one foot on the edge of the table. "I'm sorry I didn't keep you posted. You deserve answers."

"We're listening now," June says.

"Hit us with it, bro," Beers says, dropping his feet to the floor with a thud, in anticipation.

Really, there is no easy way to reveal what I've discovered. They won't like it no matter how I serve it up. The best I can do is start with a little bit of good news and ease them into the bad. "You'll be happy to hear I resurrected a full backup of the Kno-Mor database."

"That's what we expected," June says.

"It wasn't difficult."

"So?" Darah says. "What did you find?"

"I can confirm you were right when you insisted KnoMor was

a success. The original data show the gamers aced their evals." I pause. We're only a minute into this, and I've exhausted the good news. There's no getting around the first unwelcome truth: "I can also confirm your data were compromised."

She stares at me. "Intentionally?"

"Yes, someone cut the students' scores by fifty percent."

"Fifty percent?" she echoes. "You mean the data I used for my report?"

"I'm afraid so."

"Sounds like you're not calling this some fluky cyber hiccup," Beers says.

"No. Someone did this. On purpose."

The night Darah told us something was fishy with her data, June brought up a possible cyberattack, but we cold-toweled it. Now I'm saying human meddling is no longer off the table. June could easily make this into an I-told-you-so moment. And she'd be justified. At the very least, she has to know from what I just revealed that it didn't take all those hours to discover someone did in fact meddle.

"All right," June says, "who's the culprit?"

I'm glad she's not rubbing my nose in it, but I can't reveal who it is without dropping the first major bomb. So I hedge: "Three guesses."

"Obviously not an evil maid attack," Beers says. "Maybe someone in the bunker?"

"Of course," June says. "They're—"

"No," I cut in, "not the bunker."

"Then some competitor," Beers says. "Like—"

"No," I say emphatically.

Beers is stumped.

None of the others venture a guess.

"Kurt?" he says finally.

"Right," I say without thinking—Kurt has become our default

when we need someone to blame—then quickly correct myself: "Actually it was Karin."

"*Karin?*" they exclaim in unison.

"Yes, Karin," I say over their protests. I know this comes as a shock. Karin is someone we rub elbows with regularly. Her role in the penthouse takeover made her look dodgy, but that doesn't translate into masterminding a data heist.

"You're about to give us proof, right?" Even if June was thinking cyberattack before, she wasn't thinking Karin.

"Hear me out. Darah's data had only been posted to the cloud for a matter of minutes before Karin overwrote it. She deleted the backup. Meaning only someone with the highest security clearance, like me, could restore it. Fortunately I was able to trace her signature on the move. Which led me straight to the original data."

Darah looks unconvinced. Like June, if she has a list of potential suspects, Karin isn't on it. She asks what the others think. A dizzying barrage follows.

"Someone could have used Karin's ID," June says.

"Or stolen it," Beers throws in.

"Either way, without her knowledge," Nick says.

"If she knew her ID was stolen, she'd have reported it," Zack says.

"Maybe she did and we don't know." Beers looks questioningly at me, but I don't bail him out. If they toss this around a bit more, maybe they'll get somewhere. Maybe.

"Okay, say it was someone within HSys," June says.

"Except KnoMor wasn't on anyone's radar," Beers says.

"Sounds like it was on Karin's radar," June counters.

The kid is watching from the hearth. This kind of corporate politics—maybe even espionage—must be incomprehensible to him. He's snapping his head back and forth from one person to the next, like watching a ping-pong match. I find it hard not to do the same.

"Wait a minute," Darah says. "KnoMor wasn't in production. No release manager was ever assigned. And Karin's in sales."

"Yup. Frigging sales." Beers gets up and begins to pace the room. He's trying to connect the dots, anticipate where all this is going. But he's getting frustrated.

I remind myself that frustration isn't always a negative. When the trail on an investigation dries up, a little frustration can stimulate the sleuthing juices. Plus if he struggles with it himself now, he'll be more likely to accept the results when he eventually learns them. Still, I don't want him to feel too lost, so I drop a hint. "I said Karin switched the data. I didn't say she was working alone."

"So who's working with her?" Beers asks.

"Actually, it's not just one person."

"So, who?" Darah repeats.

"Forget who," June says abruptly. "If Jedd's right and Karin did this, all that matters is *why*. If we can't answer that, we won't know how to stop them."

"Good point." I tell her that bothered me too when I saw Karin's signature on the data. Why would someone in sales, with no role in KnoMor, want to blow it up?

"Or frame Selma," Darah adds.

"This makes no sense." Beers collapses back into the armchair. "Unless . . . unless by more than one person you mean this is part of a much bigger operation."

"Is that it?" Nick asks.

"Maybe we were wrong to assume no outside actors." Zack exchanges glances with Nick, the way they do when they're about to launch into prediction mode.

But a prediction isn't what we need right now. Not even if it ultimately proves correct. They've wrestled enough. It's time to spill. Time to close in on the whys and wherefores. I lift myself off the sofa and step to the middle of the room, where I can better track their reactions. All eyes are on me. "Stop me if you think I'm driving beyond the headlights here, but this is what I can tell you. Karin's actions seemed so random, and I was at a loss for motive, so I did the only thing I could: cast a wide net and hope to get lucky."

"Tell me you got lucky," Beers says.

"I did. That's what took so long. My search in Karin's HSys account was going nowhere. Nothing explained her signature on the data move. Nothing irregular, no red flags. But then a message popped up. I almost didn't catch it." I pause. Everyone is rapt. Time to drop the next bomb. "It led me to a hidden site belonging to Karin, Kurt, and Keith."

There is a chorus of oohs and wows.

NicknZack let out low whistles.

"Keith?" Darah says under her breath.

"You mean a site housing messages or documents?" Beers says.

"Both."

"Hidden as in the deep web?" June asks.

"Or the darknet?" Beers adds.

"We envisioned a bigger operation—" Nick says.

Zack finishes his thought: "This sounds way bigger."

I acknowledge it is bigger. How much bigger I don't know. "The site is on the darknet. So far I haven't detected evidence of outside actors."

"What tipped you off?" Beers wants to know.

"An oblique reference in that message to a site called"—I pause, knowing how this will sound, but there's no holding back now—"KKK."

"KKK?" June is incredulous.

Darah looks like she wants to vomit.

"Short for the three of them."

"Holy crap!" Beers says. "That's revolting."

"I was appalled too. But I had to check it out." I explain how my time in the bunker trained me to be on the alert for stuff like this, to sniff it out even if well hidden. Clearly Kurt and his cohort didn't expect anyone to find their darknet site. Though it's hard to imagine anyone at HSys using that acronym even in the most private context.

Beers stares at me, his eyebrows askew with a mix of awe and dismay. "So you stepped outside the legal bounds of your job?"

I scan the faces before me and register their concern. "My clearance grants access to company data and other docs in the cloud, as well as personal communications on the company server. This site is outside the HSys network, but it contains company information. You could call it a gray area."

"I take it you kept going," June says.

"I'd have kept going at that point, regardless," I say with half a laugh. No one smiles. "The site is pretty well protected, so it took a while to get in. Even so, I wouldn't say its owners are careful about security. If they were, I'd probably still be trying to gain access."

Beers picks up on my vague reference to owners. He wants to know who besides Karin and Kurt and Keith has access. And why I don't suspect outside actors.

"It's possible there are outside actors," I admit. "All I know definitively is the three Ks are working behind the scenes with a small, tightly knit group looking to use HSys products for their own purposes. Most likely they intend to hijack a proprietary technology." I pause before dropping the next bomb. "I can give you one additional name. Donna O'Donald."

There is another explosion of wows.

"I didn't know she'd left the C-suite," June says.

"She hasn't." I explain she's keeping her status on the down-low and intends to put a populist spin on her partnership with the Ks if anyone gets suspicious. Pretty slick really.

"Let me get this straight." Beers is racing ahead, trying to put all the pieces together. "You're saying the fuckers who stole the penthouse are the same fuckers who messed with Darah's data?"

I tell him he's right; that's what I'm saying: the two crises we assumed were unrelated have one and the same cause. "Now you know as much as I do," I say. "With a little more digging, I can pull together my findings and get them into the right hands. Of course we'll have to decide which hands, but that shouldn't be hard. Then we can sit back, relax, and watch justice being served."

June reins me in. "So Kurt isn't the upstanding dude people think he is. Gotcha. But I still have the same question: Why go to such lengths to kill KnoMor, a showpiece no one considered mission critical? Just so you can brew your morning coffee in the penthouse?! Really, nothing like that warrants conspiring on the darknet. Not even close."

"Well . . . I don't have a conclusive answer for that," I say.

"Understandable," Darah says. "It's a ginormous task. You ran out of time."

"Plus it's better done from home." Beers is always thinking of security.

"And with our support," Nick adds.

June doesn't look convinced. But she backs off. "All right, Jedd, let's see what you can find. But to be honest, I suspect you've already discovered more than you've said. You're holding out on us. Tell me I'm wrong."

"Wait a minute." Darah rises to the edge of the sofa. "Before you go further, I need to know, is this safe? You just admitted it's probably illegal."

Darah knows far less than the rest of us about the ethics and etiquette—and even basic techniques—of hacking, so I want to allay her fear that venturing into dark places will get me in trouble. And worse yet, that any trouble will be because I agreed to help her. "You're right," I say. "I have taken some risks. But I did so knowingly. And I'm prepared to take responsibility for what I've done. I told you I'd get to the bottom of your data issue, and that's what I intend to do."

Darah doesn't get past my first sentence. "So it's *not* safe?"

Before I can respond, the kid calls out, "I can help!"

All heads spin toward the hearth.

Frankly I thought he'd completely tuned us out. Not that this is routine office politics. Still, it's hardly his vibe. I can't imagine what he could add. Yet as he jumps up and rushes over, I don't have the heart to shut him down.

He crouches on the rug at my feet. "Suppose we're in a forest," he says, looking first at Darah, then at everyone else to see if we'll buy in.

I step aside to give him more space.

"Now suppose there's a fire." He marks a circle on the rug with his finger to indicate its perimeter. "It's spreading rapidly. All the creatures are trapped, their lives in danger. And you"—he points at Darah—"are a little mouse. What do you do?"

She laughs, then stops when it's apparent he's waiting for an answer. "I guess find a mousehole. Crawl into it."

Clearly the kid is a natural with analogies. But now he's being goofy, pretending to burrow into the rug. So I run with it. "That's right. If you dig a hole and hunker down, you'll be safe."

She still looks skeptical. "So you'll make like a mouse on the darknet site?"

"Yes," I say. "As a hacker, I have to think smart, stay one step ahead. Crawl on my belly if I encounter any fires. That's how I can go into dark areas of the web and not worry anyone will detect I was there."

She has more questions. "What about getting out? Can you do that safely too?"

I offer another analogy. "Suppose your enemy has a treacherous palace. You manage to get in but then you realize it's a trap. You could get seriously burned in there. I'm not saying Kurt set a trap for me. But he doesn't want me visiting his site. The question is, how do I get out safely, without anyone noticing?"

"Build a backdoor, obvi," June says, doing her best to bridle her impatience.

"June's right," I say. "That's what I did. I created a backdoor—a secret tunnel out of the palace—so I could sneak out. And go back in later to finish the job."

"I'm not sure I want you to go back," Darah says. "Is it worth the risk?"

"Of course it is," June says.

"This isn't just about your KnoMor data," Beers adds. "Now we have to think about everything that's at stake."

"Understood," Darah says. "But I'm worried Jedd will get caught."

"And I'm saying you shouldn't worry," I counter. "There are smart ways to do this. The first is a backdoor. But that's not always enough—"

The kid jumps in to build on my analogy: "The enemy knows you're in the palace. They've got you in their crosshairs. Even if you escape, they're coming after you."

"So cover your tracks!" Nick says.

"Get creative," Zack adds.

"Exactly," I say. "Which is why before you get out, you may want to—"

"—burn that palace down!" Beers chimes in with glee.

"Or one strategic chamber." The kid has turned his circle on the rug into a palace and is striking imaginary matches to start a fire.

"Right," I say. "Burn one chamber or the whole palace. The enemy's planning to set the place on fire, with you in it. So you beat them to it. Plus it won't hurt if when they search the ashes, they find a charred body or two. They'll assume you died and stop looking for you."

"Jedd!" Darah exclaims. "That's gruesome. Now you're scaring me."

I apologize. That wasn't my intention. I'm describing the tactics of cyberwarfare. Charred bodies don't mean anyone literally died.

"I get it," she says. "You can go in and damage some data but make it look like someone else did that damage. In other words, throw them off your scent."

"Bingo!" says Beers. He might not be a hacker, but he understands the basics.

Now that everyone has grasped the scope of my task, June is done reining in her impatience. "Jedd," she says, "can we please proceed?"

I tell her it's a go. I expect to find answers to her questions about motive. Then we can discuss how to get the appropriate authorities involved. "The Ks aren't getting away with a plot targeting HSys employees or HSys products," I say. "Not if I can help it."

"I want to see some charred bodies," Beers says, a gleam in his eye.

It's a joke, but Darah winces.

I reiterate that my tactics are cyber maneuvers. No one wants to physically harm the Ks, no matter how objectionable their actions are. This is about being responsible, about doing the hard work so justice ultimately prevails.

"What I meant," Beers mumbles, "was charred veggie burgers on the penthouse grill. After we get our lives back."

It's agreed I will work in the living room, and they will support me in any way they can. No one will interrupt, so I can stay focused. I'll make an effort to narrate my progress and stop whenever I find something to discuss. I warn everyone to expect long periods of silence and invite them to go to bed if they're too tired. It's going to be a late night. Likely an all-nighter.

No one budges. Except Beers, who disappears into the kitchen to reheat my dinner.

With Yudhishtira and Arjuna on his shoulders,
and his mother around his neck, Bheema picked up the twins,
and with one in either arm,
walked the entire length of the tunnel.

THROUGH THE BACKDOOR:
Jedd

I sit down on the sofa again and activate the screen on the coffee table.

June edges closer to get a better view. The twins settle back onto the smaller sofa, while Darah moves to the rocking chair, where she wraps up in her pattu shawl. The kid lights a couple of candles and places a stick of sandalwood incense on the mantlepiece, then lies flat on his back on the rug, eyes closed, with Dharma alongside him, nose on his shoulder. I can hear Beers shuffling around in the kitchen. Each of us in our own way is set and ready to go.

I immediately report no trouble accessing either Karin's email account or the darknet site. The backdoor is working nicely. Running a search on "KnoMor" generates a list of hits going back half a year. We're off to a good start. I scan through them, reading aloud snippets that offer clues as to why they targeted the project—stuff like "neutralize them" and "whiz kid won't see it coming" and "target something not mission critical."

Beers returns with my steaming hot chili and some buttered cornbread, which he places beside my screen before retreating to the armchair. "Did I hear 'not mission critical'?" He frowns. "Sounds like KnoMor."

"Ironic," June says. "They targeted Darah's project for the very reason we figured it couldn't be a target."

Beers points out that no one on campus noticed when KnoMor was terminated. No buzz at all. If that was part of the Ks' plan, they pulled it off.

"At least they think they did," I say. "Whiz kid must refer to me. Kurt was around when that was my moniker and I got all those MVH awards. He sees me as a bigger threat than the bunker. Judging by his latest comments, though, he suspects I'm already onto them."

"But you *weren't* onto them," Beers says.

"You are now," Zack says.

"Further irony," Nick adds.

Darah looks alarmed, "Jedd, they can't see you in there, can they?"

I double-check my settings. "Nope. Totally invisible."

She smiles but doesn't look reassured. The threat to neutralize us probably evokes images of our charred bodies littering the Ks' digital palace. Even knowing that cyber bodies don't really die, it sounds scary. And of course cyberattacks can and *do* kill. Literally. Attacks on the internet of things have resulted in millions of deaths. People can't get food or heat. Or water. Still, I can't sugarcoat what I uncover now. The Ks aren't going to intimidate me. We have to hang tough. Darah included.

This is starting to feel more and more like my old work in the bunker. Except instead of foreign adversaries, the perps are people we know—colleagues at HSys. The ones we call our cousins down the corridor. Unbelievable. I scan more messages as I chow down on my chili. The three Ks and Donna are discussing their strategy to kill KnoMor. It's alarming how much detail they have. Donna's C-suite status gives her essentially blanket access. I'm tempted to do a dumpster dive into her account to see if she's meddling in other projects, but that would be stretching my authorization. So I refocus and share the relevant intel: "Donna says she's keeping tabs on the KnoMor beta test and will notify Karin when the data go up. She will then enable Karin's biometric authentication so she can doctor the results."

"Why not do it herself?" Beers wants to know.

"Probably protecting her butt in case something goes wrong," I say with a shrug, then share messages from after the data move. "Donna's congratulating Karin on a job well done. Says it establishes proof Selma falsified the research. Now they have grounds to kill the project. Here's the termination notice she sent Selma."

"I'll bet that's what Selma read to me," Darah says.

"Yeah, while we stayed to confront Kurt." I pause. No one will like what I'm about to read aloud now. But I can't stop. Not even if this is about to get ugly. "Here's Kurt's next comment: 'Fire the other bitch.'"

Darah lurches forward, almost tipping the rocker. "*Me?*"

We all tell her not to take it personally. She was at the wrong place at the wrong time. Her project was low-hanging fruit, their idea of not mission critical. KnoMor may be dead, but she still has her job.

"For how long?" she counters.

I don't have an answer for that. Nor do I see any messages with an action plan to back up the threat. "It's possible someone put in a good word for you, saved your job."

Beers wants to know who.

Again I have no answer.

"This is nuts. You're all skating on speculation." June hops off the sofa and heads to the hutch near the kitchen door. She returns with a bottle of whisky and several shot glasses, which she sets beside my screen. She pours two and downs one. When no one takes the other, she drinks it herself. Then she squares her shoulders and faces me. "I'll give you this, Jedd. Let's say the bulk of what you've found is true. It's outrageous and it needs to stop. But that still begs the question: *Why* would they do any of this?"

Usually I appreciate June pressing an issue, as long as it doesn't turn into a bickerfest. Sometimes even when it does. However, we don't have that latitude now. Letting everyone hover while I work may have been a mistake. "Trust me," I say, "I'm as eager as you to uncover their motive. But their reasons aren't going to be laid out like breadcrumbs. Our best bet is to flush out as much intel as we can, as fast as we can, then read between the lines and get into their mindset."

"In other words, more guesswork."

"You could call it that. But it's educated guesswork, based on evidence they've been conspiring on the darknet and taking preemptive moves against anyone who might stop them."

"The bunker would stop them."

"True. But apparently the bunker isn't onto Kurt. If they were, they'd have protected KnoMor. Spying on employees isn't a high priority." When June doesn't clap back, I wipe my chili bowl clean with the last corner of cornbread, pop it in my mouth, and lick the drops of sauce off my fingers. I was hungry after all. "If you'll hang with me just a tad longer," I say, "I'd like to explore their second operation against us."

"VRcher?" Beers says.

"Yes. I think we may find what we're looking for."

No one objects, so I run a search on VRcher. It pulls up dozens of hits, and I scurry down the trail, narrating as I go: "Kurt's talking about the VRcher superpod, how they'll act and how we'll react. The whole event was orchestrated, starting with the invite sent only to June. All three Ks were in on it."

Beers points out that Karin was furious at Kurt. They were still going at it when we left.

"Well, it was all an act," I say. "Karin talks about staging a meltdown. Kurt says he'll throw her under the bus. They wanted us to think they were at odds with each other."

"We did think that," Nick says.

"They were convincing all right," Zack adds.

June's left knee is bobbling the way it does whenever she fights the urge to speak her mind. She's overtired and those shots of whiskey haven't helped. In such moments, a little reverse psychology often works. So instead of insisting yet again that she hang tight, I pause my search and ask what's on her mind.

She matches my conciliatory tone. "Sorry if I'm being dense, Jedd, but these clowns talk with each other in person every day. This darknet stuff has to be a joke."

"No one sets up a darknet site as a joke," Beers says.

I remind June that what we're looking at was created before the Ks moved into the penthouse. They shared space with podmates who weren't in on their plotting, so they needed a private place to talk. That's what the site is: their secret meeting space.

"Their treacherous palace!" Darah shoots me a knowing look.

June isn't as easily persuaded. "So you think they're playing us like suckers?"

"We're only suckers," I say, "if we don't verify what is true and what is not and then take responsible action to stop them. Like Darah said, I'm snooping around their palace. Before we burn it down—or set fire to one chamber—let's learn as much as we can." I summarize what we've learned so far: The three Ks have a secret agenda. Because of our skills, they view us as threats to that agenda. They're working with Donna and others not yet identified, using unorthodox strategies. They went after KnoMor to weaken our pod. Booting us from the penthouse was meant to further weaken our morale. The VRcher superpod was an elaborate smokescreen to keep us from discovering the real project they're working on.

"You're asking us to accept all this as fact?" June pours herself another shot. "I'm not ready to do that."

"No. I'm asking you to take it as a working hypothesis. Like any ongoing investigation. Can you do that?"

"We can," the twins say. Beers and Darah are nodding.

But June counters with more questions: "Who developed VRcher? Kurt markets products others create. So was it created by someone at HSys? Or by outside actors? And if so, are they also targeting us? You haven't identified any outsiders, but who could they be?" She shoots her questions rapid fire, then sits back.

They're all valid questions. I was jumping the gun to think I could bring this investigation to a snappy conclusion. "You're right, we've barely scratched the surface. The best way to get clarity is to go into the VRcher files and take a close look at the code." Since that pretty much covers it, I turn back to my screen.

But Beers has a different idea. "June's right. We need to know who we're dealing with."

"Yup," says June. "Check the metadata and see who has access."

"Wait," says Darah, rising from the rocker and joining us around the table. "How can you do that? Doesn't the darknet make everyone anonymous?"

"They *think* they're anonymous," Nick says, with a laugh. "That's why we have Jedd."

I'm about to argue for assessing the VRcher code first, but they have a point: we need to find out who the Ks are working with. My guess is pals of Kurt from his college days who now work for the competition. I've seen that scenario before. HSys employees with a hefty dose of hubris think they can pull off something nefarious and make a few bucks on the side. They think they're such darlings on campus that no one will notice. Never ends well for them.

It doesn't take me long to check the metadata and produce a list of IDs. "I've unmasked the three Ks and Donna," I say. "We already knew about them. Here are a dozen others I haven't seen in the message threads. Don't recognize any HSys people—"

"Whoa!" June leans in for a closer look, almost knocking over the whiskey. "Who's this?" She attempts to sound out a name syllable by syllable but gets tongue tied halfway through. "Khristorozhdestvenskaya. Who'd use that handle?"

"Someone from Russia?" Beers says.

June laughs.

"I'm not being funny," he says. "It's the most logical explanation."

Darah's eyes bug out. "They're working with *Russians?*"

For a minute I'm speechless. We're all speechless. If what Beers is suggesting pans out, this bomb dwarfs any I've dropped so far. Looking more closely at the names, it's obvious these aren't Kurt's college pals. They're probably not Californians. Not even Mericans. We could be dealing with Russians. Forget whatever I said about a small, tightly knit group. The Ks could be operating in the major leagues. "Okay," I say slowly. "These do look—"

"Seriously?" Suddenly stone sober, June cuts me off. "Now you expect me to believe the Ks are in cahoots with Russians. Including another K. I mean, really! Did you consider that these IDs might be garden-variety hackers with colorful names, operating from who-knows-where, and the HSys Ks are *their* victims? Before we speculate, let's find out more."

I doubt that's the case but agree we do need more info. We might as well go after it now.

She offers to use her tablet to trace the IDs while I look for signs the site was hacked or otherwise compromised. Meanwhile the others will update the kid on what we've learned while he's been snoozing.

It doesn't take June long to turn up hits. "I hate to say it, but you were spot on, Beers. Most of the IDs have IPs in Russia. A few in Florida. Only a couple I can't trace."

"The ones you can't trace could also be Russians," Nick says.

"Or bots," Zack adds.

"This gives a whole new meaning to the idea of a bigger operation," Beers says. "We've just established that an HSys pod is conspiring on the darknet with contacts in Russia and the States. Unless Jedd finds evidence of a hack, these aren't intruders. They're here by invitation."

Beers and I lock eyes. I know what he's thinking. It's what I'm thinking. My plan of going to the authorities so justice can be served is out the window. Normally when we talk about taking action—blowing the whistle, if need be—it's within the company, within our community. But a scenario of this magnitude? Honestly, if you'd told me a few hours ago we'd be looking at foreign collusion or a global cybercrime conspiracy, I'd have said you were out of your mind. Yet here we are. It's like we've stepped into a VR game that has eclipsed life as we know it. I certainly didn't see this coming.

June breaks the silence. She's still looking for alternative explanations. "All right, I'll give you the benefit of the doubt. Let's assume there was no hack. Kurt and Karin are in marketing and sales. Keith's in accounting. It wouldn't be farfetched for their pod to team up with Russian geeks on a project unrelated to VRcher."

"Then why is VRcher in here?" I counter.

"Do those three even speak Russian?" Darah asks before June can respond.

"People all over the world speak English," June says.

I confirm the messages I've seen are in English. In fact, as I buzz through more threads, I see some where the Ks aren't chatting only among themselves; they're also talking with the Russians. Khristorozhdestvenskaya goes by Krist. Like June said, another K. That makes at least four.

"Hey, bro," Beers says, "can you tell if these Russians are gamers or other kinds of programmers?"

"Oh, this gang definitely includes gamers." As I say that, I open a link in one of the messages about VRcher and find myself staring at a dazzling array of complex coding and graphics. "Look at this! Here are all the materials for VRcher. We have our answer: it was developed by the Russians, working with the Ks."

"Working . . . in the penthouse," Nick jeers.

"No wonder they needed stealth mode," Zack says.

For once June isn't ready with another question.

While the others toss around what all this could mean, I turn back to the materials. There's much more here than VRcher. I race through a maze of folders, trying to get the lay of the land, while also seeking answers to the question of motive. I suspect Beers is wondering if this is secret for political reasons. That's looking increasingly plausible. It's common knowledge the Russians have been running the States like a puppet master for years. Mericans might publicly deny it, but that's out of fear for their safety. These materials could be part of a Russian strategy to expand power. They could be using HSys to gain control over California. Still, I don't want to throw out such inflammatory ideas in the absence of more evidence.

And then I see it: a folder, unlike the rest in English, marked СЧАСТЛИВЫЙ. Auto-translation tells me that's Russian for happy. Happy? I have no idea what that could mean, except I'll be happy if I can get my hands on some solid evidence. It doesn't take much poking around to realize I have indeed hit the jackpot. The Cyrillic letters were either a feeble attempt at camouflage or a joke. This folder houses a game built on the technology used in VRcher but far exceeding it. What I see is so impressive I immediately share the news. "Hey, I've found the goods. There's a game here that's well beyond the concept phase."

June wants to know if they have a prototype.

I tell her it's right here, along with the architecture design. Programming is already underway. "All their notes"—I turn to Darah—"are in English."

"So, what's the game?" Beers presses.

"Come on," Nick says, "out with it."

Even the kid has come over from the hearth and is looking at me expectantly.

I get that they're impatient. I'm impatient too. Still, before I can say more, I need to take a closer look. "You realize, if I get cranking, we'll be here all night. It's already . . . what?"

"Almost 4 a.m.," Zack says.

"Aren't you tired?" I know they are but I need to hear them say they're still in.

"I'm exhausted," June says. "We all are. But this is far too important."

"I couldn't sleep anyway," Darah says.

"Good," I say, relieved everyone, especially June, is willing to run with me on this. "Let me do some uninterrupted digging. When I've got a handle on it, I'll report out."

Beers promises to whip up some coffee so we can keep our eyes open.

The Kauravas conspired: "The Pandavas can never be defeated in a war. But we have a weapon more powerful than steel. Without spilling a drop of blood, we shall turn their own honor against them."

9

SECRET PLOT: Beers

I return to the living room with a pot of coffee in one hand, a tray of snacks balanced on the other. Darah follows with mugs and napkins and begins pouring the coffee. Everyone dives at once for the nut brittle. Fortunately I whipped up a double batch a few nights ago, with my signature sprinkling of freshly ground jalapeños. Should keep us awake if adrenaline alone doesn't do it.

And my adrenals are pumping. Russian geeks? Are you kidding me? This is crazytown. We've gone from what was basically some rancid office politics to a secret plot unfolding on an international scale. From zero to red alert in a matter of minutes. I always knew Kurt was trouble, but this is effing unbelievable. We need to get rid of this guy—I mean that literally—before he pulls off some batshit insane stunt.

We all agreed not to interrupt Jedd. He works best that way. Unlike me with crossword puzzles. I'm used to finding obscure words while people yap at me from all sides. But now, after shifting my butt back and forth in this armchair for five minutes, I can't hold off. "Come on, dude," I plead, "spill!"

Darah cradles her mug in both hands and dittos that. "Please say something."

He doesn't so much as glance at us. He could be afraid June— or one of us—will challenge what he has to say. Or he could be trying to protect us from unpleasant news. I can't tell which. Or maybe it's a bit of both.

"Whatever it is, we can handle it," June says.

"Okay, okay," he says finally, still flipping through screens. Must be some pretty sophisticated technology. He takes a swig of coffee like it's a hard drink. "Okay," he says again. "I've only looked at a fraction of what's here. But this is what I can tell you. The Russian team is developing an app. It's not your run-of-the-mill app or even your run-of-the-mill VR app." He looks at us one by one, as if assessing our freak-out level.

"So?" I say when his eyes reach me. "What is it?"

"It's an SL app. Using quantum SL."

"Quantum smart light?" Darah enunciates the words as if she needs help spelling them. The fact that she's heard of SL doesn't mean she knows much about it. "Really, Jedd?"

"Really."

"Don't tell me Kurt's fluent in quantum computing and smart light," June says.

"He doesn't need to be," I say. "That's on the Russians."

This is serious shit, well beyond my technical capacity. No point being an ultracrepidarian. Everyone hates a dude who offers opinions outside his sphere of knowledge. And I'm not ready to weigh in from a security perspective. So I ask Jedd to say more.

He explains the app uses a cutting-edge quantum technology that incorporates smart light, an area in which, much as we Californians hate to admit it, Russia has outpaced the rest of the world. VRcher was a primitive test of a few features; this new app builds on that in a major way. Krist and the other Russians are using cloud-based quantum computing, working in tandem with game developers in Florida. All their materials are housed on this site. The Ks' pod is responsible for marketing the app.

"Wow," I say, "straight out of a spy flick."

"Except for real," Jedd says.

But June isn't buying. "You mean real BS."

"You said you could handle anything," he counters.

Normally how June and Jedd engage doesn't concern me. If constant contretemps works for them, fine. But not tonight. I can't watch them be pissy with each other while a bunch of Russians are plotting against us on the darknet. Enough already. This is as serious as anything we've faced in our lives. So I confront her: "You think Jedd's mindfucking us?"

She tosses her head as if to say she never said that. "There's a ton of weird stuff on the darknet. Even if these look like Russian IDs and Jedd's uncovered what looks like real game specs, this could still be part of a hoax. Or an elaborate con. Or some sick in-joke."

Jedd helps himself to the last piece of nut brittle, bites off a chunk, and looks up at her. "You're worried that I'm messing with you." Annoyed as he may be, he comes off as cool and collected. Totally rational. It's a skill I'll never have.

"*Are* you?" she says.

I'm about to butt in again but Jedd shoots me a glance that says he wants to run with this. "June," he says, "we've lived through so much post-truth insanity that it's natural to have doubts. I'd be more concerned if your BS antenna wasn't up."

"It's up all right."

"Keep it up. We can't drop our guard just because living in California is easy." He looks at Darah, who's nodding. "Tonight our world was turned upside down. This is happening in *our* lives. At our company. These are our colleagues with contacts in Russia and Florida. Like I said, no one in the bunker has picked up on this. It's in our hands. So please bear with me. I'm starting to see how it all connects."

His rational, logical strategy works. June mutters something about playing devil's advocate, then retreats to the sunroom to nurse a second cup of coffee, leaving it to the rest of us to pull the info out of Jedd.

Nick starts by asking if the app has a name.

"It's called Happy App."

"Did you say Happy App?" Darah looks confused.

"Yes, Happy App."

"No way!" NicknZack say in unison.

The kid plays a few trills on his flute. As if that's the only happiness app we need.

The whole idea is so screwy all I can do is laugh out loud. Not that Russian geeks and hackers are known for their sense of humor. "You're shitting me. They're full throttle with quantum SL, one of the most advanced technologies ever created, on something called a Happy App?"

Jedd confirms he's not joking. "Happy App is its production name. The three Ks could of course market it as something else down the line."

Darah asks if it's for kids.

Jedd shakes his head. "All ages."

When I ask if it's a game, he says it's more like a lifestyle app that's been gamified.

Nick points out there have been dozens of happy apps, dating back before our lifetimes. Many take a neuroscientific precept and boil it down to something marketable on a tablet. He recalls one called Happify that reframed negative thought patterns and came preinstalled on his phone in high school but he never used. Zack chimes in about one that sent happiness affirmations to his mom's phone. She read them aloud at breakfast and quizzed him at dinner. If he ever copped to being unhappy, she hit him with an affirmation.

I want to know more about how this app works.

Jedd says he was just getting to that. "Keep in mind I've only had a peek at the specs. I haven't touched the code. Obviously I haven't tested the app."

"Fair enough."

June returns to the living room. Her excuse is a third cup of coffee, but really I think she doesn't want to miss what Jedd is about to disclose.

"The app," he says, "produces a beam of smart light that enters the user's brain. It's the same light that emanates from any tablet, except programmed to transmit data. As you focus on its spotlight, it hooks you up to a quantum computer in the cloud that targets the area of your brain that's most activated when you're happy. It does this through the portal of your eye. You have no idea what's happening. You just view a simple interface that says 'Watch here . . . be happy.' Points are earned for the length of time you look at the light and report being happy." He creates a blank screen on the coffee table and diagrams the elements with his finger: the app, the cloud, the smart light, a pair of eyes, a brain.

It looks simple enough. Until you realize that could be your brain being breached. Broken into. By Russians.

June puts the concept in context. Many technologies access the brain. The most popular HSys products incorporate BCI, including some that use smart dust or neurodust. And then there's neurogaming. Plus all the wearable devices that have come and gone over the years.

Jedd is nodding. "Remember, June, what you felt during the superpod?"

"Yes, that sensation in my eye."

This is news to me. "What sensation?"

June explains that as she shot the bird, something hit her in the eye. Or so it seemed. She and Jedd discussed it at the time.

Darah looks dubious. "What hit you in the eye?"

June says it wasn't physical. What hit her eye was in the light emanating from the explosion when the bird dropped. Now it sounds like that was an early test of the technology for this new app.

"If that's true," I say, "I'm amazed they let us experience it."

Jedd acknowledges the Ks probably didn't expect June to detect anything. Most people wouldn't notice something so subtle. In all likelihood, it was due to a timing error they've since corrected. He adds that this new app doesn't use a helmet. Transmission happens entirely through the eye.

"Sounds like next-gen neurogaming," I say.

"It's incredibly sophisticated," he says. "The data travel between targeted areas of your brain and their cloud-based computer. At the speed of light, literally."

"Wouldn't that require 7G?" June wants to know.

"They designed it to work with 6G." Jedd looks around to make sure everyone is following, then continues. "Hiding its complexity is part of their strategy. While it masquerades as a feel-good lifestyle app, it can be used to program—or reprogram—thoughts and feelings. You think you're perceiving a nice image, no big deal. But messages are entering your brain and inducing you to react, and you're reacting without realizing why."

Darah is horrified. "That's mind control."

Jedd doesn't deny it.

"What message does it transmit?" I'm trying to get a fix on the level of cybersecurity threat. We tend to think of cyberattacks on computers or databases or internets, not on the human brain directly. Not on our own minds. Yes, I know about brain-hacking of medical treatments and other kinds of neurocrime, but I haven't heard of it affecting HSys products. Maybe that was inevitable.

Jedd says the message is not cognitively complex. "Remember, it stimulates the region of the brain most activated when people are happy."

June cuts in: "The left prefrontal cortex." When Jedd doesn't jump on that factoid, she adds, "I took neuroscience in college. I still recall some of it."

She may know her stuff, but showboating isn't helpful now. So I stay focused on Jedd. "Is the idea to make users feel happier or to make them feel happier *about* something?"

He spins around. "Good question, Beers. Definitely the latter." He explains that in addition to stimulating a response in the brain, the smart light is transmitting subliminal images. These functions are linked at the speed of light so the brain perceives and responds to them as a single event.

"But what, Jedd?" I say. "Transmit an image of what?"

"My guess is something that activates oxytocin release," June says. "Pics of friends and family."

"Or selfies," Nick says.

"Didn't studies find that sharing selfies makes us happier?" Zack adds.

"Photos of trees make your nervous system relax," Darah says. "That's why I put nature images on the display wall. I mean, I used to."

I try to picture the Russians choosing between trees and selfies, and it doesn't compute. The concept of a happiness app may be innocuous enough, but we're talking about devious motherfuckers. Their app must be designed to pack a punch in an underhanded way. "Wait," I say. "I bet this app doesn't use images that naturally make us happy. I'm guessing it does the opposite. Like make our brains associate happiness with an image of something we dislike."

"You're right," Jedd says.

June does a double take, realizing she's led us down the wrong alley. "So tell us: What's the image?"

"You know, don't you?" I say.

He nods.

"Stop with the tease," Darah says.

He shoots me a silent *you won't like this*, then spits it out: "The Dictator."

We all react at once. Yes, we've been talking about the Ks working with these Russians. But carrying out the Dick's agenda? Directly, unambiguously, shamelessly? This is next level.

Darah is the first to slow down enough to talk above the group. She looks pale, and I suspect she's feeling triggered. This has to disturb her even more than it does the rest of us. "You said Kurt's in contact with Washington and Moscow. But do you know whose idea this project was?"

It's a sobering question.

Jedd admits he does. He apologizes for not explaining more before, but he didn't want to alarm us in case he was misinterpreting. Now he offers to go into the site and locate the specific sources so we can parse all of them more carefully. But no one wants to wait for that. The coffee is running low and we're way too tired. So he proceeds with a summary.

"Kurt is in contact with someone close to the Dictator. I saw a message where he boasted about going to Washington to meet him, which I took with a grain of salt. Who in their right mind is proud of that? But I read more, and turns out his family has ties with the Dictator's clan going way back. One of the Dictator's cousins connected Kurt with the Russians and Floridians. The idea was to take advantage of HSys's position in the industry to launch a state-of-the-art app that advances their mutual interests. Yes, the Ks took a big risk, but the potential payoff is even bigger. Kurt and Donna also knew each other before HSys. From what I can see, the rest of their pod got pulled in by Kurt's personality. He's a master at bending people to his will, demanding absolute loyalty, and decimating anyone standing in his way."

I'm astounded at how much Jedd has pieced together so quickly. PIs take months if not years to come up with far less. "Say more about why this app," I say. "And why now?"

"The Dictator never had many supporters. Those who backed other wanna-be dictators in recent decades like him. That's about it," Jedd says. "So he negotiated with the Russians for a technology to swing the public in his favor."

"Isn't that the point of being a dictator: you don't need to be popular to stay in power?" Darah says.

"He may not need their approval," Jedd says, "but it irritates the bejesus out of him knowing people find him so repugnant. Anyway, the Russians came up with the concept for this app using their revolutionary SL technology. Most related applications—the ones we've heard about—are medical in nature, such as manipulating the brain to help people with disabilities function independently. This app isn't too great a jump from that."

"So after the Dick got this concept from the Russians, he approached Kurt?" I say.

"More likely his cousin approached Kurt." Jedd says having the app come out of Russia would look suspicious. So what better place than here? No one would suspect an app coming from HSys, deep in Silicon Valley, in the independent nation of California. "Think about it," he says. "We worked alongside Kurt, Karin, and Keith for years and never imagined they were cozying up to the Dictator."

"Nope," I say, "not a clue." And my job means I'm on the lookout for stuff like this.

"Never occurred to *me*," Darah says. I know which K she has in mind.

Jedd says that's not all. "While the Dictator wants people to like him, his endgame is more ambitious. He regrets letting California go."

I've been following this daily on the way home from work. The Dick assumed we'd become a failed state if left to our own devices, and it pisses him off to see how wrong he was. Each new success of ours adds to his humiliation. His crackdown with drones on the border led some to conclude he intends to invade. Soon. Other experts consider it a vituperative but empty threat. I tend to agree with the latter. "He won't dare attack us," I say.

"Maybe not," Jedd says. "With all the strong allies we have, he has to know any invasion would be well defended against. That's where the Happy App comes in. He's counting on its mind control strategy to lay the groundwork for a surprise takeover."

June is shaking her head. She can't accept such a far-fetched product premise. "Stimulating the brain could increase happiness. That's viable. But using it to make people like the Dictator? Reminds me of that study in which people supposedly ate more popcorn after their brain registered an image of buttered popcorn. It was debunked decades ago." She raises her eyebrows at Jedd. "We studied it in college, remember?"

"I do," Jedd says. "This app is nothing like that. It's not flashing an image of the Dictator like popcorn. It uses smart light, probably with instant BCI mapping, to influence the emotions associated with a target thought."

June concedes that's possible. She's fluent with some quantum programming languages but hasn't heard of smart light used this way. I'm sure she intends to research it as soon as she can. Probably first thing when she gets to the office.

"Okay, Jedd," I say. "Sounds like you're convinced this app could work. But let's be practical. In this day and age, who'd even want to try something called a Happy App?"

Nick ventures a guess: "Miserable people?"

"Yeah, who want to be happy," Zack adds.

We all burst out laughing. How absurd is that? Still, it's a relief to let off a little steam.

"The world doesn't need another happy app," I say.

"No, it doesn't," says the kid, with a twinkle in his eye. "But it sure could use a . . . compassion app."

"Or a courage app," June says.

"How about a peace app?" Jedd says.

"Or a cacoëthes app," I say. No one bothers to ask what that means, but I like the sound of it. Plus stirring up irresistible passion might help with their marketing problem.

The suggestions pile on.

"A generosity app."

"A harmony app."

"Maybe a woke app?"

"I think I need a nap app," the kid says with a giggle as he heads back to the hearth rug, where Dharma's waiting for him.

"We can joke about it," I say when everyone has settled down, "but I don't see people buying this thing. Not on a scale that would cause millions to stop hating the Dick."

"I agree with Beers," Jedd says. "That's the one thing they failed to account for: people won't buy it."

"Heck," Nick says, "no one will try it for free."

"Not even if you pay them," Zack adds.

"Right," Jedd says. "People aren't that stupid."

"Or maybe they are?" June goes back to playing devil's advocate.

But Jedd isn't interested in debating the fundamentals of human nature. "Even if people aren't stupid—which I believe—this app is stupid. That's what we've got to count on."

"It's odd," Darah says. "You'd expect Kurt to have thought this through."

Jedd says he saw no evidence of that in their messages. The Dick wanted this app. The rest are blindly following his orders. Full stop.

"Kurt may get a lot of mileage out of quirky advertising," June says, "but if a concept is flawed, even his best campaign won't amount to more than turd polishing."

The next question of course is what to do about all this. It's reassuring to think the app will flop on its own. But we can't bank on that. These assholes need to be stopped before their app does real damage. I'm just not sure how. "So what now?" I ask.

No one has a clear answer.

"We have to do *something*," I say.

June agrees. "Even if the app is a total fail, they're still conspiring with the Dictator, threatening California. All of this breaches company policy. If no one at HSys realizes what they're up to, it's on us to speak out about it."

"Report them to management," Darah suggests.

"The C-suite can't be trusted," June says. "Notify the bunker."

Jedd says he was considering that on his way home. He even decided which colleague to approach there. But that was before we learned about the Dictator and the Russians. "The more I've uncovered," he says, "the more ambivalent I am about our best course of action."

"Knowing the Russians are involved is all the more reason to speak up," June argues. "We can't fight them by ourselves."

Jedd bristles at that. "You think I'm no match for a bunch of Russians?!" His voice is rising from its usual calm, but he quickly reels himself in. "What I mean is, if we all agree that taking them on is the right thing to do, I'm ready to do it."

His pledge lands on me like a boost of double espresso. "I'm with you, let's do this!" I say, fists clenched, punching at an invisible happy app. "Let's squash those fuckers!"

Instead of high-fiving me as I expected, Jedd looks deflated. "Sorry, Beers, I'm afraid it's not a good idea."

"Bro, you just said—"

"I said *if* we agreed it's the right thing to do. Which also means if it's the right time. And it's neither of those." He watches me take another swing at the air and shakes his head. "Believe me, I'd like nothing more than to take them on. I'm not intimidated by the Russians. Or the Ks."

The kid sits up abruptly. I thought he was napping, but apparently he was lying on the hearth rug, eyes closed, listening the whole time. "Do the right thing," he says, "but also be smart."

"Exactly," Jedd says. "We can't go off half-cocked. If we do, we'll end up even higher on their enemies list than we already are. Then it won't be just our office space on the line. It'll be our lives."

"And the lives of many," the kid adds.

The truth of that pushes on me hard. He's right. If we take this on and they manage to launch this app anyway, countless millions will be affected. That's not a scenario we're equipped to deal with. Much as I hate to admit it, we need to take a step back, think first and foremost about ourselves. From a security perspective, that makes the most sense. Sometimes hasty actions can be lifesaving. But if you're not careful, they can be fatal. In my own haste, I didn't stop to weigh the difference.

"So what are you suggesting?" Darah asks.

She's looking at Jedd and the kid, but I want to make it clear I'm on the same page, so I answer. "We lay low. Let the Ks think displacing us from the penthouse was enough to knock us down a few pegs."

"I see your point," June says. "Laying low in this case isn't abdicating responsibility, it's just buying time so Jedd can keep digging."

"Like . . . a mouse," Darah throws in.

I reinforce that. It's critical for Jedd to stay vigilant, make sure his presence on the darknet site goes undetected. "Let them forget we exist," I say.

"I'm not sure they'll forget us," he says, "but we can give them less reason to target us. If we run straight to management, it'll be outright war. We need to come up with a counter strategy before we take direct action."

I second that. It'll be a waiting game. We need time to come up with a smart way—like the kid said—to undermine them before they can execute this crazy scheme of theirs. In the meantime, we play dead.

The first light of dawn is outshining the living room lamps. The candles on the mantlepiece burned out ages ago. We've been up all night. Even a triple espresso wouldn't help now. "Please," I say, "I need some sleep before it's time for work or I won't be able to keep my eyes open during my shift."

The kid is the only one to object. "You really have to go to HSys? After all this?"

"Well," I say, "if the plan is to lay low, we don't want to draw attention to ourselves by skipping work. People know NicknZack work from home, but the rest of us need to act normal."

The kid gives me a look that says *if you say so*. Then we all head to our beds for a short nap.

The game began. The die was cast.
The hall was silent as Yudhishtira announced his stakes:
his jewels, his precious stones, and his wealth.

THE DIE IS CAST: Darah

The four of us, too exhausted to do more than throw on our clothes and climb into the chariot, head to HSys together. Except for the fact we're two hours late, everything is business as usual. No one can suspect we're sitting on a powder keg of info.

But in the chariot, nothing is as usual. Jedd doesn't so much as glance at a video game. Beers isn't checking the morning news. No one asks what he's cooking for dinner. June doesn't suggest a good place for drinks Friday evening. Though I know the sun is painting the madrones a rich red, my eyes are shut.

I open them and break the silence when we're halfway there by worrying aloud about my ability to act like all is normal when it isn't. "I don't know if I can pull this off," I warn them.

"You can, Darah," June says. "You must."

"We all must," Jedd says. He reminds me Kurt doesn't know what we know, and we have to keep it that way. Stay off his radar.

I ask if he still intends to go back into the darknet site. I know he will, but asking channels my anxiety, evokes a sense of normalcy. Like I can handle this. Like I'm as tough as I've been telling myself I am. In fact, my whole body is on edge. It's not just lack of sleep or because Beers's 3 a.m. nut brittle is the only thing in my belly. I haven't felt dread like this in ages. I thought I'd escaped the Dictator, that he'd never touch my life again. And now this.

"Of course," Jedd says. "Like we discussed, it's essential to learn as much as we can about what they're up to, including their timetable for launching the Happy App."

Beers frowns. "Dude, you aren't planning to do it at work, are you?"

From Jedd's befuddled look, it's apparent he intended to do just that.

"Bad idea!" Beers is unequivocal: under no circumstances should Jedd access the darknet site from anywhere but home. We don't know how secure our workspace is. Kurt could have had it wired before we got there. It's far too risky.

"But Jedd already worked there for hours yesterday," I say.

"I realize that," Beers says. "We have to be more careful now, given what we know."

Jedd sucks in his breath. If he made a mistake, it's too late to undo. He agrees all his sensitive digging will happen at home, even if that means many late nights.

"But is the farm safe?" I ask. It's not a huge jump to think the Dictator's digital spies could be listening to us in the kitchen or on the porch. Recording our words, tracking our movements. Watching me asleep in the attic. The mere thought makes my skin crawl.

Jedd warns us against paranoia. He's speaking to everyone, but I know he means me. We have no reason to believe the farm is bugged. He isn't worried about his online activities being tracked, because he knows how to shield his identity. He feels safe and in control in cyberspace. Ironically, contact with the Ks in the physical world is a greater danger.

Beers mimes goggles as he does a shoutout to Kurt: "We've got eyes on you! You're not getting away with shit!"

As we pull into the HSys parking lot, I remind the others I haven't yet confronted Kurt about his butt grab. Or gone to HR about it. With everything going on, there hasn't been a good time. I ask what I should do if I see him now.

"Confront him!" For June, the only question is what I'm waiting for. Standing up for oneself is akin to a sacred duty for her. "Give a jackass a pass," she says, "and that jackass will assume he can get away with it. He'll do it again. Or worse."

Jedd disagrees. Not about Kurt being a jackass or that he needs to be confronted but about when. He points out we don't know why Kurt grabbed me. It could be his boorish nature. Or it could be part of their setup. When we crossed paths with him at the elevator, he knew what was about to go down with KnoMor. He was one step ahead. That could be true now too.

"But you told me to report him. All of you did," I argue back.

"Things changed," Jedd says. "This isn't just an issue between two employees now. It's not even just two pods. If you confront Kurt and it gets heated, you could blow our cover."

"It would be a declaration of war," Beers adds. "Even if that's not your intention."

"I'm afraid you'll have to keep up the pretense," Jedd says.

June says she hates pretense in any form but sees their point. We need to minimize contact.

We walk from the chariot to room 538 in silence, each steeped in thought. While the others napped, I didn't sleep a wink. I was struggling with the idea that the Ks are working for the Dictator. I still can't believe it. I mean, if Keith was a liar, a traitor even, surely I'd have sensed it. I'd have read it in his lapis eyes. I've gone through too much in life to miss such signs. It can't really be three Ks, I tell myself, it's only two. The third K is mine. I can go to him in secret, force him to level with me. Or wait till he contacts me, which he pretty much promised to do. Of course that would be maximizing contact. Maybe it would be better to completely shut that door. Then if Keith comes knocking, too bad.

As we stand in the elevator heading for the fifth floor, I pull out my tablet and nudge Beers. "I'm blocking some contacts," I whisper. He'll know what I mean.

And he does. "No!" he hisses, snatching my tablet and flipping it shut. "What if they try to text you? We can't make any overt moves that might trigger suspicion."

"All right, all right, I won't," I say, holding my hand out for the tablet.

Knowing what we do about the Ks, I stick even more stringently to the routine I've followed since we were ousted from the penthouse. No running out for air, even if I'm stressed. No speedwalking the loop. Definitely no lingering over lunch in the café. No lunch in the café, period. That's not hard. With my stomach in knots, food has lost all appeal. I limit myself to one blue algae smoothie, which I bring back to my workspace and drink slowly, making it last the afternoon. Feels a bit like being in jail.

Beers is the only one who can't avoid leaving our office. In fact, he took on an extra shift at the lobby scanner. He says it's a great opportunity to practice acting normal. "Like when Karin arrived this morning," he told me earlier.

"How'd *that* go?"

"She smiled when I said hi."

"Really?"

"Yup, totally normal. If she has any idea about what Jedd found, she gave no clue."

I can't imagine sitting by the scanner every day doing nothing, waiting for the Ks to show up. My nerves would be like splintered glass.

Jedd spends his evenings digging through the darknet site. He works in the living room so he can report out to whoever is nearby.

So far he hasn't come up with any major revelations about the Happy App, though he did note a precipitous drop-off in chatter about it on the site.

Beers asked why that might be.

"Maybe the Russians have all they need to finish the app," June said.

"They could still discuss marketing strategies," Nick said.

"Or their love for the Dictator," Zack added.

Jedd said he suspects the Ks aren't talking much online because they can now talk freely in the penthouse. Which means we're out of the loop.

"They still need a secure place to talk to the Russians and Floridians," Beers said. "Eventually you'll see something."

So basically we're in a holding pattern. If the Happy App launches, we're positioned to get an early warning. Then we can decide what, if anything, to do about it. And if it fails, well, we'll deal with that too. All this could take a while to sort out. In the meantime, as one day flows into the next without incident, my nerves start to settle. Somehow, I tell myself, we'll get through this. We have each other, that's what counts.

Late one afternoon there's a knock on the door of room 538.

The usual three of us are here: Jedd and June and I. Since I'm closest to the door, I get up to open it.

It's Kurt.

Really, you've got to be kidding. I mean, the dude never visits our pod. Not when we had the penthouse and certainly not here. The last time I saw him up close, he grabbed me. Now it takes willpower not to slap him. And I'm not someone who slaps people.

He brushes past me with a raucous hello, as if nothing has happened to give anyone pause. As if he's still someone we would jokingly call a cousin. "Haven't seen you guys in forever," he says. "Almost like you don't work here anymore."

"That's because we don't work down the hall anymore," Jedd says with a smile. Without even a hint of sarcasm. His ability to maintain a game face is amazing.

Kurt grins back. "Let's fix that. How about a happy hour? Nothing formal. A few drinks, a little gaming." He turns to Jedd. "You're a good gamer. You'll love it."

"Thanks." Jedd is noncommittal.

"Where's the rest of your pod?"

"Two of us work from home," June says, rising from her chair, looking down at him. I'll bet he hates that she's taller. "Beers is out on the floor."

Kurt gives a perfunctory nod, then picks up the stapler from the table by the window and turns it over in his hand, inspecting it as one would a relic. "So?" he asks after a moment.

"So," Jedd echoes, "when is this event?"

It may not be the enthusiasm he's looking for, but Kurt is satisfied. "Today. Short notice, I know. But we do great impromptu happy hours."

"All right," Jedd says. "We'll check with the others and get back to you."

As soon as Kurt is out the door, June and I pounce.

"Jedd, for god's sake!" June is livid.

"Why did you say that?" I cry. "Now he thinks we're going to his frigging happy hour."

Jedd defends himself. "We have to do what we've been talking about: act normal. I was acting normal."

"The last thing I want to do is hang out with their pod," I say.

"Same here," June says. "I wouldn't think you'd want to either, Jedd."

"I never said I *wanted* to." He looks annoyed.

"So you were bluffing?" I'm relieved. I can think of so many reasons not to go.

But he's shaking his head. "This isn't about what I or any of us want. You know I'm not a partying guy. I find excuses to skip even cool parties. This is all about us laying low. That means minimizing contact, not avoiding it altogether. Refusing a simple invite when we don't have a credible excuse will only shine a bigger spotlight on us."

At this point, Beers walks in. Jedd explains what has happened and that we're debating the best way to handle it.

"I'm with June and Darah," Beers says immediately. "Sounds like bread and circuses. No way we do this. No way in hell!" His eyes fall on the stapler, probably because Kurt moved it from its usual spot. He punches it, making staples spray across the table.

"Okay, Beers," Jedd says. "Now that that's out of your system, can we talk strategy?"

Beers plucks a staple off the peace lily and slumps into a chair. "Sorry. I'm listening."

We take seats around the table.

"If we go—" Jedd begins.

Before Jedd can say more, Beers jumps to his feet, as if he suddenly woke up. "Shh!" he whispers, looking rapidly from one to the other of us.

Instantly we all realize we've already said too much. We exchange glances, each mentally assessing the damage. If the room is bugged, we've just screwed ourselves. Being vigilant about our actions and speech is way harder than I imagined. Now even Beers has blown it.

To cover, I say the first thing that pops into mind: "I need coffee! Join me?" I make my voice upbeat, as if I'm really dying for coffee. Hopefully it doesn't sound as fake as it feels.

Jedd and June look confused, but Beers catches on. He winks. "Let's go."

As soon as we're in the elevator, we all begin talking a mile a minute.

"Hold on," Jedd says. "Let me explain why we need to do

this." As we make our way to the café, he builds on the reason he's already given: we have to act normal, not make ourselves into bigger targets. Instead let's turn this to our advantage. Learn more about the status of the Happy App and the Ks' plans. Gather intel. He has something up his sleeve, he says, to do this without arousing suspicion.

"Like what?" June asks.

"Something I can execute myself."

"I like the sound of that," Beers says.

June wants more details.

"I'll explain later," Jedd says. "At home." Then he says something that forces our hand: "I also have my own personal reason to go. Kurt appealed to me as a gamer. Call it honor, call it pride, call it what you will, it's a challenge I can't ignore. Even if I have to go alone, I'm going."

"You can't go alone, bro," Beers says. "If you're going, I'll be right there with you."

At this point, the discussion stops so we can buy our coffees. I go for a mocha. The others get espresso freddos. June pockets a bag of jellyfish chips.

As soon as we're outside again, she says, "I get that you're bent on going, Jedd, and I'll back you up if it comes to that, but I'm worried about what you're getting yourself into."

Jedd frowns. He's offended by her lack of faith in his gaming prowess. "I'm going into this with eyes wide open. You ought to know that."

Beers jumps to his defense. "Jedd's a top gamer. Kurt will never win against him."

"And if Kurt cheats?" she counters. "Because you know he will."

"So what?" Jedd says. "This is a game. Just a game. If he cheats, it will be info we can discuss afterwards. Like with VRcher."

"Maybe calling it a happy hour is a nod to the Happy App," I say. "Kurt could be testing whether we pick up on that."

THE DIE IS CAST: Darah

June thinks that's a stretch, but Jedd says it's all the more reason to go. We need to be alert to any clues about their app, even far-fetched ones.

I want to say I have a bad feeling, but we've reached the elevator and it's time to finalize our decision.

"I'm doing this," Jedd says. "Who's with me?" At least he's leaving an out for anyone unwilling to go.

"Already told you I'm in," Beers says.

"If we're doing this, let's get it over with," June says.

Jedd turns to me. "Darah?"

I'm tempted to take the out. Missing the VRcher superpod worked well for me, and I still want to stay away from Kurt. Or . . . maybe not. I've been looking for a chance to squeeze info out of Keith, to do what I can to help our cause. This could be the perfect opportunity. The elevator door opens on the fifth floor. The time for deliberation is over. "Okay," I say. "Count me in."

Jedd pulls out his tablet and texts the twins. He's short on details, only asking if they can get to HSys for a meeting in an hour. Their response is equally fast and even briefer: yes. Then a text goes off to Kurt letting him know we're on.

I meet the twins outside the café and fill them in. They're more than a little skeptical. Everything we know about Kurt makes this too risky. Jedd, I tell them, has already made his decision. He's going even if he has to go alone. Obviously none of us will let that happen.

"All right," says Nick. "If you all agreed, we'll go along."

"For the record, we think this is a bad idea," Zack adds.

I text the others that we'll meet them at the elevator, then we all head to the sixth floor.

Kurt and Karin and Keith are waiting for us.

This is our penthouse no more. The lights are on their coldest and brightest setting. The carbon-negative white carpet that felt homey when we were here feels cold and sterile. The windows have been reprogrammed to mask the setting sun. If any others share the workspace, there's no sign of them. Nor are there signs of work: nothing on the table screens or display wall, no helmets or other gear lying around. I wish I could throw up some daisies on the wall. Anything to invoke normality.

Karin ushers the six of us toward the kitchenette, where an expansive array of liquor, wine, beer, and snacks is spread out. We kept the penthouse stocked but nothing like this.

Beers pours himself a shot of rum from a large square bottle with an ornate gold stopper, tosses it down, and pours another. Jedd and the others help themselves to beers, then wander away. I pass over several premade cocktails before settling on a Bloody Mary mix. If we get stuck here, its nutrients will have to serve as dinner. I scoop ice into a glass, pour in the mix and a mini bottle of vodka, top it off with a celery stick, and take a few sips. It doesn't taste bad.

Keith has been watching from across the room. Now he strides over, his elbow brushing my arm as he reaches for a frosted bottle you might mistake for shampoo. "Most expensive vodka in the world," he says. "Made with diamonds."

"For real?"

"Yup. Wasted on a Bloody Mary," he says with a laugh.

"If it's that pricey, I guess so," I say, laughing back. I recall hearing the Dictator has a penchant for lavish vodka. Maybe that's why it's here.

"Kurt gets lots of special gifts." He picks up the square rum bottle Beers was sampling and hands it to me. The gold stopper is in the shape of two warlike bird heads, their sharp beaks pointing in opposite directions. "This is another one. If you're a fan of the good stuff, I suggest you try it."

He leaves me staring at the bottle. *Could this be from the Dictator? Is he trying to clue me in?* I need an excuse to lure him away so I can get answers. We haven't been here long enough to justify sneaking off, just the two of us, with a bottle of rum. Still, it's worth a try.

As I turn to follow him, I find myself face to face with Jedd.

"Unusual bottle," he says, holding out his hand. "Let's see."

I can't exactly refuse.

He takes it from me and fiddles with the gold stopper, trying to open it without puncturing a finger, then abruptly turns away and walks to the window. He stands there, his back to everyone. Presumably about to pour himself a drink. I'm not sure whether to go over and ask for it back—what will my pretext be?—or approach Keith with the vodka instead.

As I'm still debating with myself, Kurt makes his way to the display wall and calls out, "Hey, everybody, game time!"

That shouldn't come as a surprise: it was the focus of his invite. But I need to work my plan on Keith. If I can't do that, I'd rather go home.

So would June. She hoists her bag onto her shoulder, gives Kurt a perfunctory thank you for the drinks, and declares she's leaving.

"What's a happy hour without gaming?" Kurt shoots her an overstated pout as he dims the lighting and projects a dark screen on the wall. "This is for you," he calls to Jedd.

Jedd brings the rum bottle back to the kitchenette and places it behind the other bottles, then approaches Kurt. "Okay, I'll bite. Whatcha have in mind?"

It's the response Kurt is looking for. "I hear you like gambling."

That's a bolt from the blue. Supposedly no one except me knows about Jedd's late-night gambling.

"I won't deny enjoying a low-stakes game every now and then," he says with a shrug.

"And you're damn good at it," Kurt continues.

Jedd doesn't deny that either. He may be a humble dude, but he's not immune to praise for his gaming skills. Nor is he one to back down from challenges. He said as much earlier: it's a point of pride to play Kurt. So much for gathering intel. If he gets hooked, we could be here for hours. Judging by the others' faces, they don't like the idea either. June has dropped her bag onto a chair and is glaring at Jedd.

"One game," I say.

Kurt is agreeable. "Sure, Darah. One game. Penny stakes. Just for fun, right?" He reaches for his tablet and swipes through a few screens. A holographic image of three slowly spinning dice takes shape in front of the display wall.

"Ha, your basic retro dice game!" Jedd grins. "Love it!"

Beers asks who's playing. He doesn't look happy, but he doesn't want Kurt to see him contradict Jedd.

"The two of us." Kurt motions for Jedd to join him at the table, where Karin has placed two auto-morphing chairs on opposing sides, at right angles to the display. She removes the other chairs so the rest of us have to stand if we want a close view.

Jedd's chair reclines a few degrees, allowing him to angle his legs to the side of the table. I'm sure he's missed that chair.

Kurt projects columns on the righthand side of the display to tally their wins and losses. "We'll use one die with six sides. Each roll is win or lose."

A swift round of old-school rock, paper, scissors determines Jedd will roll first. He touches the tablet, making all the dice spin faster. One die expands and shoots to the foreground. It stops on a four. He smiles and passes the tablet to Kurt.

Kurt rolls a two.

They play a few dozen quick rounds, with Jedd winning all but a handful. He looks pleased. The tally shows him up by twenty-nine cents. "Pennies are pittance," he says. "The odds should be at least a dollar."

Kurt readily agrees.

That sets me on edge. What was supposed to be one game is now open-ended. Jedd could easily start losing. I don't know what he's counting on. His psychic ability? In that case, the twins should step in. Still, he doesn't look concerned. As long as he's in full gaming mode, he won't quit till he's won.

June looks antsy, the way she gets when games lack a technology that holds her attention.

To keep my nerves in check, I join Beers by the alcohol, where he's helping himself to rum. I pick up my Bloody Mary, and we run down priorities for the weekend. Hike along a ridge near the farm or patch those cracks in the barn roof? I advocate for the patching project. The kid has been spending half the week at the farm and half wherever he likes to wander. That will change once the rains set in. As we talk, I keep an eye on Keith. He is intent on the hologram and never glances at me.

By the time Beers and I decide we have time for both the hike and the patching, the gambling odds have risen to a hundred dollars for each roll. Jedd is down three hundred dollars.

"Hey, bro," says Beers, coming up behind Jedd. "It's getting late."

June is watching from the head of the table, the twins at her side. All wear deep frowns.

"Come on, Jedd," I say.

He doesn't look up. "I'm fine," he says in a tone that doesn't invite second opinions.

The next round is more of the same. Now he's down four hundred.

"Gosh," says Karin, wringing her hands. "I'd hate to see you lose all that. Shall we up the ante? With one roll at five hundred dollars, you can come out ahead."

I'm certain Jedd won't go for that. It's the oldest trick in the book. But before any of us can object, he agrees.

"Let's mix the game up a bit," Kurt says. "We'll use a seven-sided die and each pick a lucky number. If no lucky number comes up, the high roll wins five hundred dollars and the low roll loses five hundred. If your number comes up, you win fourfold. If both numbers are up, that round is a scratch. You in?"

Jedd concurs. "I'll take six." He must believe six will be lucky for the six of us.

Kurt takes three. It nauseates me to think that's for the three Ks. With a few taps on his tablet, he adjusts the hologram so the six-sided die in the center has seven sides.

Jedd rolls a five and Kurt a three.

Now Jedd is down twenty-four hundred dollars. He reaches for the tablet to roll again. I don't get why he is sticking to it when he's losing big. He can't possibly think Kurt is playing fair.

The five of us trade glances. We're all on the same wavelength: *This has to stop.*

Beers steps forward and slams a fist on the table, stopping Kurt from passing the tablet.

June follows by calling a timeout. Her voice is her verbal fist on the table.

Kurt sets the tablet aside. "Okay," he says. "But if Jedd quits now, that's the end of the game." He and Karin exchange looks. A slight shake of her head indicates she disagrees. "All right," he concedes, "take your break. Five minutes max."

"When we resume," Karin adds, "we raise to two thousand dollars for a simple win, eight thousand for a lucky number."

At this point, I don't care if they raise, I just want to get Jedd away from the table so we can figure out an exit strategy. That shouldn't be hard; he's always the reasonable, rational one. If he hears us out, he will do the sensible thing. And we'll be on our way home.

Jedd grabs a shot of rum and walks over to the window with us.

"What's got into you?" June demands.

"This is insane!" Beers reaches for Jedd's glass, as if drinking is the root of his problem. "Cut the crap, bro!"

Jedd downs the rum, then looks from one to the other of us.

"We don't like this," I say.

Beers seconds that. "Let's get out of here, bro!"

"Please," Jedd says. "Don't be so uptight. It's just a game."

"Just a game?" June's voice is rising.

"It's classic dice," Jedd says. "It might be beneath you. But I enjoy the simplicity."

"You're losing big bucks in a game of pure luck!" she counters.

"It's probably rigged," Nick says.

"For sure is," Zack adds.

Jedd shakes his head. "I can afford this. If it's even a real debt, which I seriously doubt. What I'm not willing to do is let him think he can fix a game and beat me."

He's betting on his integrity over any odds, no matter how rigged. I don't know how to get him to back down. Nor do the others. It doesn't help that we can't talk about why we're here: to gather intel. "We haven't *learned* anything," I say, leaning in so my words aren't audible outside our circle.

Jedd's brow puckers. If he's picking up what I mean, he doesn't let on. "You don't want them to win, do you?" he says. "Because if I quit now, they win."

At this point, Karin calls time.

Jedd breaks away, and we follow him back to the table.

"Epic fail," I mumble to Beers.

The squeeze of his hand on my shoulder tells me he agrees but feels we have no choice but to let Jedd play this out as he sees fit.

"Glad you're not quitting," Kurt says, as Jedd eases back into his chair. "You started with a winning streak. Don't see why you can't earn back what you lost. You're a brilliant gamer. I'm the one who should be worried."

"Jedd," June says in a whisper everyone can hear, "your odds are fifty-fifty for each roll."

But he isn't listening. "Let's do this!"

All eyes are on the hologram as Jedd touches the tablet. The dice spin and the central die stops at six. The six of us let out an audible sigh of relief.

But then Kurt rolls a three, voiding Jedd's lucky number.

Quickly, as if speed can bolster his luck, Jedd rolls again. It's a five.

Three numbers on the seven-sided die can beat a five. I hold my breath as Kurt takes the tablet and rolls. The die stops on three. Again.

I have to slap my hand over my mouth to keep from screaming. The tally on the screen flips to negative $18,400 for Jedd. *$18,400?* The amount hardly seems real. Not long ago I didn't have that much to my name. Total. Yet Jedd looks undaunted. He has the calm, bordering-on-zombie expression he always has when he's deep in a video game.

Before anyone can forcibly halt the game, Kurt speaks up. "Looks like I had a few lucky rolls. Here's what I propose: no more bets for money. And let's cancel half your debt right now."

Jedd shoots us a glance that says *what did I tell you?*

Kurt not treating this as a real debt should make me feel better. It doesn't. I'm sure it's just a ploy. And all the more so as he keeps talking.

"We want to keep it fair. If you're feeling good about your chances, this should take care of everything."

"I am." Jedd sounds confident.

"Good." Kurt hands him the tablet. "The new stakes are your job."

"His *job?*" Beers glowers at Kurt.

He answers without acknowledging Beers. "Lose on your next

roll and you give up your job at HSys. Win and you get the rest of your money back. One final make-it-or-break-it game. Deal?"

"Deal."

I don't like any of this, yet another timeout is pointless. There's no way to stop Jedd when he's bent on playing.

June has no such hesitance. She leans in to snatch the tablet out of Jedd's hands.

He puts up his arm to keep her away. "Let me do this," he says gruffly.

A second thrust toward his tablet threatens to turn into an arm-wrestling match. She's forced to back off.

"I don't get it," I say, drawing her aside. She's still fuming. "How can he bet on his job?"

"That's just it, he can't."

Beers joins us. "I guess he wants to teach Kurt a lesson. Like Jedd said, it's just a game."

Again, that's supposed to be reassuring but it's not. If anything, Kurt is teaching us a lesson. I glance at Keith, hoping for some sort of hint. But he's focused on the game.

"This is too crazy!" Zack grabs Nick and they retreat toward the window so they can watch from a distance. June, Beers, and I position ourselves behind Jedd.

In the meantime, Kurt has adjusted the hologram back to a six-sided die and removed the monetary tallies on the display. He tells Jedd to begin.

Jedd rolls a three.

Kurt rolls a six.

Their lucky numbers didn't even come into play. Jedd has lost again.

"Wow," says Kurt, "didn't expect that!" He looks genuinely upset. Almost ashamed. "Sorry, my friend."

For the first time, Jedd looks flustered. Evidently whatever he thought he could do to one-up Kurt isn't working. "This sucks," he says. "But I'm not ready to quit."

"No need to quit," Kurt says. "What stakes do you have in mind?"

Jedd looks to us for suggestions, but we offer none. June's face says *this was your idea, don't expect my help now.*

Kurt fills in the silence. "How about *their* jobs? Win big, and all of you walk out of here with jobs intact." He doesn't mention the outcome of losing.

Jedd might be willing to lose his own money or job, but I know he'd never drag us down with him. Even in a game. He'd consider that dishonorable. Which means we have to step up. Much as I want this to be over, I find myself saying, "It's okay, Jedd. If you feel you can win, use us."

If everyone agrees, he says, he will go for it.

No one objects.

Kurt passes him the tablet. "Four jobs get yours back. Whose will you play for?"

"June, Beers, Nick, Zack."

Again, no one objects.

Then, as Jedd's finger hovers over the tablet, Beers steps forward. "How do we know this isn't rigged?"

"You have my word." Kurt speaks as if that should be self-evident.

"I'm not taking your word. Unless you can prove it's not rigged, this game is over." Beers leans across the table, putting himself physically between Jedd and Kurt in a way that says *over my dead body, you're not doing this.*

Kurt backs down. "Okay, we'll do it the traditional way." He retreats to the kitchenette, where he rummages around in some drawers. He returns holding a white plastic die, with indented black numbering and beveled corners. I wonder why on earth he'd keep such a thing here. It's on par with a stapler.

"How do we know that's not loaded?" Beers says.

"Check for yourself." Kurt passes the die around so we can verify it's not rigged.

I barely look at it. It isn't a hologram. I'm not sure what else to check.

"Looks good to me," Jedd says when it reaches him. "Besides, we'll both be using it."

There's no turning back. Jedd blows on the die, rolls it between his palms for a few seconds and throws it down. It clatters across the table and lands with the one on top.

Kurt goes next.

I close my eyes and pray for another one. That's our only hope.

The Kaurava prince dragged Draupadi by her hair into the court.
He began to pull on her sari. It came off easily. As the horrified
audience looked on, meters of silk piled up at her feet.
Then a miracle happened. He kept pulling, yet her sari only grew longer.

STRIPPED: Darah

I stare at the die on the table. It's an unambiguous four. Just plain bad luck. It would be hard to claim Kurt rigged this. I mean, we all saw what went down: Jedd waged everything and then lost it all.

Yet I tell myself again this can't be for real. Just as the debt wasn't real, the lost jobs can't be for real. It's a game. A frigging game. Obviously Kurt has no authority to take our jobs. HSys operates according to corporate policies and procedures. This isn't a dictatorship where you cower in terror as others wield power in willful, unpredictable, unchecked ways.

Still it feels real. As real as when people in the States lost their jobs with no warning. You lived in fear, never knowing if you'd be next. That fear chokes me now, like a constrictor knot that gets tighter and tighter the more you struggle to be free of it.

Jedd doesn't take his eyes off the plastic cube, as though he expects it to roll over one more time if he stares hard enough. As our leader, we look to him to set the tone. Now that he's silent, we are too. Even June.

Kurt picks up the die, tosses it in the air, and catches it with one hand, his fist clamping shut before anyone can see the number. As if that number matters. It galls me how certain he is that he's outdone us, that he's in full control.

Both Jedd and Kurt acted like this game was all for fun, yet now they're facing off like two kids on a street corner. Or worse. Kurt needs to stop toying with Jedd, stop prolonging this train wreck. Except he's taking too much pleasure in it. I know he won't listen to any of us, but he might listen to Keith. That is, if I can somehow get Keith to take our side. It's a desperate thought. But he might do that for me.

"So . . . what now?" I throw out.

Keith catches my eye. A split second of recognition passes between us. "Jedd didn't gamble your job, Darah. You still have worth."

I want his help, but I don't like what he's suggesting. I'm not a gamer. Definitely not a gambler.

But that's what he has in mind. "Come on," he says. "Play a final round." When I don't respond, he adds, "It's not hard. Just roll the die."

He turns to Kurt, who shrugs. "If she wants to play, I have no problem with it."

Now they're all looking at me.

I can't believe I'm considering this. If I'd managed to talk to Keith earlier, this disaster could have been avoided. But I didn't. Now I'm the only one with a chance of reversing Jedd's losses. I have to try. First, though, I check in with the others one by one. The twins' eyes express their support. As do June's. The warmth of Beers's hand on my shoulder says he's with me whatever I decide. Last I turn to Jedd.

He gives a short nod and rises from his seat.

It's disturbing to see him so passive. Yet I get why. As an avid gamer, he plays by the rules. Even if a game is fixed or unfair, he won't stoop to the lows of his opponent. That is his integrity, and we respect him for it. Now he's adhering to the rule that says, having bet and lost, he can no longer participate in any way. He has nothing left to wager. He can't fight back. He literally doesn't have a seat at the table.

So I will fight in his place.

Keith suggests we go back to digital dice. For a second I think he'll take Kurt's place and flip the odds in my favor.

But Kurt keeps his seat and motions for me to join him. "Let's give this a whirl."

Beers doesn't insist on plastic dice. I'm not sure why, except that he has confidence in me.

The auto-morphing chair softens as I sit down. "What stakes?"

Kurt sizes me up. "You're not a gamer like Jedd, so let's switch things up. Stack it in your favor so you can save your pals."

Jedd might take offense at an advantage, but I don't mind. I just want to get this over with. Next time Kurt suggests a happy hour, we aren't going. Period.

He swipes through some screens, and the hologram with three dice reappears. A larger hologram forms to its left. It's not dice. It's a greater-than-life-size image of me.

"Darah?" Beers looks shocked.

"Where did you get *that*?" I say.

Kurt snickers but doesn't reply. As he makes adjustments on his tablet, we stare at the hologram. I'm wearing a long-sleeved, gray wool dress and thigh-high boots, a red cable-knit scarf around my neck. My hair hangs to my shoulders, the tips purple, as they were my freshman year at Rutgers. I vaguely recall a photo snapped by a friend outside the library.

"Nice touch with the purple," Keith says.

Normally I'd have a sassy comeback, but I'm too focused on what Kurt is planning. "Okay," I say. "You got me. How's this supposed to work?"

"You win, you get one job back. You lose and I remove an item of your clothing. Five jobs are at stake, so you get five rolls. No lucky numbers or fancy stuff. Fair?"

So essentially strip poker. Virtual strip poker. The follow-up to Kurt's butt grab. He must have had the hologram made well in advance—by the Floridians perhaps—knowing Jedd would lose and I'd be the one to step in. Or Keith would put me up to it. Either way, it's a setup. A disgusting setup.

I don't have to do this. If I'm going to back out, now's the time. Just tell Kurt to shove it. But then what? I'll have let Jedd down. It will be Kurt's big gotcha moment. I can hear him: *I knew Darah wouldn't have what it takes!* All the work to create this hologram will have been worth it to him just to see me flake.

I can't give him that satisfaction.

The only clear way out of a constrictor knot is to cut the rope. That means cutting my fear. Not allowing it to paralyze me. Not letting anyone see it. All they need to see is that I'm determined to play and win. I avert my eyes from the hologram. "Let's do this."

If Kurt is surprised, he doesn't let on, just hands me the tablet. "Tell us whose job you're playing for."

I'm about to pick Jedd but he looks crushed already. Everyone is staring at me, waiting for my pick. Except June. She has turned away and is working furiously on her tablet. What's up with that? Surely no work is so urgent she can't take care of it later.

Nick steps forward. "Start with Zack and me."

"This isn't a two-for-one," Kurt growls.

"Okay," I say. "I'll play for Nick."

"Don't worry about it," Nick says.

"We understand," Zack adds.

"What are you waiting for?" Kurt is getting irked. "It's just a game for Chrissake."

I quickly reaffirm to myself that I can do this. Even if it's not just a game, even if there is nothing fair about it, I can do this. I suck in my breath and touch the tablet. The dice spin longer than before. The die that comes to the foreground stops on a four. I exhale through my teeth. Only two numbers can beat that.

Kurt takes the tablet and rolls. Five.

I stifle a groan and apologize to Nick.

"What a pity, Darah. So close," Kurt says. "Now I get to remove one item." He approaches the hologram and pulls on my scarf. It doesn't budge. He pulls harder. "Hey, what's wrong?" he cries, frustrated after a few tries.

"Grab an edge and yank." Karin demos the motion. She seems to know what she's doing. Like she's played this game before.

Kurt yanks the edge of the scarf. It only stretches longer. "That's making it worse!"

Karin looks befuddled. She suggests trying another item.

"I'll go for the boots," he says.

"One boot," Beers clarifies.

Kurt glares at him. "The boots come off together."

Again Karin intercedes: one boot is good enough.

He reaches down, puts a hand on the bottom of my left boot, and pulls. It comes right off.

I assumed removing an item would cause that area of the hologram to go dark. That's not what happens. When Kurt removes the boot, my naked foot becomes visible. I'm not even wearing socks. How this is possible, I have no idea.

Kurt returns to the table. "Whose job now?"

"Zack's."

I roll a three. Kurt a six.

He removes the other boot.

I stare at my two naked feet. Everyone else is staring at them too. I can't take my eyes off the chipped purple nail polish on my right big toe. It doesn't matter that I often wear sandals, that people see my feet every day. I feel exposed. Violated. The thought of more flesh stripped bare makes me want to run out of the room. Except I refuse to quit. I just need to win the next roll.

"Whose job?" Kurt is so confident that he doesn't bother to sit down.

"June's."

Still intent on her tablet, June doesn't look up when I say her name. I'm taking one for the team, being humiliated, and she isn't even paying attention. You can be sure she'll hear from me about that later. Agreeing to play was a huge mistake. Kurt was never going to let me win. Keith was never going to help me out. At this point, *I need a miracle.* I'm not one to pray, but a prayer can't hurt. So I send a silent, desperate call out to any invisible power that might be lurking in some far corner of the universe, then roll again. It's a six. I look triumphantly at the others. Maybe my luck is turning.

But it's short lived. Kurt produces a matching six.

I quickly roll again, trying to keep the momentum going. It's a two.

Kurt answers with another six.

June is so preoccupied with her tablet she doesn't notice I lost her job.

"Give the scarf another try," Karin coaches.

Kurt attempts to yank off the scarf, but it only stretches more. Now it's covering much of my dress and piling up around my feet. My naked toes are no longer visible. "What's wrong?" he roars. "I should be able to grab this scarf. But it's growing!"

Karin stifles a snort. "Guess you'll have to take the dress."

If he takes the dress, the scarf will probably go with it. So much for prayers. I look at the others, wishing one of them would find a way to stop this. Keith won't meet my eye. The rest only reflect anxiety back to me. I've let NicknZack down. And June. They were counting on me. Beers and Jedd are still counting on me. Much as I want to walk away, I can't.

Kurt yanks on the hem and removes the whole dress in one stroke. Remarkably it doesn't take the scarf with it. Like long red hair cascading down both sides, it hangs there, covering most of my torso. If it weren't for the scarf, I'd be standing in my underwear.

"You don't have to keep doing this," Beers says, his jaw set, as if he wants to punch Kurt and is only holding back because he doesn't want to make things worse for the rest of us.

"Two more rolls," says Karin.

"Your pals are waiting," Kurt taunts.

I want to spit in his face. But I refuse to let him break me. I have to stay strong and roll for the two jobs. "This is for Beers," I say, swallowing hard against the nausea rising from the pit of my stomach. I roll again and get a two to Kurt's five.

Kurt stands before the hologram and leers at it. At me. This is his idea of entertainment. He circles around to the back and grabs a strap that's not covered. We see a bright flash as my bra vanishes into thin air. But the scarf isn't going anywhere. With the bra gone, its two sides cover my breasts.

I clutch my stomach to keep from vomiting. One more job remains. Everyone knows whose it is, so I don't bother to say Jedd's name before I roll.

It's a one.

No point waiting for Kurt. Even if he rolls a one, he'll win the next round. I don't want to see what happens when he removes my panties. I toss the tablet onto the table and dash out of the room.

Beers is right behind. He catches up with me at the elevator, but I brush him away.

"Wait," he says, jamming his hand against the door to keep it open until the others can get here. "We're in this together, you know."

Two seconds later, we're all in the cab.

Jedd shouts out for it to take us to the fifth floor, north wing, and the door slides shut.

"Are you okay?" Beers asks.

"What do you think?" I retort. "Of course I'm not okay. You didn't back me up."

"I'm so sorry," Jedd says. "Our hands were tied."

"That was so humiliating," Nick says.

"It killed us not to be able to stop it," Zack adds.

"At least no one saw you stark naked," June says.

"Really? That's supposed to make me feel better?" I spit out the anger that has been burning in me. "Like you give a shit!"

"Actually, yes," says June. "I did a damn good job of blocking the scarf. That should count for something."

My jaw drops. "*You* did that?"

"Surely you didn't expect me to block the entire game that fast."

So that's why June was so fixated on her tablet. "No," I say. "I mean, how did you do it? And so fast?"

"I hacked the program and mucked up the function that allowed Kurt to remove items. Don't ask me why the scarf ended up growing longer."

"Wow," I say, shaking my head. "And I thought I was praying in vain for a miracle."

"You're welcome," says June.

Jedd acknowledges how difficult it is to hack on the spur of the moment like June did. He didn't try because he was too wrapped up in his own loss. For which he apologizes again.

"This isn't over," Beers says as the doors open on the fifth floor. "Let's talk at home, figure out the best way to get back at them."

"Why are we stopping here?" June asks.

"I left my jacket," Jedd says. "Go on ahead if you want. We've got two cars."

No one moves. We don't want to break up the group. It feels safer together.

A few seconds later, Jedd comes running back. "My code doesn't work."

"That's weird. Let me try." Beers walks up to our office door and activates the code on his tablet. It remains locked.

June and the twins all try. None of their codes work.

"What now?" Beers says.

"We go home," June says.

"Wait," Jedd says. "Darah hasn't tried."

I pull out my tablet and activate the code. The door opens.

We walk into the room and stand there dumbfounded.

"You know what this means," Jedd says.

"It means that wasn't a game. They've given us the boot. For real," June says. "We've been played big-time. Every one of us."

"Except Darah," Beers says.

I'm in shock. "But how is this possible? Who has the power to fire you? And so fast?"

Jedd shakes his head in amazement. "They must have planned all this. Like suckers, we fell for it. I fell for it." He gathers up his jacket and some latest-model VR goggles, a few smart glasses and an old gamepad he still uses. "Better take your things. I don't think we'll be back anytime soon."

Beers points out that if our codes don't work, we won't be able to take company equipment through the exit scanner.

Jedd reluctantly dumps his stuff. He toys with one vintage headset, noting it predates the puke-problem solution, before setting it on the table. The only item he salvages is the old gamepad, which belongs to him. He isn't just leaving a job, he's leaving years of personal history.

I watch the others collect some wine bottles, cram various shoes and other personal items into their backpacks. "Job or no job, if you're not coming back, neither am I." I pick up the peace lily, and we all head out.

The Pandavas prepared for thirteen years of exile.
They took off their robes and dressed in garments made
of tree bark and deerskin, as was the custom.

INTO EXILE: June

The four of us in the chariot don't say a word on the way home. We tail the twins across town and onto the freeway, then fall behind as we begin climbing the foothills. I've never wished more for the chariot to go faster. It's tempting to hack the speed controls and take care of that once and for all.

My mind, on the other hand, is racing. I want to lash out at Jedd, let him and everyone else know exactly what I think of this fiasco. If there's ever a time to speak up, this is it. Yet I'm too furious to utter a word.

At the farm, we get out of the car in silence, join the twins, who're waiting on the porch, and file into the house. Dharma runs up to greet us. We walk right past him.

The kid is sitting cross-legged on the hearth rug, playing his flute as he often does in the evening. He stops midnote as I throw myself onto the overstuffed armchair. My backpack hits the floor with a thud, and the smart shoes I crammed in spill out.

Darah sets the peace lily on the hearth before settling on the sectional, along with Beers, while Jedd isolates himself on the small sofa. The twins flop onto the zero-gravity beanbags.

The kid can see something's wrong. "So?" he says. "What happened?"

Everyone turns—predictably—to Jedd for a response. He stares at his feet.

And I stare at him. Since when does the dude have a gambling habit? And why didn't we know about it? Because he couldn't control avaricious impulses none of us knew he had, the unthinkable has happened: we've been fired. I've lost my job. A job I love. I pick up one of my shoes and hurl it across the room. It crashes into the fireplace grate, narrowly missing the peace lily. Its pecan-brown hue, carefully chosen to complement my outfit, blinks pink zebra stripes. Dharma goes over and flips it with his nose. It blinks a few times and dies.

"You really want to know?" I say. "I'll tell you. We . . . we lost *everything*!"

"Our jobs," Beers says. "We lost our fucking jobs."

The kid looks incredulous. "You were fired?"

"Damn straight." I pause. "All of us except Darah."

Darah bristles at the inference. She's not going back to HSys without us, she says, so she might as well have lost her job.

The kid looks from one of us to the other. "I don't get it."

"You wouldn't," I snap.

Beers jumps to his defense. "Don't blame the kid. He didn't do this."

Of course he's right: it isn't Darah's fault and it sure as hell isn't the kid's fault. No, this is all on Jedd. I turn my eyes back on him. "How could you be so *stupid*?"

He's still staring at his feet. "I'm sorry."

"Look at me!"

He raises his head. Slowly. When our eyes meet, I see tears swimming in his. He's contrite. But tears won't restore our jobs. I need him to fight back. I need him to validate my anger with his own. "*Say* something!" I'm practically screaming.

At this point, the others step in. "You're angry, June," Darah says. "It's okay."

"We're all angry!" The bulging vein in Beers's neck tells me he's as mad as I am. He's the one with the explosive temper. I'm not sure why he's holding back now.

The twins are nodding agreement. I wouldn't expect them to display anger, except I guess by being quieter than usual.

Jedd says nothing.

I look from one to the other, then back at Jedd. They're ganging up on me, six on one, like I'm the problem. Even the kid's with them. "What the hell's wrong with you all?" I cry, jumping up from the armchair.

In the kitchen, I pour a glass of cold water, gulp half, then dash the rest down the drain. As if water could wash away my anger. The truth is I'm rarely angry. Yeah, Jedd and I bicker over stuff. That might bug the others—it's not what you'd call mature—but it's not hostile. It's how we keep each other in check, how we deal with the kind of griping and grousing that happens between friends and in families. What we're facing now is exponentially greater than all that stuff combined. We've been attacked, violated, punked by people we considered our peers. People sitting in the Dictator's pocket.

The result? My job is gone. What I get up every day and do, and enjoy doing—all gone.

I run through the projects on my plate. There's my fave, Mars Warriors. And the new Freaks game. I'm midway through fixing the delay in its BCI. No one will be able to easily pick up the coding where I left off. That's not arrogance speaking; it's fact. Infuriating fact.

I wasn't screaming at Jedd just to express fury. I wanted to provoke a reaction. To get him to bicker back as he usually does, so we'd be on familiar ground. So we could deal. Except bickering won't get our jobs back. If anything, it'll make things worse.

We're in over our heads here. I don't mean we lack tech savvy; I mean we've been outmaneuvered politically, in the broadest sense of the word—how we negotiate the complex dynamics by which some people wield power over others. Suddenly I wish I'd stayed in politics. Maybe I'd know how to get us out of this mess, how to get Kurt off our backs. But I didn't, and here we are. Our only hope is to come together as a family and sort this out. Tonight.

I pour myself another glass of water and move to the kitchen door, where I drink it slowly as I listen in.

Jedd is speaking, taking responsibility for what happened. He sounds sincere, regretful. "I'm ashamed to admit it," he says, "but my gambling cost us our jobs."

The kid says he didn't know Jedd liked to gamble.

"*None* of us knew," I throw in.

No one looks in my direction.

"Like I said, it's not something I do regularly or am proud of," Jedd continues. "It's my one addiction, a personal flaw I should never have let become our collective undoing. For what it's worth, I'm incredibly sorry."

I walk slowly back into the room and stand in front of him. "I'm sorry too," I say. And I mean it. "I may be pissed, but I know blamestorming won't solve anything." To show I've got a handle on my temper, I retrieve the pink zebra-stripe shoe and place it alongside its pecan-brown mate. I can reset the colors later.

Darah goes over and hugs Jedd. She assures him he couldn't have known this would happen.

"I should have though," he says, hugging her back.

"Dude, you were too trusting," she says. "As someone who wants to be more trusting, I can't fault you for that."

Jedd isn't so self-forgiving. "With all the crap we've learned about those bastards, I was an idiot to trust one word out of their mouths."

"So why did you?" I ask, but without an accusatory edge. At

the end of the day, we're on the same team. Agreeing that he was an idiot won't help. "You're the smartest person I know. Why did you fall for their ploy?"

"Obviously he didn't think it was for real," Beers says.

Jedd confirms that was his mindset. Kurt presented it as just a game, and Jedd bought in. He believed he could turn it to our advantage—not only by winning but by gathering valuable intel. Then he pauses. "That's where things get blurry. When I play a game, part of why I get so wrapped up is that it feels real to me. I felt that tonight too."

"That's what pissed me off," I say, still calm. "You went ahead even though you could lose big. And fail to get intel."

"Maybe it was the rum, bro," Beers says.

I can't tell if he's serious. It's not like Jedd was sloshed. More like mildly buzzed.

"You mean something *in* the rum?" Nick says.

Jedd points out that others drank it with no ill effects. We can't blame the booze. "Besides," he adds with a wry smile, "it tasted darn good."

Beers smacks his lips in agreement. "Handsome bottle too."

"Probably worth thousands," Nick says.

"Tens of thousands," Zack says.

Darah points out that would've more than covered Jedd's gambling debt.

"I'm kicking myself," Beers says. "Why didn't I just walk out of there with that bottle?"

At least we're coming together, talking as friends again. Joking even. Instead of letting our anger eat us alive, we can own that anger and direct it where it belongs: toward our real enemies. The three Ks. And the Dictator. Lose sight of that and we're screwed. More screwed than we already are. "Let's move on," I say. "We need to be united on this."

Everyone is on board. Even the kid looks engaged. We decide

to recap what happened, nail down any details that might have escaped notice. I start by asking Jedd if the dice game came up in any darknet messages or if he saw any clues that our jobs might be on the line.

He shakes his head. "If I'd seen anything like that, I'd have told you." He reminds us he's only reviewed a small portion of the site. There is still so much we don't know.

"I bet Donna was in on this," Beers says. "Probably holed up somewhere, keeping tabs on the score, waiting to drop the hammer."

"She does have the power to fire us," I say. HSys employees aren't under contract and can be let go without warning or reason.

"She sure moved fast," Nick says.

"No kidding," Zack says. "By the time we got to the fifth floor, we'd already been booted from the system."

We're processing everything now with a large dose of hindsight. It's obvious we were duped. I lead us through what happened, step by step. First they lured us up to their workspace on the pretext of a casual party, a happy hour. We couldn't say no without arousing suspicions. So we agreed, even though none of us wanted to go. As soon as we got there, they plied us with alcohol. When we were loosened up, they initiated a little gambling.

"Kurt letting me win early got me comfy," Jedd says. "By the time he fixed things in his favor, I was hooked. His offer to cancel my debt reeled me in another notch."

"Every move was strategically aimed to take advantage of your vulnerability," I say. "I wonder how they figured that out? Our office must have been bugged after all."

Darah turns to Jedd. "Or they saw you gambling online—"

"What?" I don't try to hide my surprise. "You gambled online? Recently?"

"After we lost the penthouse," Jedd says quickly, as he and Darah exchange glances. Apparently he didn't expect her to mention that.

I push aside my annoyance at this you-did-what moment and focus on the implications. "Your online activity could have given them ideas."

Beers looks dubious. "Tracking Jedd online would take serious resources."

"Then maybe it was just good guesswork. Everyone knows Jedd's an avid gamer," I say. "Either way, they were counting on their ability to manipulate his underactive brain reward system. If he has reduced ventral striatal activation during monetary reward anticipation, he'll be drawn to gambling to stimulate those pathways."

Jedd frowns. "No need to get so technical."

Darah takes me literally. "Are you saying the dice game used AI?"

That stops me for a second. I mean, AI is used in practically everything these days. But I was just dredging up neuroscience facts to be a smart aleck. "The hologram was sophisticated," I say. "But no, it didn't have a digital brain."

Jedd agrees. "Kurt's pod must have had outside experts create that thing."

"The Floridians," Beers says.

"Most likely," I say. "Not to mention they needed holograms for the rest of us in case Jedd lost Darah's job. Someone spent a pretty penny getting all that together." At some point I want to get his thoughts on why my impromptu hack disrupted the scarf in such a bizarre manner. But this isn't the time.

"They had pics of me from college," Darah says with a shudder.

I've been so focused on sussing out their strategy so we can respond that I didn't consider what she must be feeling. Once again she took the brunt of Kurt's assault. Though she doesn't appear freaked out. She might want us to believe she's tougher than she really is. "Darah," I say, "are you okay? I mean, really?"

Beers reaches over and puts a hand on her knee.

She waves off the attention. "Don't worry about me. I'm fine," she says, adding that it helps that we're together, debriefing in the security of our home.

Which brings us back to our immediate predicament. "Okay," I say, "we're starting to spin our wheels. We're still acting like we can waltz in tomorrow and get our jobs back."

"Can you?" the kid asks.

Beers pulls out his tablet and does a reality check. "I'm still locked out."

I also check. "Me too."

Jedd says he doubts we'll get our jobs back. To think otherwise would be to fall for Kurt's double-talk. Then he turns to his tablet and starts poking around. It occurs to me he's cyberslacking, playing a video game since he doesn't have a strategy to get us out of this. He's also doing that annoying habit of his, sucking his teeth clean with his tongue. At the rate he's going, he'll put our dentist out of business.

We may be no more than a little band of techies—including one teenager—but we can't just do nothing after we've been personally attacked. If Jedd won't take charge, someone has to. "Our jobs are gone," I say. "We need to figure out how to fix this mess."

"No shit," says Beers. "This is war!"

Without looking up, Jedd reminds us he warned it would be outright war if we stood up to the Ks. Now things have gone beyond that. It's war for real.

"I say we storm the penthouse. Bash in their heads!" Beers illustrates by slamming one fist into the palm of the other hand. "Never claimed I was a pacifist."

"Some pacifists are the angriest people," the kid observes.

"Don't worry," I say, "we won't beat up on anyone."

"That's not who we are," Jedd says.

But philosophical chitchat won't get us anywhere. We need a

smart strategy that levels the playing field and allows us to out-maneuver the Ks and their partners. I try again to refocus. "Okay, how do we handle this?"

Jedd is still engrossed in his tablet. The others look shell-shocked.

"What are we waiting for?" Beers says finally. "Let's go to the authorities."

"The police!" the twins say together.

"Some form of law enforcement," Darah says.

I couldn't agree more. "What they did was illegal. This is California. Companies can't fire you based on a dice game. At a minimum we should file for wrongful termination."

But the kid is shaking his head. "I wouldn't do that."

"Don't turn them in?" Beers pivots toward him. "You must be kidding. No way we let them win and take our jobs."

"I'm not saying let them win. But if you act impulsively or out of revenge, you only hurt yourselves. Then they win for sure." This is the first time I've seen the kid take such a passionate stand.

"What are you suggesting?" I ask.

"Keep doing what you're doing. When it's time for open war, you'll know it."

Jedd looks up from his tablet. "I agree with the kid. It's too risky to go public with this now. Think about who we're up against. This isn't just Kurt or Donna or some jerks at HSys. We're up against the Dictator, for god's sake. And we don't yet know who else. Could be the Russian mafia. Or international crime syndicates. If any of those characters see us trying to fight back, losing our jobs will seem like small stuff." He stops and looks around to see if we get his point, then adds, "We aren't setting foot in that building until we've won this battle."

It's hard to argue when he puts it like that. I mean, a wrongful termination suit presupposes a normal, sane reality. Talking to the authorities—even in California—assumes they can protect us against the Dictator. None of us are that naïve. I ask what Jedd has in mind.

"I was thinking about this on the way home, coming up with a plan." He nods toward his tablet. "I've just been checking a few details." So that's what he was doing when I presumed he was cyberslacking.

"Better be good, bro," Beers says.

"What is it?" Darah asks.

"We're going into exile."

You can count on Jedd to come up with good ideas. I don't know what he means by exile, but I'm open to it. Heck, he just convinced me to do a one-eighty on running to the authorities. From the looks of it, Beers is open to it as well.

"Tell us what you mean," Darah prompts.

"I mean we'll disappear," he says. "Totally disappear. They won't be able to find us, because we'll make that close to impossible."

"So hide out somewhere that's hundo percent safe and secure?" Beers sounds skeptical. From a security perspective, not many places are reliably safe these days.

"I like it," Darah says. "Let's go somewhere nice. Maybe Mexico?"

Nick suggests Hawaii.

Zack prefers somewhere farther, like New Zealand. If we can get last-minute tickets.

Darah points out that paying for our living expenses will be hard without any income. We need to go somewhere affordable.

"Don't worry about cost," Beers says quickly. "I've got that covered."

"Hold on," the kid says. "I didn't hear Jedd say anything about going into exile physically."

Darah looks puzzled. "Then how do we disappear?"

"The kid's correct," Jedd says. "No need to go anywhere. We

have the means to disappear while we stay right here, safe and protected right within our own home."

I'm starting to get his drift. This could be an entirely virtual exile. Brilliant! "Meaning we'll be here, but anyone looking for us will think we left," I say. "We're not running scared. We're outwitting our enemies and protecting ourselves so we can take action from here."

"Ha!" Beers is also catching on. "Love it."

The kid is grinning ear to ear.

Jedd confirms that's his plan. "For this to work, I need to get on it right now. It'll take all night to implement, so don't feel you have to stay up."

It's hard to believe it's past midnight. We've been talking for three hours.

"I'm not tired," Darah says. "Will you update us as you work?"

"We might have input," I say. "These are our lives too." I understand Jedd prefers to work alone in silence. Still, he owes us this much after everything that happened tonight.

The Pandavas traveled fast. The only thought in Yudhisthira's mind was to get away from Hastinapura as fast as they could. Upon reaching the shores of the Ganga, tired and famished, they took refuge beneath a spreading banyan tree.

THE JOURNEY: Jedd

I invite the others to look over my shoulder as I log into all our accounts. Programming on my largest tablet and projecting it onto the coffee table allows for a big image everyone can cluster around. Even the kid squeezes in. It's good to see him feeling part of the family, contributing to our plans, especially now that we'll all be spending so much time together. Dharma can't find space to lay his head on my knee, so he moves to the hearth, where he can get some sleep.

"All right," I say after a few minutes. "I've got all of us up on the screen. I'm ready to start moving our digital locations."

"How do you do that?" Darah asks.

I explain that each of us has a unique identity. Our physical location is tied to that identity. I'm reprogramming our IDs so all of us will move in unison from the farm to a yet-to-be-determined destination in Canada.

The twins are excited. "Canada? That's dope!"

Now that we're working together on a plan to save ourselves, I feel less guilty about the horrific mess I walked us into. Tempers have cooled. Even June is pretty chill.

"I see what you mean about taking all night," she says. "For this to be convincing, each ID has to move along the route in real time. Let's say we go to Vancouver, how far is that?" She pulls out her tablet and runs her GPS.

I've already clocked it. "Fifteen hours."

"Geez, that's more than all night," Nick says.

"And more than fifteen hours if we're taking the chariot," Zack adds.

I clarify that we are taking the chariot. Then I continue typing code while the others stare at the table, waiting to see their IDs move.

"You should just run this as a program," Beers says. "Then we could all get some sleep."

June nixes his idea. Rightfully so. In theory I could, but under the circumstances it's too risky. As my fingers fly across the tablet, I explain that we'll need to keep monitoring the environment, so if anything unforeseen occurs, I can jump in and correct course. It's too important. We can't take chances.

"We've already taken way too many chances tonight," she says.

I let her dig stand. Really, I deserve it.

"Won't they think all of us in one vehicle is a lot?" Darah asks. "I mean, if anyone tries to track us."

I have a ready explanation. "The chariot is big enough. It's crowded for six, but if we swivel the seats, it's doable. Especially in an escape scenario. We're fleeing without luggage, just our compression sleeping bags. And toothbrushes."

She frowns. "One of us isn't going?"

I remind her somebody has to take care of the farm. All the more so since we'll actually be here. Someone will have to go out for supplies.

Darah falters, as if I'm asking for volunteers, as if someone is really being left behind. I understand it can be a challenge to juggle the parallel worlds of physical and virtual reality.

"I'll stay," the kid says. "No one will guess what's up."

"That was my plan," I say.

Darah is nodding, making the necessary mental adjustments.

I tell the kid I'll have to set up his ID.

Clearly pleased to have a consequential role, he pulls out a plastic California ID and hands it to me.

June laughs. She hasn't seen one of those in a while. None of us has. The use of digital identification and biometric authentication allowed us to discard our plastics years ago.

I examine the card, which fortunately is up to date. I'm almost surprised to see the kid has a legal name and a birthdate. And that he's old enough to drive a car, as well as purchase alcohol. If California hadn't voted to follow Canada's and Europe's legal drinking age, we'd be looking at a very dry exile. After I set up his digital ID and establish his location on the farm, I'll wipe an old tablet and reprogram it so he can start making purchases.

I enumerate all the things the kid will be responsible for as our caretaker. We can pay the big bills, such as insurance and taxes, from wherever we are, but he'll have to buy our food and any small stuff we need.

"We have enough food for a week, two max," Beers says. "If we scrimp."

"No restaurants," Nick adds. The twins like to get takeout when Beers doesn't cook.

The ramifications of going into exile are beginning to sink in. For the plan to work, we need to stay hidden. We'll be stuck on the farm. Literally. It may be an attractive prison, but it will be a prison. Each of us will have to deal with the effects on our mental and emotional state. The prospect is daunting.

"We could plant a garden. Maybe get a cow," the kid says. "That way we won't need to buy as much food."

Beers says he's always wanted a garden, just never got around to putting one in. His grandparents had cows in the barn. Though we probably don't want the burden of feeding one.

June points out that whatever we grow won't be ready for a while.

She's right. But I tell her that's not a problem. The kid can start making purchases as soon as his ID is linked to my bank account. Anyone who comes looking will see we went to Canada but also left someone in charge here. His minimal digital profile will work in our favor.

"Won't it look suspicious that he's buying enough to feed seven?" Darah asks.

"Maybe use cash so it isn't traceable?" Nick says.

"Cash?" Beers laughs. "Where can you pay with cash?"

He's got a point. The kid has been using cash for his own small purchases, and I usually keep some on hand for stuff like tipping musicians. But expecting to pay for all our household needs at a market that takes cash will be limiting. Still, I'm glad everyone is chipping in with ideas to cover what I haven't thought of.

"What about transportation?" June asks.

"He can't ride a horse," Nick says.

"Or that cow," Zack adds.

We all laugh. It feels good to relax a bit.

"How about your car, Darah?" I ask after the laughter has died down.

She's fine with that, as long as he doesn't mind an old model that takes ten minutes to charge. Which of course he doesn't.

That reminds me we should stop now to charge the chariot so that's on record. I ask them to help me find a station.

June is shaking her head. "If only I had the model with a self-charging solar roof instead of a simple sunroof. We could sail through."

"More like good thing you *don't*," Beers says.

June gives him a quizzical look but quickly catches on. "Right. Charging the chariot will help create the real-time record Jedd is talking about."

"You got it!" I say.

They all lean in to the coffee table. June immediately spots the pulsating blue dot. The chariot is driving through San Francisco. Specifically, it's at a light on Nineteenth Avenue, on the edge of the park. Beers finds a station a few miles north of the Golden Gate. There's enough time to hack it before we arrive.

"Okay," I say, "a partial charge is plenty. Let's pay and be on our way."

"Lucky dudes," says Beers.

"Yeah," June says, "scored a nice wad."

"Don't you think that looks suspicious?" Darah asks.

"Nope." I quickly make a few additional moves on my tablet. "Not only did we charge the chariot, but we paid for snacks at the convenience store. Should alleviate any suspicions."

"I like protein chips on a road trip," Beers says. "Not those 3D vending machine snacks. And definitely not those jellyfish chips you like, June."

"Noted, protein chips for the rest of the journey," I say, then turn back to Darah. "I guarantee no one will track whether those chips really came off the shelves or those meters recorded actual electric charges. The trail of our payments as well as the movement of our IDs from here to there should be enough to create the illusion of our trip."

The mention of chips sends Darah's mind in another direction. Beers isn't the only one who loves them. "What about Dharma?"

"I'm afraid he stays."

Even as a virtual reality, that pains me. Dharma and I are inseparable. If we were really going to Canada, I wouldn't go without him. He's my bred-in-the-bone canis fidelis. I often say I'd refuse to walk through the gates of heaven if he couldn't come too.

June wonders if Kurt's hacker colleagues are already hot on our trail.

"Well," says Beers, "it's morning in Moscow."

"I bet they think we're panicking," Nick says.

"And went straight to the police," Zack adds.

"Yup," I say. "They're probably tracking our IDs as we speak, expecting us to be caught in 4K."

"If you tried going to the police," the kid says, "you'd never make it there."

That's a chilling thought. And it reinforces why he steered us away from running to the authorities. I'm glad we took his advice. Kurt could easily have mafioso types waiting in the shadows, ready to swoop in and disappear us.

"They might think we've contacted our lawyers," June says.

"Which would be easy to do from anywhere," I say. "Fortunately we don't have to worry about any of those scenarios. When they track us—which I'm sure they're doing—they'll see we're already north of San Francisco. And if they hack to see whether we've contacted a lawyer, they'll find we've gone offline. Except for the positions of our IDs and my few purchases."

"Wait," says Darah. "What's to stop Kurt from driving over here and discovering we didn't go to Canada?"

June sucks in her breath. She didn't think of that.

But I did. "They won't. Not in this digital age. No one would drive all the way here without first checking our online locations. And they won't send a drone either."

"Are you sure?" Darah persists.

"A thousand percent," I say. Normally I'd say I'll bet my life on it. But any form of betting, even in jest, has to be absent from my vocabulary for the foreseeable future. "It won't cross their minds that we could execute a disappearance like the one I've set up. They're not that clever."

"Can you confirm they're tracking us now?" Darah asks.

I say I could but don't want to take the extra time. "You'll have to trust me when I say they're hot on our tails, confident they can keep us in their sights."

"So they think they've won the battle," June says.

"We've got them where we want them," I say. I couldn't be more pleased with how all this is unfolding. Kurt may think he won tonight, but this game is far from over. I ask if everyone's ready for the journey.

There is a chorus of agreement.

"But first," I say, "how long before you'll need a potty break?" I listen to their answers, which average out at five hours. That will put us in southern Oregon for our first pit stop.

While the others wander off for snacks, June keeps her eyes on my tablet. I'm working exceptionally fast, and she wants to make sure no careless errors mess up the illusion.

I measure three segments of five hours, scout out rest stops in the vicinity of each end point, and proceed to program our full itinerary. I postdate every movement and coordinate all the purchases so the chariot's progress triggers the next event. Accidents and traffic reports will be factored in as they occur in real time, and everything will automatically be reprogrammed accordingly. Really, Beers was right: my presence won't be necessary after it's all set up. Except I'm someone who can't just walk away. I will hover. Just in case. It never hurts to be fastidious, to go the extra mile. For us, the latter is literally true.

After a couple hours, I place my tablet on the coffee table. "That's it," I announce. "Now we sit back and watch."

The others drift back to the living room. Dharma, who's been sleeping on the hearth, rouses himself, then resettles at my feet. He's back to sleep within seconds.

"When do we reach Canada?" Beers asks.

"This afternoon. Barring any major traffic or bad weather."

"How will we cross over?" Darah asks.

"Easiest would be via a back road," June says.

I acknowledge we could do that. But the border between Washington—well, technically, the nation of California—and Canada is very porous. It wouldn't be hard to hack into an official checkpoint and have us on record as crossing over.

"You mean give Kurt irrefutable evidence we're in Canada?" June says.

I tell her that's what I'm leaning toward. I haven't programmed it yet, so we can wait to decide if it's worth the effort to create that evidence.

In the meantime, the others agree to take turns keeping me company through the night. Nick opts for the first two-hour shift, and Zack the second. In practice, that means they'll do the first two shifts together. June sets her alarm to go off for the third. Beers says he'll be up early anyway, so no need to schedule a fourth shift.

It is still dark when I hear footsteps on the stairs. June comes into the living room, rubbing her eyes. She's wearing the one-piece bioceramic fleece she always sleeps in.

"Hi there," I say, sitting up and rubbing my own eyes.

"Where's Zack?"

I tell her NicknZack went to bed a while ago. There wasn't anything for them to do, and they were nodding off anyway, so I insisted they get some sleep. I resisted the temptation to do the same.

She sits down beside me and stares at the screen, squinting to focus. "Where are we?"

I point to the pulsating blue dot. "Cottage Grove."

"In central Oregon? I thought we'd be farther."

"We're pretty much on track." I explain that the only storm remained to the north, so we've picked up speed. Otherwise we'd be behind schedule due to roadwork around Shasta. In fact, we're cruising at a lively ninety mph, twenty miles over the posted limit.

"You're not worried about getting caught?"

I laugh. These days any vehicle, even an aero car, exceeding the limit is zapped with a ticket. No need for police on the scene. As someone who grew up with all the anxieties of driving while Black, I appreciate enforcement being more equitable. Still, not even the most advanced ASE system is equipped for the automated speed enforcement of a virtual vehicle.

"How realistic does this need to be?" she wants to know.

And she's right: the chariot could only go this fast if we disabled the speed controls. I weigh the odds. Whoever is tracking us is unlikely to know the enabled speed of a vehicle they're tracking. But moment-to-moment traffic flow would show on their screens. "I suppose we'd better slow down," I say. "Besides, we're getting close to Portland city limits."

I slow to seventy mph and resume monitoring the chariot's progress. It's a bit like watching clothes dry in one of those old-time dryers, before laundromats installed the ultrasonic kind. I can't believe I made it through the night without any sleep.

By the time we hit Portland, it's the beginning of rush hour. The storm has closed in, and rain is coming down hard. The blue dot is barely moving. All we can do is wait it out.

Feeling antsy, June checks her tablet for new texts. Her VA—which she hasn't disabled—has already tagged a few. She previews them, then asks, "Have you thought about what to tell your peeps?"

I admit that's been on my mind. I think we should deal with different people in the ways most fitting to each. We'll have to give a reasonable explanation to friends and family but shouldn't respond to anyone at HSys. Let the company handle that. Unless of course those coworkers are also friends. That won't be much of a problem though, as our work and personal lives are quite separate. I can count on one hand the number of HSys people who've been to the farm. Ever. That's because even before we had pods, we always went to each other first.

"Are you talking about folks at work?" Beers zips up his hoodie as he strides into the room. He looks more awake than June and me combined.

"Yeah," I say. "People may wonder why we're ghosting them. But staying silent puts the burden on HSys to explain where we are. I'm sure Donna will be happy to oblige."

"What do you think she'll say?" Beers asks.

"I dunno. Maybe that a special offsite project came up?"

June points out that an entire pod doesn't typically go out of town at the same time. Not to mention it would be hard to think of a project that requires Beers to be offsite.

"If she says it's in stealth mode," I say, "no one will ask questions."

"Whatever she comes up with, she'll be covering her own ass as much as ours," Beers says with a chuckle.

"Ironic, isn't it?" says Nick, as he and Zack join us. Darah isn't far behind.

Beers volunteers to make waffles. We have nothing but time on our hands. Hell, we can have waffles every day. The kid has arrived from the barn, and the two of them head for the kitchen.

While we wait for the waffles—and then while we feast on them—June keeps an eye on her tablet. Texts are now flowing in a steady stream. "My VA is going nuts, tagging everything as urgent," she says, then reads off a veritable litany of cyberslaps: "wau??" "meeting started 5 min ago. thought u expect us 2b on time?" And "still w4u . . .where the frick r u?"

"Yikes," Darah says. "I'm afraid to look at mine."

Beers frowns. "Jedd, I hope no one can see she's reading those texts."

I explain we can still view our messages but are otherwise

invisible. We can't respond either. I included that safeguard when I set up our IDs. If one accidental emoji slips through, it's game over.

I want to check my own messages, except I'm too busy keeping tabs on the Portland traffic. It's finally thinning out and the storm has passed, so I increase the chariot's speed. We'll be able to whizz through now.

June scans a few more texts, then turns off her VA. Normally she lets her VA run her day. This day is anything but normal. Still, it's hard to refrain from checking. Before she's finished her waffle, she looks again. "Here's one: 'hey June,' followed by a string of frowny faces. And another: 'jw where r u??? tb when u can.'" She sets her tablet down and shakes her head. "This might be dope if I wanted reassurance everyone loves me."

With Portland—and a plate of waffles—in our rearview mirror, I take out my mini tablet and start scrolling. My peeps aren't as salty as June's. I read a few aloud: "'did u get my text?' 'thought u were on this.' And one from Andrea, whose security issue I was supposed to fix today: 'not like u to miss an appt.' And an hour later: 'i'm worried.'" Plus a couple from Naomi I don't care to share with the others. Not replying to her will put me in the doghouse. Permanently. It's a sacrifice I hate to make, but I don't have a choice.

There is a loud ping from my tablet. "It's Andrea again," I say. "'donna said ur pod shipped off on a sp wow!!! will miss u but HSys lucky to have talent like u.'" There's a second ping, and I read her follow-up: "'since no1 seems to know i will spread the word. guess u didn't have time to do that b4 u left.'"

"Well, that last is true." June shakes her head. It's amazing how quickly our coworkers have figured everything out. Or at least Donna's version of everything.

"Yup, all handled," Beers says. "And it's not even lunchtime."

I point out that dealing with family will be trickier and

suggest we wait to contact them until we've come up with a strategy.

"Speaking of strategy," June says, "we're getting closer to the border. What did you decide to do when we get there?"

I gave that more thought while the others were sleeping. "I've changed my mind," I say. "I'm inclined to avoid an official crossing. That way we can keep things loose in Canada."

"By loose you mean make our location hard to pin down?" Beers says.

"Precisely. If we fake an official crossing, we'll have a destination on record that we're tied to. Makes us too easy to trace. Obviously we're not getting a rental in Vancouver."

They all see the logic of that.

"So what's the best place to cross?" June asks.

"After Ferndale," I say, "we can leave Route 5 and find a side road. I suggest we head for Vancouver Island. Vast areas, especially up north, are still pretty remote. It won't be hard to get off the grid."

June reminds us that without solar charging, the chariot won't fare well off the grid.

"Understood," I say. "The idea is to stay near one of the towns, like Ucluelet or Winter Harbour. Make occasional purchases here and there, and at the same time, create the appearance we've gone into the wilderness. There's plenty of forested area for camping. And nice beaches."

Everyone likes the idea.

The kid says he's heard surfing is epic up there. He makes us promise to send good pics. If that's not too much work.

As they sat on the front porch of their ashrama,
Draupadi could not hold back any longer.
She cried to Yudhishthira, "My body burns day and night
with grief and humiliation! How can you be so calm?"

14

AT THE FARM: Darah

After we cross the border, Beers brews up a batch of mulled cider. At least for now, we've pulled off our escape. Outsmarted our enemies. It feels like a victory, and the cider, spiked with brandy, is a treat. We've been living on snacks, as if driving rest stop to rest stop for real. To be honest, I'm not even hungry.

Jedd locates a campground in a regional park north of Vancouver city limits. He says he'll register the chariot and pay for a campsite. We'll set up camp, sit around a campfire, sleep till dawn, then take off to catch the ferry to Nanaimo.

June argues that's too risky. He'll have to register the number of campers. The rangers will notice that six campers didn't show up.

"I'm sure they have no-shows all the time," Beers says.

"Especially this time of year," Jedd adds.

June says that reinforces her point: we might have the campground to ourselves. Our physical absence will be glaring. We'll be on record for not showing up. Defeats our whole purpose.

"Hey!" the kid calls over from his usual spot on the hearth. Even when you think he isn't listening, he is. Now he's chuckling. "Did you bring a tent?"

Beers turns and gapes at him. As do the others. Tracking all the details to avoid continuity errors is harder than we imagined. It takes seven alert brains.

Jedd is the first to recover. "We'll buy one on the island," he says, as if that's what he planned all along. "A big one, since it won't have to fit in the chariot."

So we drive to a remote corner of the park, where we can pull off on a dirt road, without attracting attention, and be snug in our sleeping bags in the chariot. Anyone desiring more space can sleep under the stars. Either way, we should be good since no rain—or snow—is forecast. This isn't the Bay Area, Jedd reminds us.

As I sip my cider, I keep checking the screen, reconfirming we're still there. The whole situation feels precarious. Suddenly I have an alarming thought. "What if the chariot gets hacked? What if the Russians hijack us?"

"Don't worry, Darah," Jedd says. "They won't."

June points out he doesn't know that.

"Not with absolute certainty," he says. "However, I've taken every precaution to ensure our location is visible but not hackable. I also set up notifications to alert me if anyone tries to mess with my program. Even in the middle of the night. Especially then."

He sounds calm, not a bundle of nerves like I am. Still, I find it hard not to keep checking the pulsating blue dot. By now the sun has gone down and the temperature has dropped to thirty-six degrees. We're in for a cold night.

"How long will all this take?" I ask. "I mean, before we can go home?"

"A couple months?" Beers says.

The twins look at each other. Nick says, "Thirteen is the number that comes to us."

Jedd is nodding. "That sounds about right."

"Weeks?" I clarify.

"Could be," he says. "Or months. Anyone's guess."

That's a sobering prospect. I've never been anywhere for a week, let alone a year or more, without the ability to hold a job and support myself. Certainly not without being able to get in a car and go whenever I want. Or see anyone I feel like seeing. Even in the dictatorship—the early years at least—people had freedom of movement. I wouldn't be here now without that.

Beers reminds us we need to figure out what to tell family and friends. The sooner the better, before anyone gets suspicious.

Jedd says he's not going to contact anyone. At least not yet. He has never lied to his parents, and he's not going to start now. He doesn't mention Naomi. They've been getting close lately, but apparently he's willing to sacrifice that for the sake of our safety. I'm not sure I'd be so noble.

I say I won't call anyone either. Mom is still missing, and I have no reason to expect good news about her. In the unlikely event she tries to contact me from Afghanistan, Jedd says we'll immediately drive the chariot into town.

June's parents divorced when she was in college. Her mother lives in New York, her father in Texas. She's had only minimal contact with him and her brother since moving to California. "I have to let Mom know," she says, reaching for her tablet. "She stays up late. I can catch her now."

"You mean tell her you're in Canada," Jedd says.

June freezes. "I can't lie to her."

"You have to," Jedd says.

"She's in the States. It's too dangerous to talk on the phone," Beers adds.

June objects that if she lies, her mother will know. After weighing all the pros and cons, she decides not to call. Depending on how our exile develops, she can revisit that decision.

The twins are in touch with many family members and friends, mostly in LA. After listening to June wrestle over whether to contact her mother, they opt to follow a similar plan.

I don't expect the kid to phone anyone.

Jedd says he'll set up an outgoing message for all of us that says just enough for people to think we're away on business, without causing them to worry we've been disappeared. Which shouldn't be a worry in California anyway.

Beers insists he has to inform his parents. He isn't wild about lying but doesn't have a good alternative. His parents own a vineyard in Napa and could drop by the farm unannounced. They also expect him to visit a few times a year. He's overdue for that.

"Your ID is set," Jedd says. "You can call now."

Beers picks up his tablet, starts to call, then abruptly sets it down. "Maybe tomorrow."

"Just get it over with," June says.

Beers dials and reaches his father. He doesn't use the speakerphone, so we only hear his end. "Hi, Dad . . . Glad to hear that . . . Uh-huh . . . Sorry I haven't made it up. Actually, that's why I'm calling . . . This will come as a surprise; I'm not at HSys . . . Right, not working . . . It's fine. I need a change . . . You won't believe it, but I'm in Canada . . . Yeah, spur of the moment. Drove up with friends. Always wanted to check out this area, get off the grid. It's beautiful . . . You'll tell Mom?" He talks a bit longer, mainly about the vineyard. He encourages his dad to text rather than phone, and not to worry if Beers is slow to respond. When he hangs up, he looks shaken. "That was tough."

"It had to be done," Jedd reminds him.

We reassure Beers it went as well as could be expected. He sounded convincing. For me, though I don't say so, he's lucky just to have parents he can call.

"You know," he adds, "I'm glad I called. But they need to be warned—"

Jedd anticipates where he's going. "You mean about an attack on California." Beers is nodding. "Gotcha. If we get there, we'll figure it out. But nothing's happening now."

"I wish we knew that for sure, bro." Beers slaps his thighs, then lets out a long, low growl. Somewhere between menacing and rattled. Dharma raises his head, ears pulled back, until he realizes it's just Beers.

Beers stands up, still growling, and walks toward the French doors.

June stops him. "Where are you going?"

"To ululate at the moon." He throws his head back and howls.

"That might be okay in the wilds of Canada," she says, guiding him back to the sofa. "Here, not so much."

She has a point: even without close neighbors, we can't risk a noise disturbance. Beers says he'll put his excess energy into another crossword puzzle. His tenth of the day.

The rest of us head to our beds.

As I crawl under the covers, I imagine myself by the side of the road, under towering cedars, on a frigid British Columbia night. The liner of my sleeping bag is on its hottest setting. If this is what it takes to escape the Dictator, you won't hear me complain.

Jedd is the only one whose schedule is unchanged. If anything, he's working longer hours, taking fewer breaks. He's up early and spends all day and late into the evening at the coffee table, on his tablet, only stopping to eat and sleep and throw a ball down the driveway for Dharma. Then he's back at it, sifting through item after item on the darknet site, tracking progress on the Happy App. He has no problem taking one for the team, he said the first morning, since he's the reason we're in this mess. Plus, he knows it's only temporary.

"Consider it an unexpected vacation," he said. "Don't you always gripe about being too busy?"

Beers took that as impetus to tackle some maintenance projects he'd put off for vacation time he never managed to take. With frequent crossword puzzle breaks of course. The twins began clearing brush to make a track around the perimeter of the property so they can run every day. Only June chose to stay by Jedd's side, reading along and offering comments. You can hear the two bickering over their interpretations of a new discovery.

A forced vacation is the last thing I want. I'd rather be interviewing for jobs, putting HSys behind me. I spent the first day sorting my wardrobe: one pile for wearables that need reprogramming, another for smart fabrics that are buggy, like the leggings that only change color on one leg. In the end, I shoved everything back in the closet because I didn't want to ask June to fix my electronics.

Today I'm sitting on the porch steps, vacillating between boredom and anxiety, watching a train of ants cross the bottom step.

The kid plops down beside me. "Hey," he says, as if we always hang out at 9 a.m. on a Tuesday. "What's up?"

I don't have a good answer, so I fall back on a factoid I recall from the KnoMor game. "Did you know there are ten quadrillion of them?"

"Of what?"

"Ants in the world."

He follows my gaze to the bottom step. "All busy, I suppose."

I sigh. "Wish *I* were that busy."

"If you're up to it," he says after a minute, "you could help start on the garden."

I'm not really up to it, but anything beats counting ants, so I follow him to the barn. We go online with the tablet Jedd refurbished and buy some seeds. I select what will grow well in winter: lettuce, broccoli, beets, carrots, kale. He adds celery and places the order, opting for drone delivery.

Then he rolls up his sleeves, ties back his hair, and runs out to start prepping the earth behind the house. I join him. The rains have loosened the soil, so it's easy going. Even so, the seeds arrive before we've turned over more than a few square feet. Beers, who's putting a coat of paint on the porch railing, spots the drone and yells at me to get indoors so I'm not visible. By then, of course, it's too late. The others come out when they hear the ruckus, and Jedd adds a new restriction to the kid's use of the tablet: no drone deliveries.

The twins offer to help dig. Between us we have two shovels, a pickaxe, and a rusty hoe, but we get the job done. Seeing the kid in his element, dancing around the garden, singing at the top of his lungs, puts a smile on my face, helps me relax. Just what I need. Somehow we'll be okay at the farm. This exile will keep us safe.

At mealtimes, Jedd gives us pep talks. Today, as we scarf down Beers's soba noodles, he says, "Like it or not, this is our new reality. We can deal with it. We've outsmarted the Dictator. And we can win this war. We do it by taking care of each other, like family. By refusing to let being stuck on the farm get us down."

"It's an effing bummer," Beers says.

Jedd agrees. "Big inconvenience, to put it mildly. But not the end of our world. We've hit a rough patch, that's all." Nor do we have to be heroes, he says. It's not on us to rid the world of the Dictator, to be self-appointed saviors. We didn't cause any aspect of this catastrophe, and it's not up to us to solve it. We just have to hang on, to survive. Eventually the proper authorities will take matters into their hands. In the meantime, we stay alert and follow what's happening, yet refrain from obsessing over it.

Everyone laughs at that last bit, and he has to walk it back: as a geek, he's obsessive by nature. Being a hacker makes him doubly so. His obsessiveness is what enabled him to crack the Happy App so quickly. If he had to, he insists, he could reprogram it from scratch. Not that we take that claim seriously. He's not trained in quantum SL.

Beers asks for an update on what the Ks are saying on the darknet site.

"There's a reason I haven't given updates," Jedd says. "Ever since they've had a secure place to talk in person, that part of the site has been a dead zone."

"We're seeing progress on the app," June adds, "but we have no idea about their marketing plans—promos, price point, nothing."

Beers frowns. "That puts us at a severe disadvantage."

"True," Jedd says. "Except I have a solution. I haven't had a sec to implement it till now."

We all want to know what it is.

"Let's say a certain rum bottle did the trick," Jedd says.

"Kurt has a thing for rum," Nick points out.

"Fancy-pants rum," Zack adds.

"We saw that at the dice game," Beers says. "But it's no help to us now."

"Or maybe it is," Jedd says.

Suddenly I flash back to that night. Right before the game started, Jedd snatched the rum bottle from my hands. I thought he was going to pour himself a drink. But now I recall him standing by the window with it. "Oh my god, you bugged the penthouse?"

Jedd answers with a grin.

"With one of those nano mics?" June high-fives him across the table. She's matching his grin, but I bet she wishes she figured it out herself.

"Nasty, dude!" Beers is impressed.

Jedd explains that when he told us before the happy hour that he had something up his sleeve, a way to gather intel, that was his plan. On our way out, he grabbed a couple inches of nano microphone tape and stuck it in his pocket. At the penthouse, when he thought no one was watching, he affixed a mic to Kurt's rum bottle. "Anyone who inspects the bottle will think it's a piece of transparent tape, part of the label," he says. "If they even notice it. Which I doubt." He reaches into his mini tablet case and pulls out what remains of the nano tape. When a mic is peeled off, it exposes the QR code that gives access to whatever that mic records.

"Why didn't you tell us then?" June asks.

"Losing our jobs wasn't part of my plan." Jedd looks sheepish. "If I'd told you I left a nano mic on a rum bottle, when all you were thinking about was your job—"

"You're right," June says, "I wouldn't have wanted to hear it."

"When do we start listening in?" Beers asks.

"How about now?" Jedd leads us into the living room, where he puts his tablet on the coffee table, activates the mic's code, and motions for us to listen.

After a short silence, a woman's voice can be heard in the distance: "Seen my lip balm?"

A male answers: "Check the counter."

"Geez," Beers says, "if they can't even keep track of their lip balm, we'll be fine."

We listen to some back-and-forth about where the balm might be. Then a deeper voice suggests she adjust the humidity controls at her table to lessen the need for balm in the first place. I recognize Keith.

"Is this live?" I ask as Jedd cuts the sound.

"Sure is!" He's proud of himself.

June points out we'll have to sit through hours of lip balm talk to catch anything of value.

"Time isn't something you have a shortage of, is it?" Jedd laughs. "Actually, whatever the mic picks up is automatically transcribed. Of course it will take time to review the transcripts." He asks if June will take the lead on that.

Beers offers to help as well. He'll do crossword puzzles while he listens. Maybe work on a new project he started the other day: carving a chess set out of redwood.

From now on, Jedd says, he'll give a three-part report at each meal. First he'll talk about progress on the app. Then he'll summarize what's been said on the penthouse audio. Finally he'll relay any news he's come across about the Dictator's plans.

I've always avoided following the news. It's too anxiety producing. But now it's more anxiety producing not to be able to check anything at all. So I ask Jedd if he'll set us up with anonymous IDs, like his, enabling us to access more than our personal messages.

Initially he's hesitant. But Beers seconds my idea and together we convince him to give us specific windows a couple times per week during which we can pop online.

The next day, Jedd announces our first window. "Your IDs are set up," he says. "Let's take the chariot into Ucluelet."

We sit around the coffee table and watch the pulsating blue dot inch down Pacific Rim Highway, then turn onto Peninsula Road. As soon as it stops in front of the co-op store in Ucluelet, we grab our tablets and rush online to research whatever we've been wondering about for days. When I don't see anything noteworthy out of Afghanistan, I focus on researching gardening tips for winter vegetables.

Jedd uses the time to pick up enough supplies to get us through the next few days. He even buys a wetsuit and surfboard he saw advertised at a discount. When the kid questions the value of a single suit and surfboard for the whole family, Jedd shrugs and says he'll look for more suits and boards on a later trip. In the meantime, we'll have to share.

After an hour, he shouts, "Time's up!"

We close whatever we're looking at and cluster around the screen to watch the blue dot glide out of town. And we're back off the grid.

I thought I'd be able to settle into our new normal. That being with family and caring for each other would be enough. That I could tough it out, get through this. Yet as we enter the second week of exile, I find myself more and more disturbed. Those old symptoms I believed I'd beaten are back.

The garden is planted, including lettuce in flats in the sunroom, but I don't care if the seeds come up. I don't care if the sun itself comes up. Each morning when the first light is reflected on the redwood beams in my attic room, I pull my pattu shawl over my head and tell myself I'm not getting up today. As if reality would disappear if I didn't face it. But then I hear everyone in the kitchen, talking and laughing. Eating the awesome breakfast Beers cooked. It's only a matter of time before one of them comes to get me. So I force myself to go down.

Every day, Beers gets up before dawn, assesses the ingredients on hand, and gets to work. We have waffles twice a week. Other specialties are avocado toast and chia coconut granola and soufflé pancakes with cricket lemongrass syrup.

As soon as I sit down at the kitchen table, he slides a plate in front of me.

I start eating, and it's delicious. Then I hear Jedd giving his report. It's not that I don't care about it or think it's important. I do, and it is. But I don't want to hear it, don't want the anxiety it brings.

This morning he mentions audio from the penthouse in which Kurt joked about how easy it was to steal our jobs and run us out of town, gloated about how we're now stuck in some shithole country. When I hear that, I want to barf. Literally. Kurt isn't the Dictator, but he might as well be. I'm flooded with images: the dice game, the hologram, Kurt grabbing my bra, Keith doing nothing. Along with that, visions of Mom being arrested. I can see it as clearly as if I'd been there. I see the Dictator's smirking face, hear his bullying tone and insulting, vitriolic words. He lies and cheats and kills, does whatever it takes to stay in power. Nobody fights him and wins. It doesn't matter that I've taken pains since coming to California not to watch him. The scars live on within me.

Suddenly he isn't thousands of miles away. I can feel him stomping around the farm, his guards with guns loaded surrounding the house. My stomach lurches. I break out in a cold sweat as I run to the bathroom and hurl everything I just ate into the toilet.

Something similar happened that April afternoon when I heard Mom had been picked up. I was on my way to an ecology class. If our neighbor's call had come five minutes later, I'd have missed it. When I hung up, my whole body was shaking. I got in my car and drove north on Interstate 95 while I tried to figure out where she was being held. I ended up at a facility in Elizabeth, only to learn she wasn't there. She wasn't at the Newark facility either. A guard told me detainees weren't allowed visitors anyway. I got back in my car, unsure whether to drive to our place in Palisades Park or back to Rutgers. I couldn't face school, so I drove home. But I didn't make it. I had to pull over and throw up at the side of the road.

Now, like then, I'm ashamed of my lack of emotional bandwidth. I can't hold it together the way the others can. It may feel like an unexpected vacation to them; to me it's unexpected hell. But I don't want anyone to know. I don't want them to see me as weak, as a victim. And I don't want their pity.

Panic hits without warning, at random moments, often at mealtimes. When I have to run from the table, I make excuses. "Sorry, just remembered . . ." I exclaim and disappear to do whatever that might be. Except I don't. I rush to the bathroom and lock the door and throw up.

I hope no one will notice. Of course, nothing at the farm is so pressing it warrants jumping up from a meal. I'm counting on the others to see me as hardworking, conscientious Darah, to think old habits die hard and leave it at that.

The kid is the first to figure it out.

Today as I emerge from the bathroom, hoping to crawl back up to the attic before anyone sees me, he's waiting on the bottom step of the staircase. He shoots me an are-you-okay look and suggests I bring my flute to the barn.

Since we've been in exile, he's been too busy with the garden and trips to town—and lately I've been too upset—to think about flute lessons. I'm still upset, but I want to prove to him I'm not. So I agree to meet him.

When I climb the ladder to the loft, he is playing one of the first songs he taught me. He wants me to join in, but when I do, it's as if I've never played before.

He stops and looks at me.

"I don't know what's wrong," I say.

He reminds me: "Your heart, not your ears."

I tell him that's not working now.

"Let the music flow through you," he coaxes. "Don't try to create it, let it create itself."

That sounds nice, but I tell him it's not helping now either.

"Too much stress, I get it." He suggests I listen to him play and join in if I feel moved to. If I don't feel it, that's okay too.

So I close my eyes and listen. He plays one long, drawn-out note, letting it warble before fading into silence, then pauses before beginning another. It rained hard earlier, and beneath each note, I hear the slow percussive *plunk-plunk* of water dripping from the eaves, marking time against the rushing water of the creek. The sounds of the flute and nature play off each other. It's not a melody as much as it is just pure sound. Gradually it calms my nerves.

I pick up my flute and answer with a series of deep, pure notes, punctuated with long pauses. It's like he said: the music creates itself.

By the end of our lesson, I feel restored in a way I haven't in weeks. I ask the kid how soon we can play again.

He suggests this afternoon.

There is no queasiness in my stomach at lunch. The others are riled up about Jedd's latest report, but I'm too focused on my next lesson to listen.

This time, as soon as we start playing, my notes flow strong and clear. I play and the kid listens. Then I pause and he plays. Then we play together. Each echoing the other.

I can imagine us inspiring everyone. Instead of letting the Dictator control our lives, we can make our exile a special family time. We can play music, have concerts, dance to our songs, be creative. We can do more with the garden, such as learn about native plants. It all starts with the joyful sound coursing through me.

We're still at it when we hear the windchimes clanging on the porch. Since meals have become the main markers of our day, we all crowd into the kitchen before the food is ready. If anyone is slow to arrive, Beers shakes the chimes. Now I don't care if he's serving champagne and caviar, I'm not ready to give up the peace I'm feeling.

The kid puts his flute down, stands, and moves toward the ladder.

I don't budge.

"Let's go," he says.

"You go."

"Darah, you have to eat."

When he refuses to go without me, I set my flute aside and follow.

Outside, darkness seems to accentuate the world of sound. As if the notes we created are living beings carrying me as I float along the path. I can hear melodies reverberating in the redwood branches, harmonies in the gurgling creek. All my senses are heightened. As we pass through the field, I can smell the grass growing. Taste the moonlight. Silky and sweet, it melts the instant it touches my tongue. I move slowly, soaking it all in.

The others are already seated around the kitchen table. I take the chair next to Beers and wait for the serving dishes to make the rounds. Curried lentil soup, herb focaccia, mixed greens. The first baby lettuce from the trays in the sunroom. As I fill my plate, I can still hear our flutes, feel their pure sound surrounding me. Like golden armor, invisible but impermeable, keeping me calm and free. I can still taste the moonlight. This is how I want to live.

I haven't yet taken a bite when Jedd starts his report. "Before we get to the app," he says, "there's some ugly news—"

"What'd the Dick do now?" Beers cuts in.

"Let me guess," June says.

Poof! My golden armor vaporizes. I'm exposed, defenseless against the ugly news, whatever it is. Against all the scary feelings that will come pouring in with it. The Dictator might as well be sitting across the table, leering at me with his pinhole eyes. "Stop," I cry. "Just *stop*."

Jedd looks confused. "Stop what?"

"Do you have to do this while we're eating?" I say, as if mealtime reports aren't our daily diet. "Can't we eat in peace? Whoever wants to talk can do it afterwards!"

They stare at me. I know what each is thinking: *She's lost it.*

"I'm sorry," Beers says. "We should be more sensitive—"

"Don't patronize me," I snap. Who cares if he means well, I'm desperate to recapture the serenity I felt. I push back my chair and yell at them all to carry on without me.

In the loft, I light the kerosene lantern and crouch against the wall, close to the solar space heater. I thought if I played my flute, I'd get the magic back. But I can't even bring myself to pick it up. Nothing feels the same. The *plunk-plunk* from the eaves sounds annoying now, like a leaky bathroom faucet. I stare at a large damp spot on the rug that I didn't notice earlier. It seems like forever since Beers and I discussed patching the roof.

I hear the barn door slide open. The kid mounts the ladder, then lies down on the rug, arms behind his head, propping it up, his feet resting on the damp spot. He looks at me without saying a word.

"Doesn't all the negativity bug you?" I say when it's clear he's waiting on me.

He shrugs, then sits up to face me.

"Well," I say, "it bugs the heck out of me. I know what it's like to live in terror of the Dictator. It's not a virtual reality. You can't turn it off and on. You can't grab democracy back once it's gone. But everyone here is lounging around in a cushy farmhouse, following along on a computer. They think it's a vacation. It's like a game for them."

He looks surprised. "You really think so?"

I can't believe I'm arguing with the kid. But I've reached a breaking point. I need to feel okay again, like life is normal. Maybe it's unrealistic to expect to get over years of PTSD in one afternoon. But I thought the others would get where I'm coming from. Honestly, I'm starting to think they're still the five, and I don't belong. "They aren't bothered by ugly, threatening, scary stuff," I say. "They thrive on it, knowing they have the privilege to walk away if it gets too tough."

"They lost their jobs," he points out. "For real."

"So they get new jobs."

"Not in exile. They're stuck here like you are."

"Then they can go to Canada for real."

"And you can't?"

I pause. As a Californian, I do have a choice. I'm free to get in my car and drive to San Jose or maybe LA or Canada. If I want, I can go back to teaching science. Yes, the Dictator's agents might track me, but they'd probably lose interest if I was no longer linked to Jedd. Except that isn't the point. The point is I'm tired of watching the Dictator find new ways to wield power in my life. "Maybe they don't mind it," I say, "but I don't want to live like this."

"What are you saying? You want to leave?"

I ignore his second question. "I'm saying stop all the negativity, toxicity, fear."

He tells me nobody wants those things. N-o-b-o-d-y.

The way he says that, it's hard to argue. The problem is that even if they don't want negativity, they're choosing it. It would be different if they had the power to stop the Dictator, but they don't. They feed off the negativity at every meal. Since the kid apparently doesn't get this, I try another angle. "You're a peaceful person. Don't you want others to be that way too?"

"Of course, Darah." He frowns. I don't think I've ever seen a frown cross his face. "But peace isn't a weapon. I can't use my own peace as a shield, as a way to keep others out."

I'm shocked. If that's what he thinks, he doesn't understand me after all. Earlier I imagined all the ways we could make our lives on the farm better. I assumed the kid would be on board. Welcome it. Instead he's acting like there's no difference between playing the flute and obsessing over the Dictator, between songs of the heart and raw hatred. Between whether we live or die. Like he's equally at peace with both. Like I should be too. Newsflash: I'm not. I never will be. Maybe I don't understand him that well either.

I excuse myself and head back to the house.

Jedd is alone in the living room, bent over the coffee table. I take the back stairs to the attic so I don't have to talk to him.

In bed, I close my eyes and reflect. I'm not ready to sneak off to LA. I'll stick it out at the farm. I'll practice the flute every day and learn how to fortify myself with more durable armor—not as a shield against others but to block the negative news and toxic thoughts. To feel happy again.

Bheema was angry and frustrated.
The sight of Draupadi's suffering only made his misery
more unbearable. He ground his teeth in helpless rage.

POISONED: Beers

Beep, beep, beep, beep! It's the middle of the night and an alarm is going off. Jedd's alarm.

I roll out of bed, reach for my hoodie, and meet June in the hallway, both of us racing toward the stairs. Lights are already on—if they ever went off—in the living room. As we round the turn in the stairs, we can see Jedd bent over the coffee table.

"What's up?" June asks.

"Don't tell me we've been hacked," I say, squinting in the brightness.

Jedd grunts in the affirmative as he begins typing furiously on his tablet. The familiar pulsating blue dot is nowhere to be seen on the coffee table screen. The chariot has been hijacked. Really, we're god damn sitting ducks. The fact that it's 2 a.m. doesn't help.

The twins arrive a minute later, and we all gather around. Except Darah. The alarm didn't reach the attic. Fortunately. I hope for her sake she won't wake up. This is not a crisis she needs right now.

"How serious is it?" I ask.

Jedd is still typing away but not so frantically that he can't talk. "They got into the chariot's odometer."

"The odometer?" June looks dubious.

"Not to mess with our mileage. They wanted to disable the vehicle, and that was their point of entry."

"You mean disable it or control it remotely?" I wonder aloud. The latter seems more probable. I mean, we're talking about Kurt. About an evil, sadistic mind. I imagine the six of us in Canada, cruising in the chariot, confident in its self-driving mechanics, only to have it suddenly career off the side of the road going a hundred miles an hour. It would be over so fast you wouldn't know what hit you.

Except that kind of spaghettification wouldn't be cruel enough for Kurt. So maybe his hackers just tweak the alignment five degrees to the left. With no steering wheel, we'd be helpless. But no, Kurt still wouldn't be satisfied. He'd go next level. Tell his hackers to make sure the chariot has a full charge and we're all inside, then autolock the doors and windows and drive us to a predetermined destination. A dead-end dirt road somewhere in the British Columbia wilderness. Where no one will find us. The terror of that ride is unthinkable.

Yes, Kurt is one sick puppy. That's putting it nicely. June and I have spent hours poring over the penthouse tapes, listening to the crap that comes out of his mouth. I can't blame Darah for taking a pass on that. It requires a stronger stomach than she has. Yesterday Kurt and his pals joked about Jedd playing strip poker in the cold Canadian tundra. Hope that was just a velleity. They'd better not be planning to act on it.

Still, our willingness to listen to their crap has paid off. We now know for a fact they believe we've gone to Canada.

We also know it has taken them all this time to figure out why Kurt couldn't get a clean grab on Darah's scarf. You'd think they'd be busy working up a marketing strategy for the Happy App. But no, Kurt was obsessed with Darah's scarf. Karin kept insisting it was an error by a programmer in Florida. Eventually he convinced her June was the culprit. Says she's the most dangerous one in our group. If we dare to resurface, he's going after her first.

June shrugged when she heard that. Called it her badge of honor. Now as she scrutinizes the odometer reading on Jedd's screen, she says, "We're lucky your alarm went off."

"Yes," he says. "Another half hour and we'd be looking at a different outcome."

"So what now?" Nick asks.

Jedd explains he has stemmed the bleeding. The chariot is back on the map, back under his control. He just needs to patch up any vulnerabilities. "Should take a couple hours," he says. "I'll be fine. You can all go back to bed."

Which we're more than happy to do.

"I'll be up early to make beer pancakes," I call out from the foot of the stairs. It's the least I can do.

Of course, Darah hears all about the hack at breakfast.

Since nothing disastrous happened, we downplay it, say it was a good thing actually. Allowed Jedd to plug a hole. Shows we're on top of this.

Everything must have a positive spin for Darah these days. We've always watched what we say about the Dick around her, but this goes way beyond that. The other night, she had a major freak-out for no apparent reason. The slightest negative sets her off. I've been making a big effort to counter that. When I see something good, I tell her about it. Like the old ukulele I found in the attic. Or how the dish of beer I set out is keeping slugs from eating the young lettuce. When someone reports bad shit online, I make sure she doesn't hear about it.

Mostly, she hangs out in the attic or the barn and plays her flute. Yesterday she played for six hours. I try to include her in projects that will get her mind off stuff. We've finally gotten around to patching the barn roof, using sealant the kid picked up in town.

I miss the old Darah, the playful Darah. The one who sang along with her nature sound apps as if they were karaoke. Who said my cooking was delish even when I over-spiced or under-spiced. Once a big splash of soy sauce ended up in my chocolate mousse and she ate it anyway. Said she loved it.

Not that I haven't changed in some ways myself. I'm angrier and more irritable. Faster to fly off the handle. When it's in response to the Dick or the Ks, I feel justified. When it's about small stuff, not so much.

Like right now, at this jentacular moment in the kitchen. In the middle of the night, I promised to throw together beer pancakes. So I got up bright and early, and I'm standing at the fridge, and guess what? No beer. Not one bottle. None in the pantry either.

"What the fuck!" I scream. The kid is in my line of vision, so I take aim at him. "How am I supposed to make beer pancakes with no fucking beer?"

He stares back with a look that says *how would I know?*

"You were in town. Why didn't you buy beer?" I'm being unreasonable, but I can't dial it back. I've been practically tasting those pancakes since 2 a.m.

At this point, Jedd steps in. "There was a bottle in the fridge yesterday."

June confirms seeing it too.

"I wonder," Darah says quietly, "who drank it."

That stops me cold. She knows who drank it. So do I. And it wasn't those pesky slugs in the garden. After dinner last night, I was chilling on the porch, nursing that beer—a full-bodied milk stout, perfect for pancakes—when she passed by on her way to the barn. I suggested we watch a movie I'd downloaded while the chariot was in Ucluelet, a rom-com called *Honey Moon*. A couple of newlyweds go to the moon as tourists. She put me off with "maybe another time."

Now I fall all over myself apologizing. I'll make banana pancakes. I'm just frustrated the beer is gone and we're limited to what one person—the kid, who doesn't even drink—could believably purchase and consume. None of which is an excuse for being a total butthead.

My anger toward the Dick is like a poison roiling in my belly. It can erupt at any moment. Of course, this anger isn't new. Or exclusively mine. Most Californians have felt it for years. The difference is I can no longer stuff it down. I can't laugh it off with a sick joke. Before it was about the Dick. Now Kurt gets to me just as much. Not that he's as bad as the Dick, but he's nearby. And getting worse by the day. Nothing energizes Kurt more than mocking June or belittling Jedd. It's more than crude remarks about poker on the tundra; it's ugly, vicious, mean shit. Really, the guy has no filter, no decency. And what's most enraging, no one is holding that bloviating piece of human detritus accountable. No one.

Fuck this laying low, hiding out, following a smart strategy, waiting for the right moment. Enough is enough.

Sometimes I think about driving to town and hunting Kurt down. Not only sometimes, I think about it at least once a day. I don't have a plan; I don't even know where the SOB lives. I fantasize about catching him unaware in the HSys parking lot after dark and letting loose. The only thing that keeps me from going there is knowing the extreme distress it would cause Darah when she finds out.

This evening, Jedd and June are hard at work in the living room, as per usual. The kid is on a run to the store he assured me will include beer. The twins are off doing whatever they do. Darah and I are alone in the kitchen.

She's putting away the dishes and I'm popping popcorn. Before she can take off for the barn, I repeat my offer about *Honey Moon*. I've watched it twice now. It's innocuous fun. I wouldn't mind seeing it again. With her.

To my surprise, she agrees.

We go up to my room, where I usher her toward the corduroy couch. I brought it up from the barn so I could watch movies the old-fashioned way—across the room on the wall over my bed, painted with digital wallpaper. Nothing dope like Jedd's setup.

"Let's get cozy," I say, cradling the bowl of popcorn on my lap. I don't mean cozy as in cuddle. We've never done anything like that. No, popcorn plus a good movie defines cozy for me.

But as the movie begins, Darah rests her head on my shoulder. She's just seeking a shorter distance from bowl to mouth for her popcorn. Still, it's close to a cuddle. Toward the end, as the space travelers, in their sexy, skintight spacesuits, are boarding their return flight to Earth, and all seems good in the universe again, I stretch my arm across the back of the couch. She leans in. Now we're in actual cuddle territory. I feel like a teen on my first date.

A couple days later I offer another movie. She accepts again. And so it becomes our thing, cuddling on my couch over popcorn and a movie. Sometimes two or three movies. Plus the occasional beer.

I can't say I'm less angry. Nothing about our predicament has changed. But I've found an antidote in late-night dates with Darah that takes the sting out of the poison at least temporarily.

Jedd has been digging in the darknet site for weeks now, and we aren't any closer to a plan that would nail Kurt and his goons and get ourselves out of this mess. Feels like we'll be stuck here for life. Jedd says he's accessed the SL technology and has a sense of how the app works, and I believe him, but we have yet to see a demo. I keep asking if we'll ever see the damn thing.

Now for the first time, at dinner his answer is yes. The app is in beta. It's obviously a closed beta, with a small group in Russia or Florida. But it's live on the site, functioning off the cloud-based quantum computer. He and June tried it out earlier.

"No shit!" I say. "Why didn't you tell us?"

"We're telling you now."

Neither of them will say much because they want us to try it with a clean slate. So we drop our forks on half-eaten lasagna and rush into the living room, where we gather around the coffee table. Even Darah. She doesn't volunteer to try the app, but she'll watch. I'd like to believe our time alone has helped her feel it's safe to join in again, like the old Darah.

Jedd has the demo ready on his large tablet, which he hands to me. "Beers, you first."

"What do I do?"

"Follow the prompts. It's pretty intuitive."

The words *Be Happy* are splashed across a bunch of balloons. I touch the screen and a question pops out of a white balloon: "What's your favorite color?" Answers are floating around in smaller balloons of different colors. I choose red, which refreshes the screen with new balloons and a new question: "What's your favorite number?" Looks like something put together by kids in a middle school computer club. Not sure what I expected, but this isn't it. I turn to Jedd. "What's the point?"

He tells me not to get hung up on the questions.

"Note the less-than-awesome user experience and keep going," June says.

"I thought this was supposed to make me like the Dick?"

"What did you expect, dick pics?" June can be sarcastic when she's impatient.

"Okay," I say. "I'll keep going." The questions don't improve, but I make my choices. My favorite number is five. For the five of us, though we're seven now. My favorite animal is a polar bear.

My favorite food is popcorn. After a while, I stop giving a shit about my choices. My favorite dance is a waltz. Favorite sport comes down to archery or kickboxing. I choose the latter.

The final question is "Do you want to be happy?" My finger circles the no button.

"It will throw you out," Jedd warns.

"Stop messing around, Beers." June reaches to tap yes in case I don't.

I tap yes.

Now I'm instructed to keep my eyes fixed on the center of the screen. I comply and a weird combination of my favorites flashes before me in 3D. The polar bear is red. Five boxes of popcorn appear to be kickboxing. "Is this supposed to be funny?" I ask.

"I don't think so," Jedd says.

By then it's over. The only thing on the screen is a single balloon with the number one hundred.

"A hundred what?" I ask.

"Those are your points," Jedd says. "Your happiness points. And no, they don't get you anything."

"Did you notice any effects?" June wants to know.

I can't say I did. More to the point, I haven't suddenly found love for the Dick. Like that's ever going to happen. I pronounce it a total bust.

Zack takes the tablet and runs through the same series of questions. His choices include purple, the number two, ice cream, acoustic guitar and—after we all agree extinct animals should qualify—sea turtles.

"Now be quiet," Jedd says when Zack reaches the final screen.

Everyone is silent as he stares at his little movie. Like mine, it's over in a matter of seconds.

"Well?" Jedd prompts.

"Can't say I have any warm fuzzies for the Dictator," Zack says. "But I did feel a sensation of some sort."

"Like what?" June says.

Zack furrows his brow as we anticipate what it might be. "Like . . . maybe . . . little Russians running around in my brain?"

Everyone laughs.

June reminds us she felt a sensation in her eye during the VRcher superpod. But nothing today. "As you saw, the app doesn't produce any flashes. They probably recalibrated the smart light to avoid perceptible effects. So you shouldn't feel anything. Of course, some sensitives pick up stuff. You and Nick are very sensitive."

Before I can object to the inference I lack sensitivity, Nick has snatched the tablet. Not surprisingly, he picks the same favorites as Zack. After we've watched the identical video, he confirms he felt nothing. "My hate for the Dictator," he proclaims, "is as strong as ever."

He passes the tablet to the kid, who says that since we've tried it, he doesn't need to.

"So," I say, "the app is a failure. We all still hate the Dick. End of story."

"Hold on," June says. "We know far too much to be able to evaluate this app as if we were your average dude on the street. Plus, we only tried it once. We don't know how many exposures are needed to change someone's reaction to the Dictator."

I push back on that. "Quantum smart light was never going to work in a rinky-dink app. No way. No matter how many times you use it."

Jedd cautions that we'd be naïve to assume that. The interface is deceptively simple. The app is still doing its work within the brain.

"Then everyone should be equally affected," I argue. "Everyone with a brain, that is."

"Not necessarily," June says. "Think about drugs. Even if a drug acts directly on the brain, people still respond differently, depending on their neurochemical predisposition."

Darah follows her reasoning. "So unhappy people might respond more than happy people?"

"Or vice versa," June says. She adds that knowing what the app is supposed to do could have influenced our responses. When she tried it earlier, she was monitoring her feelings about the Dictator. That in and of itself could have made her less susceptible.

Jedd says we're in uncharted territory. No one knows what to expect in a gaming context when smart light is applied to the brain via a quantum computer. All we know is the Russians started with VRcher as a simple pilot, then developed the technology to sway public feeling. "They're counting on people being desperate for a little happiness, willing to try anything," he says. "Like thirsty people desperate for a drink of water."

The kid, who loves analogies, is off and running with this one. "The app is like a lake. People thirsting for happiness flock to its shores."

"To get a drink of happiness," Jedd adds.

"But," says the kid, "it's not so easy. There's a bird guarding the shore. That bird makes everyone answer its questions before they can drink the water."

Jedd builds on that. "If they give a wrong answer, the water becomes poison."

"If they drink the poison, they die," the kid says.

Jedd looks at each of us. "So you've come to the shore, desperate for a drink. How do you answer the bird?"

"Depends on the question," Nick says.

"If it's Kurt's game, I shoot the bird," Zack throws in.

"If I'm desperate," Darah says, "I'll give whatever answer it wants."

"Forget the questions, forget the answers," I say. "I'll drink the effing water!"

The kid turns to me. "Except, Beers, for this bird, giving

192

no answer is the same as giving a wrong answer. Either way, the water becomes poison. Either way, you die."

"Like the app," Jedd says. "If you don't answer its questions, it kicks you out."

"Okay, okay," I say. "I played along, didn't I?"

"You did," he says. "But the app is tricky, like the bird. It's smart, but not the same way."

"It's the smart light!" the kid interjects.

"Yes, and its premise," Jedd continues, "is that people are dying for a blast of happiness. They'll try anything. The questions serve as the app's cover. Unlike the bird's questions, there are no right answers, no wrong answers. But don't be fooled: behind the questions and that innocuous little video, the smart light is doing its work."

"Like an insidious poison!" Darah says.

"Exactly." Jedd wheels around. "The app is like poisonous water. Kurt and his crew are counting on people not to suspect what's happening in their brains while they're quenching their thirst. It might take time, but that poison will eventually kill you."

It's a gruesome image: poisoned people collapsing and dying by a lake. Or next to their tablets. Poisoned by the Dick. Even if a few are immune, millions are at risk. It's hard to put a positive spin on that. Even so, I'm relieved Darah looks no more agitated than the rest of us.

As we digest all of this, the kid says he'd like to give the app a try after all.

Jedd hands him the tablet.

He taps through a few balloons, then looks up. "If I were designing this, I'd use better questions."

"Like what?" June wants to know.

"Like . . . what's more plentiful than grass?"

We all laugh.

"Wait," says Darah. "Why are you laughing? I like that. It's positive."

"I like it too," June says. "Even if I don't have an answer."

Of course that means we have to think of answers. Good ones.

"Plentiful round here? I'd say thistles," Nick says.

"Spider webs," Zack suggests.

"Boredom," Darah says.

The kid doesn't like that. "You're bored? Really?"

She walks it back, says she didn't mean to sound negative. She's only bored on some days. And less often than before.

"If we're talking about *plentiful*," Jedd says, "how about crimes on the darknet?"

That gets me started. "Attacks on democracy. The Dick's lies. Kurt's hypocrisy. Keith's farts."

"Beers!" Darah exclaims.

But Jedd is chuckling. "You all are awesome. Realistically though, only a rare person would answer philosophical questions on an app."

"Only a dumbass would answer these," I say, pointing to his tablet.

"Which," says Jedd, "brings me back to what I've been saying: nobody will go for the Happy App. Having tried it, I believe that even more strongly. What do you think, Beers?"

"The user experience sucks," I say. "Even if it's meant to poison minds on a mass scale, I don't think we have much to worry about."

Everyone is nodding.

"So what's next?" Darah sounds relieved.

June explains that Kurt and his pod intend to launch the app this week. It will come out as an HSys product and operate on 6G.

"They haven't put together any sort of promotional campaign, at least not that we've seen," Jedd adds.

"I predict a total flop," Nick says quickly.

Before Zack can second that, Jedd says, "I think you're right. This thing will go nowhere. Classic case of the Dunning-Kruger effect. Kurt thinks he's a lot smarter than he actually is; he has seriously overestimated himself here. As soon as this all plays out, we can discuss our next strategy. In the meantime, we wait."

Bheema said to Yudhishthira, "This talk of dharma is pointless.
Our enemies have wronged us, so we must destroy them.
A thorn must be removed by another thorn. It's time to
march on Hastinapura and take back our kingdom."

LAUNCHED: Jedd

The sooner the Happy App bombs, the better. I'm counting the minutes till it flat out fails and this whole travesty is over. That's when things will get interesting. Kurt will have played his hand and lost. Assuming he continues to keep the bunker at bay, we'll be the only ones who know what he has done. Which means we'll have leverage. I haven't yet thought through our best course of action.

In the meantime, Beers is hankering for revenge. June isn't vengeful but she wants to see some form of activism. Even the easygoing, peace-loving twins want to do something. Now! I keep putting them off. Let the app fail, I say, then we can decide what we want to do.

Initially when I said that, they didn't push back. But now that the app is about to launch, they've stopped giving me any benefit of the doubt.

"Bro, we can't let Kurt skate," Beers declares as I finish my dinnertime report and he dishes out apple crisp around the table. "First it was a butt grab. Now he's about to get away with murder."

I ask what he expects us to do.

"Stop the fucker!" he says. As if how we'd do that is obvious.

"We have to do *something*," June echoes. "Have you forgotten what's at stake?"

I tell her I haven't forgotten. Trust me, I haven't forgotten.

She doesn't take my word for it. "Millions of brains are about to be invaded. Our civil rights, human rights, democratic elections—all that trashed. If we don't do anything soon, it'll probably be too late. Even if we save ourselves, think of all the suffering, the torture, the persecution. All those who will die—"

Beers whips around. "Then what're you waiting for?"

June resents the implication she's sitting on a fix. She may have scary-good skills—like hacking holographic scarves—but this is different.

Beers looks at me and back at June. "You're telling me that between the two of you, you can't hack this sorry-ass app?"

"Okay," I say, "setting aside the fact that this sorry-ass app uses smart light and runs on quantum computing, suppose we do manage to hack it. Think about it. When they discover the app was hacked, who'll top their list of suspects?"

"All of us," Beers says quickly.

"Me," says June.

"Not only that, our escape to Canada will be sus," I continue. "They'll know we couldn't pull off a hack of this magnitude while spending days at a time offline, hanging out in wetsuits, polishing surfboards." I glance at the kid. I haven't made good on my promise to buy more equipment. "Not even with one suit and board between us."

Beers acknowledges these are reasonable concerns.

As everyone works on their apple crisp, I build my argument. First we have to consider what happens if we lose our cover. Right now we're secure at the farm. But if our enemies realize where we are, they could show up on our doorstep. Second we have to consider the value of hacking their app. Yes, it could delay the launch. But it would only be a matter of time before they get it up and running again. And with tighter security. In a cat-and-mouse game like that, we'd lose.

Darah, who hasn't lobbied for hacking the app—I wouldn't expect her to—looks discouraged. "So you're saying you can't stop the launch."

"That's what I'm saying."

It takes a bit more convincing, but by the time we've finished the crisp, everyone has agreed the smartest strategy is to do what we've been doing—namely nothing—and wait for the app to fail. Which it's bound to.

Day to day, waiting for the app's launch is nerve-wracking. So much is at stake. This could mark the beginning of the end for our country. It kills me to think of all the people going about their business a few miles from here, with no clue that their lives are in peril. That their world may implode. And I can't stop it.

I spend every waking minute monitoring the progress of the app on the darknet site, keeping track of chatter in the penthouse, and safeguarding the chariot. It's a proverbial three-ring circus. I'm so busy that I lose track of which supplies have run low at our beach camp. I only remember when I notice everyone gathered around, staring at me.

"Winning your game?" Darah asks.

She knows I'm not playing a video game; she's just trying to get my attention. They're all waiting for me to green-light a trip into town.

I drop what I'm doing and program a run into Ucluelet. I also realize I haven't played any games since we've been holed up here. I knock out a few spacecraft over my bed before I fall asleep. That's about it. Not that gaming has lost its appeal because I no longer work at HSys. Once a gamer, always a gamer, as they say.

But my focus is on our real life-and-death situation. All day, every day, for the foreseeable future.

After our trip into Ucluelet, it's time for dinner. Over stir-fry and mixed greens from the garden, we discuss marketing plans for the app. Or rather, lack thereof. Which makes no sense, considering Kurt is a PR mastermind. I'm dying to see how he plans to persuade the masses to purchase such an obvious dud.

June says she reread the most recent transcripts to see if we missed anything about a promo campaign. But nada. "We should do more," she says.

I ask what she has in mind.

"Listen to the audio stream in real time."

"In the living room? Twelve hours per day?" I can't believe she's suggesting that.

But Beers is on board. He can use the time for the chess pieces he's carving out of redwood. More importantly, listening in real time will cut our risk of missing critical info. "Without more info, we'll never get a leg up," he says. "Even if someone's inconvenienced."

By "someone," he means Darah. But I can't argue with his point. We need to be on top of the intel. Out of respect for her, we promise to keep the volume low until we pick up something significant.

It doesn't take long for that to happen. First thing after breakfast the next morning, as soon as I tune in to the penthouse, I boost the volume.

June and Beers come running.

"It's promo copy," we hear Karin say.

"Finally!" June says.

"Hope she reads it aloud," Beers adds.

That hope is dashed by Kurt's response: "Don't worry about it."

"What?" June's jaw falls two inches.

Karin doesn't sound pleased either. "I'm not *worried*," she whines. "I just want your okay before I post it."

"Don't post it," Kurt says.

Other voices pile on in the penthouse: "Why not?" "Whatcha mean?"

"That's what I want to know," Nick says as the twins join us.

Kurt is emphatic: "Like I said, we're not posting anything."

We listen as his pod-mates push back. Without publicity, they say, the app is doomed. It's their job to generate buzz. Negative buzz is better than no buzz. They're so vocal, it sounds like a crowd of twenty. But it's only Karin, Keith, and Donna.

Kurt shoots them down. "What are you? Slaves to the media?"

Suddenly the penthouse gets quiet. My first thought is the nano mic has failed. But then I realize we're listening to the silence of acquiescence. Kurt is a master at using hyperbole and ridicule to bend people to his will. "You're freedom fighters!" he crows when it's clear they've backed down. "History will love you. Everybody's gonna love this app."

I'm glad Darah is off in the barn with the kid. She doesn't need to hear any of this.

Beers is shaking his head. "Asshole thinks his app will sell itself."

"Yeah," I say. "If he doesn't promote it, fine by me. Let the thing die."

I say that aloud, but I'm suspicious. Kurt is a marketing genius. He's quirky, a maverick. Yet there's nothing quirky about failing to promote a product. Something else is going on. Perhaps they'll talk outside the penthouse and concoct some eleventh-hour crackerjack plan. I set up additional alerts to notify me the instant any promo goes out for the Happy App.

After a few days, however, there's still no sign of marketing. Just endless penthouse chatter anticipating the launch. I'm continually cranking up the audio to hear better. June suggests leaving it up, even if Darah has to make herself scarce. So I do. The gist is they intend to launch ASAP. I warn the others to be prepared for that today. Beers guesses it will be more like a week.

A couple days later, instead of a launch, we catch them discussing revisions.

"They want to reprogram at this late date?" June says.

Kurt, it turns out, has received a directive from HQ. The first time we heard them mention HQ—after we'd turned on the nano mic—it took a bit to figure out who that might be. It wasn't HSys HQ, that much was clear. Then June noticed that while the Dictator's name appears in darknet messages, they never say it aloud in the penthouse. Presumably out of an abundance of caution. They use HQ as a code name instead.

Now Kurt reports HQ is unhappy with the photo programmed into the smart light.

"You saw the pic, Jedd. What could be wrong?" Beers asks.

"No clue," I say. "Let's listen; maybe they'll discuss it."

But they don't. All we can deduce is they're looking for a pic that will please HQ.

June talks back to the audio stream as if the Ks can hear her: "Idiots! You're using smart light to transmit messages to the brain. Images must be simple, familiar, recognizable."

"Sounds like this is about flattering the Dick," Beers says.

The Ks continue to debate pics, with Keith lobbying for one that's younger, more handsome.

Karin—as if she heard June—points out younger pics will be harder to recognize.

Kurt suggests adding a flattering frame. He didn't get the memo about being simple.

In the end, we aren't sure what they decide. If anything.

Beers suggests I watch the darknet site for any changes the Russians or Floridians make, but I don't see that as time well spent. All we really need to know is when the damn app launches.

New pic, old pic, flattering pic, ugly pic—I can't wait for all this to be over and done with.

As it turns out, we don't get any advanced warning. My alert—several pings in quick succession, followed by a ping-alarm—goes off as we're sitting down to breakfast the next morning.

"That's it!" I exclaim.

"What?" Darah says.

"The app. It's launched." I jump up from my waffle, spraying chia coconut syrup onto the table, and sprint to the living room. The others follow. The coffee table screen is already lit, the Happy App announcing its immediate availability for purchase. One click and it's yours! Like every other HSys app on your tablet. Only the backend of this one is on a darknet site linked to a Russian quantum computer.

I stare down at it in horror.

"Aren't you buying it, Jedd?" Beers says.

June is also waiting for me to take the plunge. "What's wrong? Did you think it wouldn't launch?"

I don't quite know what I thought. Probably I was a fool to think it would fail before launch. Or that someone at HSys would blow the Ks' cover, and then we'd be able to come forward and testify we knew about it all along. None of that has transpired. And now here it is, like any innocent new app, birthed and ready to meet the world.

"Should I buy it?"

"Of course!" they say in unison.

"Why?"

"To see how it works?" Count on June to be a master of the obvious.

"We already know that," I say.

"We don't know what they changed," she argues.

"If they changed a photo, running the app won't tell us that," I argue back.

"Dude, why are you fighting this?" she says.

"If you won't buy it, I will," Beers says, knowing full well we'd have to drive into Ucluelet so he could get online to make the purchase.

The kid volunteers to buy it on his tablet.

Since I'd rather not be an identified buyer—even in Canada—I tell him to go ahead.

He downloads the app, then passes his tablet to Beers so he can do the trial run. June, Nick, and I also take turns. Everything appears just as before. Red polar bear and all. We've learned nothing new.

"Satisfied?" I say, somewhat vindicated.

"Yes," June says. "I'm glad we checked."

"I still hate the Dick," Beers confirms. "With a passion."

"There's no reason to think it will be a hit," Nick points out.

"We don't predict that," Zack says.

"Even if it's a flop," Nick adds, "the Dictator is here to stay . . . unless some little guy comes out of nowhere and dethrones him. Like we've said all along."

We all laugh at their standing joke about the little guy from nowheresville. Beyond that, though, it's hard to disagree. The Dictator doesn't need higher favorability ratings to stay right where he is. To do what he wants. To attack California, if that's what strikes his fancy. App or no app, he has total power. He's invincible. No one is in a position to challenge that. It's depressing.

"I wonder what they're saying in the penthouse," June says.

Beers suggests we turn up the audio stream.

Again I drag my feet. I've gotten to the point where I don't give two shits what they say in the penthouse. I can't stomach any more of Kurt's gloating. "I'm sure they're celebrating. Do you really want to hear that?"

"Not really," Darah says. "I mean, not at all."

But the others won't let it go. To their credit, I should say. I'm the one flaking out.

"We owe it to ourselves, to everything we've done, to continue monitoring," June says. "Are you willing to back off now, Jedd?"

"What are you afraid of?" the kid asks.

It's a pointed question. And I have an immediate answer: nothing. Kurt's gloating may disgust me but I'm not afraid of it. On the other hand, we might hear him say something important. So I turn up the audio. Everyone stops talking so we can listen. We listen for a full five minutes. Crickets.

"They're not there," Darah says.

"Like I said, they're celebrating," I say. "Probably stayed up late partying."

June frowns. "You can't be serious. You've been around hundreds of product launches. People don't go MIA the day of a launch."

"They've got to track the ranking, monitor for bugs," Nick says.

"Which means they need to be in the penthouse," Zack adds.

"You'd think," I say. "We listened to them just fine yesterday. So there must be another explanation." I'm beginning to suspect what that is. Except I don't want to admit we've lost contact.

Beers is following my thought. "I bet the mic's dead."

June suggests I check for issues on this end.

"Or maybe," Darah says, "they drank all the rum and tossed the bottle?"

Beers lets out a whistle. "Didn't think of that."

"Except then," June says, "we'd hear broken glass at the recycle center. Or some sound wherever the mic is."

"Didn't we figure that bottle was worth tens of thousands?" Nick says.

"No empty bottle is worth that much, even with a gold stopper," June says before anyone can respond.

I do a quick mic check. "From all appearances, it's live. Just not picking up sound."

June offers to review the transcript to see what was recorded last.

While she takes my tablet and settles into the armchair, the rest of us retrieve our cold waffles, then return to the living room to finish eating them as we discuss options. Even if we can't listen to chatter in the penthouse, there's plenty else to do. Starting with checking the app's ranking. I pull up the list on our screen and everyone bends over to see where the Happy App has landed— our eyes starting at the top and moving down.

"I don't see it," Beers says.

I refresh and we all look again.

"Dude, it's not there!" Darah exclaims.

No HSys product in recent history has debuted at less than fifty among the top one hundred, so I refresh again, assuming there was a Wi-Fi glitch. We check again. Still nothing.

"Are you sure it launched?" Nick asks.

"We bought it," Zack says. "Clearly it launched."

Nor was it a soft launch, a fact I confirm with an online search. People may not be hopping and jumping to buy it, but the app is out. The only explanation I can offer is that this is what happens when a product is launched without any publicity. No promotion translates into no sales. Even a nerd like me knows that. Which brings our question full circle: Why did Kurt go that route?

June interrupts with the results of her review. Normally transcripts stop at the end of the workday, but she found something after midnight. Only one word was transcribed: "yeah." But it's confirmation the mic is still live. Like I thought.

"After midnight?" Beers says. "They were in the penthouse that late?"

"Before a launch, I don't see why not," June says.

"Then why was nothing transcribed?" Nick asks.

I don't have an answer for that, so I suggest we listen to the full recording and see what we can decipher.

June sets playback to start at midnight and we gather around to listen. It's immediately clear why no transcript was produced. The sound isn't people talking, it's music—some electro-techno mix I've never heard. It's so jarring that Dharma lets out a howl. Darah stands up and does a few dance steps, almost like she recognizes it.

Beers looks at June. "Still think this is the penthouse?"

She shoots back a *got me* look, then puts playback on fast-forward so we can search more efficiently for signs of human life. At about the one o'clock mark, the music stops and a male voice can be heard in the background. I motion to June to raise the volume.

"Yeah . . . yeah . . . uh-huh . . . ." The voice is slurred. Sounds half asleep. To be expected at this hour.

"Must be on the phone," I say.

"Who would he talk to so late?" Beers wonders.

The voice continues: "Yeah . . . done." Most of his words are too low to distinguish, then, "Yeah . . . like you said."

"Kurt can barely get a word in," Nick says.

June points out it's the first time she's heard him so muted. So uncommunicative.

Beers laughs. "Big improvement if you ask me."

"Except we need to hear more." I still can't tell if this is the penthouse. Heck, it could be a nightclub. "If Kurt—"

"It's *not* Kurt," Darah cuts in.

"What?" I turn to her, as does everyone else.

"It's not Kurt," she repeats.

The sound quality is poor, but it never occurred to me we might be listening to anyone other than Kurt.

Beers is nodding. "She's right. It's Keith."

As soon as he says that, it's obvious: Keith is a softspoken, almost monosyllabic guy, and his voice is deeper. We all should have known right away. Everyone starts speculating about how we could have mistaken his identity.

"Sounds like he's been drinking," June says.

"The rum?" Nick says.

"Dude, what else?" Zack says.

"Quiet!" Darah shushes us. "Let's listen."

By now the conversation is over. June has to backtrack so we can hear the last part again.

"Okay," Keith says, "I'll tell him . . ." Then something unintelligible. "Yeah . . . done . . . Yeah . . . like you said." And the sound cuts.

"What's that squawking noise?" the kid says.

June plays it again and we listen more closely. A screechy sound can be heard between the words.

"Sounds like a parrot," I say.

"Sounds like Keith squawking, 'Happy, happy, happy.'" Beers does a high-pitched imitation.

"Could be part of the Happy App," Nick says.

"I bet his favorite animal is a parrot," Zack says. "That's his app video."

"Or they have a parrot in the penthouse," Beers says. "Part of some promo?"

Really, we are at a loss.

June says she could care less about the parrot; she's convinced Keith is talking to HQ. "My guess is that person reports directly to the Dictator. He's confirming they made the revisions HQ wanted and the app has launched."

"We don't know that," I say.

"No we don't. I'm giving you my take."

"You still think this is the penthouse?" Beers asks.

She pauses, but only for a second. "Where else would it be?"

"I dunno. Keith's house?"

"You really think he'd call HQ from his house?"

"Why keep insisting it's HQ?" Beers counters. "He's probably talking to Kurt. Or Karin."

"He said it was *done*. As in over, done, finished. Clearly he's talking about the app to someone who needs to know that," June says.

"Or he's talking about something else."

"Like what?"

"How should I know?" Beers says. "Maybe . . . the rum."

They go back and forth for a while. In the end, all we can conclude is that we don't know. We agree to keep monitoring to see if the mic's location becomes apparent. If it is in the penthouse, that should be clear soon enough. And if it's somewhere else, well, we'll deal with that. The good news is it didn't land in the garbage, and we're still in contact with the Ks.

Over the next few days, we watch the app like hawks. It's going nowhere fast. By the end of the week, it finally makes the top one hundred. To be precise, ninety-seven. And stays there.

As much as I'd prefer never to hear another peep out of the penthouse, we really need ears there now. Hearing Kurt curse the app's poor performance would tell us all we need to know. But the nano mic has produced nothing new. Or I should say, nothing new that's meaningful. Music was recorded again, without any voices, for brief interludes on a couple of late nights. After that, silence.

Beers declares this is all the proof he needs to conclude the mic isn't in the penthouse. He doesn't want to waste any more time monitoring it.

The others aren't convinced. Nick thinks the mic could be picking up interference in the penthouse. Zack says he's heard of bizarre cases where Li-Fi messes stuff up. Technically speaking, I'm not sure that's feasible. As much as I want to agree with Beers that Kurt is cursing the app outside audio range, I have to admit other scenarios are equally likely. Bottom line, we are back where we started: we don't know what's up.

Nor can we forget this isn't just about the Ks. We're dealing with the Dictator. With his malicious whims. With his determination to crush any sign of democracy. California has been a thorn in his side, and now the news—which I still check daily—suggests he intends to recapture it. Recapture *us*.

Californians on social media laugh this off. They say the fact that there've been no deaths at the border, despite all the hype about drones programmed to kill, is evidence he only wants to annoy us. "Fight lies with laughter" is the latest buzz phrase. Let me tell you, I'm not laughing with them.

And there's his ongoing barrage of insults directed at California. A new insult every day. People here are tired of it. They brush it off as hot air and a further sign he can't do us real damage. Our democracy will protect us. I'm not falling for that either.

With the Dictator, things are never what they seem. He's all smoke and mirrors: get people to think one thing, then shock them by doing the opposite. Now he has managed to get Californians to let our guard down, to feel we're on top. That we've won. What better time to strike?

Still, it seems ludicrous to think the Happy App could be the Dictator's means to strike. An app? Seriously? I keep telling the others we have nothing to worry about. The app is doomed. It can barely hang onto last place in the top one hundred, a pitiful performance for an HSys product.

To tell the truth, I'm not nearly as certain as I let on.

Yes, we're familiar with the app's atrocious user interface, not to mention Kurt's nonexistent marketing strategy, but there's no denying the Russians' technology is among the most sophisticated on the planet. Silicon Valley may be number one overall, but the Russians own us in the arena of quantum SL. And there's a bigger problem: they're miles ahead when it comes to dealing in deviousness. For all I know, they're minutes away from launching a devastating strike.

I avoid sharing this with June or any of the others. They'd want a plan of action. Which I don't have. These worries will have to remain my burden to bear. For now.

One evening a week later, while Beers is making dinner, I check the app's ranking. It's predictable at this point: somewhere between ninety-nine and ninety-six. That's it. No rise, no fall. I'd rather see a quick demise, but I'm resigned to waiting out its slow but inevitable death.

Now as I look at my screen, I do a double take: the Happy App is at fifty-one. "Hey!" I call out. "Look at this."

A second later, they're all in the living room.

"Better be fast," Beers says. "The mac and cheese is almost out of the oven."

"Geez, it went from ninety-six to forty-nine since breakfast?" June is incredulous.

"To fifty-one," I say.

"It says forty-nine."

Before we can get into a serious bicker, I look more closely. Sure enough, the app has risen two more notches.

"What do you think's going on?" Beers looks worried.

"This sudden bump," Nick says, "why now?"

I'm at a loss to explain. But they're all looking to me for direction. Even June. "Could be Russian bot activity. Maybe that was Kurt's plan all along: see if the app took off without publicity. If it didn't, then troll up the rankings."

That's pure speculation but everyone finds it plausible. All the more so as we watch the rank jump to forty-six.

"Wowzers!" Beers wants to know if I have access to sales figures to verify what we're seeing.

"Nothing on the darknet site. I'd have to hack into HSys's

financial data. But even if we saw the numbers, it wouldn't prove anything. People have gotten away with inflating sales and similar scams for decades." As I speak, I take a sniff. "What's that?"

The kid is sniffing too. "Mac and cheese?"

"Oh shit!" Beers bellows as he darts toward the oven. I don't think I've ever seen him move so fast.

We follow so we can continue tossing around ideas as Beers scrapes off the burnt edges and dishes the surviving mac onto our plates, along with kale from the garden.

The twins think we should continue to lay low. When the app gets past this false bump in rankings, it'll self-destruct. They point out that fake sales won't achieve the Ks' goal. The Dictator doesn't gain anything if a million more fake people like him.

June feels we don't have enough info. "If this rise is due to bot activity, then laying low makes sense. But what if their strategy is to boil the frog so people's beliefs change gradually enough to go unnoticed until—tada!—they've reached critical mass?"

She's right, there are many possibilities, and we need more info to assess them. I suggest we take our food into the living room because I have an idea I'd like to try.

When everyone is settled, I say, "Okay, I'm programming a trip into Ucluelet."

"Now?" Beers is surprised.

"Yep, this can't wait. No guarantees, but it's worth a try."

"I take it we're not buying supplies," he says. "Or having a few drinks at the pub."

"What do you want us to do?" Darah asks.

"Research. We're going online to assess chatter about the app. We need to find out what's driving its sudden rise." I explain I'm creating temp anonymous IDs for everyone. Yes, we could do this from the farm. Going to Ucluelet is precautionary in case anyone slips up.

"Sounds ambitious," June says.

"It is. That's why we need all hands on deck. We're going to dig deep enough to distinguish between bot responses and genuine human reviews."

Even before we've finished the mac and cheese, we pick up our tablets and get to work. Kitchen cleanup will have to wait. June, Beers, and I gather around the coffee table, while Darah and the kid sit on the rug. The twins are on the small couch. I will also keep an eye on the app's ranking. It's still on an upward trajectory: forty-one is the highest I've seen.

After about an hour, we stop to compare findings.

"I see no reviews in California before yesterday," Darah says. "Now there are a ton."

"Same for Canada," says June. "All the reviews are recent and not fake. People are talking about their experiences, tallying their happiness points, praising the app."

"There's a huge buzz in the States," Beers says.

"#happy is trending like crazy," the kid says.

"Some dude claimed he has a thousand happiness points," Darah says.

"I saw someone claiming a hundred thousand points," Beers says.

None of this is good news. If it's a real and sustained buzz, the app might be taking off. For real. It took a while to get here because Kurt—or someone in his ear—decided against even the most basic advertising, but now we could be on the verge of realizing our worst nightmare.

June points out the app's focus on happiness builds on the HSys mandate for nonviolent game genres. People like that. They trust it. The Ks are leveraging that trust. Which makes the app's true purpose all the more subversive.

"Listen to this," Nick says. "'Clean fun, getting this app for my kids.'"

"At least no one's posting about the Dictator," Darah says, looking for a positive spin.

June reminds her that may show up after people have used the app longer. And they wouldn't associate it with the app.

"Here's a good one," Beers says. "This guy—Roadkill is the handle—likes the app because it doesn't pretend to be smart."

Not only is that the height of irony but it blows our theory out of the water. We've been counting on the app's stupidity to cause its failure, not skyrocket it to success.

June voices the question on all our minds: "How is this even possible?"

"It's possible," I say, "because people *can* be that dumb. They can be outright ignorant."

After batting this around for a while, we realize stupidity is the only explanation. It's how the Dictator got into power in the first place. We were so sure no one would fall for his bullshit, but then it happened. Just as it did years ago with one of his predecessors. Only worse now.

Each of his moves—targeting people of color and women and immigrants and scientists and political dissidents and ultimately democracy itself—seemed like it must be the limit. People were too savvy, too decent, too woke; they'd know where to draw the line. They'd realize what was at stake. But they didn't. They unquestioningly bought into things that were against their own best interests. They willingly gave up their rights. What could be more stupid? We so much wanted to believe they were smarter than that, yet time and again they proved us wrong.

What we're seeing now depends on the same broad base of stupidity. Regardless of its sophisticated technology, the app appeals to the lowest common denominator. And if anyone thought gen beta would bail us out, that's not happening.

"Users don't even need to feel happier to keep using the app," Nick says. "They'll use it simply because everyone else is using it."

"Yeah," Zack adds, "it's enough for them to be *told* it makes them happier."

"What I don't get," says Darah, "is why Californians don't know better."

"You have to remember," June says, "they think this was created by a trusted Silicon Valley tech company."

"There's no reason to associate this app with the Dick," Beers adds.

That is all true.

We go back into another session of research, working into the wee hours to see what else we can learn about the app's appeal. By the time we're ready to turn in, all we've done is reinforce our original conclusions. The app is taking off. No doubt about it, the buzz is spreading like a solar storm around the world. I was so sure it would fail because no one would buy something so dumb, and now I'm eating my words. People actually like it *because* it looks dumb. The world doesn't realize it yet, but the Dictator has scored a huge victory.

By morning, the app has reached the top ten. Everyone wants to try it. People are blogging and vlogging about it. Major news outlets are posting articles about it. HSys stock is going through the roof.

"Oh my god!" is all I can say as I join the others for breakfast. Having never entertained the possibility the app would succeed, let alone in a massive way, I gave no thought to how we might handle that. Now I have no idea where to start. I feel utterly powerless. That's what I tell everyone.

"Prepare yourself, bro. It'll make number one," Beers says.

He's right. By the end of the day, the Happy App is the world's top-selling game. With no sign of peaking.

We sit around in the living room, despondent. Beers offers half-heartedly to make popcorn with caramel, but no one is interested. He slumps in the armchair and Darah leans against his legs, her knees up, and buries her head in her arms.

The kid stares at his flute, on the rug in front of him.

Dharma nudges my elbow, as if he feels responsible for raising the mood.

Nobody says anything.

"Looks like it'll stay number one," I say finally. "The Dictator must have known all along it would catch on."

"That's why he told Kurt to skip the PR," June says, then adds, "Good thing the mic worked long enough for us to deduce that."

"Good thing we can't hear their happy hour celebrations now," Beers says.

June ignores his corollary and continues: "They knew one blast of the smart light wouldn't be enough. It needs extended exposure. With everyone talking about the app and so many using it, the effect will be cumulative."

"Which means," I say, "what we're about to witness is not a sudden, artificial favorable swing in the Dictator's direction but a slow-building, long-lasting groundswell. It's exactly what he wants."

For us, it's the absolute worst scenario. Total defeat. None of us, not even NicknZack, saw this coming. I have no idea what we are going to do now.

Draupadi set her plan in motion. Touching Keechaka's arm, she said, "You shall have what you desire. My husbands need not know. Wait for me late tonight in the king's dance hall."

UNDERCOVER: Darah

I can't sleep. If I doze off, I'll have a nightmare. One of *those* nightmares. It's been a while since I had one, and I thought I had them beat. Until tonight.

I pull the covers over my head and lie in bed, trying to come to terms with what is happening. The Happy App is a bestseller. Millions around the world are using it. Probably soon to be billions. As Jedd said, the Dictator has won. I can't imagine better fodder for nightmares.

Before today, you could assume Mericans not standing up or speaking out publicly didn't mean they lacked reasonable feelings and opinions. Within their hearts and minds, most were as horrified as you were. Now even that inner world has been invaded by the Dictator. And people have no idea. Really, that's the scariest part. If I found out my mind had been breached like that, I don't know what I'd do. It freaks me out to imagine walking down a crowded street where everyone harbors warm feelings about the Dictator. And not just Mericans. Now Californians are also falling under his power.

Even more insane is the fact that we're the only ones able to fix it. Well, obviously not *me*. Jedd and the others.

Except I'm not sure I want them to try. This might sound like privilege talking, but I've finally found peace on the farm. Life in exile is good here. I play the flute every day, help in the garden, chill up at Boulder Point. I'm winning my battle against toxic thoughts. If I hear the others being negative, I go off in nature and reconstitute my golden armor. All this is progress I'm not willing to give up.

No closer to sleep, I decide to make kava rose tea. I wrap myself in my pattu shawl, then tiptoe down the stairs. As I round the corner, I see Beers's light on.

I can't imagine these past weeks without Beers. He talked me into late-night movies. It was the fluff my nerves needed, and he knew that. He's always been the brother I never had, and now we're even closer. If you told me we'd be cuddling, I'd have said no way. Of course, they're innocent snuggles. No sex. I don't recall Beers dating, so this has been good for him too.

I tap on his door and he opens, surprised to see me still up.

"I can't sleep," I say.

"Me either. Too flippin' *mad*!" His eyes are puffy and he's practically frothing at the lips. Usually he damps down his anger for my sake. Not now.

I sit on his corduroy couch and listen as he rants about how the Dick will own California, own our minds. How we're totally fucked. I want to talk him down, but he's not wrong.

"Don't ask for a positive spin on this," he says, anticipating my pushback. "There isn't one. You're gonna have to suck it up, face shit like it is."

That puts me on defense. I'm listening, giving him space to vent. That has to count for something. "You want to fight over who's angrier?" I retort. Not that it's a fight I'd win.

In response, he grabs a blood orange—one I picked off the tree by the barn so he could enjoy it—from his end table and tosses it from one hand to the other. Nervously, like he wants to weaponize it. I step forward and take a swipe at the orange. If he's not going to eat it, I want it back. But he catches it in one hand and holds it out of my reach, closing his fist around it like a vise. His nose and then his wholes face turns red as he squeezes, slowly, deliberately, mercilessly. Pulp oozes between his fingers as the juice drips onto the rug. I know what he's thinking: *This is the Dick. I'm pulverizing him.*

That does it. I mean, how will destroying a piece of fruit solve anything? I pick up a bath towel draped over the couch and thrust it toward him. "Dude, clean up your mess."

Downstairs I make my tea, then take it to the sunroom and drink it in the dark. The kava, along with the pattering of rain on the glass roof, calms me. Restores my golden armor. Too bad Beers isn't a fan of kava.

It annoys me he said to suck it up. Like I haven't been. Like I can't be tough when I need to be. Like I'm useless. He has no idea. In fact, I'm sitting on a huge secret: the nano mic. No one has figured out why it stopped recording properly after the app launched. Jedd thinks it's still in the penthouse. Everyone except Beers agrees. They're wrong. It's not there. The parrot was a dead giveaway. And the electro-techno mix. I tried to act like I'd never heard it in Keith's helmet. Only thing I couldn't do was let them think that was Kurt speaking. Kurt, really?

Telling them everything I know would mean revealing how I know it. Which I can't. Even if keeping quiet hurts our cause.

We need a reliable flow of info to have any chance of stopping the app, of stopping Kurt and the Dictator. Of stopping the theft and desecration of our democracy. Ultimately that's what's at stake.

I have the power to help. If I can figure out how to use it.

Draining my last drops of kava, it occurs to me that learning where the mic is has no value for Jedd. What matters is that it's reliably recording sound. Which means I don't have to divulge my secret. All I have to do is make the mic work again.

With that, I have an idea.

It's the middle of the night, but this can't wait. I wrap my shawl more tightly around me, put on my tall boots, find an umbrella and flashlight, and go out the back door. It's cold and wet as I cross the field, so blustery the umbrella is useless. No light is on in the barn. Even knowing I will wake the kid, I crack open the barn door.

He hears me instantly. "Who's there?"

"It's me."

"Darah?"

I apologize for waking him.

"What's up?" He lights his lantern so I can climb the ladder, then helps me over the top rung. "You're soaked."

I remove my boots and sit down on the rug. He takes a blanket from his bed and throws it over my shawl. "What's up?" he asks again.

"I wouldn't bother you if this wasn't important," I say. "Are you getting supplies in Mountain View tomorrow?"

I know what he's thinking: *Why do you need to know now?* But he confirms he is.

I pause. "Can I ask a favor?"

"Sure."

"Take me with you."

Even in the dim light, I can see his eyebrows draw close. "You aren't planning to run away?"

I promise I'm not. And reiterate my need to go into town. I realize I'm not telling him much.

He responds by saying I don't have to leave the farm. He'll get whatever I need.

"I don't need you to get anything."

I can feel him trying to figure this out. If I don't need anything, why am I insisting on doing something that's off-limits? "Okay," he says, "you want to meet someone."

"Please don't ask who," I say, admitting he's not wrong. "Just let me come with you."

For a long moment he doesn't say anything. Then he agrees.

I stand up and hand back the blanket, then put on my boots and step toward the ladder. He is already under his covers when I look back. "One more thing. Nobody can know I'm going."

"Understood," he says. "Get some sleep. We'll figure it out tomorrow."

When I meet the kid at the barn for a flute lesson in the morning, I expect him to say he's reconsidered and won't take me to town. But no, if anything he's more supportive, almost conspiratorial. He suggests we go in the evening. I can slip out during kitchen cleanup, go to the car, and he will join me shortly. No one will suspect I'm gone.

If the kid thinks less of me for sneaking around, he doesn't say so. Most likely I'm the one judging myself. I feel bad lying to Jedd, jeopardizing our safety. I have to keep reminding myself this for his benefit. For everyone's benefit. Maybe the kid intuits that.

After dinner I excuse myself. "I don't know why, but I'm really fatigued," I say. "Going to turn in early."

It's an obvious lie but no one questions me. I dash up to the attic and change into dark clothes. As I throw on my black soysilk cloak and slip a pair of shield sunglasses into its pocket, I visualize my golden armor surrounding me, strong and impervious. I can do this. No one may believe it, but I can.

I step into an old pair of biocouture mules, then tiptoe down the back stairs and out to the car. I can hear the others in the kitchen, laughing as they clean up. As far as they're concerned, I'm safely tucked in bed.

The drive to Mountain View is uneventful. It's weird zipping along a road after all these weeks, not to mention as a passenger in my own car. The kid has to be wondering what I'm up to. But he doesn't ask. He parks in the market lot, and we agree to meet in forty-five minutes, an hour max. He makes me promise to be prompt. The others are waiting for their supplies.

As soon as he disappears into the market, I get out of the car and survey the scene. People are going about their business, picking up groceries, chatting with friends, window-shopping after dinner out. A woman gets into a yellow aero car parked next to us and lifts off. It's an ordinary evening. No one is lurking, waiting to expose me.

I realize there's one place Keith might be: El Carnal. He once said that bar is his go-to after work. It's just down the block, on the route to his condo.

I pull up the hood of my cloak—though it's a dry evening—and hurry along the sidewalk, weaving between people. A man is holding his tablet inches from his face. A teen is laughing as she hops off the hoverboard she just landed. A couple outside the hyperloop station sway to music I can't hear. Could these all be users of the Happy App, their minds brimming with pleasant notions of the Dictator? I don't want to think about that now.

Inside El Carnal, I let my eyes adjust to the darkness. Sure enough, there is Keith, seated alone at the bar, nursing a drink. There's still time to slip out unnoticed, abort this insane mission. I take a deep breath, spot check and reinforce my armor, and push my hood back onto my shoulders.

As I come up behind Keith, I say hi. Quietly so he has to turn to see who it is.

"Darah!" He looks me up and down, clearly taken aback. Hesitating as if he doesn't want to say the wrong thing. "I thought you were on a special project?" He last saw me running away from my almost-naked hologram, but he's going with the official HSys position that I'm still an employee, just out of town with my pod. If he knows we fled to Canada, he doesn't let on.

I answer in a way that supports both narratives. "Yeah,

here for a few days taking care of personal stuff, leaving in the morning."

"Cool." He motions to the empty stool beside him. "Join me?"

I take a whiff of his drink. "Whisky on the rocks? We can do better!"

"Sure." He laughs, raising a hand to signal the bartender. "You name it."

Time to put my plan into action. I lean in, head close to his, and lay a hand on his arm. It goes against every instinct, but I do it. Without flinching. "No. I mean *you* have something better."

He startles. "Me?"

"Yes, you." I give his arm a little squeeze. "Like . . . five-star rum maybe?"

Now he's getting the idea: I'm hitting on him. He's pleasantly surprised. A quick last swig of his whiskey and he stands up. "Hell yeah. I still have some of the really good stuff. Let's get out of here."

He reaches to put his arm around me, but I'm already two steps ahead, moving toward the door.

It takes five minutes to get to his condo. I'm keeping track of time. So far so good. As soon as he leads me into his bedroom, the holographic parrot starts squawking. Like before. Except now I realize I heard it wrong. It's not "Happy! Happy! Happy!" It's "Happy App! Happy App! Happy App!" I guess Keith never thought I'd catch on.

He's already peeling off his shirt. Like me, he's in a rush. But for a very different reason.

I kick off my shoes and drop my cloak by the door and scan the room. If it weren't for the light of the frigging holographic parrot cage, we'd be in total darkness. The bed is unmade, and dirty clothes are piled on the floor. An assortment of liquor bottles crowds the light cage on the nightstand.

Keith is reaching for me, and I have to think fast.

"Where's the rum?" I whisper. If the mic is here, it will pick up my voice. This has to be a conversation with very few words. Fortunately Keith is known for his economy of speech.

"Rum?" Either he's already forgotten or he took that as merely my code for hooking up.

I break away from him so I can examine the bottles. I have no plan B if the rum isn't among them. Thank god it is. I pick up the large square bottle with its gold bird head stopper and hold it to the light. It's almost empty. *Almost.* A day or two and this would be a vastly different scenario.

Triumphant but silent, I wave the bottle in front of Keith.

"Yeah, that's the good stuff." He's trying to humor me, sitting on the bed with his pants unzipped, hand on his crotch, while I obsess over his rum. "Your buddies liked it."

I walk toward the dresser, my back to Keith, pretending to study the bottle as best I can in the dim light. My finger searches for a small piece of tape on the label. A couple passes over the surface and I feel it in the lower left corner. I'm worried it will be hard to peel off, but one flick of my thumbnail does the job. I grip the mic firmly between my thumb and index finger, hoping that will mute it. Then I spin around to face Keith and gesture with the bottle. "May I?"

"Be my guest."

Standing at the foot of the bed, holding the bottle high, I mime pouring rum into a glass. It looks like I'm curving my left hand to form a glass, but really I'm clutching the mic. I need Keith to bring me a glass, but I don't want to say it aloud. I raise my invisible glass and drink some invisible rum. As sexy as I can.

He plays along. He has some shot glasses, he says.

I set the bottle on the nightstand, then lie down on the far side of the bed. I pull up the sheet as if I'm eager to get under the covers. To get this party started. He can't have any doubt that I'm all in.

He hitches up his pants and heads toward the kitchen.

As soon as he's out of the room, I jump into high gear. Everything is going as planned. I found Keith. The rum bottle is here. The mic is in my hand. And I got Keith out of the room without saying more than a few words. But none of this will matter if I can't get the mic where it needs to go.

I have a plan for that.

As I was counting on him to do, Keith took off his shirt. I pick it up from the floor and check the pocket. He likes to keep his mini tablet there so people can see its handsome holographic snakeskin case peeking out. Sure enough, there it is now. I open the case and carefully apply the mic to the back of the inside flap. I was worried it might not be sticky enough to read here. But it is. Of course now we will be recording all his activities, but that's the only way I can think of to get the mic back to the penthouse. Keith's a pretty quiet guy, so maybe there won't be any embarrassing moments. And if there are, who cares? I close the case, return it to his pocket, and drop the shirt back on the floor.

The sound of running water in the kitchen suggests Keith has located the glasses and is rinsing them off. With mere seconds to spare, I grab my shoes and cloak and speed-tiptoe down the hallway. His back is to me as I pass the kitchen, and the sound of the water gives me cover. I crack open the front door and slip out, leaving it slightly ajar to avoid the click of it closing.

Still barefoot, I sprint down the walkway, past the other condo entrances, around the corner, along the far end of the pool, and out through the condo gates. Only here do I stop, breathing heavily, and look over my shoulder. No sign of Keith.

He must have discovered by now that I've bolted. Most likely he assumes I had second thoughts about hooking up and figures it's not worth pursuing me. He has no idea that hookup was *never* going to happen. Nor any idea what I've pulled off. He's probably putting his shirt back on, making sure his tablet is secure in the pocket. Yes, I'm the one in control now.

I step into my mules, put on my cloak, and draw the hood low over my face. This might be the moment for sunglasses. But when I put my hand in my pocket, it's empty. They must have slipped out in my rush to leave Keith's bedroom. A small price to pay.

It's just past the forty-minute mark when I reach the car. The kid is waiting in the driver's seat, nibbling protein chips, getting in a few bites ahead of Beers.

He smiles at me as I sit beside him and close the passenger door. "Ready?"

"Let's go home."

Really, the kid is hard to read. I'm not sure if he thinks he knows where I went or he just doesn't care. Most likely he suspects I saw a boyfriend. That's okay. Let him think whatever he wants as long as he's willing to keep my secret.

As we approach the farm, it's not that late but I feel fatigue setting in. Real fatigue this time. Espionage is exhausting. But it will be worth it when I watch Jedd and the others realize they have live sound in the penthouse again.

Ideally I'd wait a few days to lessen the chance of June rewinding the audio stream and putting two and two together. However, considering the circumstances, I'll take that risk. First thing tomorrow I'll find a way to tip them off.

*As he surveyed the Kurukshetra battlefield, Arjuna said,
"O Krishna, drive my chariot between the two opposing armies. I
need to have a good look at these warriors I am supposed to fight."*

CONSENSUS: June

For the first time since we've been cooped up, Beers doesn't make breakfast. No waffles, no scramble, not even coffee. He shrugs it off when he comes downstairs and finds the twins and me waiting in the kitchen. Darah isn't up yet.

I make myself instant coffee and bring it into the living room, where Jedd is already staring at the Happy App's ranking.

He doesn't try to mask his gloom. Nothing has changed. The app is on track to become the biggest craze of the decade. Of the century. It was translated into a dozen new languages overnight. This very instant, zillions of brain cells around the globe are being sizzled by its smart light—even as the users have no idea that's happening. Which of course was the Ks' plan: clothe sophisticated technology in a deceptively simple package and let her rip.

Who'd have imagined some dumb app could put the final nail in the coffin of democracy.

Judging by the lack of recent activity on the darknet site, the Russians and Floridians consider their jobs done. Still, new products never get everything a hundred percent. This app should require at least one update. Probably sooner than later. Which will generate new chatter on the site. Since we lost audio, the site is our only source of info, our only link to the penthouse.

Jedd and I are grumbling about the malfunctioning nano mic when Darah joins us. She looks ragged. If I didn't know better, I'd say she's hung over from too much partying. In fact, she went to bed right after dinner. Maybe she's hung over from too much sleep.

Instead of telling her she looks like crap, I ask how she's doing.

She ignores my question and instead asks, "When did you last check the mic?"

Jedd tells her we've given up. There's been no meaningful sound, nothing transcribed. Continued checking is a waste of time.

She suggests another try.

Jedd shakes his head. "These mics are flimsy. It was going on the fritz sooner or later."

"Hey," I say. "Get yourself some breakfast. You'll feel better."

She opens her mouth as if to dispute that, then stops herself and retreats to the kitchen. A few minutes later she's back with a platter of fruit, which she sets on the table for us to share. As she bites into an apple, she turns to me. "Did you try yet, June?"

"Try what?"

"The mic."

It's pointless, but she's not giving up. So I pull up the audio stream, check the settings, and turn it on. Just to humor her.

And lo and behold, we have sound.

The three of us let out a collective whoop. To be honest, had there been more than a few seconds of dead air, I wouldn't have left it on.

Beers and the twins come running.

"The mic works!" Jedd is practically bouncing on the couch. "Don't ask me how."

"You mean it really never left the penthouse?" Beers says.

"Sure sounds like it." No point making this into a gotcha moment.

"I didn't know you were still checking," Beers says.

"We weren't." I point to Darah. "This is all on her."

The twins ask if she's getting psychic.

Darah brushes that off, says it's about not giving up so easily. "I checked the KnoMor data daily for weeks. Right up till Jedd's investigation."

Nick suspects the mic never stopped working, even if the sound was too poor to transcribe.

"Let's rewind, see what we missed," Zack says.

That's a great idea but Jedd is already on it, bent over the table, listening intently, motioning for us to be quiet and do the same.

The first voice to emerge over the crosstalk is Kurt's. "I told you, didn't I?" he roars. "The whole world wants us!"

Hearing his boastful, bellicose voice almost makes me wish the mic stayed dead. Yet we need to hear what he's saying. Even Darah, who usually walks away from anything to do with the Ks, is spellbound as Kurt goes on about the glories of the app, about the accolades flowing in from all corners of the globe.

His words are punctuated by a repetitive "Yeah . . . yeah . . . yeah" from Keith. Though he's a softspoken dude, and this sounds like under-the-breath muttering, Keith is coming through louder than everyone else. He must be in the kitchenette, literally hugging the rum bottle.

Donna starts talking about how they're in a position to take control of HSys. Their pod will seize company profits. I've been so focused on what the app is doing within people's brains, how perceptions of the Dictator might change, that I'd almost forgotten about her. Clearly she's been biding her time, ready to cash in. The app is her gateway to personal, professional, and political gain. As it is for the Ks. No wonder all of them are so psyched.

"What's our next step?" Keith booms over the others. This

isn't softspoken Keith. I'm beginning to wonder if extended exposure to smart light can alter personality. Make a reticent person bombastic, for example. If so, we're even more screwed than I imagined.

Kurt says HQ will put their plan in motion as soon as the adoption rate reaches a certain percentage. Which is being calculated through algorithms for market penetration and degrees of exposure. He almost sounds like he knows what he's talking about.

Beers asks Jedd if he's seen any such algorithm on the darknet site.

He says no. But if HQ ordered it, he wouldn't expect to see it. They don't need Russian assistance to run adoption algorithms.

The download rate is eighty percent, Donna says. Better yet is the two hundred percent increase in the favorability index. She doesn't say favorable to what or whom. But we know.

As Kurt and the others cheer, I nudge Jedd. "That's pure mumbo-jumbo." He quickly dials back the audio so I don't have to speak over it. "The app works subliminally, activating biases in the left temporal lobe. Even if it succeeds, it's happening below people's threshold of awareness. Huge swings in the population couldn't happen so fast. It's impossible." I don't mention my speculation about personality changes. I don't want anyone getting unnecessarily worked up.

"So you doubt their results?" Beers says.

"Damn straight I do. This is HQ. His people aren't capable of legit research."

The others are nodding.

"June's right. They're using fake stats as an excuse to push their plans," Jedd says.

"We need to know what those plans are," Beers says.

Jedd turns up the audio again just as Kurt gets to HQ's plans. "Begins with a blackout of California. Wipe them off the grid so fast they won't know what hit 'em."

He doesn't say much more, but he doesn't have to. Beers is already filling in the gaps. "Holy crap! The Dick will control everything once the grid comes back up."

"No one will have a clue what happened," I say.

"What a fucking catastrophe!" Beers is wiping his brow as the enormity hits him. "We'll be at his mercy, struggling to secure basics, like water and electricity and Wi-Fi. Forget about democracy."

"It'll be a digital-age bloodless coup," Jedd says.

"That's the app's purpose," I say. "If people's subconscious minds see the Dictator as their savior, they won't resist. Except he's banking on it working much, much faster than I'd predict."

By this point, chatter in the penthouse has shifted to the best Mountain View restaurant to hit up for ribs, so I volunteer to monitor the audio while Jedd watches the darknet site and the others go about their chores.

When I hear the Ks leaving for lunch, I decide to take a break myself. Stepping into an old pair of self-cleaning shoes, I venture outside. It's drizzling but not too wet for a run. I sprint up and down the driveway, leaping over small potholes, skirting the big ones. The terrain is more like a pockmarked battlefield than a track. At least it's not as muddy as the twins' perimeter trail. As I complete my second loop, heavy drops start falling, so I abort the run and return to my post at the audio stream.

Though it's been less than an hour, Kurt is talking. Obviously they wouldn't take the rum bottle with them. So either they never left the penthouse or they're speed eaters. Even if they opted for takeout when they got there, they'd still be driving back to HSys. I should know; I lived that crunch-time scenario more times than I'd like to recall.

As I dial up the volume, Beers comes in from the kitchen, where he's been trying to redeem himself for breakfast. Followed by the twins. Darah and the kid are in the barn.

Kurt appears to have new info. The latest stats, he says, confirm they've reached their target adoption rate.

The response in the penthouse is animated: "Woohoo!" "Hit the big one!" "Time for the killer app?" All against Keith's incessant "yeah, yeah, yeah" and a dull roar in the background that makes everything harder to hear.

"Hold on," Kurt says. There's a pause, presumably as he checks his tablet.

"What's all that background noise?" Beers asks.

"That dull roar?" Jedd is wondering too.

"Sounds like the ocean," Nick says.

"Sounds like traffic," Jedd says.

Traffic in the penthouse, seriously? I'm about to ask if he's forgotten the windows don't open, but Jedd is hushing us so we can hear Kurt.

"HQ wants an update to the app," we hear him say.

"Now?" Karin sounds frustrated. "It's already done what it's supposed to do."

Kurt grunts what sounds like a—rare for him—admission of ignorance, then quickly adds, "Doesn't matter. We do what they tell us. You know that."

"Okay, okay. Send me the ask and I'm on it," Karin says.

There are a few muffled words, followed by what—if I didn't know better—I'd say was the sound of a car door slamming shut. Then the audio stream goes quiet. Even the background noise mysteriously disappears. I assume Karin is busy drafting instructions for their colleagues in Russia. The others must have left for a late lunch.

I make a mental note to talk to Jedd about using a nano camera if we ever, god forbid, find ourselves in a similar situation. Sound alone is too confusing. Then I wonder aloud what this update could be.

"Maybe a more flattering photo," Jedd says.

"Anyone catch that about a killer app?" Beers asks.

"Sure did," I say.

The others shake their heads.

But I could swear I heard it. What comes to mind is an app that uses smart light to stimulate murderous instincts in the brain. Or that can kill target populations by paralyzing critical neuro-cognitive centers. All of which sounds extreme, so I just say I want to know more about the update.

"One way to find out," Jedd says, turning his attention back to the darknet site. After a short while, he reports a message posted by Karin. No technical specs, only a basic request to the Russians. In a nutshell, the updated app has to deliver a double whammy: not only must it boost the Dictator's favorability ratings, but it must whip up a frenzy of hate against California.

"Like that'll make us #happy?" Beers scoffs.

We all agree it sounds nuts.

Leave it to the Dictator to come up with something batshit crazy. I try to imagine how this could work. The smart light could stimulate aggression by targeting the ventromedial hypothalamus while simultaneously presenting images of California. That might create some degree of self-loathing among Californians. Not so sure what effect it would have on others around the world. Alternatively, they might reverse-engineer those anti-aggression therapies that stop bullies from getting pleasure out of bullying. Theoretically, that could be achieved by decreasing basal forebrain activation and increasing lateral habenula neuronal firing. Both shady hypotheses, I know. Really, I'm at a loss. Not wanting the others to jump on me for snowing them yet again with pseudo-neuroscience, I simply say, "When you use smart light to mess with the brain, who knows what'll happen."

Beers wonders what pics they'll use.

"A map of California?" Nick says.

Zack suggests California poppies.

"For what?" Beers counters. "To make them hate poppies?"

But Jedd is shaking his head. "This is seriously flawed. What's to prevent the app's signals from getting crossed in the brain and generating a frenzy of hatred toward the Dictator?"

"Like that's a problem?" Beers says.

"Of course not," Jedd says with half a laugh. "My point is we're talking about more than a minor update."

"Which works in our favor," I say.

"Precisely," Jedd says. "Gives us more time to prepare our response."

Beers's eyebrows shoot up. "Dude, what response? Update or no update, the app is out there. It's not like we can do anything to stop it."

Like Beers, I flash my brows at Jedd. This is out of our league. No matter that we're the best at what we do, we're not stopping it.

But Jedd has other ideas. To him, nothing is out of our league. "I argued against taking action before because I was sure the app would fail on its own. But I was wrong. Now we're in a unique position to stop it. And by stopping it, to stop the attack on California. This is a new reality," he insists. "We haven't even begun to think about how to proceed."

"To be clear," Beers says, "you want us to take action?"

"I do."

"Like what?" I say. It's hard to imagine how we could deter an attack on California.

Nick searches Zack's face for ideas.

"Warn our families?" Zack says.

Jedd is shaking his head. "If we reach out to family, they'll become targets too. However, if we do what I'm proposing, none of that will be necessary."

We stare at him, trying to figure out what he has in mind.

"You mean hack the app?" Beers says.

"That's what we need to discuss."

Beers gets up and heads to the porch, where he gives the windchimes a vigorous shaking. He hasn't been in the kitchen, so it would be premature to summon the others for food. When I ask, he says, "If hacking the app is up for discussion, all of us need to be here."

A minute later, Darah rushes in, followed by the kid. They drop their wet jackets and muddy shoes by the door, all the while sniffing for a hint of what's cooking.

Beers clarifies this isn't about lunch. We're here to talk as a family.

We've been sitting in a circle for the past hour. So far all we can agree on is that we have a decision to make. Even if that decision is to do nothing. Much of the discussion has been between Jedd and Beers, and it hasn't been fruitful. The kid hasn't said a word. Not that I'd expect him to; he's probably only sticking around for the food. We'll have to eat eventually. All of us are starving, but no one wants to admit it.

Sensing our frustration, Jedd steps into his leadership shoes. "Let's drill down. This isn't about whether there's a killer app out there that will end civilization as we know it. Or whether the bunker must have spotted the darknet site and started monitoring the Russians. Or how little HSys employees know about quantum SL, since the company has yet to use it in any products. Or any of the other stuff we've been tossing around. I know I'm as guilty as anyone for going down those rabbit holes. But it's time to get serious."

"What are you suggesting?" I ask.

"I'm saying we have to take the Dictator seriously," Jedd says. "He has a secret weapon, an app using mind control that will eviscerate democracy if it isn't stopped."

"Bro, we know that," Beers cuts in. "And we are taking it seriously. Question is, what do you want us to do about it?"

"It's not what *I* want. It's what we all want." Jedd stops and I sense he's stalling because he isn't clear what that is. The only thing that's crystal clear is we all have very different ideas.

"Then let's approach this democratically," I say.

"You mean go around the circle?" Beers says.

"Yes. We can each speak our mind, say what course of action we recommend. Get all our ideas out on the table. Then decide what's the right action." Since we've been in exile, our discussions have been spitballing sessions, without the need for a formal consensus. That worked because we were in a holding pattern, waiting for the app to self-destruct. Time was on our side. Now time has run out.

Jedd sets the ground rules. Everyone will listen and only ask clarifying questions. No judgment or censorship. He hopes this will get us unstuck, allow us to reach a consensus.

Beers volunteers to go first. He stands up and immediately walks back what he said earlier, that there's nothing we can do. There *is* something, he says, and we must do it. "This is killing me!" His voice thunders across the room as if it were a stadium. I've never seen him so riled up. He's literally panting with fury. "I'm a prisoner in my own home! We gotta *do* something to take back our lives!"

"Okay," Jedd says. "Like what?"

"Like . . ." He hesitates but only for a second. "Plant a bomb."

The twins jump. "A bomb? You don't mean a real one?"

Beers says that's what he means: a real bomb. He sits down abruptly, recognizing this will be a hard sell. But he's rolling now, not about to let our opposition sway him. "I'm not talking about a mass event. Just a simple device, homemade ingredients, easy to assemble, easy to deliver. Maybe we can't take out the Dick or stop him from seizing California, but we can do some damage. Move on his people. Really fuck with them. Those Ks won't see it coming, guaranteed."

The rest of us stare at him in disbelief.

"If this is about killing people," Nick says, "count us out."

"No way," Zack adds.

But Beers won't let it go. These are desperate times, he says. Our anger has to fuel our response. We need strong, explosive action. He says he has a plan but doesn't want to lay out too many details because he doesn't expect us to be directly involved. "I'm willing to carry the burden, do whatever it takes. Those fuckers aren't getting away with this shit—"

The twins jump up before Beers can finish.

When Jedd asks where they're going, Nick grabs Zack's arm and moves him toward the door. "Like we said, we won't be party to violence."

"Hold on." Jedd jumps up as if he intends to physically block their exit. Except he does it with words. "No one here is agreeing to violence. That's a given. But we did agree to let each person speak and to hear each other out. Can you do that?"

NicknZack exchange looks, communicating as they do between them. If they walk out now, any consensus will be dead in the water.

"Your thoughts are important to all of us," I say. "Please stay." They must know I also have zero tolerance for violence. It's an inherently undemocratic form of action.

Reluctantly they sit back down.

Jedd turns back to Beers. "Do you want to say more?" It's a polite question, phrased not to fault anyone, while keeping the process on track.

Beers wipes the sweat from his brow, though it's anything but hot in the room. "Not right now. You go ahead."

Jedd looks at the twins, then veers back to Beers. "This isn't comfortable for any of us, bro. I know it wasn't easy for you to put it out there like you just did. So thank you. But before we move on, I want to clarify: If the rest of us come to a consensus that differs from your preferred action, will you support it?"

Beers pauses, and I sense he wants to leave his options open. He's already indicated he won't wait for a thumbs-up from us to act however he sees fit. Withholding support now would make it easier to do his own thing, if it comes to that. Nevertheless he doesn't push it. "If everyone supports a decision," he says, "even if I don't agree, I will support it, yes. I understand that's the democratic way."

With that, we move on to the twins. Nick says he'll speak for both. "We already said what we won't support. Here's what we will. Let me pose it as a question: Why not stay here and chill, like we've been doing?"

"We like it here," Zack throws in.

I honestly didn't expect this from the twins. From Darah, yes, but not these two. I thought they'd defer to Jedd, ask him to propose a plan, then declare their support. From Jedd's clenched lips, I see he wasn't expecting this either. Chilling isn't his idea of a plan. But he encourages them to keep talking.

Nick explains it's taken time to adjust to being in exile, but we have. In a sense, we're over the worst. Of course we miss our amenities, but at least we're safe. That counts for a lot. "If the Dictator annexes California," he says, "we can ride it out. The farm is remote, and we can exist entirely off the grid if need be."

Jedd and I may have been caught off-guard by their response, but Beers is livid. "What the hell? Don't tell me you're cool with the Dick taking over?" He practically shouts his question.

"Excuse me." Jedd is calm but firm as he faces Beers. "Clarifying questions only."

"That is a clarifying question," Beers says, lowering his voice but not his intensity. Now it seems like he might be the one walking out. If he does, none of us will be able to talk him down.

Jedd is about to intervene, but Nick says, "It's okay. We get that you're angry, Beers. Obviously we don't want the Dictator to invade. That would be cataclysmic. But here's the thing: it's not within our power to stop him."

Zack points out there are only seven of us.

"Be realistic," Nick says. "Seven people can't take on a world superpower. Derailing the app's launch would have been ideal. But we didn't pull that off." He reminds us the twins always said the Dictator was invincible. That hasn't changed. And there was never going to be a little guy from nowheresville. "Now our best action is to protect ourselves. Instead of panicking, play the long game. The time will come—yes, we predict—when we can put all the info we've gathered to good use. In the meantime, let's hang tight."

"There's plenty of upside," Zack says. "Good food. Good music. Good movies. Picnics at Boulder Point. Evenings in the hot tub. Life isn't bad here."

Nick is nodding and anticipates Jedd's question. "And yes, if the group comes to a different consensus—provided it's nonviolent—you can count on us to go along."

Darah is next. She starts by saying her main concern is how safe we'll be if the Dictator does make a move on California. As she looks at each of us, I see the fear in her eyes. Unlike the twins, chilling isn't top of her mind. "The dictatorship never disrupted life here the way it did in the States. You don't know what that's like. Things could get tough in ways you can't even imagine. The farm might end up not being as remote as we wish."

"So what do you recommend?" Jedd asks.

"Canada. I'd like us to go to Canada." She says she'd feel safer and jokes it's almost like we're already there. When Jedd doesn't hide his surprise, she adds, "What did you think, that I'd want to stay here?"

He says he didn't realize she felt unsafe.

"I do feel safe," she says. "But not if the Dictator attacks. Which is what you expect, or we wouldn't be discussing this." She explains she's proud of the personal work she's done while we've been in exile. She plays music every day, keeps her mind steady, avoids negativity. Plus being with all of us feels safe. She says all of us, but she's looking at Beers. I find it ironic that despite his anger, he's the one who makes her feel most safe.

Darah is the kind of person who'd run into a burning building to save a stranger. So this isn't about lack of courage. Or lack of caring. No, what I hear is powerlessness. She's afraid her little boat will capsize if she doesn't cling to positive thinking. The twins are in a different boat altogether. They're opting for the path of least resistance. Succumbing to apathy.

Jedd is about to turn to me, but she stops him. "I'm not trying to run away, if that's what it sounds like." Then her voice gets very soft. "But I will say this: when someone's life is in immediate danger, their only choice may be to flee."

"Like your mom," I say. "Before you were born."

She nods.

"Of course," Beers says.

"We understand," Jedd says.

Really, there are no words. So we sit quietly, holding Darah's mom in our thoughts. Things would have been so different if she hadn't been forced to run for her life. She could have fought for women's rights. Raised her daughter to be strong and free. Even the ability to resist, I realize, presupposes some degree of a functioning democracy.

"And you, June?" Jedd says, coming back to our discussion. I know what he has in mind: the kid can speak after me—or just flash his smile—and then Jedd will have the floor. Going last will allow him to channel us toward his vision. Right now we're all over the place. Beers is ready to detonate a bomb; the other three want to retreat. That's a wide gap to bridge. Jedd doesn't see doing

nothing as an option and assumes I don't either, so he'll build off whatever I recommend. What he doesn't realize is I'm not riding with him.

After staring each other down for a minute, I say, "Go ahead."

"Fine," he says when it's clear I'm not saying more and the kid isn't clamoring to speak. "Here's what I think. Going into exile was about our survival. About making sure the Dictator doesn't come after us. About staying safe, like the twins and Darah said. We're not trying to be superheroes. I always figured we'd go to the authorities after the app failed. After it became clear the threats to democracy were vacuous. Well, that didn't happen."

"Sure didn't," Beers says.

"No. And now the danger is exponentially greater. To our country. To people's sanity. To their lives. Much as we might want to hang out here or in Canada and wait for things to blow over, we no longer have that luxury. Nor can we respond out of hatred or anger or the desire for revenge. That's not who we are." He pauses. The kid is nodding but the others are just listening, neither agreeing nor disagreeing. "No point second-guessing whether we should have hacked the app's launch," he continues, with a glance at Nick. "That ship has sailed. We have to move forward, take action now. And we have to do it here because we don't have time for travel."

"But do *what?*" Beers pushes back.

Now Jedd is on the other end of the question he posed to us. He leads with what we shouldn't do. "Running to the authorities is still not an option. There's no one we can trust for sure. And we can't expose our Canada cover. Our best bet is to work within the darknet and find a way to counterpunch the Russians."

He's clearly talking about some sort of hack, maybe pushing out an altered app with their next update. "We have no idea how long before they update," I say.

"Could be soon," Beers adds.

"Could be," Jedd says. "Which is why we can't sit on this."

"On *what*?" I echo Beers.

He looks at the two of us as if he expects us to be mind readers. "Okay. I admit I don't have a specific strategy, but this much I'll say: we need to commit to a hack."

So there it is. He wants us to hack the app. To stand up for democracy by taking on the Russians and their quantum SL code.

"I don't think—" I start to say.

But he cuts me off. "June, I'm not saying it will be easy. But we have to try." He explains we need to reach a consensus: all of us must be on board. None of us can sit this one out. No one can be off doing their own thing or offer half-assed support. Even if we don't yet know what it is, we have to agree to take action. To stand up to what is the greatest technological and existential threat of our lifetimes. We will examine our options, build a strategy, and then pool our skills to make it happen. He's careful not to denigrate any of the ideas offered so far and asks us to consider this as a compromise.

I don't see how it's a compromise since he is asking us to go along with his vision, but that doesn't stop the others from consenting.

The twins say they'll need more specifics but will compromise if everyone else does.

Beers doesn't say anything, but it's obvious he was merely venting earlier. He knew no one would condone any sort of bomb. Except perhaps a logic bomb. In fact, Jedd might want to use one of those on the Happy App.

Darah and the kid are nodding.

Satisfied the others are on board, he turns to me, calm and collected: "So, June, I take it you're good?"

His question doesn't have the effect he intended. My thoughts are running on a different track. Suppose we sabotage the app with a logic bomb or some kind of slag code, and that fails? Our failure will pave the way for the Dictator's success, his total domination. Not just our loved ones and families, millions will suffer. And it will be our fault. *My* fault. Yes, some of us have quantum computing skills, but I'm the only one who knows much about smart light. And that's only because I jumped on the research when Jedd first told us about the app. Even if he hasn't said so, he's counting on me to lead the charge. Which means I'll be front and center when the Dictator's agents come looking for us after the hack fails. Jedd is proposing an operation in which failure is unthinkable. And yet failure is the only outcome I can visualize. Failure and the death of everything I care about. I don't know why the others aren't as freaked as I am.

I shake my head. "Sorry, dude, I'm not ready to sign on. Think about all that could go wrong. We've been cautious for so many reasons we'd be idiots to ignore now."

"But June—"

I signal that I'm not finished speaking, then count off the reasons on my fingers. There's a reason we decided to lay low. There's a reason we haven't gone to the authorities. There's a reason we haven't even talked to the bunker. There's a reason we have fake IDs. There's a reason we've stayed offline, off the grid even. There's a reason we're lying to family. I'm already on the fingers of my second hand, and I'm just getting started.

As soon as I pause to take a breath, they argue back.

"The app's launch puts everything in a new light," Nick says.

"Its unprecedented success sure does," Zack clarifies.

"Jedd has a point," Darah says. "We need to fight for California, for democracy."

"Wait," I say, "you three were fine a few minutes ago with hiding out here or running to Canada. Now you're giving me a hard time when I say we shouldn't rush this?"

When he sees I'm not backing down and we're starting to polarize, Beers suggests taking a breather. Everyone is hungry anyway. He starts moving toward the kitchen, promising to rustle up some veggie burgers.

"As long as it's a quick break," Jedd says as he pulls up the app on the coffee table to check its status. "June, look—" he says.

But I'm not looking. I'm focused on the untenable position Jedd has put me in. With everyone else in agreement, what we do comes down to what I decide. Normally I'd be first on board to hack anything malicious. I'd do it with relish. Even now, no one is more eager than I to destroy the Happy App. No one would be more elated to see the Dictator go down in flames. Still, I can't get past the fact that if I give the go-ahead and it turns out Jedd was wrong about his strategy, its failure will be my fault. When we realize democracy has died because we were just flying on hubris, I'll be a murderer.

My every instinct is screaming to slam on the brakes. *I can't do this. I have to back out now, before it's too late.*

Still, explaining myself won't be easy. I need to figure out what to say. I can't just say no. I can't just say what I'm against, what I refuse to do. I also have to say what I support. Is it going to the authorities? Is it fleeing to Canada? Is it something we haven't thought of yet? Really, my mind is all over the place. I need time to think.

I slip outside so I can take my breather alone.

Arjuna threw down his Gandiva bow and sat silent,
refusing to fight. Krishna said, "O Arjuna, it is your duty
to fight. Do not be sad. The eternal soul is neither born nor can
it die; weapons cannot destroy it and fire cannot burn it.
Knowing this, treat pleasure and pain alike, victory and loss alike."

IN THE CHARIOT: June

I head straight to the chariot.

It's my go-to spot when I need a quiet place to think. While its cyber ID has tooled around Vancouver Island, redwood needles have piled up here on the sunroof and windshield, creating a cave-like feeling. Now it's quiet but also cold and damp. The faded-pink fuzzy dice are starting to look moldy. An old Cal Bears navy sweatshirt is draped on one seat, where I left it months ago. As I pull it over my head, there is a tap on the window.

It's the kid.

I ask if Jedd sent him.

He shifts from foot to foot, as if that will stop the rain from soaking through his thin jersey, and says he came on his own. Begs me to let him in.

I can't exactly refuse, so I open the door and retreat to the far-side seat. "You know," I say, "it's cold in here."

Cold, he insists, is not a problem. He got used to cold while living on the streets. Hunger isn't a problem either, he says as he sits opposite me. He shakes off, spraying wetness in all directions, then looks at me hard. "You aren't leaving, are you?"

I'm surprised he'd think that. Darah might split in a moment of weakness. But me? Not a chance.

"Good." He smiles as he relaxes into the seat. "You had me worried."

I tell him I'm out here to weigh the pros and cons of hacking the app. So he doesn't think I'm talking down to him, I throw in some technical jargon about smart light, while making it clear I need to sit with this. By myself. Quietly. Unpressured. Free to reach my own conclusions. I say everything short of the truth: I've already made up my mind. I'm against the hack. All con and no pro. Trying to persuade me otherwise will be futile.

He doesn't take the hint. "Without you," he presses, "there's no consensus."

That's what I'd expect him to say. Whatever Jedd suggests, the kid will blow with the wind. Despite his denial, I am sure he's here because Jedd sent him to rope me in, gently, probably with the instructions *don't say I sent you*. Which means it'll be hard to get rid of him. "Sorry," I say, "I'm not rubber-stamping a consensus."

A frown flits across his brow. "No stamp, June. We need you fully behind this."

"I'm not," I say bluntly. So much for feigning an open mind.

"You're not?"

"No."

I watch as he digests this.

"So you're scared?" he asks after a moment.

I can see how he might think that. But I'm not afraid. I'm an activist, a hacker. A warrior. Fear isn't a warrior's MO. Warriors are confident, in control, intrepid. "It's not about fear," I say. "It's the fact that everything is stacked against us in a situation where failing is not an option."

"The Russians are beasts," he concedes. "Out-coding them will be an epic battle. Their whole army versus a handful of us."

"Then you agree it's stacked against us?"

"Sure. But that makes it more important for you to work your magic. You have the quantum SL skills. It'll be a race against time, and you're the fastest coder." When I don't respond, he pleads, "Come on, June."

I had no idea he cared so much about what we did. These can't all be Jedd's ideas and Jedd's words. Apparently the kid has views of his own. Maybe even his own strategy. Still, if he expects me to fall for it, he couldn't be more wrong. "Honestly," I say, angling to wrap this up, "being fast, writing awesome code, carrying the team on my back—none of that's enough now. This isn't a project where you assess your errors and try again. It isn't a game. One wrong move and we'll be toast. Maybe we'd have time to flee the farm and save our skins. Maybe. But by then, where would we even go?"

He doesn't have a ready answer for that. We sit in silence as a redwood sprig inches down the windshield, dragged by a rivulet of rain. At the bottom, where you'd have wipers on a gas car, it rear-ends another sprig, forming a little dam.

"People always look out for their own skins," he says finally.

Like he thinks I'm being selfish. I remind him my activist friends gave their all to the resistance. Look how that turned out. The Dictator is more powerful than ever. And my friends? Dead. I'm not willing to risk that now. I don't want to die. I don't want any of us to die. "Sometimes one has to view things more objectively," I say. "That isn't selfish."

"I'm not saying you're selfish. I'm saying there's a better way."

"The best way I know," I counter, "is to be smart and pick my battles. The Happy App hack is one battle I'm not picking. Period."

Instead of taking my word as final, he shoots me a look that says *we'll see about that* and swivels to face the dashboard. He gives the fuzzy dice a twirl, as if summoning good luck, then extends both hands to grip an imaginary steering wheel. "Let's go for a ride, June!" he chirps.

"Do I have a choice?" Really, I'm in no mood for jokes.

"Humor me," he says, jamming an imaginary key in the imaginary ignition and making engine-revving sounds in his throat. Then he cranes over one shoulder as if turning the car around and guns it.

I ask where we're going.

"To the cyber battlefield!" His normally melodious voice, like an echo of his flute, is suddenly strident: "We're gonna stop that stinkin' app!"

You get three minutes, I think. *Max.*

He bounces high in his seat as we hit imaginary potholes, then white-knuckles the wheel, yanking it left and right so violently the chariot must be riding two wheels down the mountain.

"Phew!" he exclaims after a dozen sharp turns. "Let's get those freakin' Russians!" He gives the fuzzy dice another twirl, then weaves like a maniac through traffic, narrowly missing oncoming vehicles, all the while emitting piercing squeals and screeches. He must have watched a lot of old-school high-speed chase scenes.

Except this is about the hack. A task predicated on accuracy and precision. The ultimate stealth operation. He's expending so much energy when what he really needs is to be cool and stay off the Russians' radar. I tell him that.

He pauses as if considering my input, then abruptly hisses, "June, git down!"

"Why?"

"Smart beam attack!" He hugs up on the imaginary wheel as he dodges beams. Then he ducks lower, his forehead almost in his lap, the wheel above his head. He narrates as he goes, jumping cars and doing wheelies. "Oh, shit!" he exclaims, glancing in the rearview mirror. I figure it's the police. But he says it's Kurt. He's trying to catch us before we catch the Russians.

Three minutes aren't up, but I've reached my limit. His antics could be amusing another time. I had no idea he was such a ham. But I can't lose sight of the fact that the Russians are finishing their update—right now, for real. Not to mention they could have detected Jedd on the darknet site and be closing in on us. I have to let the others know what I've decided so we can come up with a plan B that doesn't involve a hack.

"You know," I say, "the cool dudes all drive SDVs." Implying the kid is uncool as a way to stop his clowning may be a bit harsh. I'll have to do damage control if his feelings are hurt.

But he jettisons his imaginary wheel and grins at me. "Yes, yes, June!" He's practically crowing. "Having a steering wheel in a self-driving vehicle defeats the whole purpose, doesn't it?"

"Sure does."

He's grinning ear to ear. "So you get my little demo?"

We were talking about my decision not to hack the app, and his demo was about a car chase. "Sorry," I say, "no."

He looks disappointed. But only for a second. "Then forget the demo. Let me explain."

Since he won't take no for an answer, I play along in spite of myself.

"It's like . . . this," he says slowly, as if choosing his words for a remedial student. "Driving an old-model car—even without any Russians around—takes a lot of work. You gotta steer, give it gas, brake. All of that."

"Obviously."

"You are the car," he says, as if that's also obvious.

But it isn't. Not to me anyway. "I am?"

He explains it's an analogy, it's what he was trying to get across with his demo: he wants me to imagine myself as a car. "I know you drive an SDV," he says, "but think of yourself as a gas car. Can you do that?"

I tell him I'll try.

"Okay, so your body is the car. It's what you move through life in. Now imagine your mind as the car's steering wheel."

That's a bit of a leap. But it's not like I've forgotten how to steer a car, how to turn left or right to get where I'm going. I guess my mind serves a similar function. "Makes sense," I say.

He builds on this. "We can also say your ego, your sense of *me*, is the steering wheel."

"When I'm behind the wheel, I'm in control," I say. "Got it."

"Exactly." He pauses to make sure I'm ready for more. "Now, the steering wheel is connected to the car's wheels."

"Which should be on the ground at all times," I say.

But his mind isn't on chase scenes anymore. "You have five wheels, counting the spare. The five senses through which you experience the world are those wheels. Your mind—that is, the steering wheel—keeps your senses from running off the road and getting you in trouble."

"In that case," I joke, "forget about staying on the ground. My mind's steering an aero car. Much faster. More fun!"

We both laugh.

He tells me I'm getting ahead of myself. His analogy is meant to compare a gas car with a self-driving vehicle. No aero cars. "In an SDV," he says, "you sit back while the car drives itself."

I consider that. After calculating that one year of commuting to HSys equaled an entire workweek behind the wheel, I bought the chariot to reclaim my time. "In an SDV," I say, "the driver becomes a passenger. It's less stressful."

"Yes," he says when he sees I'm following. "Your five senses—your wheels—still perceive the world and navigate through it. You've determined your destination, but now you're not steering every move."

"I trust the electronics."

He explains that electronics represent a greater power. "You trust that power to get you where you want to go. While you relax, the electronics do the work. There's no ego trying to look out for itself. No mind to steer you in the wrong direction."

"The world runs on electronics," I point out. "It's crazy how much faith we place in it."

"Except that's not true faith," he says quickly. "We take electronics for granted. But the whole time, we act like we're the ones in control—" He stops himself. "But let's not go there. This isn't about people who *own* SDVs. I'm talking about the SDV itself. About *being* an SDV."

"Being an SDV?" I echo.

"It sounds weird, but yes. This is about a choice between two ways of going through life. You can go through life like a steering wheel, with your ego-mind running the show. Or you can go through life like an SDV, where your mind takes a back seat and you place your faith in the car's power." He stops and looks at me. "So, June, which is it for you?"

It sounds like the punchline of a convoluted joke, but he's posing a serious question. And I know the answer. I may own an SDV, but I'm going through life like a steering wheel. No doubt about it. I like the feeling of being in control. Being a programmer keeps me in control. Using a kick-ass VA keeps me in control. Speaking my mind keeps me in control. Making Jedd wrong and me right keeps me in control. Even now, forcing the others to wait while I sit here and worry about the probable failure of a hack is my means of control.

If you like to get technical—as I do—the sense of *me*, the steering wheel, is generated in the anterior cingulate cortex. The inability of the right supramarginal gyrus to correct egoistic tendencies reinforces it. You can learn this geeky stuff in school yet never have a clue how it plays out in your life minute by minute.

The kid is watching, waiting for my response. "I'm a steering wheel all right," I say. Yep, even right here, in this bastion of faith that's my SDV. What irony.

"It's habit," he says. "We all want to feel like we're in control. For Darah, it's about fear of more trauma. That fear makes it hard to take action or support others' actions. For Beers, it's about anger. He gets so flipping mad, he could kill someone. His anger clouds his thinking, makes it harder to choose the right action. For the twins, being in control means preserving life as they know it."

"And Jedd?" I say. "He's very inclusive. That's not controlling."

"With him it's less obvious. But don't tell me he doesn't think, *I want to be seen as a good leader.*"

Which of course reminds me Jedd is waiting. So I ask what all this means for us now. The kid had better have a good answer, considering how much time I've given him.

"Say you hack the app," he says. "If you go into it as a steering wheel, it's all on you. Everything is in your hands. Literally."

"But it *would* be all on me." When we first dug into the dark-net site, I assumed we'd come up with a way to fix the mess. Either we'd inform the authorities and let them handle it or we'd pool our skills and get it done ourselves. That was before I knew quantum SL was involved. Before I knew about the Russians. When I saw the magnitude of the mess, everything changed. "That's why I freaked," I say. "Jedd expects me to go toe-to-toe with an army of Russians. Me!"

"If you go in feeling it's all on you, the hack will be hard. Like I said, there's a better way."

"Which is? Be an SDV?" It sounds ridiculous when I say it.

Not to the kid. "The better way is to stop acting like you have to be in control. Yes, put forth your best effort, but lean into faith."

"Faith in what?"

"In a greater power."

"Which is?"

"I guess you could say a higher power." He stops to weigh his words. I doubt he explains this sort of stuff frequently. If ever. "I don't mean it's higher or lower than anything else. It exists in every corner of the universe. Including within you. And it's aligned with the greatest good in every situation."

I like the sound of that. He's not talking about faith in a simplistic religious sense. Or as a good luck charm, like fuzzy dice. In truth, I do believe in a greater power that holds the universe together. I might not experience it moment to moment, but I see it as intrinsically good. Trusting in it might help with the hack. At the very least, I'd stop focusing on failure. "So you're saying do the hack," I say, "but without worrying about the outcome?"

"Exactly! If you do your best and it still fails, you won't be to blame."

"And if it succeeds, I won't be so quick to take credit."

He high-fives me on that.

"Don't make it so personal," he says. "We see our lives and the world as separate. It's not like that. If each of us does our part, we can all contribute to the greater good. We can move forward in sync, part of a larger whole."

"You mean like traffic in a world with only SDVs?"

"Yeah." He smiles. "Imagine a driverless car with road rage."

We both laugh at that.

"Okay," I say. "I get it. In a sane world like you're describing, we'd base our decision to hack the app on what benefits the greater good, not on our fears or other feelings. Not even on the objective odds of success."

"In a sane world, you wouldn't hesitate to do what you know in your gut is right."

"Except this isn't a sane world."

He doesn't dispute that. "Even so, you want to do the right thing."

I point out that my idea of the right thing isn't necessarily what someone else sees as right. All activism isn't equal. Kurt would call his actions the right thing. So would the Dictator.

"Of course," he says. "People engaged in self-serving actions may call themselves activists. But I'm assuming you can figure out the decent, honorable, just, courageous, and compassionate action in any situation. That's what you'd want, right?"

"Absolutely. Still, even if my gut is telling me what's right, I can't snap my fingers and grow some faith. I can't just drop my need for control." I turn his analogy back on him. "The chariot may be self-driving, but it won't start unless you activate home on the dashboard. In the driverless version of me, where's the home button?"

He chuckles and tells me there are techniques for that.

I ask him to explain.

One technique, he says, is to focus on the breath. "Breathing is like the flow of electricity that powers an SDV. It's not something you control. If you focus on the brief gap between breaths, you can find the source of that power."

When I don't jump at that idea, he offers another. "Or you can look beneath your thoughts. The mind is always running, but there's a quiet space below our thoughts. It's much like the gap between breaths."

I still look unenthused, so he tries again. "Or try to find the one who, when you wake up, knows you were asleep."

This one grabs me. Obviously it's not a part of myself I control. "Awesome," I say. "But it sounds like a lot of work. It could take years to nail down."

He acknowledges it could take a while. But there's a shortcut. "For now, just *act* as if you've nailed it."

"Even if I haven't?"

"Even if you haven't. Think of it this way. You don't have to know how the stomach digests food before you bite into Beers's nut brittle. You don't have to know how a car's engine works to feel comfortable getting behind the wheel."

"Or activating its home button."

He shoots me a wry smile. "We do many things without fully grokking them. Doesn't stop us from acting. Especially when we know it's the right thing to do."

When he says that, something shifts. I can't say I have more faith, but whatever previously said no within me is now saying yes. It's an open yes, a free yes. It doesn't depend on a predetermined outcome. It simply knows what the right action is for me in this moment. "Alrighty," I say slowly. "I'll work on the hack. I can do it based on the conviction we must do whatever we can to stop the Dictator. To protect democracy. I know in my heart that's the right thing. It's clearly for the greatest good. And I can act without feeling it's *me* doing it all. I mean, I'll still be doing stuff, but I won't be wrapped up in the feeling of doing it."

"That's the idea," he says. "Free yourself so you can act."

I stare out the window as I sit with this sense of freedom. This open yes. It isn't totally unfamiliar. It's like the old June—the old Rose, the committed activist—has reawakened, only in a new, more inwardly empowered way. "Hey," I say, glancing at the kid. "What you're saying about faith in the greater good is true of democracy itself, isn't it?"

He's nodding. "Democracy works when people value the collective good not just their own interests. When they aren't always looking out for—"

"—their own skins," I say, bringing our discussion full circle.

I know what I have to do. My agreement will enable the consensus, and we can begin the hack without further delay. Jedd is probably chomping at the bit, if he hasn't already started on his own. Yes, we can do this, far-fetched and improbable as the entire operation may seem.

The rain has tapered to a drizzle. The redwood sprig that slid down the windshield is no longer distinct from the mound of needles at the bottom. Even if I wanted to, I couldn't pick it out of the collective whole.

"Okay," I say, turning to the kid, who's waiting patiently. He still doesn't look cold. "We're doing this. Let's go tell everyone."

The conches had been blown. The first move was from the Kauravas. Then the Pandavas sprang into action. The fight between their armies was fierce, all of them excellent archers. By day's end, the number of dead was too great to be counted.

THE BATTLE: Jedd

No two ways about it, we need to hack the app. Sure it's risky. No denying that. But I'm glad we reached a consensus. Or I thought we did, until June threw a wrench in it. She literally walked out. I didn't see that coming, not after the two of us worked side by side all these weeks tracking the app and monitoring the Ks. Any minute now she could return and call this whole thing off.

I don't know why I couldn't convince her our time for debate is over; it's time to act. Her skills are critical for any hack, but I guess she doesn't care. I do know forcing the issue never works with June. She pushes back harder, and whatever we're tussling over ends up taking even more energy. Which is why I didn't run after her, tempting as it was.

I tinker on my screen, checking our IDs, double-checking the chariot's coordinates, the status of supplies. We've been flat out of beer since yesterday, and we're low on bread and toilet paper. Except programming a run into Ucluelet isn't my priority. Let the Russians think we gave up booze and are foraging at our campsite. Dining on grilled sea asparagus and laminaria-wrapped oysters works for me.

In fact, I'm going ahead with the hack, consensus or not.

The first step is to clone the Happy App and export it to a secure site where we can work on a parallel update. The move requires total concentration. There can be no flub of any sort.

While the others are preoccupied with their veggie burgers, I access the darknet site. Immediately I notice I'm no longer invisible. Notifications are flashing across my screen, informing me the Russians are in here, programming their update. They must be getting alerts on me as well. Evidently they've amped up security to guard against intruders. Like me. Under normal circumstances, I'd return when the coast is clear. But I can't afford to wait. Plus they've already shown that they work at all hours of the day and night. The coast will never be clear. So, hacker bandit that I am, I waltz into my settings and make myself invisible. Then I snatch a copy of the app and hightail it out of there.

I have no idea if the Russians noticed. We'll deal with that later.

With the copy dropped into a secure site I keep for personal use, I close my screen and release a pent-up exhale as I look around the room. The others are still focused on their burgers. Rather than mention my close call, I pick up the now-cold burger Beers left on the coffee table, bite into it, and ask, "Anyone seen June?"

No one has.

"Nor the kid," Beers says.

"They're probably in the barn," Darah says.

Nick offers to fetch them.

As he's getting up, the front door swings open and in walks June, trailed by the kid. She's wearing an old Cal sweatshirt, collar turned up, her long hair tucked inside. It must have been cold in the barn.

We all stare at her, trying to read her mood. I think I see the old fighting spirit in her eyes. Like she brought to our final exam in algorithm theory, the all-out effort that earned her class honors while I was runner-up. Like she brought to HSys projects over the years. If anything, it's stronger now. Still, given how she ran out earlier, I'm prepared for the worst.

"Hey, Jedd." She sheds the sweatshirt, sits down opposite me, and smiles. "You can relax. I'm in. All in."

I want to ask where the heck she's been, why she was holding out on us. How she could possibly justify caving to the Dictator. But this isn't the time to get into any of that, so I say, "We've got work to do. Glad you're on board."

"Me too!" Beers gives a whoop, then runs to fetch two burgers he was keeping warm. While mine chilled on the table. But hey, I'm not complaining.

Now everyone wants to know what exactly we're going to do.

I ask permission to lay out my plan. Taking the lead isn't a problem now that everyone has bought in. Though I make a mental note to be extra careful to include June at every step.

They all nod approval.

Even the kid. He's over by the fireplace, scarfing down his burger while Dharma eyes each mouthful. The kid has already spent more time listening to us today than he typically does in a week. I expect him to slip out shortly.

I start by laying out our goals. "We're not going to shut down the app or seize control of user data or reveal its proprietary technology. We won't divert its revenues or personally profit in any way. None of that. We're not black hats. We'll want to expose the Ks at some point, but right now our purpose is to neutralize the app's effect. We need to reverse the rising public regard for the Dictator that's emboldening him to attack California." I turn to June and invite her input so she knows our skirmish is in my rearview mirror: "How do we execute this?"

"Disable the Dictator's photo," she says, speaking with confidence, showing me she's also moved on.

"Just disable it?"

"Correct. We need to prevent the smart light from transmitting his image to the user's brain and stimulating a neural response."

"What about the frenzy of hate he wants to whip up against California?" Nick asks.

"That could mean multiple photos to disable," Zack says.

"Yeah, remove *all* of them," Nick says.

But June is shaking her head. "I don't think so. No way the Russians had time for the complex coding such a strategy would require. Not even working around the clock. So let's not worry about it." She looks at us with sudden intensity, as if her brain has gone into overdrive and generated all the code for this hack, and she's staring at it. "Please," she says, "I need to trust my gut on this."

"What's your gut say?" Beers asks.

"It says act with courage. Do the right thing. Don't fall prey to doubts and fears." She looks at the kid, like he has something to add. Which of course he doesn't. "That means unlink the Dictator's photo and leave it there. Keep it simple. And trust we can replace their update with ours before they release it, which I'm guessing will be soon."

"As long as the Russians can still see the photo," I say, "they won't suspect a hack."

"If the interface doesn't change, most users won't even notice there was an update," Beers adds.

I'm pleased June shares my vision and that our task is being defined narrowly. It looks doable. After all is said and done, I want to hear what transpired today to transform her outlook. I'm also relieved Beers isn't insisting on a vigilante approach—for example, plant an indiscriminate logic bomb. Or reprogram the smart light to generate aggression toward the Dictator. We can't risk the app's signals getting crossed in the brain, potentially causing who-knows-what damage. There's already too much hate in the world. "The less we do," I say, "the faster we can do it."

"How will you handle the quantum computing?" Darah wants to know.

It's a reasonable question. HSys uses quantum computing for some AI products, so we're fluent with various quantum programming languages. "We'll draw on June's expertise," I say. "A QPL translation program should handle most of the job if we stick to unlinking the photo and don't try to mess with the smart light."

In case this isn't clear, I diagram it for Darah on my screen. The app's interface is a square at the center. Behind it is another square: the app's home on the HSys site. Behind that is a third square: the darknet site. The Dictator's photo sits within that last square. An arrow runs from the photo to a big wavy circle at the top of the diagram, representing the quantum computer in the cloud.

To the left of the app's interface, I draw a user's head. The spaghetti-like blob inside represents the brain, which is connected by a line to a large eyeball facing the app. To show the user looking at the app, I add a dotted line that starts at the eyeball and ends with an arrow tip at the outer edge of the first square. The user sees whatever is displayed on the app's screen. A second dotted line runs through the first, second, and third squares and ends on the Dictator's photo. I retrace the arrow running from the photo to the cloud to show how the user is directly connected to the quantum computer. Then I add a solid line coming back down from the cloud. This is the smart light. Its first arrow tip lands on the photo, where it picks up the image. It continues through the sequence of squares and out the other side, with a second arrow tip on the eyeball and a third tip ending in the brain, completing the circuit.

June extends a finger and draws a loop around the arrow tip as it hits the photo. "We target the hack here."

"Wait a minute, dude," Beers says with sudden alarm, pointing to the second square. "I can't believe I didn't think of this before. The frigging app is housed on a dedicated HSys site."

"It has to be so people can buy it," I say. "But that's just cloaking."

"Okay, a false front. Still, HSys maintenance programmers have access," he says. "What's stopping them from noticing its link to the darknet, from realizing it's cloaking?"

I've mucked around enough to have an answer for that: "The Russians heavily encrypted the link to prevent anyone at HSys detecting it."

"Gottcha," he says.

"But thanks for bringing that up. We'll need to be alert for encryption issues." I put my finger on the loop June drew and tap it, turning it red. "I agree with June: we target the hack here."

She sets her empty plate on the coffee table and wipes her hands rapidly back and forth against each other. "I'm amped! When do we start, Jedd?"

Since she's deferring to me, I explain what I envision. "First we reprogram the app so it doesn't transmit the Dictator's photo to users' brains."

"In other words, create a bypass around the photo," June says. "Sweet."

"The coding will be done using a clone in a secure sandbox. Once that's completed, we'll move our update back to the darknet site."

"That's the trickiest part," Beers says.

"Yes. The switch out—replacing the Russians' update with ours and linking it both to the false front on the HSys site and to the quantum computer in the cloud—has to be swift, seamless, undetectable." The good news is that as long as we execute it before the update rolls out, we should be home free.

"How long will you have for the move?" Darah wants to know.

"HSys releases updates at midnight," Nick says.

Zack says that's arbitrary.

"We don't know if the Russians will follow HSys protocol," I say. "They could be under pressure from HQ to release the update ASAP when it's ready."

"Meaning there could be no time for that last step?" Darah says.

I admit it could be very short. For all practical purposes nonexistent.

"Then let's prepare a hack to delay the update's release," Nick says.

"As a backup, just in case," Zack adds.

June immediately objects that while such a backup would be ideal, we have too much else to handle. "We have to trust our skills are good enough to pull this off superfast."

"And trust we have enough runway?" Beers screws up his face. "I don't think so."

"We have to trust," June says. "Along with put in our best effort. I'd call that the definition of courage: trust plus hard work." She looks around the room to see if we agree. I don't think I've ever seen her so inspired. Whatever got her to this point was worth the wait.

But Beers isn't buying. He declares he'll start working on a backup hack himself.

"No way, dude," I say. "We need you on more important stuff."

He's about to argue back when a voice pipes up from across the room, causing all heads to turn toward the kid.

"I'll do it."

"You'll write the code?" I'm surprised, though vaguely recall he once admitted to being a hacker. I think he said he could hack if he approved of the situation. Apparently this qualifies.

He extricates himself from a sleeping Dharma and joins us. "If you're okay with it."

Since I wasn't counting on him to help in any other capacity and this is a nonessential task, I don't see a downside. I tell him by all means have at it. He can use his tablet as long as he works offline. Then I turn back to the others and make a confession. "While you were on break, I made a clone of the app."

I expect blowback for acting without a consensus, but there isn't any.

"Blazing fantastic, bro," Beers says.

"You pulled it off without a hitch?" Nick says.

In response I display the backend of the cloned app on my screen. "June and I can start coding right away. Then the rest of you can jump in. Everything will have to be checked and double-checked."

"Don't worry, we're not going anywhere," Beers says. He agrees to monitor the audio stream and will let us know of any signs the update is imminent.

Darah acknowledges that without coding skills, there's not much she can do. Except make sure we don't run out of hot coffee.

We've been working steadily for hours, and everything's going well. I'm glad we're doing the simplest possible hack. This has a decent chance of success. I've already given the twins code to check while June and I plunge ahead. It's cute seeing the kid on the hearth, programming away like a pro, stopping occasionally for a quick tug of war with Dharma over his favorite sock. He's a good kid. Whatever he said to June earlier at the barn is probably what persuaded her to come around.

Beers is sitting across from me, monitoring the audio stream. We've gotten surprisingly little intel recently. Honestly, it's hard to believe they haven't finished that rum yet. Beers jokes about going there and polishing it off himself. He suspects Kurt stuck the bottle on a back shelf, perhaps after scoring an even classier one. That would explain the reduced sound quality but not the weird noises it picks up at odd hours. Or the fact that the transcription stopped. I think the issue has more to do with the mic than the rum. Cool as that nano technology is, it's meant for disposable, onetime use. We're fortunate it's working at all.

I'm deep in coding when Beers rips out his earbuds and squeals, "Bro, listen to this shit!"

"What?" I ask without looking up. Better be important to interrupt me now.

"They're fucking coming for us!"

Darah runs out of the kitchen to see what the ruckus is about. "I didn't think you were still on the audio," she says.

"Good thing I am."

"At this hour?"

"It's not even ten o'clock."

"Turn it up," I say. We need to hear this live, not debate whether it's too late to listen in.

As the others gather around, we hear Kurt say, "Like I said, everything synchronized. Stun the losers. Soon as the grid's down, obliterate 'em."

"And us?" Keith's voice is unusually loud. Has been for a while. I've been meaning to ask June her thoughts on that. Not now obviously.

"We'll be fine," Kurt says.

"Our line to HQ?"

"Secure. We've got the app, remember?" Kurt laughs. "They need us!"

"So we just play along?"

"Yup. Act as shocked as everyone else." Kurt says it will be fun.

Beers is getting more agitated by the minute. "This is gross!"

"It is," I say. "But we need to hear more."

He cranks up the audio as Kurt describes how HQ will take out key infrastructure in California—power, water, all forms of communication cut at the same time. No one will see it coming.

"We'll be effing sitting ducks," Beers says.

"It'll be anarchy," Nick says.

"Total chaos," Zack says.

Keith is on the same wavelength—only with a positive spin. "With all the chaos, it'll be easy to take power."

Kurt confirms that's the plan. While people scramble for basic necessities, the Dictator will grab the wheels of government.

"An invasion?" Keith asks. "Or send in B-21s?"

Kurt says no, nothing like that. Everything will be done remotely. No state of emergency. No outer show of force.

He doesn't give more details. It's unclear how the Dictator will seize power without violence, but perhaps commandeering the current leaders' IDs will be sufficient in the absence of telecommunications. Or maybe this is where the mysterious killer app comes in. There are lots of unanswered questions.

Then we hear something that sets us even more on edge.

"When will HQ strike?" Keith asks.

Kurt shrugs that off. "Whenever they're ready."

"Like, before the update?"

"Before or after, who cares—"

June whistles through her teeth. "Dude, did you hear that?"

"We could be in for a surprise strike," I say. Now that the Dictator is satisfied with the level of his public support, the app has done its job.

"If this is true, our hack will be too little too late," June says.

Based on what we just heard, I can't deny it. We may have missed our chance.

"It's the ultimate zero-day attack," Beers says. "We're fucked. Totally fucked."

Everyone is silent as this sinks in. Really, the consequences are mindboggling.

I find myself grasping for options. "Unless . . ." I stare down at my screen, at the code that looked so stellar only a few minutes ago. "Unless we shift strategies."

"How?" the others want to know.

I don't have anything specific in mind, so I turn to June. She's been on fire since this afternoon. Maybe we can draw on that energy now. "What do you think?"

"There could be a silver lining here," she says. "I mean, this forces us to hone our strategy, give our hack more teeth."

"How?" the others repeat.

"Well," she says, clearly thinking on her feet, "we assumed disabling the Dictator's photo so it isn't transmitted to users' brains would lead them to quickly unlearn their neural responses to the app."

"They'd see the Dick for who he is again," Beers says.

"That's what we assumed," June argues. "And in the interest of doing something quick and dirty because time isn't on our side, it made sense."

"You're rethinking that?" I say.

"Yes. I'm realizing our premise could be flawed. With the photo disabled, the smart light will stimulate the brain in an untargeted way. That's dangerous. Users could feel good about whatever crosses their mind, whatever they happen to see while using the app. Something random. Even something they actually hate."

"Like the Dick," Beers grunts in frustration.

"That's my point. We shouldn't be messing around with untargeted smart light."

"So, June, what should we do?" I ask.

"More than disable the existing photo."

"Like what?" I press.

"I haven't gotten that far," she admits. "Maybe substitute a different photo."

I point out that the Russians will spot an unfamiliar image immediately.

"Only if they're alert," she counters.

"Based on past behavior, that's a big if," Beers says. "I say we go on the offence. No more playing defense."

Nick brings us back to Kurt's disturbing new info: there may not even be an update. All this may be out of our control.

But June isn't fazed. "Then we force an update."

"Could we?" Darah asks.

She's looking at me, as if I have the definitive word on this. "It's possible," I say. Pretty much anything is possible; the question is how complicated forcing an update would be, and if we could do it fast enough. Not wanting to explain all this to Darah, I say, "Let's assume the update will happen before any attack."

June agrees. No point solving something that may not be a problem. "Let's just do the most effective hack we can. We're the best at what we do. Have faith in that."

I'm surprised to hear her mention faith. It's not a word you normally hear June use, not the kind of leg you expect her to stand on. But I agree: when it comes to hacking, we're the best. Unbeatable. "Okay then. Let's say we're doing this. You do realize a more complex hack will require more quantum programming."

"Of course."

"And that programming will be on you."

"Understood."

I'm not trying to discourage her, just making sure we're fully on the same page. When it seems we are, I say, "What image do we use?"

Beers suggests a cartoon of the Dick. Or something funny.

June nixes that. Any attempt at humor could backfire. "We can't count on the area of the brain the app is stimulating—presumably the left prefrontal cortex—to parse a joke. The app would have to target the extrastriate cortex. And our hack can't change what it targets in the brain."

Beers isn't willing to abandon what he calls a "bad Dick pic strategy." He suggests the Dick's decapitated head. When that is met with strident opposition, he says, "Don't we want people to *like* that?"

"Beers!" Darah says.

"No pics of the Dictator," Nick says.

June is nodding. "We want to give the hack teeth without going violent. Without letting random smart light loose in the brain. I think we go with something neutral."

"How about photos of nature?" Darah says.

No one objects, so we run through options.

"Redwoods," Nick says.

"Like I said before, poppies," Zack says.

Darah lobbies for Monet's waterlilies. She still has the images she used in the penthouse.

I'm about to say go with the redwoods since Nick said it first, when the kid speaks up. "Hold on!" For a sec, I think he's talking to Dharma about his sock, but he means all of us. "A new photo isn't enough. We can do better."

"It'll have to be enough," I say. We're not going back to square one, we gotta keep rolling.

"Wait, Jedd," June says. "Let's hear what the kid has to say."

I'm surprised she's taking him so seriously. But I guess a few minutes can't hurt. Besides, we want to maximize impact, and there's a chance he's onto something. "Okay," I say. "Shoot."

"We can use sound," he says.

"Sound?" NicknZack express their disbelief in unison.

"You mean music?" Darah says. "Like a song?"

"Sure, let's rickroll 'em!" Beers says. "Couldn't be more harmless."

"How's a song better than a photo?" I ask. "Besides, if the app suddenly starts making music, it'll be a dead giveaway it was hacked."

"Not a song," June says quickly. "We can't pump sound into people's brains. We don't want to create an earworm."

"She's right." The kid giggles as he sticks a finger in one ear to shake loose any worms. "I'm thinking of a natural sound vibration they can't actually hear."

June turns to me. "I can tell you why that's better than a photo. A photo requires the brain to interpret its meaning, whereas pure sound is nonverbal. More direct. We all have personal associations with sounds, but there's less likelihood of a natural sound triggering unintended subjective responses."

"A fart, then," Beers says. "We're talking about the Dick, right?"

Darah swats away his suggestion as if it were a verbal gnat. "I have a library of nature sounds. Waterfalls, waves on the beach, forest rain, songbirds, crickets. Take your pick."

But the kid is shaking his head. "We need a vibration that's universal."

At first I think he's referring to the global hum. Except that phenomenon was debunked decades ago. So I ask what he means.

"I mean the original vibration that underlies all sound," he says matter-of-factly, as if that's something we listen to every morning over our first cup of coffee. Then he elaborates. "It's what emanated from the Big Bang at the creation of the universe. The primordial sound. But it's also in our world here and now. *You* know what I mean," he says, looking at June.

"I think I do," she says. "I know that acoustic wave phonons underlie sound. Coupling them with qubits allows quantum computers to work at room temp instead of near absolute zero." She stops to consider how that's relevant for us now. "What you're saying is that sound vibrations exist in every object, even though we don't hear anything with our ears."

The kid is nodding. "We can produce that kind of soundless sound for the app."

"How?" Darah asks.

He hums a deep note, then replicates it on his flute, deep and steady and pure. I notice it has an uncanny effect, almost as if the more absorbed in it I become, the more it seems to dissolve into silence. "Do that again," I say.

He plays another long note on his flute.

We all listen for what he called the soundless sound.

Again I sense the sound dissolving. I hear the flute. But I can also perceive it as just vibration. Maybe my lack of musical ability has finally come in handy. "You're referring to the subtle vibration?" I say.

"Yes," the kid says. "I mean put that in the app."

I'm still not sure I understand, but June is excited. "If we convey that vibration via the app," she says, "people won't know what hit them."

"Hit them?" Beers says. It's obvious what he's thinking.

But June is shaking her head. "Not physically. I mean hit in a good way."

"Okay," I say. "But we'd have to program it into the smart light."

"Good luck with that," Beers adds.

"No problem!" the kid exclaims. "Programming sound and pics is interchangeable."

"It's all qubits," June says.

"Yes!" The kid is practically jumping up and down. "We'll be programming sound into light. Don't you love it!?"

I give them both a *hope you know what you're talking about* look and remind myself I'm the kind of leader who gives everyone a full say. This is an inclusive process. I just wish it wasn't a life-or-death moment. Really, the prospect of a devastating strike on California has changed everything. Instead of the simplest, fastest hack, we're about to attempt what could be the most sophisticated hack in Silicon Valley history.

The two of them continue to build their case. I recall the kid talking about a formula that paired sound frequencies and colors when he first came to the farm. I thought he was pulling our legs. Now I'm struggling to keep up. I turn to June: "So you're sold on this?"

She nods. "Yes, the universal sound has a unifying effect on consciousness. That means the app will generate calmness."

The kid flashes a grin. "Happiness, created by the Happy App! Perfect!"

Beers is still skeptical. "So users will get a blast of smart light and be enlightened by the sound of Om?"

The kid laughs. "I doubt anyone will be enlightened by an app."

"Of course not," June says. "To be clear, yogis and mystics aren't the only ones who believe in the effects of sound vibrations. Scientists do too. At the very least, users of this app will become more relaxed, get a sense of peace."

"I guess there's zero risk that would boost the Dick's favorability ratings," Beers adds.

"My concern," says Darah, who's been listening intently, "is whether this could be considered another form of mind control. I mean, we'd be doing it with a compassionate intent, but we'd still be interfering with people's brains."

June immediately objects. "There's a big difference between blasting them with the Dictator's ugly mug and transmitting a pure sound vibration."

I agree and elaborate. "The Dictator's image is a covert influence users wouldn't expect to have pumped into their brains when they purchase an app. It's invasive, deceptive, plain dirty. That's what makes it mind control. However, if the vibration is outside the frequency range of audible sound yet can generate happiness, then users are receiving what they purchased the app for."

"Don't forget, the primordial sound already exists everywhere," the kid says. "Including within every user. You aren't giving them anything they don't already have."

I like that.

Darah and Beers and the twins are satisfied too.

All that remains is to determine whether we're committed to carrying it out. A simple voice vote answers that.

Although everyone assumes I will continue in the lead role, that no longer makes sense. This more ambitious hack requires more quantum computing expertise than I bring. June is the logical one to manage it. I ask if she will step up.

"Sure," she says, and adds one condition: the kid must be her righthand person.

"You got it," I say. "Now please put the rest of us to work."

*Krishna said, "Bheema did the right thing. Even if he
did not follow all the rules of fair fighting, his actions cannot
be compared to the crimes of our enemies. Duryodhana was a cheat
all along. Leave him to his fate, and the Pandavas to theirs."*

UPDATED: Beers

We've been working nonstop. The kid is at June's elbow, coaching her along. That's a shocker, no? June is managing the operation and doing all the coding, but I'm not fooled. He's the brains behind this, with his vision of reprogramming the app to use sound. Including doing it with effing QPL. Fortunately June has the skills to follow his instructions.

The new code produces inaudible sound waves he calls "universal sound." June is embedding it in the smart light. Bleeding-edge stuff. It makes sense when he describes it, though I think June is the only one who fully gets it. Of course, none of them thought *I'd* get it, not after I ranted about planting a bomb. And I meant it when I said it. Every word. Nothing would satisfy me more than blowing the Dick to smithereens. Wipe out that kakistocracy for good. Ultimately though, my rant was just a rant. When Jedd and the kid came up with a wicked cool strategy, I simmered down. I mean, we're all entitled to our moments. But I'm no lunatic.

Under normal circumstances, I'd drop everything and watch what June and the kid are doing. Offer to assist so I could learn.

But my assignment is listening to the audio stream, and I can't break away.

It was past midnight when I started monitoring. There was nothing but dead air, so I suggested we stick to daytime surveillance. But June insisted we've already caught Kurt outside office hours and can't risk missing new info. Like I said, she's calling the shots. Which means I have no choice but to sit here and listen all night.

Darah is by my side, dozing occasionally, then perking up and giving me shoulder rubs. It can't be easy to sit on the sidelines while the rest of us work. Or at least do our best to stay awake. In her perkier moments, she pokes around in the kitchen and comes out with snacks. Mostly sliced fruit. Somewhere in the wee hours, she realizes we have pistachios and all the other ingredients for gosh-e fil, a pastry from her childhood. Piecing together her mother's recipe from memory so she can make it now should keep her awake for a while.

This hack is a long shot. We're talking about a teenage geek outsmarting an army of Russian quantum programmers. Our odds of success are what? Ten percent? One percent? Which translates into a ninety-plus percent chance of the unthinkable: release of the Russians' updated app, followed by a surprise strike on California. The only worse scenario would be if they skip the update and simply attack.

Our lives are already upside down. Living in exile is like an altered reality, where we obsess day in and day out over threats we never took that seriously, that personally. Sure, as a security guard and an informed citizen, I tracked everything from office politics to international politics. Still, I didn't let any of it define my life. Now it does. Everything has escalated. We're not anonymous hackers watching world events like flies on a wall, we've got skin in this game. We're the chefs de cuisine for this hack. Even if its success is about as likely as pancakes growing on a palm tree.

The kid doesn't seem too concerned though. Being cool is his trademark. He acts like he could care less about the outcome.

His cool has rubbed off on June. Especially considering how unglued she became earlier. Her trademark is speed. No one codes faster than June or multitasks more ambidextrously. Not only is she hacking the app at top speed, but she's taking what amounts to a crash course in reprogramming smart light. When June does something, she gives one thousand percent. For all I know, she'll come out of this fluent in Russian as well.

I hear the kid coaching her, making comments like "Take it line by line. Don't stress about the end result." And "All we can do is do our best and see what happens." And "Remember, like an SDV." That last makes no sense. This isn't about hacking the chariot. But I could learn a thing or two from the rest.

Shortly after sunrise, as I'm listening to the audio in a hypnagogic state, my eardrums receive a sudden electro-techno jolt. There'd better be a special spot in hell for the jerk who plays this mix at odd hours in the penthouse. If I ever have the chance, I'll make sure he gets there. Now I dial down the volume to avoid an encore.

Little of consequence is said in the penthouse all day. The Ks banter about the new Happy App logos on their espresso lattes. About who misplaced their lip balm this time. Keith announces that he's doing laps in his condo's pool this weekend. Hardly sounds like he's expecting a strike on California. If anyone is, they don't mention it. Basically they're in the same boat we are, awaiting news about the update's progress.

Jedd, who's been keeping an eye on the darknet site while he codes, says he can see Karin popping in and out, presumably looking for word from the Russians. Who seem to be ghosting her. On my end, I hear her bitching about this to Keith. The irony is Jedd knows more than she does, as he's moving freely around all corners of the darknet site, staying abreast of the Russians' progress.

As the second day dawns—another day, thank god, without a surprise strike on California—I realize it's Saturday. The days have blurred so much I've almost lost track. Which may not matter much for our hack but matters for monitoring the Ks. They have lives in the real world, and even with everything going on, I wouldn't expect them to show up at the penthouse today.

When I point this out to June, she agrees to put me on a new assignment, helping Jedd and the twins lint and clean code. It's crunch time and we need to catch any and all bugs. "If you don't mind, keep one ear on the audio," she says. "Just in case."

The code turns out to require such intense focus that I can't manage to listen with more than half an ear. It's like trying to follow live basketball while cooking an elaborate recipe—you miss the best plays, at least if you want to be able to eat what you've cooked. Till suddenly I'm blasted. This time it's not electro-techno. No, sounds like someone landed a bellyflop on my eardrums. "Listen to this," I say, turning up the volume for the others.

"You're kidding," June says. "They're swimming?"

Nick rolls his eyes. "In the new penthouse pool."

"Or Keith took the rum to his condo for a dip," Zack says.

He's being facetious but it's the most logical explanation. Unless you think Keith scraped the mic off the bottle and pinned it to his shirt. Or his swim trunks. Which would mean he had to find it first. And we know it was essentially invisible.

Muffled voices are audible in the background, then a child: "Daddy, gimme a towel?"

For some reason, Darah looks embarrassed. Like we just caught someone naked.

So I turn down the volume and tell everyone to go back to

catching bugs. Really though, it's whacky, this dude taking the rum wherever he goes. Gives new meaning to rumdum.

We work through the weekend, putting in long shifts, with brief naps for those who need them. If the Russians can work around the clock, so can we. I'm good with one nap each night. June and the kid, however, stay on the hack straight through to Monday morning, when they announce the job is done.

The version of the app that transmits a universal sound vibration instead of the Dick's pic is ready to export from Jedd's sandbox to the darknet site. All we have to do is wait for the Russians to load their update so we can swoop in and replace their version with ours. We know the timing will be tricky. But the lion's share of hard work is behind us. We did it!

In honor of the moment, I run outside and shake the windchimes. It's the best celebratory salute I can come up with.

"Outstanding job!" Jedd is thumping the kid on his shoulders when I step back inside.

The kid, however, isn't interested in our fuss. "No big deal," he says. "I just ran some calculations to produce the universal sound. And June let the code flow through her fingers." You'd think he has an allergy to praise. A contagious allergy, considering June has caught it.

"Did you test it?" I ask.

June confirms they did as much as possible prior to hooking up to the quantum computer.

"And?"

"Everything's working."

"Could you hear the universal sound?" Darah wants to know.

June says that's impossible. It's not an audible sound, it's a vibration in the brain. Even sensitive people won't hear anything when they use the app.

Which reminds me how insanely hokey all this is. Our very

lives are riding on something so flimsy, so implausible, so out of control. It kills me to be this out of control. I may be just a security guard, but I know programmers double-check and triple-check their work. We should be doing that now, not relying on the kid's word. Even if we can't test the backend, we can look for obvious user-interface glitches.

When I mention this, Jedd takes a peek at the darknet site and reports the Russians haven't added any new code in the past hour. The update's release appears imminent.

"That could be two minutes or two days," I say.

Jedd acknowledges it's hard to know. "Okay, we have a window, so let's do some front-end testing, like you suggested, Beers."

The twins second that. "The more eyes and ears, the better," Nick says.

"The more brains, the better," Zack adds.

The kid agrees. Not that he's the one making this call. Jedd has already opened the app on his tablet to begin testing.

He hasn't gotten much further than tapping the first balloon when my attention is diverted by voices in my ear. The penthouse crew are back on mic. No splashing today. "D-day!" I hear Karin exclaim. My guess is she's referring to the update.

"Hey, bro," I say, "check the site."

Jedd hops off the app and onto the site and immediately confirms the Russians' update has been linked to both the quantum computer and the HSys dedicated site. They aren't following HSys protocol: release is scheduled for noon. In less than an hour. There's no time to check let alone double-check our work.

There's a brief scramble as the twins lobby for finishing just this one test, and June says all our focus needs to be on replacing the Russians' version ahead of the scheduled release.

"I'm making an executive decision," Jedd says. "We've taken too many risks. We go with what we've got."

Nick looks at the kid. "Didn't you write code to delay its release?"

"I did," he says.

Jedd points out that was in case the Russians scheduled an immediate release. Which didn't happen. So there's no reason to program a delay. "Though if I run into a snag," he adds, "we may still need it."

With that, he gets on task.

The digital gods are smiling on us. Jedd is able to seamlessly replace the Russians' update with our doctored version. He has all his bases covered and then some. Not only does he remain invisible on the site while he works and makes sure our version is invisible to the Russians, but he throws in code so our version carries the Russians' timestamp. In case they snoop, they'll have to probe very deep to realize they aren't looking at their own update. Things couldn't go more smoothly. He pulls out with five minutes to spare before noon.

We sit around Jedd's tablet and count down the minutes, then seconds.

At noon, Jedd opens the app on his tablet. Sure enough, it reloads, indicating an update has taken place. We already knew from notes on the darknet site it's a forced update: if you don't get it automatically, you have to manually download or your app won't work anymore.

"Good. It updated," I say. "How do we know it's our version not the Russians' version?"

"We don't," says Nick quickly.

"I have a hunch it's our version." Zack sounds unsure.

"No need to rely on hunches," the kid says. "June added a signature for that very reason."

"Good thinking." Jedd projects the app onto the coffee table screen so we can find it.

The kid leads him through the app, stopping at the "What's your favorite color?" screen, then instructs him to magnify the purple balloon in the top right corner.

"What are we looking for?" Darah wants to know.

June points to a red dot in the sea of purple.

Jedd blows it up a bit more, revealing a tiny red A.

"A for Ansirk," Nick says.

"Or for Ahmadi," Darah says shyly.

"Either way, nice touch," Zack says.

"Yeah, nice," I echo. "Or not. It's a bug we should have caught while checking code."

"You weren't supposed to catch it," the kid says.

"Since we didn't," Jedd says, as the kid nods, "hopefully neither will the Russians or anyone else." The real news, he says, is our version made it into the update. We pulled this off. Kurt and his goons got pwned. Totally pwned!

Although we've hardly slept for days, everyone is too excited to relax.

The kid picks up his flute, goes over to the hearth, and starts to play.

"No need to listen to you anymore," I say. "If we want pure sound, we can use our Happy App."

Of course everyone knows I'm teasing.

Darah brings out the last of the gosh-e fil, and we sit around and speculate. How long before we see results? Will users feel or behave differently? Will they notice the update? Even if it's not possible to hear the sound, will some users report weird sounds? Will the Dick still try to attack California? If he doesn't, can we claim credit, say our hack made the difference?

I'm concerned we'll never know the answer to that ultimate question.

June suggests we might find clues in the early reviews. She uses Jedd's tablet to check what's been posted. I tune in to the audio stream. Neither of us turns up anything.

Nor do we have greater clarity the next morning. While the others gather in the living room as Jedd checks his tablet for news related to the app, I prepare a fancy breakfast. Black forest waffles with cherries and whipped cream. Except we don't have either cherries or cream, so I substitute a rose water and strawberry compote. When it's ready, I set everything on the kitchen table and summon the others.

"Find anything?" I ask as I serve Jedd a waffle with two dollops of compote.

He shakes his head.

"Wonder if their update had code to create a frenzy of hate, like HQ wanted," June muses.

"We'll never know," Jedd says. Technically he could go in and check. But it doesn't sound like he's about to.

After breakfast, we return to the living room and continue to scan for clues. Since we're limited to Jedd's tablet, he does most of the checking while June and I take turns with the audio stream. We hear a few comments about how the update was a slam dunk, about HQ being pleased. After that, the mic seems to go on the fritz again.

Really, it's a big heap of nothing. Nothing notable on the darknet site. No action on the audio stream. No change in the app's popularity. No burst of reviews or discussion about it. Nothing from official State news sources. Nothing from alternative or California news. No surprise attack. That last is of course the best news.

Bottom line, we're in limbo.

Over lunch, we discuss options to pass the time as we wait.

I'm grumpy because all the projects I had in mind have already been done: patching the barn roof, planting a garden, painting the porch, hanging a basketball hoop on the redwood. The redwood chess set I carved is ready for two of us to find enough time to play. We could do that.

Darah has another idea: fill the potholes in the driveway. Since the kid is the only one who drives to town, it's odd she would think of that.

"You mean," June says, "so we can get out faster if we have to flee?"

Jedd squelches that. "We're not going anywhere."

I offer to take some measurements. Then the kid can order materials.

"Aren't you worried that'll look sus?" Nick asks.

The conversation shifts to whether a sole caretaker living here would take on a substantial road repair project. And whether it's safe for me to be at the far end of the driveway, where the deepest potholes are, visible to cars passing on the main road. In the end, we can't reach a consensus.

After a couple days, uncertainty has eclipsed any relief we felt after stopping the Russians' update. Yes, we pulled off a historic hack, but all that work was a waste if the kid's universal sound hasn't reached users' brains. Which we don't know.

Nor do we know if or when California could be under attack. That appeared imminent a few days ago. Yet there's been no sign of a strike. Maybe HQ is still waiting for a shift in favorability ratings or other app user analytics. Maybe they're readying the killer app. If there is such a thing. Or maybe, just maybe, our hack inspired someone in HQ who's been using the app to grow a conscience.

Today after breakfast, I check the audio stream. It's been dead since shortly after the update. I don't know why I bother to sit here listening to silence. Really, there are only so many crossword puzzles even a cruciverbalist can do.

I'm thinking of venturing down the driveway to measure the potholes, to hell with safety, when Jedd—who continues to spend each day online, scouting news related to the app—says, "Hey, look at this!"

I remove my earbuds and ask what's up.

"A story out of the States." Mostly we only get State-run

media, but this is from an alternative source that sometimes sneaks stories through.

I read the headline: "Protest Draws Thousands." Photos show a large crowd assembled at the Arizona border wall.

Jedd summarizes what it says: "Despite heavy drone coverage in the area, people converged on both sides of the Arizona border to stage a nonviolent protest. Spontaneously. No indication of any organized effort." He checks social media and says a briefer version of the story is currently trending.

"This could be something," I say.

We summon the others and fill them in.

Darah immediately asks the obvious: "Was anyone killed?"

Jedd skims the report, as well as others that have popped up since. "Apparently not."

I speculate that if it was spontaneous, the authorities may have been caught off guard.

Darah is having a hard time understanding this. "Why weren't they afraid of the drones? They're programmed to kill, right?"

After we've tossed this back and forth for a while, June responds with another question: "Could this be an effect of the Happy App?"

Jedd says we can't rule out the possibility.

The twins look skeptical.

"Were people there even using the app?" Nick asks.

Jedd reads the original report aloud. There's no mention of the app. People are voicing their outrage at the wall, at being prevented from reuniting with family. At the drone threat. Some in the photos are holding or waving tablets, but that tells us nothing about the app. They could be taking photos or inviting friends to join them.

"No mention of the app doesn't mean there's no connection," I say, aware how much I want our update to succeed, how desperate I am for any sign of success.

June reminds us that the app could be having an effect at a neurological level, below conscious awareness.

"No one's mentioning the Dictator," Darah says. "That's gotta be a good sign."

The kid has been listening quietly. Now he asks, "Is this the only event?"

"Only one I've seen," Jedd says.

"No point speculating," I say, turning to Jedd. "We can find out if there are others."

He says he'll check. Of course there could be others that are never reported, that we'll never hear about.

"Dig deeper," I say.

He says he's on it.

While Jedd investigates, the rest of us discuss how unusual an event like this is in the States. Darah explains it's not technically illegal to attend public gatherings but going is too risky. So people don't. You never know when an instant crackdown might occur. The Dick of course holds his own events, usually with people bussed in to inflate the crowd. She knew people who attended a gathering and were disappeared while there. That was years ago. It's likely worse now.

Jedd is still looking for signs of another event, not finding any. Eventually if nothing surfaces, we'll have to write this off as a onetime affair.

We don't have to wait long, however. The next day there's a second event. This time it's in NYC, with students and teachers taking to the streets during lunch hour. First it's one school in Brooklyn, then a couple schools in the Bronx, then schools all over the city. We're looking at upwards of ten thousand in the streets.

Jedd finds live coverage on social media that has managed to bypass State media control. "Look," he says. "They're protesting the ban on teaching science."

While we're watching that, reports come in about an event in DC. And one in Chicago. And smaller events popping up around the country. Some focus on the lack of funding for schools, others on government control over what teachers are allowed to teach.

By afternoon, an expanded wave of events has appeared online. These are focused on the desire to reinstate democratic elections. Crowds are protesting the Dictator's life term, protesting the loss of their right to cast a vote to determine their own leaders. And along with that, all the laws stripping them of other basic democratic rights: a fair judicial system, a free press, civil rights and economic justice, the right to nonviolent protest.

Over the next few days, the events get bigger and more frequent. As well as more widespread. And in apparently random locations. Chillicothe, Ohio. Spirit Lake, Idaho. Hartland, Vermont. Blessing, Texas. The official State media denounces all gatherings as criminal and threatens severe consequences for anyone participating. Yet with literally millions showing up at unpredictable times and in unpredictable places—hospitals, daycare centers, retirement homes, clinics, factories, parks, parking lots, malls, warehouses—enforcement is nothing short of impossible. We watch all this, jaws on the floor. What the fuck is going on?

When it's clear this is not a one-time-only or even a hundred-times-only event, I ask the big question: "Is this just coincidence?"

No one has a clear answer.

Jedd sums up what we know: "A few days after the updated app was released and users started receiving the universal sound through the smart light, there was a massive uprising in the States. Outrage that was simmering silently for years burst onto the streets. About the Dictator. About free elections. About free speech and the crackdown on resistance. About racism and social justice. About gun violence. About schools. About health care. About science and the environment and climate change. On so many issues, people are saying enough is enough."

"It sure is enough," I say. "But why now?"

"Today's the seventeenth day since the update," June says. It's not clear whether she thinks that's long enough for the app to have had an effect.

"I want to believe it's the app," Darah says.

"So do I," June says. "But there's no way to prove it."

"Maybe go with our hunch?" Nick says.

I'm not willing to do that. Nor are the others. So I keep raising the question: Is it more than coincidence?

June points to the fallacy of *post hoc ergo propter hoc*, which she translates for those who didn't study Latin or logic as "correlation does not equal causation." All we have now is the former.

We go around in circles, debating whether the exposure people's brains have had to the universal sound was enough to alter their feelings, beliefs, and behavior. That of course was the purpose of the hack, and now people are suddenly doing what they were terrified for years to even think of doing. And they're doing it without leaders or any form of coordination. It's like a grassroots movement but without any roots. Clearly something has changed. If the app didn't cause it, what did?

We continue to toss that around. Still without good answers.

Finally the kid says, "Let's be real: we humans can't always know things for certain."

He has a point. Frustrating as it is, we may never know if the Happy App is causing this. All we know is that people are standing up everywhere, with conviction, with unity, and almost entirely without violence. We just don't know why. Nor, for that matter, do we know the status of the attack on California. Best case scenario, the protests have taken all of HQ's attention and resources, forcing them to abandon a strike.

The next day we discover a website listing reports of events, as well as an app to locate one near you in real time. Since they're all spontaneous, the list changes by the minute. Some in the States use code words to preserve anonymity, but they're not hard to figure out. Like "free concert" and "rock on" and "flash dance."

Darah points out many of the code words involve music or sound. Of course that doesn't prove anything.

We check for events in California. There's one in San Francisco right now, though it's midmorning on a workday. Reports suggest a hundred thousand people.

"My god!" says Darah. "What are we waiting for? Let's go."

The kid points to one that's closer, in Palo Alto.

"Then let's go there," she says.

I love seeing the old Darah, up for anything. But we can't forget a key fact: we're still in exile. Mericans may feel freer, but our situation is different. We have Russian agents tracking us. "I don't think it's a good idea," I say.

Jedd reinforces that. "We're still in Canada."

But the kid wants to go.

"Your ID is officially here," Jedd says. "Nothing's stopping you."

"Then I'm going," he declares.

I'm surprised when June takes his side. "If this is the kind of historic turning point we all want to believe it is, we should ease up a bit. We can still keep our IDs in Canada. No one will notice if our physical bodies show up briefly at a local rally. Especially if it's a huge crowd."

In the end we compromise. The kid will take Darah with him. I'll go along to provide security. To be honest, I'm going because no way I'm going to miss this. And because I want to share it with Darah. Jedd and June will stay and monitor the news and the darknet site. The twins aren't into large gatherings of any type anyway, so they're happy to stay.

"Remember to take photos," Nick tells the kid.

"We predict you'll have the time of your lives," Zack adds, as the three of us head for Darah's car.

The potholes are deeper than the last time I was this far down our driveway. Maybe because of all the rain we've had lately. Certainly not from heavy traffic to the farm.

There's no rain now. Just blazing sun and clear blue sky. And bumpy clay dirt. It's strange to be in a car after so long. Thirteen weeks. I don't know why Darah is acting like it's no big deal, like she drove here yesterday.

As the kid heads down to the freeway, then north on it, the two of them chatter about how this is the breakthrough we've been waiting for, evidence our hack worked. Both are stoked. It's hard not to be swept up by their gusto. Except I'm not convinced. These events could be another way the Dick is duping people.

The app for locating events put this one in downtown Palo Alto. As we get off the freeway at Page Mill and cut across toward El Camino, I find myself second guessing our decision. If we really want to see what's happening, we're short-changing ourselves in a small place like Palo Alto. "Should we go to the city instead?" I ask.

"What's wrong with Palo Alto?" Darah counters.

"Probably only a handful of people. Someone could notice us."

The kid offers to get back on the freeway.

But Darah wants to stick with it. "If it's a small crowd, we can hang on the outside and get a feel for things. We don't have to stay long."

It's risky but I see her point. Besides, after being holed up at the farm, a large crowd could feel overwhelming.

Traffic is moving slowly as we continue east on Page Mill. No cars are heading west. When we reach the intersection where we plan to turn north on El Camino, suddenly we're faced with a roadblock. Beyond it, the road is filled with people.

"Holy crackamoli!" I say. "Look at that."

Darah turns to the kid. "Keep going straight. We can bypass this mess and get to the event."

The kid and I respond in unison: "This *is* the event."

"But downtown is more than a mile away," Darah objects.

It takes a minute to convince her we are, in fact, at the outskirts of the event. I couldn't have been more wrong in anticipating a small crowd.

In the meantime, the kid has jumped the curb on Page Mill and parked between cars already left there. We get out and walk north on El Camino, following the crowd. The online reports described these events as decentralized webs of humanity that begin with a few people protesting at one location and grow from there, stretching in all directions. That seems to be the case here. The original protesters tagged the event in downtown Palo Alto, but we'll probably never see them or know who they are. Not that it matters. We can see from signs being carried and hear from the chants around us that people are here to support those rallying in the States, to support their cries for freedom and justice and a new government.

Darah grabs the kid's arm. "You did this!" she exclaims.

"We did," he says.

Either way, that's not something we should be discussing in public, so I hush them. I remind the kid to get good pics with his tablet. At the same time, I remind myself to stay in active security mode. It's been a while since I've done that in the physical world.

In fact, this is nothing like the tame environs of HSys. I try to scan everyone we pass, but it's literally impossible. Too many people, all moving too fast. Not to mention I'm not sure who or what I'm looking for. On a personal level, we want to avoid detection, avoid the possibility someone spots us and relays that to our enemies.

Then there's the broader concern of a disruption at the event. The news has reported peaceful rallies. But one never knows. This could be the one event that blows up. For no predictable reason.

Or maybe there is a predictable reason. These are the first

events in California. What if the Dick intends to use them as an excuse to launch his surprise attack? I didn't think of that while reading reports online. Or when I agreed it was a good idea to drive down here. But here in the crowd, it makes total sense. Hit us with a few dirty bombs at the same time as dropping a blackout on California. The perfect recipe for chaos. For a successful takeover.

That thought sends my pulse into overdrive. In this sea of people, I may be the only one aware of the possibility. To make matters worse, we've reached the confluence of El Camino and Stanford University. So many are pouring out of the campus that we can't go farther without pushing and shoving. No one is moving fast anymore. It's gridlock.

I've been keeping a hand on Darah's arm so we don't get separated, while relying on the kid to stay with us. Now I pull her closer and check if she's okay.

"More than okay," she says. "Can you believe the vibe here?"

I agree it's upbeat. I may not be feeling it, but that's definitely the vibe. People are literally dancing in the street, even as they're pressed up against each other. I'm glad Darah isn't freaked by it. I don't want her worrying about dirty bombs either. That's my job. But my pulse is still racing, and I'm not about to let my guard down. In addition to continuously scanning the crowd, I decide to approach some folks, gain a little intel.

I ask a student next to me why she's at this rally.

She scrunches her nose like I asked her to eat bubblegum ice cream with hot sauce. "I wouldn't call it a *rally*. I'd never go to a political rally. Not my style."

"Then why are you here?"

"Because I have to be. It's like—" She stops to search for words. "Like we're aware of our power now. You don't want to miss that."

Her friend leans in and adds, "I always felt one person can't make a difference. I still do, actually. But all of us together can. That's our power."

"Yeah, dude," a third says. "All of us united are so much stronger than the Dictator."

Still seeing no evidence of a dirty bomb—not that it's clear what that would look like in this crowd—I turn and ask another student why he's here.

He shrugs. "Everyone's outraged, so it's chill."

I ignore the cynicism. "But why now?"

"Timing," he says, getting serious. "You can't keep stomping on people's freedom, on their lives. Eventually they won't take it anymore."

"We've been sitting tight for years," someone else says. "No more!"

The way he's holding his tablet, with the sunlight reflecting off it, it's hard to tell, but I think I see colored balloons. "Hey," I say, "you know the app that's so popular?"

"The Happy App?"

"Yeah."

"What about it?" The edge in his voice suggests he won't admit to trying it.

"Dunno. Just curious if it has anything to do with what's happening here."

He gives me a can't-believe-you-said-that sneer and dismisses the idea as idiotic.

His friend is equally dismissive. "Who cares, bro? Do we look unhappy? We're doing the right thing now, that's what matters."

Which is pretty much the answer I expected. Even if the app is working, people won't be aware of it. We'd have to zap all of them with effing brain imaging to prove what's going on within their skulls because of the app.

I turn back to Darah and the kid, who are also talking to

people. One woman pushing a stroller says she's hopeful her child can meet their grandparents in Texas for the first time.

An older man says he was afraid he'd die before he saw a day like today.

His partner says it's not like they'd given up. They wrote thousands of postcards to random strangers in the States, believing that would bring the Dictator down. He laughs. "Now we realize those cards only made *us* happy. We had no idea how to really make a difference."

I wonder if this couple might be using the app. It's possible, right? But I don't pursue it.

By now the crush around us is thinning. There may not be a dirty bomb after all. We may actually make it out of here alive.

Then, as we start moving again, I spot a face to my left, about two layers deep in the crowd. It's Keith. Fucking Keith! His ice-blue killer eyes are trained on Darah. This can't be mere coincidence. He must have tracked us here. My security instincts kick into high gear. I grab her arm and spin her in the opposite direction, muttering something about all the happy faces. Thank god she didn't spot him.

The kid follows as I steer us away from Keith.

After a few minutes, I glance over my shoulder and scan the crowd. We seem to have lost him. Still, I worry it's too late. The damage is done. He's probably already reported to HQ that we're not in Canada. They must be dispatching agents to the farm right now. I need to warn Jedd and the others.

I suggest as forcefully as I can to Darah and the kid that it's time to head home. I don't tell them why. They'll find out soon enough.

As we push through the crowd, I picture us in a race against the agents. We need to make it to the farm first. Our family can't be split. But I have no idea what to do if we make it back. Destroy our computers? Run and hide in the underbrush? I'm kicking myself, realizing we never made plans for this kind of scenario.

Then it occurs to me Keith probably had agents with him. Even if we lost him, they must be tailing us. Most likely they'll jump us just as we reach the car. I'm starting to think we'd be safer staying in the crowd, using it as a shield—I mean, how could they harm us in the midst of all these happy people?—when a thunderous roar goes up around us. It doesn't start slowly and build up, it just erupts full force out of nowhere.

Fucking shit!

All I can think is *it's happening.* A dirty bomb has gone off. Somewhere close by. The attack has started. Our effing worst nightmare. Forget the agents; we're all in the same boat now. This is how democracy dies. And we haven't even made it home.

"The car!" I scream at Darah and the kid.

The roar is so loud they can't hear me.

I scream louder: "The car!! Get to the car!" Reaching out with both arms, I try to shepherd them toward Page Mill.

But they push back. To my astonishment, both are grinning.

The kid pulls my face so close to his that our noses are practically touching. "What's wrong, Beers?" he shouts.

His eyes are glistening. These are unquestionably tears of joy.

That stops me in my tracks. I listen more carefully to the sound around us. In fact, it's gleeful. Jubilant. The roar is coming in waves now. Like a crowd at a sports event. People are jumping up and down, and their jumping creates physical waves in the crowd. They're not feeling terror. They're happy. Ecstatic.

This can't be about an attack. There is no bomb.

I breathe deeply for the first time in what feels like hours. "What's going on?" I shout.

"Something's happened?" Darah shouts back.

I suggest the kid look at his tablet since neither Darah nor I have one. He's been using it to take pics but doesn't receive news alerts.

He looks now and immediately flashes it at us. A huge banner covers the screen: DICTATOR OUT!

At the same moment, a text comes through from Jedd: "did u see news?"

I snatch the tablet out of the kid's hands—I know, rude of me, but he doesn't mind—and text back: "omg yessss! fr?"

"for real!!!"

Within a matter of minutes, we piece together what has happened. The Dick has been ousted. Thrown out on his ass. Suddenly, unexpectedly. But oh-so mercifully. It's not clear whether he went willingly or unwillingly. One woman next to us says it's because of the rallies. Someone else says it's not just the crowds in the streets, but people in the government have also had enough. Another says there's been a coup. One man believes the Dick was executed.

This is of course lots of speculation. It will take time for the full facts to emerge. All we know right now is the Dick is gone. The people are free. We are here and we are safe. Which. Is. No. Small. Thing.

As the truth sinks in, I grab Darah by the waist, plant a wet kiss on her forehead, then hoist her high in the air. And together we howl our happiness to the whole wide world.

*In the grand city of the immortals, Krishna sat on
the highest throne. By his side was Arjuna. All the Pandavas
were there, as was Draupadi. As soon as they saw Yudhishthira,
they rose as one and welcomed him to heaven.*

22

HAPPY: Darah

After science club is over and the last student has left, I pop an
image of the constellations onto the ceiling. It's spring and Ursa
Major is high over the horizon. Since no one else is here, this is for
my pleasure. I like knowing the stars will light up the classroom
all night.

I've been teaching environmental ecology. When all was said
and done, there was no way I could return to HSys. Anyone who
knows anything about PTSD will understand. Instead I took
this job in a Mountain View middle school. They're constantly
upgrading their science program and wanted me to start immediately, though it's spring semester.

It's an awesome ending for a nightmarish year. All the trauma
I thought I'd escaped was suddenly a visceral reality again. Day
to day, I was never certain we'd come out okay. Yet we did. Better
than okay. Beers is a big part of what makes life better for me.
But it's more than Beers. It's everything I learned about myself
during those thirteen weeks of exile. I have greater trust now—in
my friends and family, but also in humanity.

For a long time, I thought the roll of Jedd's die that awful night in the penthouse was a curse on us. So much rested on one single die. If it had landed another way, we'd have avoided exile. But now I also see that keeping our jobs—in that untenable situation—might have robbed us of the chance to defend democracy.

And I'm continuing to see things in new ways. I talked with the kid about that night I almost left the farm, when he acted like playing the flute wasn't any better than obsessing over the Dictator. "I don't get how you could see those as the same," I said. "Like there's no difference between whether we live or die."

He said that wasn't quite what he meant. Of course we want some things and don't want others. That's only human.

"Then what?"

He sized me up, as if to see if I could hear now what I couldn't then. "I was trying to show you a different way to look at things. Not just as positive or negative, good or bad. We don't have to pigeonhole life like that."

"Even though the Dictator is bad—entirely bad?"

"Yes. He can be bad, but you can look at his badness from a quieter place within yourself."

"You mean a place where I don't freak out or run away?"

"Exactly. I wanted to help you find that place."

I told him I did find it. At least some of the time.

He high-fived me. Then he turned serious. "I think we sometimes get confused between what it means to live and what it means to die. As I see it, there's a part of us that never dies. Even if we don't realize it. Or you could say we're part of something that never dies. Either way, if we can find that place within us that never dies, and get comfortable in it, then the world looks different. And we can make different choices." He paused. "Am I making any sense?"

"I think so."

He told me to chew on it.

I've been doing that. I'm still not sure what he's referring to that doesn't die. It seems like one thing you can count on about everything that's alive is that sooner or later it will die. But I do see how life in the dictatorship pushed me into a corner where my only protection was to pretend bad things didn't exist. At the farm, I created armor to protect myself. Yet it turned out that armor was just toxic positivity. It led me to reject everything happening in the world, to believe dealing with it wasn't my responsibility.

Another thing the kid said stayed with me: "Don't keep your vision so narrow." He used the example of a house. We see our own personal life like a small house. We shut our doors and windows, thinking that's how to weather a storm. But that only creates a permanent state of exile. "Darah," he said, "even if it feels small, your house is vast. It has no doors. It has no windows. It's wide open. All our lives are bigger than we imagine. Everything happening in the world is part of our lives. It's not separate from us."

No doubt about it, I'm part of the world now.

When I came to California, I told myself Mom would want me to flee. Really, there wasn't another option. But now I can see the value of staying to fight for what's right. When there is absolutely nothing you can do, then fleeing may be the only course of action. But if there is a chance to help make things better, then it's your duty to stay and fight. I guess wisdom lies in the ability to see the difference.

Beers says I'm back to my old self. I'm more solid, more centered. More purposeful. I have greater faith in myself.

It's true. Instead of armor, I tune in to the universal sound so I don't freak out when I hear negative stuff. I don't need the Happy App for that. I just play my flute. Or I stop and listen for the pure sound at random moments during the day. I quickly discovered it's easy to hear it in my nature apps. But it's also there as a silent vibration in my body. In my breath. In everything else in the world. Maybe becoming aware of that is what the kid meant when he talked about a place within myself that doesn't die. I'll have to ask him.

I also think about Mom's death. I was afraid to do that before. Afraid to admit its reality. Now I hold her in my heart and imagine what it is like to die. No one wants to be tortured by an enemy, die from starvation, or suffer an excruciating death during a pandemic. But I don't believe death has to be that way. When it's my time, I want to die in peace. I want to die knowing the place within myself that doesn't die.

I tidy up my students' tablets and rearrange their chairs in the few minutes before I have to leave to meet Beers at El Carnal. It's funny he picked that spot for us to meet today. But I have no worries because I know we won't run into anyone.

Yes, Keith was at the rally. It was a shock to see him. When our eyes met, I read an unmistakable message, clear and blunt and final, etched in lapis lazuli: *Goodbye, Darah.* I have no idea how he found me in that massive crowd; possibly it was pure chance. But there he was, for a split second before he disappeared. I suspect he felt the walls closing in and realized his best option was to flee. For all I know, he went to Canada.

Luckily Beers didn't notice. He didn't get his much-desired pretext to deliver a punch. Or a swift kick to the groin. Not that he would actually have done either of those on what we've come to jokingly call Happiness Day. The angry Beers is gone. He even swears less. He still gets mad at moments—we all do, we're human—but he's not waking up angry and going to sleep angry. There's no room for anger when he's so proud of what we did, of how we stood up for democracy.

Like me, Beers didn't go back to HSys. Since he didn't need the money to begin with, that wasn't a surprise. His plan is to spend more time on home projects. He started with the potholes. Grander plans are underway as well. Like renovating the barn. The kid talked about getting a cow, but it looks like that won't happen. Instead Beers is turning that area into office space. Jedd will need it.

Right now Jedd is working out of his bedroom. I thought he'd return to HSys as soon as he could. I couldn't imagine him anywhere else, doing anything else. The others thought the same.

"Dude, what's stopping you?" June said when he announced he wasn't returning.

"Zero desire to be there," he said.

She pointed out he could expose the Ks and the Russians. He could tell the truth about the Happy App, assuming the bunker hasn't discovered it yet. He could demand his old job back and maybe even regain the penthouse. Really, his full kingdom awaits.

"Sweet revenge," Beers called it.

Jedd immediately clarified that sweet revenge holds no interest for him.

"Okay," Beers said. "Then bitter revenge or salty revenge. Or revenge under any other name."

Nothing we said made a dent in Jedd's position: he's not returning to HSys. It's not so much about what he doesn't want as it is about what he does want to do. Everything that happened, he said, showed him what that is. He's going into business for himself—with a clear goal, plan, and mission. We learned so much while in exile about the vulnerabilities of cyberspace, about the inability of technology to deal with evil, especially when it's disguised as benevolent. He's convinced he can develop a product that will be lifesaving for our country. For the world, really. "It's a huge task," he said. "But I'm up for it."

He's been working long hours. Which of course is nothing new. Except now when he needs a break, he doesn't limit himself to VR games on his tablet or chasing spacecraft on his canopy screen. Or even throwing balls for Dharma. He and Beers have been playing chess with the redwood set Beers carved. Some days he goes into town and reconnects with friends. He's working on Naomi, seeking a second chance for them. I hope she'll grant it.

His biggest disappointment is that June wouldn't go into

business with him. He tried hard to convince her. They're unstoppable as a team. She has mad skills. He even gave a blanket promise to defer on any and all bickers. But it fell on deaf ears. She is set on a different path.

June has always sworn she'd run for office. Someday. Now there's no excuse. With the Dictator gone, so much must be done to safeguard our rights and freedoms. Not to mention what's on everyone's mind: Will California remain independent? She picked an open race in our district and is laying the groundwork for her campaign. Unafraid to speak her truth in any situation, she'll be an amazing candidate.

We're seeing a new and improved June—less insistent on being right, more open to considering all sides of an issue. When we heard California was being attacked, she dug her heels in and refused to hack the app. I didn't expect that from her. Jedd certainly didn't. I guess we all had some excuse, some reason to avoid stepping up. Hers was the most pivotal though. But then she had an epiphany. Once she committed to the hack, she gave it her all. Yet without getting stressed. Almost like she wasn't invested in the outcome.

I asked her afterward how she was able to do that.

She pointed to the kid. "That's how he lives his life."

And she's right, he does. We've all learned from him. Even Jedd, who was always so cool and levelheaded, is extra cool now.

I intend to work on June's campaign. We all will. In the meantime, though she still lives at the farm, we hardly see her. She's out every day and most evenings meeting with community groups.

We've seen even less of NicknZack. You might think they'd had enough after being cooped up with the rest of us for thirteen weeks. But it wasn't like that. They simply wanted to be on their own, just the two of them, for once. So they moved off the farm. They're also the only ones who went back to HSys. Beers tried to talk them out of it, said they'd feel awkward around the Ks, and even more awkward if the truth about the Happy App comes out.

But they insisted they always liked working there and wanted to see if they could get their jobs back.

Turns out that was easy. After they settled into their new apartment, they paid a visit to HSys and spoke with HR. The next day they had their old jobs again. No questions asked.

About once a week they drive to the farm for dinner, and we catch up on everything. Last time we saw them, they had joined a pod in the R&D building.

"Here's something that will surprise you," Nick said. "Keith left HSys."

Since this confirmed what I picked up at the rally, I wasn't surprised. For some reason, Beers didn't seem surprised either.

But Jedd was taken aback. "Really? Completely out?"

"Yup."

"How do you know?" Beers asked.

The twins said they had a hunch when they saw Kurt and Karin walking across campus. They checked the HSys directory, which showed that Keith had left a few weeks earlier, without providing forwarding info. Kurt and Karin are still in the penthouse and Donna splits time between their pod and the C-suite. The twins promised to stay alert and let us know if they hear anything about the app. So far that's nothing beyond what the whole world knows: it's the best-selling app of all time.

The only one in our family we haven't seen lately is the kid.

Travel was high on his bucket list, but he could never afford to go anywhere. One night he was listing places he'd love to visit: Iceland, Uruguay, New Zealand, Taiwan, Mauritius, Ukraine. Not the States, at least until the government stabilizes.

Beers offered to fund his travel.

The kid said thanks, but he couldn't accept that.

Beers responded with the classic mi casa su casa argument. "Besides, bro," he said, "think of all you've done for us. Do I need to make a list?"

In the end, the kid decided to start with short trips to Canada and Mexico, with the farm remaining his home base. Work on Jedd's office space in the barn started as soon as the kid left, but the loft will remain his spot. He'll stay here in between trips, work on projects with Beers, then head out to other, farther destinations. I'm pleased his life is so full of adventure. But I'd be lying if I said I don't miss him.

I miss playing flutes together. I miss climbing up to Boulder Point and watching for aero cars. I miss weeding the veggie beds. I miss his smile. I miss thanking him every day for his ingenious fix on the app that saved our lives. That may well have saved democracy.

There haven't been any more spontaneous events. The rally in Palo Alto was the largest in this area, and one of the last. I guess some phenomena peak and then fade away. The Happy App itself has become part of the culture. At least a dozen times a day, I have to tell kids to put it away during class.

Of course, the big question is does it work?

Beers says that ultimately doesn't matter. What matters is the Dick is out. People are happier simply because of that.

June believes the smart light technology works, at least as far as its ability to stimulate parts of the brain. The code they created to expose users to the universal sound was brilliant, and she sees no reason to think it wasn't successful. Over time, users may well feel happier. She jokes the kid deserves a Nobel Prize for his contribution. I think she's serious about that.

However, she's dubious when anyone suggests the rallies were a direct result of the app. It doesn't impress her that #happy is right up there with #savedemocracy and #freeelections. "It was all too accelerated, just eighteen days," she says. "We knew the effect on the brain would have to be cumulative. It couldn't have happened so fast." She's also quick to point out that people still have arguments and bad days, so we shouldn't proclaim any miracles.

I disagree with her on that. I mean, she wasn't with us in Palo Alto. She didn't experience the crowd, feel the energy. In that moment, anything was conceivable. Even miracles. Especially miracles. Of course, that's not scientific. But in my heart of hearts, I believe it.

When I walk into El Carnal, Beers is already at the bar. On the same stool where I found Keith that night. He notices me before I have a chance to sneak up on him and greets me with a hug.

"I took the liberty of ordering for you," he says, sliding a margarita toward me.

"What're you having?"

"Moscow mule with spiced rum."

We don't have much time this evening, because the twins are coming for dinner. June will be there too. Beers prepped the meal earlier—egg pp, for old time's sake—and set the oven timer so we only need to get home a few minutes ahead. Besides, the twins are family. They wouldn't care if he served leftovers.

Beers comes into town a couple times a week so we can meet for drinks after I leave work. Now he holds my hand as we chat about our respective days and asks how my kids responded to the lesson on sea level rise in the San Francisco Bay that he watched me prepare last night. He steals kisses between sips of rum. At home we keep a greater distance, out of habit, out of deference to the others. Though it's no secret he sleeps in the attic most nights.

As we walk to our cars, he puts his arm around my shoulder and asks simply, "Happy?"

I tell him he knows I am.

Conversation around the kitchen table starts out light and easy. Not because anyone is tiptoeing, afraid of triggering me, but simply because we aren't in crisis mode anymore. We may not have all the info and answers we'd like to have, yet the entire situation has changed. The Dictator is out. The whole world is happier, and so are we. We talk about our new jobs, about where June should take the chariot for maintenance, about planting raspberries, about installing Li-Fi in the barn. About the miracle that is Beers's tiramisu classico.

We get all the way to dessert without mentioning the huge secret we're still keeping.

Of course I'm keeping my own secret about the nano mic. I have no problem with that. Someday I'll tell Beers and we'll laugh about it. In the meantime, no one is worse off not knowing.

Our secret about the app is a different story. When we went into exile, we decided against going to the authorities, and we've stayed that course. No one knows what we know about why the app was created, who created it, and why and how it was hacked. Lately though, Beers has been making the case it's time to change this. Jedd is amenable, but only if we do it the right way. I imagine June is all for going public since she's an advocate for speaking out. However, she hasn't been home during our recent discussions. Tonight is the first time the six of us have been together in a while.

June eases us into the topic by asking the twins about life at HSys. Then she asks what they've heard about the app.

"It's pretty much a joke around campus," Nick says. "You don't see employees using it, though I guess they're proud of it as a company product."

"They like what it means for their bonuses," Zack says.

"But do they think it works?" June wants to know.

"Does your average HSys flunky really believe it makes people happier?" Beers prompts.

Nick says no. From what he's observed, techies and gamers aren't buying that. They think it's a piece of fluff that lucked out.

Zack says he hasn't heard any conjecture the app might run on more than the most basic technology. Certainly no mention of quantum computing, let alone smart light or the fact that it's operating off a Russian darknet site. "Talk on campus supports your dumb and dumber theory, Jedd. People are dumb, the app is dumb, therefore people love the app."

"Or maybe no one's dumb," Jedd counters. "Having used the app for a while, maybe people love it because it actually makes them happier."

"I've been trying to tell you that," June says.

"You have. But you stop short of saying the app could have inspired the rallies. Let me ask you this: Why do you think those events took place when they did?"

Of course she doesn't have an answer.

Jedd points out that even if the events weren't a result of the app, they are widely believed to have paved the way for the Dictator's demise. He was firmly in power. Until he wasn't. We don't know what happened to him or where he is now. We may never know. Still, the mood of the country—not just California, the States too—is undeniably upbeat. "Here's the irony," he says. "He may have been ousted with the help of the very app he commissioned to consolidate his power. Yet no one suspects he had a role in creating it."

"Not only that," Beers says, "nobody in the bunker is investigating."

"Or if they are," June adds, "we don't know."

Nick points out there's a lot we don't know. For example, when an HSys product soars, normally those who developed it are instant celebs. Not in this case. No one's taking public credit. Kurt has walked away from it altogether.

"Probably why he didn't promote it," Jedd says. "He was hedging his bets."

"Yeah, waiting for the Dick to invade so he could collect a huge payoff," Beers says.

We go on like this for a while, covering a lot of ground—the app, the rallies, the Dictator, HSys—but without getting to the crux: what to do about our secret. I know this is on everyone's mind. Do we keep quiet about our hack or go public? It's like a final exam where you rush through all the questions but skip the toughest one, figuring you'll answer it last. But then you run out of time.

When Nick suppresses a yawn, I realize our time is running out. "Wait," I say, "I know you're tired. But what's next?"

They all know what I mean.

Beers jumps in immediately. "Thanks, Darah, for keeping us on track. We can't put this off anymore." It irks him, he says, knowing it's business as usual in the penthouse. The longer we wait, the more likely the Ks will get away with what they did. One left already. How long before the other two slither away? "I don't care if their plan backfired and they actually got the Dick out. They need to be held accountable."

Nick is suddenly wide awake. "Even if the Ks go scot-free, the world needs to know about the Russians and Floridians and the threat to California."

"And the app's technology," Zack says.

"And the mind control in their brains," I say. "They need to know about that."

Beers piles on: "The bunker needs to know about the darknet site. They should be digging into it, seeing how the app really works. If they'd been more on top of things from the get-go, so much could have been prevented."

"We have to make sure nothing like this ever happens again," June says.

As we keep talking, reenergized, it's hard to understand what has held us back, why we've been sitting on this for so long.

Zack states exactly that: "I don't know what we're waiting for."

Jedd has been quiet, listening to us, as he often does before speaking. Now he looks around the room and says, "I agree. It's belated, but I'll contact the local authorities first thing tomorrow. That should be a good place to start."

Everyone is on board.

Beers points out Kurt and Karin will probably go to prison.

I can't say that would bother me. In fact, I'm pleased with myself for forcing a discussion on the issue, relieved we've finally come to a decision.

Until June cuts us off. "I don't disagree that the world needs to know about this. But we never do anything without full consensus, and there's one voice we haven't heard tonight."

"Sorry, but he's not here," Beers says, as if that makes the kid's contribution moot.

"He isn't carrying a tablet," Nick says.

"No way to ping him," Zack adds.

June says she realizes that. But his input matters. We can come to a preliminary consensus and run it by the kid when he gets home, which should be early next week. Then she throws out a question: "What do you think he'd have us do?"

"He'd want us to go to the authorities," Beers says quickly.

"That's what *you* want," June says equally quickly.

"Fair enough. But he wouldn't advocate doing nothing. He believes in the value of taking right action."

"When we went into exile, he told us to wait," I remind the others. "When it's the right time to act, he said we'd know."

"We did know," Beers says. "We hacked the update at the right time. You can't deny that was major."

June says no one's denying that. But hacking the app and going to the authorities are different matters.

Beers doubles down: "Now is our moment to go public. We have all the evidence. The authorities will investigate and see the undercover work we did. We'll finally get some credit. Even the kid will. It will be a huge exposé that prevents anything like this from happening again."

"Valid points," Jedd says. "I agree, the kid wouldn't want us to sit idly by now."

"I'm not so sure," June says as all eyes pivot to her. "He might feel it's better to keep the secret."

Beers stares her down. "You don't really think that, do you?"

"We should at least consider it."

"For god's sake, June!" His hands fly to his head, gripping it on both sides, as if he could pull hair out of its smooth surface. "I can't believe you of all people are afraid to rock the boat. Tell me one thing that could possibly be gained by staying silent now."

"Well," she says, "for starters, the kid always says to have faith—"

Beers pounces on the word. "*Faith?* In what?"

June stares back at him. "If you'd let me finish—"

"Let her finish," I say. I have my own ideas about what the kid might say but I want to hear what June thinks.

Beers drops his hands, then reaches for the twins' plates. Moving slowly, he stacks them on his and aligns the silverware on the top plate.

June takes this as a signal he's willing to keep his mouth shut. When she has our full attention, she starts again: "The kid looks at all angles. At what we can do for the sake of the greater good, not just for our personal agenda. He'd be against seizing center stage, against making heroes out of ourselves."

"Nothing wrong with a little credit where credit is due," Beers mumbles.

June glances at him, then continues: "What we did with the app was nothing short of monumental. Let's not undercut that by making this about *us*. It's about something bigger. That's what the kid calls the basis of faith: you do your best, acting on what you feel is right, knowing it's for the greater good."

When Beers doesn't take issue with this definition of faith, she says, "Horrific as the dictatorship was, when you look at the big picture, you have to admit the problem wasn't just the Dictator. It was bigger than that. It was every last person who helped put him there, and then every last person who failed to do anything to remove him. Even now, it's every person who doesn't give the preservation of democracy and the very life of this planet as great a priority as they give their personal wants and desires."

"No argument there," Beers says. "We need to educate people. Starting with the young ones—" He looks at me.

"Young and old both," I say.

"Yes," June says. "It's a lot of work, but that's how we rock the boat."

"The only question," Nick says, "is whether going to the authorities aids that work."

"And whether exposing the Ks and holding them accountable is helpful," Zack adds.

"Maybe this doesn't have to be either or," Jedd says when it's clear we aren't any closer to a consensus. "We could be anonymous whistleblowers. My message doesn't need to reveal our identities."

Beers argues that could be problematic. "An anonymous tip won't give the authorities access to all the evidence. There's no guarantee they'll successfully uncover it on their own. Not to mention it could take forever."

Nick suggests Jedd send an anonymous tip to the bunker instead.

Zack thinks they would guess who sent it.

"Yeah," June says. "Who but Jedd could have uncovered a darknet site at HSys?"

Beers opens his mouth, then quickly snaps it shut.

"What?" I say.

"Huh?"

I laugh. Really, it's funny he doesn't realize how transparent he can be. "Dude, you were about to say something. What was it?"

"You know me too well, Darah," he says, laughing back. "I

was looking at all the angles, like June said the kid does. There's one we haven't mentioned."

"You mean a reason to keep the secret?" I say. How ironic if Beers was the one who persuaded us to stay quiet.

"I wouldn't go that far. But it's a reason to be cautious about going to the authorities."

"We're listening," Jedd says.

"Suppose we do go to the authorities," Beers says. "Either anonymously or straight up. And suppose we report Kurt for hijacking an HSys product on the Dick's behest—"

"Like *you've* been pushing," June says.

"Yeah. And like Jedd agreed to." He pauses. "You realize, if we do that, we'll also have to come clean about our own hack of the update. All of it."

June is nodding. "That's the deal. Everything will come out."

"All the darknet digging. And the nano mic. Even the universal sound." Beers looks at Jedd. "Is any of that a dealbreaker for you?"

"Normally, yes," Jedd says. "As a hacker, disclosing my secrets goes against the grain. In this case, I did everything to keep my work under wraps." He stops to clean his teeth with his tongue. All of us sense a but coming.

June voices it: "But?"

"But I thought about all this from the start." He looks at me. "Remember the mousehole in the forest?"

"Crawling into the hole keeps you safe." I smile as I picture the kid drawing a circle on the rug. It feels like a lifetime ago.

He nods. "A good hacker knows how to mitigate risk. At the same time, you know what can happen when you emerge from that mousehole. If the fire is still raging, it will burn you. To a crisp. If the fire has passed, you must face the ravaged land. Either way, the safety you enjoyed in that hole doesn't nullify the consequences. It doesn't erase accountability."

"So you're prepared to face any consequences?" Beers says.

"I always assumed that if I broke any laws, I'd take full responsibility." Jedd gives us a look that falls somewhere between *I hate this as much as you do* and *what did you think I'd say?* "It will all have been worth it."

It's an honorable stance. None of us can question that.

Except Beers. "Bro, I'm not willing to see you go to prison. Or god forbid, the kid. Not for breaking some cyber law when that was the only means to take the Dick down. Sorry, no way."

I ask if he really thinks prison is a possibility.

Beers and Jedd answer at the same time.

"It's possible," Beers says.

"It's low probability," Jedd says. "I like my odds."

I think it's the first time since the dice game I've heard him speak of odds. He doesn't mean it lightly.

June immediately agrees with Jedd. "I'm not worried about legal jeopardy. Considering the threats we were up against, our hack was benign. It might even still be doing some good."

And so it goes. In the end, we don't have a decision before it's time for the twins to leave.

Once Beers is persuaded the odds of Jedd or any of us facing prison time are low, he restates his preference for bringing everything to the authorities ASAP. We should go to the media too, he says, so the whole world knows what happened and we get recognition for what we've done.

The twins are split about going to the authorities or the bunker first. It's a rare moment of disagreement between them.

June is leaning toward alerting the authorities anonymously. She thinks we could find a way to protect our identities while still getting the important information to the public.

I tend to agree with her, though I want to think about it a bit more. I also want to think more about how we educate people. So much can be done on that front.

Jedd says whatever we decide, June was right when she said we need to get the kid's input first. He reminds us we do everything as a family. This is no exception.

I have no doubt we'll get there. Maybe it didn't happen tonight, but it will happen sooner than later. We will do the right thing, at the right time, in the right way. And we will feel right about it.

It's a school night, so after the twins depart, I brew a cup of kava tea and climb the stairs to the attic. Beers is waiting.

While I sip the tea, we lean back on our pillows and look up at the skylight. It's a moonless night, and stars are twinkling above the redwoods. I could point out how bright Ursa Major is. But I know Beers is already looking at it.

He could give me his take on this evening's discussion. But he knows I don't want to hear it right now.

There will be plenty of time to talk about all that. About whether our secrets need to be revealed to the world. About the potential for future cyberattacks. About whether Jedd's work can prevent those attacks. About June's campaign. About whether the science I'm teaching will be enough to slow climate change. About the future of democracy.

In this moment, though, I just want to be silent and appreciate that this crazy world, which for so long seemed to be spinning out of control, may have gotten a little bit less crazy.

I'm so proud of us for stepping up. For taking responsibility. I see now that, for democracy to survive, every person has to feel as if they're the one on whom the fate of the nation rests. As if without *their* right action, democracy will die.

You might think I'm saying everyone needs to see themselves as an activist. No. All of us aren't going to become full-time activists. That's for people like June. What the rest of us need to do is stop thinking so much in terms of me and mine and start thinking more in terms of us and ours. Of humanity. Of the planet.

That's the expansion I think the kid was talking about. It's the house without windows and doors, where we can create change in this world without sacrificing our sanity. Where it's possible to stay happy while also knowing we're profoundly connected to both the joys and suffering of the ten billion other humans on this planet. All of us together on this little globe spinning through space, one hundred and eighty light years away from that big bear in the sky.

AUTHOR'S NOTE

I want to offer my gratitude to Kamala Subramaniam, born exactly a century before I sat down to write this book, whose retelling of the *Mahābhārata* (which contains the *Bhagavad Gītā*) has inspired and sustained me since I began studying it four decades ago.

I've always seen this epic as highly relevant to life in our modern world. I envisioned a futuristic novel that could convey its timeless wisdom to readers unfamiliar with it—and do so without requiring them to know all the layers of the story. Then, in 2016, as I watched the increasing ascendance of totalitarian, nationalist, fundamentalist, and fascist forces in the United States, India, and elsewhere, I felt compelled to write that novel. Drawing from favorite stories scattered throughout the epic, I leaned into its teachings about right action. I also deeply considered what keeps us from full engagement with our world, even in times of crisis. Whether fear, anger, apathy, fatigue, rationalization, or something else holds you back, my hope is you find the inspiration to step forward and join with others working toward a just, free, and democratic future on our fragile but miraculous planet.

BOOK CLUB QUESTIONS FOR *THE DIE*

1. With which character in *The Die* do you identify most closely? What about them—and about you—leads you to feel this way?

2. Imagine and discuss what your life might be like under an authoritarian regime. How would it be different than your life now?

3. What are your thoughts about the current state of democracy where you live? In the world? What do you see as your role in preserving democracy?

4. If you are familiar with the *Mahābhārata*, what parallels do you see between its story and characters and the story and characters in *The Die*? What differences do you see? What subtle references and symbols did you notice?

5. Why do you think Jedd insisted on playing the dice game? If he were your best friend (or, depending on age, your child), what would you say to him? Imagine that discussion.

6. As June points out, many people see politics as inherently dirty. Do you agree? Why or why not?

7. How do you determine the right (or dharmic) course of action in any given situation?

8. How can you both be an activist and follow a spiritual path without compromising your values or feeling overwhelmed?

9. Are you going through life more like a steering wheel or more like a self-driving vehicle?

10. What piece of wisdom expressed by one of the characters has stuck with you? How might you apply it in your life?

11. If you were to, as Darah mentions, think more in terms of "us and ours" instead of "me and mine," how would you act differently in the world? What would you do?

12. At the end of the book, it is unclear whether the friends will go public with what they know. Do you think they should? Why or why not?

ACKNOWLEDGMENTS

My deepest thanks to those who, each in their own way, were steadfast companions on this journey: Liz Cunningham, Niranjani Forrest, Penelope Shackelford, and Dan Woodard. Great thanks and admiration to Brooke Warner of She Writes Press/SparkPress for her revolutionary vision and contributions to the publishing world and to all the dedicated members of her publishing team. Many thanks also to Julia Drake of Wildbound PR, who showed me at our very first meeting that she totally got my book.

Gratitude to Bharatiya Vidya Bhavan for permission to include epigraphs adapted from the *Mahābhārata*, by Kamala Subramaniam (Mumbai, 1988).

If you enjoyed this book, please consider leaving a review on your preferred site. New authors, indie authors, and books like *The Die* can only thrive with the support of wonderful people like you who take the time and energy to let others know about them. Feel free to spread the word in whatever way feels good to you.

ABOUT THE AUTHOR

Jude Berman grew up amid floor-to-ceiling shelves of books in many languages. In addition to a love of literature, her refugee parents instilled in her a deep appreciation for cultural diversity and social justice. Jude has a BA in art from Smith College and an EdD in cross-cultural communication from UMass Amherst. After a career in academic research, she built a freelance writing and editing business and ran two small indie presses. She lives in Berkeley, CA, where she continues to work with authors and write fiction. In her free time, she volunteers for progressive causes, paints with acrylic watercolors, gardens, and meditates. She blogs at https://judeberman.org.

SELECTED TITLES FROM SPARKPRESS

SparkPress is an independent boutique publisher delivering high-quality, entertaining, and engaging content that enhances readers' lives, with a special focus on female-driven work.
www.gosparkpress.com

Riding High in April: A Novel, Jackie Townsend, $16.95, 978-1-68463-095-0. *Riding High in April* takes us across the world as one man risks it all for a final chance to make it big in the tech world. At stake are his reputation, his dwindling bank account, and his fifteen-year relationship with a woman grappling with who she is and what really matters to her.

Cold Snap: A Novel, Codi Schneider, $16.95, 978-1-68463-101-8. When a murder shocks her peaceful mountain town, Bijou, a plucky house cat with a Viking spirit, must dive paws-first into solving the mystery before another life is taken—maybe even her own.

Those the Future Left Behind: A Novel, Patrick Meisch, $16.95, 978-1-68463-079-0. In a near future in which overpopulation, resource depletion, and environmental degradation have precipitated a radical population control program, people can volunteer to be culled at a young age in exchange for immediate wealth.

A Place Called Zamora: Book One, L B Gschwandter, $16.95, 978-1-68463-051-6. If an eighteen-year-old boy must risk his life in a motorcycle race to the very edge of a forty-story rooftop, his bike better be the one with brakes. That's what Niko faces in this dystopian story of love and survival: a race to the death that, if he survives it, will get him the girl of his choice and a kingdom of wealth laid out for him in an endless buffet. Except prizes like these come with strings in a city where corruption permeates everything, and there is no escape. Or is there?

Echoes of War: A Novel, Cheryl Campbell. $16.95, 978-1-68463-006-6. When Dani—one of many civilians living on the fringes to evade a war that's been raging between a faction of aliens and the remnants of Earth's military for decades—discovers that she's not human, her life is upended . . . and she's drawn into the very battle she's spent her whole life avoiding.

Firewall: A Novel, Eugenia Lovett West. $16.95, 978-1-68463-010-3. When Emma Streat's rich, socialite godmother is threatened with blackmail, Emma becomes immersed in the dark world of cybercrime—and mounting dangers take her to exclusive places in Europe and contacts with the elite in financial and art collecting circles. Through passion and heartbreak, Emma must fight to save herself and bring a vicious criminal to justice.